THE HUNTER

JOHNNY MORICE

authorHOUSE®

AuthorHouse™ LLC
1663 Liberty Drive
Bloomington, IN 47403
www.authorhouse.com
Phone: 1-800-839-8640

Published by AuthorHouse 8/15/2014

ISBN: 978-1-4969-1203-9 (sc)
ISBN: 978-1-4969-1202-2 (hc)
ISBN: 978-1-4969-1206-0 (e)

Library of Congress Control Number: 2014908606

This book is dedicated to my three

ACKNOWLEDGMENTS

First, I'd like to thank my three. To Amy, my strong, beautiful wife who helped make this book what it is. To my children - Mackenzie, my princess warrior, and Jaden, my own personal superhero. Your pure love and joy has encouraged me to be stronger, to love more, and to believe in myself. I love you!

To Joe, your abundance of knowledge and kindness has given hope and help to a man who was in need. I thank you continuously for your friendship.

To Dustan and Rob, my fishin' buddies, whose ongoing bro-support will always be remembered, and our friendship strong. Fish on!

To Alyson Dubler, who made my vision of The Hunter come to life on the cover of this book. Thank you.

And to God, thank you for helping me choose the right path.

CHAPTER 1

UNIQUE

The sweet summer scent of lilac trickled in through the open windows, filling the house like no air freshener ever could.

"What a crappy day," Geraldine thought.

It's one of the hardest things to do, watching your child pack and get ready to go out on their own. Geraldine Cormie was dreading this day.

She was a strong, beautiful, independent woman, and was very proud to have raised such a fine, young man. Geraldine was brought up by her aunt after her parents died in a tragic car accident when she was only seventeen. Her aunt had a son, Gary, and they were raised as brother and sister.

It was hard on Geraldine raising a son without his father. It meant that she had to be both the mother and father figure for Brogan. Brogan learned at a young age that his father had chosen his name; it was the only thing he had ever given him, besides his light brown hair and unique blue eyes. Sure, Brogan had his uncle Gary, but the true father figure was still missing. The subject of his father wasn't discussed much while growing up, there wasn't much to say. It's not that Brogan wasn't interested in knowing about his father; he didn't ask questions because he could sense the pain it caused his mother to talk about it.

After graduating high school, Brogan decided to take a couple years off to contemplate his future; basically to weigh his options and continue working to help his mother.

"Do you have your dress shirts and ties from the other closet?" Geraldine had a hard time asking without breaking down crying. It was an emotional time for her. She had watched Brogan grow, and now her only child was leaving.

"Yes mom, I got 'em."

Geraldine stared at him, shaking her head, as he folded his clothes and packed his suitcase. "Oh, it feels like only yesterday that I held little baby Brogan in my arms."

"C'mon mom, don't get all emotional. I'm twenty years old now."

"I don't care how old you are, you will always be my baby boy."

Brogan was like his mother, very independent. And although he would never admit it, he liked it when she fussed over him.

"You were such a beautiful baby," Geraldine continued.

Brogan still packing threw an affectionate glance over his shoulder at his mother.

"The doctors and nurses couldn't believe their eyes when they saw you! I even heard one of the nurses gasp. I later learned it was because no one could believe how alert you were."

Brogan's mother always stated with emphasis how the doctor had said, out of the hundreds of babies he had delivered, "Brogan was unique"; and how all the nurses came to her room to see unique baby Brogan for themselves.

Tears welt up in Geraldine's eyes as she continued, "Then they placed the sweetest little bundle of joy in my arms, and we shared a long, loving stare; it was almost as if you already knew who I was."

Brogan almost always got embarrassed when his mother told that story, especially if anyone was around to hear it. Lord knows he had heard it hundreds of times already, and could probably recite it word for word with her.

"Did you grab your vitamins from the bathroom medicine cabinet?" she asked wiping her tears away.

"Yup, but I've gotta go to town and pick some more up before I leave."

Geraldine sat on Brogan's bed watching an exceedingly, decent, young man move around the room, packing his belongings, as he prepared to venture out on his own; and wondered how she was going to survive without him. They had always been very close; after all, it had been just the two of them for the past twenty years.

"Why out West Brogan? Why so far away? That's over 3000 km!"

"Actually mom, it's 4404 km."

She sobbed a little and stuck out her bottom lip. Brogan went over and sat on the bed beside her. "I have to do this mom. I just feel it's what I'm supposed to do."

"You did nothing wrong honey."

"I know mom, but, it's…well, I just have that feeling. You know, I just know I gotta go."

Geraldine stuck out her bottom lip again and gave Brogan her best puppy dog eyes. Brogan took his mother's hand and placed it on his chest over his heart. It didn't matter how many times she heard or felt his heartbeat, each time she was amazed.

Brogan looked into his mother's eyes with much love, "Mom, if every time I thought of you a rose came to mind, I'd walk through a garden forever."

Only a second went by and both of them started snickering. Geraldine punched her son playfully in the arm, "Go on and finish packing, you cheese ball."

Brogan, still chuckling, jumped up and continued to pack.

Feeling Brogan's heartbeat reminded Geraldine of the heated discussion she had with her doctor the day Brogan was born. She never told a soul what her and Dr. Merder discussed that day. But Geraldine recalled every word. "Hello Doc, where's my baby? Is he ok?"

"Your baby is down the hall with the nurses, and is doing fine. Now Mrs. Cormie, when a doctor, like myself, stumbles across something…"

Geraldine even remembered the short pause, as if Dr. Merder knew something but didn't want to reveal it.

"If a doctor discovers something they have never seen or heard of before, then they're obligated to ask permission…"

"Permission for what?"

"Basically to run further tests."

"What kinds of tests? What are you talking about?"

"Well, first I would like to contact a few of my colleges to help me come up with some theories. Then we'd have to decide on the proper tests, that would in turn lead us to the more imperative and specific tests!"

"Specific tests?"

"I'm sorry Mrs. Cormie. Any and every test that would extract beneficial and crucial information, missing links so to speak, that we don't posses yet! I'm talking about possibly taking the next evolutionary step!"

Geraldine could still recall growing impatient with Dr. Merder's rambling explanation.

"Ok, I'm confused. Did I miss something?"

"Once again I have to apologize Mrs. Cormie, you'll have to excuse me; I'm just very elated! Your baby's heart rate is, well, let's say it is abnormally misleading."

"How do you mean?"

"His heart rate is comparable to no other. Mrs. Cormie, I listened to your baby's heart rate for five minutes straight, at ten different times, and it never slowed once."

"What does that mean? Is Brogan alright?"

"Fine! Better than fine! His heart rate is faster than an Olympic sprinter's would be after a race. This, and the fact that his pupils are extremely dilated, convinced me to get an MRI done. Incidentally, we all watched as one of the nurses tried to put drops in Brogan's eyes. He kept moving his head...purposely! That's unheard of! No one here has ever experienced such alertness from a newborn."

"And are his eyes good?"

"I'd have to say your son's eyes are exceptional! I know this might sound strange Mrs. Cormie, but...well, every time I walked past Brogan's incubator crib...it was...well, he watched me. It seemed as if he recognized me from the delivery and was...watching me! It sounds extremely ludicrous, and virtually impossible, I know!"

"Ok, so Brogan is alert and his eyes are fine?"

"Mrs. Cormie the MRI indicated that Brogan has two aortas running to and from his heart. His ventricles...his internal set up is...it's extraordinary! It's beyond anything I have ever seen or even thought relatively possible. Everything is amazingly peculiar, and until now, undiscovered...hell, even unprecedented! I'm very excited about the potential breakthroughs your son could provide for..."

"Potential breakthroughs?" Geraldine interrupted. "I'm sorry Doc, did you say you ran all the basic tests that needed to be done?"

"Yes, and a few extras to make sure Brogan was stable, and that the readings we retrieved were accurate."

"And is my baby healthy?"

"Exceptionally…beyond healthy! Mrs. Cormie I have to be blunt, if you refuse to allow me to run more tests, then you could very well be depriving others, maybe even sick patients, of having a better chance!"

"A better chance at what?"

"Well we won't really know how or what could be accomplished until we run further tests."

"Is there any other reason why you think Brogan should remain in the hospital, besides what you are asking?"

"No Mrs. Cormie but…"

"Then I would like to take my baby home as soon as possible."

"I strongly disagree with your decision…"

"Look! If Brogan and I are both healthy and able to go home, then that's what we're going to do."

"Listen, Brogan is unique. He could very well be the next step on the evolutionary ladder!" Dr. Merder said trying to convince Geraldine to allow further testing.

"You said he is healthy and everything's normal, right?"

"Yes! He is healthy and intriguing, especially on the inside!"

"No offence Dr. Merder, but my baby will not be a guinea pig!"

"Mom…MOM!"

"Oh…what Brogan dear?"

"You were just staring at me, like you were in a trance or something."

"Sorry dear, I was reminiscing. What do you need honey?"

"I need to borrow the car. That was really freaky. What were you thinking about? Definitely something more than reminiscing; you ok mom?"

"Yes dear, I'm fine. Take twenty dollars out of my purse, the blue bullet needs refuelling."

"I've got money."

Brogan kissed his mother and grabbed the keys.

Geraldine smiled as she watched the best part of herself leave the room. She was very proud to have Brogan as a son. He was a tough, confident, caring, young man. If there was one thing Geraldine had done right in her life, it was the way she had raised Brogan.

When Brogan was nine he realized that his mother was having a hard time keeping up with all the bills. In the winter she would hang wool blankets up in the doorways to help keep the heat in certain rooms of the house. That's when Brogan started taking on any and every odd job that he could. He knew the extra money eased the stress on his mother. During the winter Brogan would shovel driveways. The rest of the year, he would rake leaves, paint fences, mow lawns, whatever needed to be done. The extra money made things easier, and Geraldine let her son know all the time. Not only did it help with the bills, but it also paid for some of Brogan's countless activities. In fact, Geraldine knew she wouldn't have been able to afford all the sports that Brogan competed in, without the extra money.

It was Brogan's superb work ethics and amazing athletic gifts that lead to his small town fame. He was an all-star in everything he participated in, which was a complete mystery to Geraldine. She had played softball back in her day, and yes it was fast pitch; she was also named MVP all four years in high school. But she knew Brogan was in a totally unique league, one that only god like athletes dare strut their stuff. Geraldine always wondered how Brogan came to be so athletically blessed, and often thought it must have something to do with what Dr. Merder had discussed with her that eventful day.

Geraldine sat on Brogan's bed staring at all the trophies he had won over the years. She was amazed that one kid could win so many, and still be so modest. Looking at the wall of awards reminded Geraldine of a conversation she once had with her brother Gary.

"Where are you exactly?"

"I depart for Iraq in two days little sis, I'm just packing now. How's my favorite nephew doin?"

"He's your only nephew, and he's doing great. Gary, you've gotta see him playing sports now! You'd be astonished at his speed and agility."

"Yeah, Brogan's always been a fast kid."

"Oh, but since he's hit puberty, it's like night and day!'

"What do you mean?"

"I mean he's fast Gary, fast as in don't blink!"

"C'mon sis, you remember how quick and strong I was at his age. And my buddy Ryan, you remember him? He was quicker and stronger than me."

"Sorry Gary, but there's no comparison. When he's running full out, it's like he changes gears, followed by a lot more horse power, then poof... gone!"

"Well, I'll come see him play sometime when I'm back for a visit. What sports is he playing right now? I'll bring him something for every sport he's in. That would be a nice surprise, eh?"

"Everything."

"What?"

"He's playing everything. Literally any and every sport. Not only that, he's also filling in for any and every position the team needs covered for that game."

"Wow! Ok, find out if there's something specific he wants, and I'll try to get it for him. That might be easier."

Eventually Brogan's uncle made it to one of his high school football games. Geraldine remembered Gary being so excited that his voice actually cracked. "You gotta get him in professional sports! Hey! Geraldine! Do you hear what I'm tellin' you? He's a freakin natural! No! He's a freak of nature! The money Geraldine, sign him up!"

Still sitting on the bed, Geraldine smiled as she recalled what she had said to Gary. "He is unique, and there's no doubt in my mind that Brogan is meant to do great things. He'll do what makes him happy."

Brogan participated in every sport that he could. And excelled like no other. In high school Brogan quickly became friends with all the coaches; sometimes before becoming friends with his own teammates. Some of the older jocks did not appreciate what Brogan had to offer the team, mostly because he was a young player with natural abilities and was outperforming them. And Brogan did not appreciate the hazing the rookies had to endure. He wasn't out to change everything, just the things he felt in his heart were wrong. So, even though he himself was only a rookie, Brogan started sticking up for them. This of course led to some confrontations and altercations with the older players. But, after a short period, the bad hazing stopped. The worst thing the rookies were made to do was run the hill with a lineman on their back.

Brogan had also involved himself with martial arts at the tender age of eight. He started to live and breathe every type of martial arts that was available to him in his small home town and the surrounding areas. By the age of eighteen Brogan had successfully completed and received the highest degrees in Judo, Karate, Taekwondo, Jujutsu, and his favorite Muay Thai; the nine body weapons, surpassing not only his peers but his sensei's as well. Brogan also dabbled in boxing and made an example out of everyone in and out of his weight division.

Brogan had scouts from numerous colleges and universities checking him out ever since he started high school sports. As well as working to help his mother with bills, Brogan spent the two years after high school trying to decide what school he wanted to attend, and make sure it was the right choice for him. Even though he had a pick of any college or university, he was quite positive that if he did decide to continue with his education, he would go to his home town university. But he still teased his mother about attending a school away from home. Geraldine was very impressed with the amount of scholarships Brogan had received. But the scholarships weren't enough for Brogan to just dive into college or university right after graduating high school.

Finally after two years of pondering schools Brogan decided to take one of the scholarships and put it to good use. On the last day of registry, Brogan enrolled at his home town university. That same night, Brogan got a phone call that would not only change his decision about university, but also alter the course of his entire life.

It was his Taekwondo instructor, Master Elvis Cros. He made very little small talk and proceeded to explain that he wanted to put on an exhibition bout that Friday night, between some of his best students, to demonstrate what his Taekwondo classes entailed. However, because Brogan had surpassed all his other students, and because several people had suggested it before, the main and final fight of the evening would be between himself and Brogan. Master Cros had said that Brogan was his best student, and he wanted everyone to see his prodigy. Brogan was reluctant but Master Cros became aggressively persistent, and pointed out that no one but Brogan could come close to matching his skills. Brogan, feeling obligated, agreed.

The arena was full. There were dozens of wannabe fighters interested in joining the Taekwondo classes, and Master Cros wanted to put on a good demonstration for these potential clients. Also, nearly the entire town showed up to watch the exhibition fight between Master Cros and Brogan; because they always wondered who would win.

The final demonstration started with an assortment of kicks, punches, and a flurry of fancy moves; all thrown by Master Cros. After every strike he would give a brief explanation to the crowd of what he was trying to accomplish with that particular move or strike. Brogan did what he was supposed to do for the first part of the demonstration, block and avoid.

After Master Cros finished giving his final verbal spiel to the audience, the plan was that a heads up would be given, then he and Brogan would start sparring. This particular exploited demonstration was so everyone could see the coordination and discipline Master Cros' self defence course had to offer. But before Brogan got the heads up, in the midst of his explanation, Master Cros lost focus. Maybe Brogan was doing too good a job of blocking and avoiding, causing Master Cros to get mildly frustrated. Maybe it was the excitement of so many people watching that caused Master Cros to forget about giving the heads up. Whatever the reason, the strike was uncalled for.

Brogan and Master Cros had sparred several times in the past at half speed and force. However this time, a couple head shots and a side kick to Brogan's left rib cage, and the fight was on. The three strikes given by Master Cros had a lot of power behind them, making them sting, consequently spoiling the social shindig. Like so many times before, Brogan felt a hot rush surging through his entire body, which would later end in a severe headache. When the next strike was thrown, Brogan side stepped releasing a single kick; unintentional, but done. The bottom of Brogan's right heel connected with Master Cros' gut. The impact sent the instructor flying backwards before landing on his back sliding along the arena floor.

Four fractured ribs, three herniated discs, and a severe case of whip lash was a part of Brogan's decision. It wasn't the same anymore. Being shunned by most of the community would cause anyone to pick up and move. It was an honest mistake, one that Brogan could not explain; and no one would understand for that matter. If anyone had a beef with Brogan, it should've only been Master Cros, but the majority of the town held the bigger grudge. Although, it was Master Cros that turned quite a few people against Brogan in the hopes of keeping his reputation as a prominent Taekwondo instructor.

Geraldine knew it wasn't Brogan's fault. Even though she would not admit it, she understood why he needed a change. His whole life, Brogan went above and beyond expectations and was all about helping others. Whether it was helping one of his neighbours with chores, or giving his all in every sport he played. But none of this mattered now. Brogan knew he had severely injured Master Cros, unintentionally and regrettably of course, but that did not register with the community. It was one of the contributing factors that helped Brogan make up his mind to leave everything he had ever known behind. Part of the reason was that he felt betrayed. Betrayed by the people that cheered for him over the years. Betrayed in the sense that everything Brogan had sacrificed for his small town sports teams meant nothing now. He could not be bothered with the fame that came with being an exceptional athlete. His main focus growing up was to have fun and help out. Now there were feelings of resentment, and not by Brogan.

He didn't explain to his mother *exactly* why he decided to move out West. Although he had a feeling she already knew. Most people assumed it was because of what he did to Master Cros. But that wasn't the main reason. In fact, Brogan himself could not explain the dreams and random thoughts he was having. Not actual thoughts, more like visions and feelings that he should be doing something else with his life. Brogan knew he wasn't clairvoyant, but the images were definitely distracting him. He would see highway signs flicker in his mind. Certain buildings that he had never seen before would flash through his head, as if he were driving past them. Brogan was freaked out by this, but there was more to it. He couldn't begin to describe what he was feeling, he just knew. He knew exactly where he was headed; Saddleback City.

Saddleback City was a huge, beautiful city with a population of 4.4 million, and growing. It would be quite a change from the small town of seven thousand. But easy enough to get lost and try to find oneself.

"How can I explain to mom the real reason I'm leaving?" Brogan thought to himself as he headed home from the store. He put more than twenty dollars in his mother's car. He knew she would notice the gauge reading 'full' and be upset that he hadn't taken the money from her purse earlier, but he couldn't help it.

As Brogan drove, he could see his old high school in the distance; beside it, the football field. It suddenly took him back to the last game of his high school football career. Brogan remembered how the sun was shining in everybody's face that day. Even some of the spectators in the stands put black under their eyes. They were playing the Blue Cats, who were considered the "all star team". The smallest player was almost 200 lbs, and he was their safety. Most suspected the team was on steroids. In fact, it was once said that the Blue Cats could very well have beaten the home town university football team.

Brogan's team, the Titans, were down by five. They had fought with all their hearts and souls that final game, but it seemed futile. The Titans could not let the Blue Cats score on their last drive. When the fullback came through the line Brogan, who was playing middle line backer, hit him so hard it stopped both the fullback and running back, who was carrying the ball, dead at the line. Brogan smiled as he remembered how the fans jumped to their feet, their energy firing the team up in the final moments of their last game.

The Blue Cats were forced to kick the ball. They tried to run the time down, but there was still ten seconds left on the clock. Everyone knew Brogan was going to get the ball, especially the other team.

Coach Bowmin called for Brogan. "Brogan, no pressure here, but there's only ten seconds left in the game and we're down by five. I don't care what you have to do, just score will ya! When the ball is kicked to you, and you know it's gonna be a doozy, try catching it on the run. Now go kick some ass!"

Brogan ran to the huddle and looked at his teammates. Although they had seen Brogan do amazing things to win games throughout the season, this time seemed less likely. Despite their energy, there were looks of despair, lost hope, and even some words of discouragement.

"Brogan dude, not even you can save us."

"If I were you I'd let the ball fly, don't even touch it!"

"Think about it man, this is the last play, they're gonna try to make an example out of all of us!"

A smile came to Brogan's face as he recalled the pep talk he gave to try and motivate his team. "Listen up! We didn't make it this far on bullshit luck. We deserve to be here and we're gonna play this final play to win! Boys, this is the last play of our last game…shit, it's our last year! And I'll be damned if I let anyone walk into our house and make an example out of us!"

"The coach give you a trick play or something?"

"There's no trick play, there's no certainty that we're even gonna win," Brogan said honestly.

"Then what Brogan, what are we supposed to do? What are you gonna do?"

Brogan remembered how his eyes narrowed and his nostrils flared, followed by a somewhat sadistic smirk. Those who witnessed the smirk would later describe it as scary.

"I tell ya what! I'm gonna catch that ball when it comes down, and I'm gonna head toward the end zone. If any son of a bitch gets in my way, they'll be eating through a straw for a month!"

Brogan then recalled the feeling he got as he took position on their twenty yard line. As he stared down the opposing team he felt the rush again, except this time it felt as though his heart was going to explode. He was sure he was going to have a heart attack right there on the field.

There had been times, over the years, when Brogan was in a tight or scary situation; he would feel a rush of extra energy surge through his body. Although he knew it was more than extra energy, he couldn't describe exactly what it was. As time went on, the adrenaline rush of energy would last and stay with him longer. Each time it happened, he found himself getting faster and stronger. Unfortunately the energy surge was always followed by a horrific headache, that he endured while trying to hide it from his mother.

The kick was a big one. It soared through the air so far that Brogan had to back pedal out of his own end zone. As the football came down towards him, that unearthly feeling rushed through his entire body. This alien adrenaline rush made his muscles seem more unified, more connected to his mind than ever before. Brogan watched as the ball streamed down on top of him, his eyes were fixated on it, and the rush started to get stronger.

Brogan's grip on his mother's steering wheel got tighter as he recalled the events of that day. A small squeak escaped between his knuckles.

The ball landed in his hands and he shot to the left of the field. His speed could not be matched, and he ended up passing his blockers. Once Brogan was all the way to the left side, he looked up field and could see only blue jerseys. The entire Blue Cat defence had flanked Brogan to that one side. Without any hesitation, or loss of speed, Brogan changed directions and shot for the right side of the field. Two linemen made it through the blockers and had Brogan in their sights. Brogan dropped his left shoulder and hit one of the 270 lb linemen in the hip. The impact was low and deliberate, not to mention heard and felt in the stands. The lineman's legs shot out from under him causing him to helicopter-spin in mid air. The momentum threw the lineman into the other causing four more players to pile up on the already fallen Blue Cats. Some nice blocks were thrown and Brogan, now on the right side of the field, started up the side line towards the end zone. He ran in for the touch down that won the game and spun around to celebrate, only to see everyone staring at him. His teammates and the opposing team were still on the field just looking at him. It was as if time was standing still. Brogan's eyes panned over to the crowd and the same thing, not a sound; no cheering, no clapping, no celebrating. What was only a few seconds of silence, felt like forever. Brogan later learned everyone stood in disbelief because he had run so fast for the end zone that every other player on the field looked as if they were in slow motion.

The first person to cheer was Brogan's mother. She had seen it in him all along, and knew he was fast, but this moment was considerably faster than any time she had ever seen him run before. In fact, it was so fast that Geraldine found herself, like everyone else at the game, awestruck.

But since she had seen Brogan do so many amazing things, she quickly snapped out of the crowd's zombie like state and started cheering louder than she ever did before. She was hoping it would snap everyone else out of the trance, and it did. Within a couple of seconds the entire place went crazy. Hats flew into the air along with every type of food and beverage you could think of. It was a giant food fight with no intended targets. *We Will Rock You* started playing over the loud speakers, and the fans rushed the field. Scouts were falling over each other trying to hand their business cards to coach Bowmin. Reporters scampered across the field to get more information on this phenomenon. Later that week, all the papers called Brogan the "Titan Juggernaut!".

"Just another meaningless memory," Brogan thought as he turned the corner heading back towards his mothers.

As he turned into the driveway he noticed a black and yellow Volkswagen Bug parked in his spot. "Who the heck is this now?" Brogan thought.

He parked behind the Bug spotting the dual exhaust, hard to hide but still not too noticeable. Brogan took his time walking past it. As far as he could tell, it didn't appear to have any extra body work, just a nice paint job. Actually, the car looked like it had just rolled off the assembly line, except for the fact that it had been lowered. After studying the inside, and spotting the high output exhaust, Brogan was right; it was a sleeper. He was very impressed with the amount of work that was put into it. Someone went to a lot of trouble to add all the extras, and keep it looking like a normal Bug. Brogan took one last glance before going into the house. He was still curious who it belonged to and what they were doing at his mothers.

"Hey there Brogan, how's it going?

"Uncle G! Good to see you! I thought you were off somewhere in South Africa fighting rebels!" Brogan joked.

"Naw, plan went south, no pun intended."

"Well I'm glad you made it before I headed out."

"Me too Brogan. So, you all ready for the trip? Your mom said you were heading out first thing in the morning, and you're goin by bus, right?"

"Yeah, the bus leaves at 8:00am."

Brogan quickly changed the subject thinking of the vehicle parked in the driveway that he had just been admiring. "So, that's a little different set of wheels than the army issued Jeeps! Is it bullet proof?"

"Yes it is a lot different, and no it's not bullet proof, smart ass. But if I tell ya a little secret, you keep it to yourself. It's freakin' fast Brogan!"

"What made you pick that ride? The speed?"

"You know, when I first started workin' on that car all my army buddies made fun of me. They thought it was the beginning of a midlife crisis. But, pretty soon they were all pitching in to help. It became our project when we were stationed at the base. In fact, most of us spent all our free time workin' on it. We, you could say, got emotionally attached to it."

"That's cool Uncle G. How fast is it?"

"I tell you what Brogan, when you come home for a visit you can let me know, cause I've been a little timid to push it past 115.

"What?"

"115 mph, that's as fast as I've had it goin'. But don't worry, there's still a lot more under the hood."

"I don't understand?"

"I'm talkin 'bout horse power boy!"

"I know what you mean about the horse power, but what you said earlier, I..."

"Brogan listen to me very carefully," Gary interrupted. "Your whole life you have done everything you could to help your mother. But it's not only that, it's everything you do for other people too and ask for nothing in return. You see, I've been tellin my army buddies 'bout you and they think you're an awesome kid. You got shafted by the whole town Brogan, and I believe it's time you got a little something back. So, to make your trip a little more exciting, we designed and modified until there was nothing left for us to do. Well, except give it to you."

"You've...you've gotta be kidding me Uncle G!" Brogan stuttered.

"No kiddin' Brogan, she's all yours. This is something like a reward that you never knew 'bout. All those years of working when you were growing up, instead of just being a kid, and handing the money over to your mom; not asking for anything, not even keeping a little so you could get a treat for yourself. Brogan I gotta tell ya, my army buddies and I think you're one hell of a young man! And hopefully this car will save you money and headaches. Lookin' for an affordable vehicle and havin' to take the bus or subway to get around is all stressful. This way you don't have to worry 'bout those little things."

Brogan never said a word, he didn't know what to do except grab his uncle and give him a huge hug. He spent the rest of the evening listening to his uncle's stories, smiling back at his mom, and checking out his new ride as he packed the Bug for his long journey.

Brogan would miss his mother and uncle tremendously. A part of him would miss his home town, a small part. In order for him to find his calling in life, he had to find himself first, or at least part of himself. For one to truly know oneself, would take a lifetime. Brogan understood that you could live a long life and still not truly know yourself, so he wasn't looking for all the answers, just a few. He did know two things for sure, at his young age; that no matter where he went, the path he chose would be full of mystique, and no matter what he did he was definitely unique.

CHAPTER 2

THE CURE

For some the journey to work is enough to keep them in bed. But for those lucky enough to have a purpose or a reason, other than bills, it is much easier. Five thirty in the morning and the alarm only rang twice before being shut off. A lone figure rolled out of bed and headed for the bathroom.

Brogan's morning routine was pretty much like clockwork. He started off with a hundred push-ups and the same amount of sit-ups; and would usually throw in a few sets of pull-ups and whatever else, just because. Although this part of his morning routine was not necessary for Brogan to follow, he still enjoyed the warm up before work.

Never having to work hard at gaining muscle or staying in shape, Brogan always assumed it was related to his unique internal setup and unexplained adrenaline rushes. Standing 5'11" and weighing 190 lbs, Brogan was effortlessly stacked.

His exercises were followed closely by a protein breakfast, before heading out to battle the morning traffic. Ten kilometres of go-cart racing and another fifteen of slug like movement, not to mention dodging the crazy bastards driving all over cutting people off. And yet, Brogan did not mind at all. The majority of drivers would get frustrated and make gestures, even threats. But Brogan refused to give into the almost inevitable road rage that would overtake morning drivers. He was very mature for the most part, he always had been. Most men his age were looking for a good time or the biggest party to crash, until of course they found someone to tame their wild hearts. But not Brogan, he was the exact same as when he first moved out West five years earlier. Just a lot happier. It really didn't matter what Brogan had to endure, he figured it was well worth it. Love does strange things to people. Why else would he put up with all the bullshit in the big city if there wasn't something much more important to focus on.

Brogan never use to drink coffee, but the first day he arrived in Saddleback City, five years earlier, he was hooked. Brogan had checked into a hotel before venturing out to look for an apartment and work. He didn't really have a plan, but figured he'd check out what was around the hotel and maybe pick up a newspaper to take a look at the classifieds. While Brogan was wandering around he noticed a bulletin board through a coffee shop window, and went in to check it out. The board was full of posters and ads of every kind. Fate played its part that day. Not only did Brogan find work and a place to stay, he also found his reason. Since that day, Brogan has spent every second in love.

Geraldine knew there was a girl even before Brogan had told her, mothers just know. "You have to bring that girl home to meet your mother before you two get married," she said when Brogan told her.

Little did Geraldine know, Brogan was planning to do just that, very soon.

Rita Lorraine was a small redhead who indeed had the personality to back up the rumours. Not only that redheads have tempers, it was her passion for the cause that intrigued Brogan; whether it was rescuing mistreated animals or saving the planet one can at a time. Actually, it was the whole package. Brogan had had dates in the past, but nothing ever went beyond that. Rita was different. Brogan felt weak every time he was near Rita; and at the same time he felt invincible. From the moment their eyes locked in the coffee shop that fateful afternoon, Brogan knew that Rita was the one for him and Rita felt it too.

Brogan often played that day over in his mind. It was by far the best day of his life, and it amazed him how everything seemed to fall into place. Rita was still working at that same coffee shop, JoJo's Java House, and Brogan was still drinking black coffee.

JoJo's Java House was the place to go if you wanted the best coffee and donuts. But for Brogan it was the service, one server in particular.

And every morning he had to see her. Where else could he find peace with himself and escape the cruel impractical world, if only for a bunch of minutes.

Brogan started work as a construction laborer for Mocor the day after he met Rita, and had been working for them since. The company started in 1940 and was still growing. It was a dangerous fabrication job that involved heights and heavy machinery, making it a high paying job with a high turnover rate. Every employee had to put their life in the hands of a co-worker sooner or later. It was part of the job. Rookies would come in and get cocky and careless after a few weeks and end up getting injured, or worse, there were even fatalities. Most would say, "If you're lucky, you'll still be able to work after you fall". Basically saying that if you work there, you will fall at some point. Even veteran workers had their bad days, except for Brogan who still had an accident free record.

Brogan quickly won the respect of his co-workers, foremen, and supervisors. Even the owner paid a visit to the plant after Brogan saved two more people from certain dismemberment, maybe even death. This brought the total number of people he saved to a staggering one hundred and three. In all the years of operation no one had ever seen or heard of this, especially by one individual in only a five year span. It was a part of the job that Brogan excelled at and seemed to enjoy the most. He had been asked several times how he did it, and would answer the same every time, "In the right place at the right time I guess."

But most everyone who worked with Brogan knew it was much more than that. They didn't know what it was or how exactly he did the things he did. Most assumed it was because he was in phenomenal shape with cat like reflexes, or because he had a big heart and couldn't stand to see anyone get hurt. Others would say that he was very aware of his surroundings and had an eye for safety hazards. This was all true.

Everyone wanted to work with Brogan, not only because they thought he made the work day go by faster, but mostly because they would be a lot safer working along side him. When employees requested a shift change to work with Brogan, the supervisors would respond, half jokingly, that "someone else needs saving, wait your turn".

Brogan started getting nicknames such as Superman, Man of Steel, Reapers Rebellion, and the Catcher of the Steel. Every week he would receive some sort of baked goods, home cooked meals, or be invited over for supper from co-workers who he had helped or rescued. At first Brogan felt guilty about accepting anything, but it had become a normal occurrence, and Brogan was very grateful for everything they did. Plus, Brogan was saving for a wedding and a down payment on a particular house, so every little bit helped. Though, Rita had no idea what Brogan was planning.

Taking the last gulp of his protein shake, Brogan grabbed his keys off the hook to set out on his mission. Starting the 1977 Volkswagen Bug at precisely 6:00am every morning upset some neighbours; others appreciated the wake-up call having to go to work themselves. Allowing the Bug to warm up for a few minutes each time he started it had proven healthy for it, and Brogan. Three minutes for the Bug to warm up was also three minutes for Brogan to fix any imperfections in the rear view mirror. He made sure there was nothing in his teeth, or hanging from his nose. If anyone saw Brogan's goofy smile as he checked his teeth, he might be construed as disturbed or unstable. But like a barber to his blade, Brogan demanded sharpness.

With much excitement and anticipation Brogan popped the Bug into reverse and backed out of his parking stall. As desire oozed from his thoughts, Brogan found first gear and proceeded to blat down the street.

To understand Brogan's mission you had to look through his eyes and see what beauty they absorbed. You had to be witness to the green eyes, the red hair, and a smile that would bring any war, in a man's heart, to an end. Brogan was sure he wasn't the only guy out there that had been affected by Rita's smile and beautiful personality. He still got butterflies every time he was near her. If for some reason his morning objective was not achieved, he knew there would be a huge void in his day. Although it had not happened yet, the thought of missing the most amazing sight the Lord had ever partaken in ran through Brogan's mind. A dull ache set in and surrounded his chest making it feel tight. His foot got heavier and the Bug, now being pushed, accepted the challenge.

For Brogan there had only ever been one true love. One woman who could soothe all historic pain and make him realize his potential. For five years Brogan had followed a strict game plan that had neither faltered nor failed. Every morning he had gone to see Rita to get his coffee before heading off to work. And for five years Rita had yet to deprive him of his waking hot beverage, or his much needed ten minutes of serenity. Seeing her was a treat, seeing her and not being able to hug or kiss her was torturous, especially when she would subtly caress his hand when passing him his order.

Ordinarily Rita worked in the back making donuts and cookies, but for just ten minutes every morning, the entire front of the java house shone. For those ten minutes, Rita would come to the front and serve customers until the next shift came in, and Brogan had yet to miss a shift change. This might seem a little pathetic to some people. Actually Brogan had called himself pathetic just for that reason alone. But he could not help himself, he had to see her. For those ten minutes every morning Brogan would sit and drink his coffee, inhaling the long, loving glances known only to him as pure sweetness.

There are few people who get the chance to experience unconditional love, the kind of love that is stronger than any other force, stronger than jealously, stronger than addiction, and strong enough to endure all time. Brogan was one of those lucky few, and what made his relationship even more sincerely romantic was that the feeling was mutual. Rita declared her love for Brogan the day they met. Only not with words, but with her eyes. Fate, meant to be, written in the stars, call it whatever; it was the kind of love that most people wouldn't ever experience in their lifetime.

Many people had asked Brogan why him and Rita hadn't moved in together, and Brogan always had the same answer, "We're doing this the old fashion way. Besides, her dad is huge!"

Everyone at his work would laugh when Brogan said this, not only because it was funny, but because no one could see Brogan being intimidated by anyone.

As Brogan drove to work that Friday morning, he tried to figure out when he should pop the question; and wondered if the Lord would have mercy, allowing him the passage to heaven on earth with Rita's hand in marriage. Brogan knew the only way he would live a happy, fulfilled life was to marry Rita. And now that he had the ring, the only thing left to do was put it on her finger. It was a beautiful ring with a huge diamond, and a lot of sentimental value. It had belonged to Geraldine's mother. Geraldine sent the ring to Brogan the day she found out he was thinking of buying one.

SWOOSH

"What the…"

Not even a millisecond went by when Brogan spotted an orange hockey ball shoot across his windshield.

"This early in the morning?"

Suddenly Brogan saw the black tape on the blade of a hockey stick in front of his car, followed closely by a young boy who emerged from between two parked cars. He cranked the wheel left missing the boy by inches, then quickly jerked to the right to avoid the boy's dog, before slamming on the brakes. The Bug reacted perfectly. The tires made an eerie squawking noise, like something you'd hear in a Canadian horror flick. Brogan now stopped, his car facing the right curb, looked back to see that the boy had already returned to playing his hockey game.

"That came out of nowhere!" Brogan thought as he took a minute to regroup.

Brogan was already behind schedule because of a huge accident on his route that morning. It happened from time to time, you almost had to expect it in a big city. But this one seemed to set him back longer than any other in the past, and now this.

Glancing at the time, Brogan began to panic, "I can still make it!" he said trying to convince himself. "If I hurry!" He quickly corrected his direction and took off down the street.

Brogan briskly geared down as he spotted a police cruiser hiding behind some bushes. "I don't have time for this!" he said starting to panic again. He checked his watch as he was forced to slow down and obey the traffic laws.

Brogan shot an evil eye at the cop as he passed him, "You best not make me miss her!" he mumbled.

Once he was out of sight of the badge wearer, Brogan found out exactly what was under the hood. With a few twists and a couple turns Brogan could feel how well it held the road. As he turned into the parking lot, the left fishtail he generated by cranking the wheel without slowing down, surprised Brogan. Almost as much as the squealing tires surprised all the people going into JoJo's Java House. Brogan felt a little embarrassed, but not enough to detour him from his mission.

"Pulling into the parking lot at 65 km/h was not part of the plan," Brogan thought to himself with a smile. "Sometimes you have to improvise."

Brogan quickly jumped out of the Bug and noticed it was parked in the stall perfectly. Two guys drinking their coffee stared out the window looking for a camera crew, thinking there was a movie being filmed and Brogan was the stunt driver. With no time to waste Brogan headed for the java house.

"Only one purpose and the rest of the day will fall into place." Brogan thought.

Not realizing, Brogan almost ripped the door off as he barrelled into the shop. Without looking, he apologized to the couple he almost bumped into and made his way to the counter. He didn't look at the clock on the wall because he knew the bitter truth. He also knew that when he looked up from the floor, chances were it wasn't going to be Rita standing there. He cleared his throat and tried to act normal.

"There goes the rest of my day!"

"I'm sorry sir...could you repeat that please?"

"She must be new here," Brogan thought not recognizing the lady taking his order.

He mustarded up a smile. "Extra large black, one sugar, please," he said looking past her into the back, hoping to catch a glimpse of Rita. Hoping that if she saw him, maybe she could quickly come out to say hi and set this horrible day back on the right path.

Everything seemed to be in slow motion now. Brogan's breathing became rapid and heavy. His brain felt like it was stuck in molasses. Realizing that for the first morning in five years he had missed seeing her, Brogan started feeling extremely exhausted and emotionally drained.

As Thelma brought Brogan his coffee she noticed his demeanour. "Are you ok sir?"

Brogan took a deep breath, nodding to her frivolous question. A whimpering sigh almost broke loose from his lips as he exhaled.

"That'll beeee, $1.80 sir."

Brogan slid a toonie across the counter, "Keep the change," he said in a harsh whisper.

"Thanks, come again!"

"Just a little too cheerful right now Thelma," Brogan thought to himself.

He grabbed his coffee off the counter and proceeded to mope past his regular seat; where he sat every morning, for ten minutes, to regain the concept of the purpose of life.

Brogan was not mad at Thelma, or the cop for that matter. He was definitely not upset at the boy and his dog, or the accident. Brogan just needed to see Rita every morning. Some people go for a jog, others need their caffeine or nicotine fix first thing. Brogan needed to see Rita. Basically, seeing her made the day so much more meaningful. It gave him a beautiful reason for being at work, besides paying taxes in the huge out of control city. A reason for all reasoning. Brogan did not consider himself a pessimist, but he knew the rest of his day would not be the same now.

Rita was a busy, important woman. She was always donating her time and energy to good causes. Thursday nights she volunteered at the homeless shelters, and would spend various Friday nights at the animal shelters. Brogan knew it would be difficult for them to find time to spend together; Rita had explained that to him when they first started dating. He understood it then, and he definitely understood it now. But not seeing her that morning really aggravated him, more than he thought possible. Maybe because it had been three days since they had spent any time together, except for the quick morning coffee pick ups, but that didn't count.

Brogan knew him and Rita were meant to be from the get go. But there was something missing, and he knew Rita felt it too. Picturing her smiling face, he believed there was only one good thing that transpired that morning. Feeling the void of not seeing her made him realize he could not live without her for another minute. He had to pop the question soon.

For the next ten minutes Brogan shared the news and his coffee with the Bug. Sickened by the turn of events that morning, Brogan started to dream of Rita to help him cope. Rita, so sweet and pure, she was the only cure!

CHAPTER 3

UNSETTLING

"Well, at least it's Friday! Aren't you glad it's Friday Brogan?" Those were the first words he heard as he got out of his car at work. Brogan turned to look at Harold, a short, pudgy man who he had saved six times in the two years they worked together. Brogan knew Harold wasn't trying to be annoying, he just came across that way naturally. He was so appreciative of how many times Brogan had saved him that he was more affectionate than he should be.

"Morning Harold. How's the family?"

"Really good Brogan, thanks for asking. The wife, Carol, wants to see you…have you over for supper again soon. And the two little rug rats want to see you again too."

"That sounds like a good idea Harold, we should set a date and time and I'll bring Rita."

Brogan started walking towards the plant because he knew Harold would sit and talk his ear off. Harold followed quickly behind him, jogging a bit to catch up.

"Yes, that's a good idea, bring Rita. You know Brogan, the wife and I were talking again this morning about how grateful we are for what you have done for our family." Harold stared at Brogan the whole time they walked, he was always staring. Brogan even noticed Harold staring at him from the opposite end of the building sometimes.

Still upset about the turn of events that happened that morning, and not being able to see Rita, Brogan had a short fuse. He stopped and grabbed Harold by the shoulder. "Dude, you know I love ya Harold, but you gotta let this thing go man. I mean, everyday for almost the last two years you have been thanking me! You're welcome! Now let's not say another word about it, ok?"

"That was kinda demanding," Brogan thought as he released Harold's shoulder and started walking towards the plant again.

Harold immediately rushed up beside Brogan again, "I'm sorry Brogan, it's just very touching for me…everything that you've done."

Harold stopped, grabbing Brogan by the shoulders, and stared into his eyes. Brogan could hear Harold's voice starting to crack as he continued to explain himself through tears, "You are the man Brogan. I can't begin to express how grateful I am. You will always be treasured by my family, as family."

"Harold, pull yourself together man, people will see you," Brogan said feeling a little awkward.

Letting go of Brogan's shoulders, Harold stared at him with more tears streaming down his chubby checks. "I get to watch my babies grow up because of you Brogan, that's everything to me," Harold said in a soft, sincere voice.

Brogan's awkward feeling was replaced with a strong buddy connection as he continued to walk with Harold, who was now walking with his head down a bit. Brogan put his arm around him, "Oh Harold, you big, softy you."

The truth was Brogan was the reason, many times over, why a lot of kids still had both their parents. It wasn't that Brogan didn't like the gratitude given by people whose lives he'd saved, he just preferred feeling the gratification that came with helping someone.

On a regular work day there were approximately a hundred men and women fabricating, designing, and building pieces for specific uses. Brogan had shown from the first day that he was versatile and could work any and every job that was assigned to him; but the higher authorities kept Brogan close to the more dangerous jobs on purpose. Brogan knew this, but did not mind at all. Although, he did wonder what would happen when, or if, he didn't make it in time to save that one person; would people hold it against him? Could he continue working there if something did happen?

The morning seemed to slip by fairly quickly, quicker than Brogan had expected given the earlier events. Although he knew the afternoon would go by more slowly because of the piece they were building next. It was part of a huge job they were working on which, once complete, would stand forty feet tall and eventually become computer operated in a factory in Toronto. The top piece, which weighed about a tonne, was the final piece to be added; but was the most dangerous part of the job, because it had to be hoisted thirty feet so they could mount and fasten it.

Three sets of scaffolding were set up around the fabrication with five people working on each to make sure everything went smoothly. Ben and Peter were two of the biggest guys on the shift, so naturally they were assigned to the floor work where most of the heavy lifting was.

It took a lot of practice and safety precautions to stay out of each others way when working in close quarters like they were on the scaffolding. Even though safety was the company's number one priority, workers on the scaffolding were told not to clamp their safety harnesses onto anything unless otherwise instructed. They were told they needed to move around freely without having to worry about tripping over their own, or someone else's safety line. Also, there had been employees, in the past that had gotten injured from being tied off.

The piece had been hooked and was being carefully lifted with the hoist. When it was halfway to the top a loud crack suddenly echoed through the shop. The supervisor quickly stopped the hoist to check everything over. Within a few minutes he deemed things "good to go". The workers on the scaffolding had their pry pins and bolts ready to start fastening the pieces together as soon as it was mounted. Forty-eight foot ceilings gave the workers plenty of height to work with, but the weight of the piece was a major concern. All safety precautions were taken; the hoists were checked everyday for wear and tear, along with every tool or piece of equipment used for the job, and safety meetings were held religiously every morning.

"Only two feet to go and we'll be able to slide it into place," one of the workers on the scaffolding yelled.

Communication was a key factor in the safety of this or any lift. Especially when lifting something this heavy.

Brogan was on the top of one scaffolding when another ear popping crack rang out across the shop. It was so loud that workers in the other rooms stopped using their power tools, questioning the sound. Instantly Brogan realized what was happening and was on the move. One of the thick chains on the hoist had snapped, and the one tonne wrecking ball was swinging straight for Brogan's scaffolding. Before anyone realized what had happened, Brogan grabbed a chain that was connected to a pulley. He ran past the four other workers on his scaffolding, hooking onto their safety harnesses before jumping to the next scaffolding, fifteen feet away. In mid flight Brogan grabbed the other end of the chain, feeling it go tight as he gave it a quick, hard yank. The four men jolted straight up, swinging outward underneath the pulley they were now attached to, before starting their descent. The chain zipped through Brogan's gloved hands as he landed, but he was able to take enough weight of the men to slow their fall. Without delay Brogan headed for the next five workers.

The shop was in chaos, everyone was yelling as the one tonne piece blasted through the first scaffolding like it was built out of toothpicks. The five workers on the third scaffolding were now on their way down, frantically, but at least on their own accord. Brogan knew it would only be a few seconds before the one tonne widow maker had the second scaffolding in its sights. Everyone was panicking and trying to figure out what to do, then noticed Brogan running flat out. It was faster then anyone at his work had ever seen him move before.

Two of the five workers on the second scaffolding were female and known for always attaching their safety harnesses, even when instructed not to. Brogan ran by shoving both girls over the side knowing their safety harnesses would drop them down, and eventually fetch them up before they hit the concrete floor. Before the girls had reached the end of their lanyards, Brogan was headed for his next two targets.

"Excuse me!" Brogan said zipping past Harold.

Harold was bewildered to what was happening, until he saw the huge chunk of steel swinging out of control. Suddenly Harold was stricken with devastation thinking Brogan had left him behind.

Brogan reached his next two targets just as the one tonne chunk of steel reached its full pendulum swing and headed for the next scaffolding. Without slowing, Brogan grabbed a chain with his left hand and planted his right palm in the chest of the man he thought could take a harder hit. The force of the impact sent his co-worker flying straight back off the edge of the scaffolding. Brogan then grabbed the other guy by the back of his safety harness and jumped off the scaffolding, catching the first falling co-worker between his legs. Holding one man with his right hand, the chain with his left, and the other man with his legs, Brogan swung toward the third scaffolding.

In mid flight, Brogan yelled at the two men, "When we hit, you two head for the floor and go help the girls."

As they landed, Brogan let them go and pushed off, swinging back toward the second scaffolding. The swing was hard and fast as Harold came into Brogan's view. He was scrambling, trying to figure out the fastest way to safety, when he saw Brogan swinging towards him like Tarzan. Brogan couldn't help but smirk when he saw Harold's chubby, teary-eyed face, and his arms extended like he wanted a hug. The wrecking ball was heading straight towards him, and Brogan raced to reach Harold first. As Brogan swung closer to Harold he pulled his knife out of its sheath with his free hand, and noticed the look of concern on Harold's face as he swooped in. His legs hardly went around Harold, but Brogan was still able to snag him. As they swung through the scaffolding, Brogan reached out and cut the two safety lines that the girls were dangling from. Co-workers were ready below, as the girls dropped several feet to the floor.

"It's probably a good thing you can't see this Harold!" Brogan said noticing his eyes clenched shut.

"What!" Harold squealed nervously, his eyes popping open as he held onto Brogan for dear life.

Harold screamed like a girl as he watched the swinging chunk of steel wipe out the scaffolding he had just been working on. As it crumbled to the ground, the one tonne piece continued its destructive course towards the remaining scaffolding. Surprisingly no one was injured from the debris raining to the floor.

Because of the speed at which they were swinging, Brogan was unable to slide both Harold and himself down safely to the floor. And now, the one tonne chunk of steel was heading straight for them. The only thing the workers on the floor could do was watch as Brogan and Harold collided with it. Brogan managed to absorb a lot of the impact with his legs as he grabbed Harold with his left hand and bounced off the piece like they were repelling down a wall. Dangling from the chain, both men started spinning out of control. Brogan noticed a somewhat clear spot to land, and started to let the chain slip through his hand. Their decent was awkward and fast, but they both hit the floor and ran straight for one of the open bay doors.

It took several minutes for the one tonne mass to slow its momentum and the workers to get it back under control.

Brogan had to help Harold sit down because he was shaking uncontrollably.

"You ok me buddy?" Brogan asked Harold.

"N…n…n…no! I'm…n…n…not…ok!"

Brogan gave Harold a pat on the back as he walked inside to help clean up. Not much was said for the rest of the work day while everyone cleaned up and assessed the damages. Thankfully there were only a handful of injuries. Harold was sent home early because he could not shake the shakes.

Brogan replayed everything over in this head as he put his coveralls in his locker and packed up for the day. Despite the rough morning, and the intensity of today's events, it had been a fairly normal day.

It didn't matter what job Brogan was doing, he always felt as though he was wasting his time. He never truly understood the feeling, although he did understand that the bills had to be paid, and the concept of working for your money. But that didn't change the fact that he felt as though he should be doing something else with his time rather than working. He could not explain it, therefore he never told anyone about it. Whether he was saving someone or merely carrying groceries for an old lady, these were the times he felt as though he was doing what he should be…fulfilling his destiny so to speak. He didn't consider himself a superhero or anything like that, but he always thought that working at a job that involved saving or helping people would be great. And to a certain extent his job at Mocor allowed him to do just that. At times, like what had occurred today, it made the feeling of wasting his time diminish. Even if only for a while.

Brogan had considered working for the police force, and the army like his uncle Gary. He even thought about being an EMT. But for some unexplainable reason each and every time he planned on joining, or tried to join, something always came up to persuade him not to; or made it virtually impossible for him to get to his interviews on time. It seemed there were obstacles thrown at him each time he tried getting a job that would put him with the heroes of society. Like the time he went to sign up to be a volunteer fire fighter. "That was brutal," he always thought.

That day he had received a phone call from his mother and was disconnected just as she was trying to explain that she was having chest pains. After spending half an hour trying to get his mom back on the phone, he was late for his interview with the fire chief and ended up getting a speeding ticket on the way there. To top it all off, he also got a flat tire before making it to the fire hall. Needless to say, he was very late for his appointment! Yes, he remembered that day vividly, mostly because of what the fire chief said to him. "Life happens fast boy, it ain't gonna wait for you to catch up."

Brogan often thought of those words, which at the time didn't seem like the smartest thing to say, but really no other words could be more true.

Brogan was just locking his locker when he felt his cell phone vibrate in his jacket pocket. He scrambled for it hoping it was Rita texting him to say she didn't have to work all weekend. Brogan finally reached his phone and realized how selfish he was being. He couldn't help it, he wanted Rita all to himself and all of her time too. But sadly, Brogan knew that an angel such as Rita would have to be shared with all the other people who needed her help.

He looked at the number and read the text out loud as though it would help him figure out whose number it was. "How's it going?"

Brogan smiled as he replied. "I see you figured out how to use your cell phone! I will call you."

The phone only had a chance to ring once, "Hello."

"Hey ma, what's up? Mom...you have to talk slower...mom...mom I can't...yes, I'm fine. How are you doing? No I'm not trying to change the topic...yes, there was some excitement at work today...well let me finish. To make a long story short, some scaffolding gave out and I saved a couple of people. Yes, I'm fine, and everyone else is too...yes, every single person has thanked me...yes, they are all grateful. Thank you mom that makes me feel good."

Brogan rolled his eyes, and chuckled to himself as his mother raced to the next topic as if she was an auctioneer.

"No, Rita has to work all weekend...I know she's always working. No I haven't asked her yet...cause the time hasn't... Yes, I went and got the ring cleaned. Actually, I got it cleaned five times, they had a special on... no I didn't mom, I didn't get it cleaned that many...yes this is me being funny. Ok mom, love you too...k...bye."

On the drive home Brogan couldn't help but think about how wonderful his mother was. She always knew what to say when something needed to be said, and had a mother's intuition like nothing he had ever heard of before. Brogan did not think his mother was psychic or could see into the future, but for the most part he became use to the fact that she would have some sort of feeling when something happened to him. Geraldine could not explain how worried she would get about Brogan whenever she had these feelings. She could sense the pain with whatever he was battling, and for Geraldine this was unsettling.

CHAPTER 4

INSTINCT

No matter how bad life seemed to get, talking to his mother always made him smile. Brogan was in a better mood than what the morning had brought on. He remembered how his mother helped him learn to cope with his anger; to channel it and use the aggression in a positive way, such as helping others. There were a few people throughout Brogan's life that had helped him along the way, but Geraldine was the one who opened his eyes to doing good things. Brogan could remember the first time he had helped someone; he was hooked from that point on. The pleasure he felt each and every time he did a good deed, and seeing the smiles on people's faces, was enough for Brogan and made it all worth while.

"Sure the day started off rough, but you got through it," Brogan said out loud as he shifted gears. "Now I just gotta get through this pounding headache."

Despite his excruciating pain, a smile spread across Brogan's face as he recalled the day's events. The fact that he saved all those people helped his mood, and his headache. He didn't know when he was going to see Rita next, so not seeing her in the morning threw him off. But the adrenaline rush of the afternoon's events helped straighten him out a bit. As he pulled into the parking lot of the Grab n Go Store, he still felt revved up. Like a kid that had eaten too much chocolate, he had a lot of piped up energy.

Brogan shut the Bug off and pushed back in his seat reaching into his front pocket. He pulled out twenty five dollars and some change. "Good enough," he thought, but grabbed his wallet just in case.

Brogan stopped before fully getting out of his car. Staring at the big green neon sign he tried to gather his thoughts. "Grab n Go Store n More," he read out loud trying to idle down his bottled energy.

Brogan couldn't figure out why he was still so revved. "I'm still fired up, but I'm in a good mood…I've gotta simmer down," Brogan said, his voice getting louder as he spoke.

He took a few more minutes to try and gather his thoughts.

The store was exactly that - More. It had everything you could think of, and then some. Brogan had been shopping there since he moved to Saddleback City. They carried everything a person needed to survive in the big city, or the wilderness. From bread and milk to duct tape and fishing supplies. It was by far the best all-around store for anyone with an appetite for a hobby.

As Brogan shut the door to the Bug he felt cool specks of rain hit his cheeks. The cool mist instantly took him back to when he was a kid. As a young boy he would try to keep his eyes open to catch a glimpse of where the raindrops were falling from. He stood there looking up, letting the small, cool memories splash on his face.

A smile streamed across his face and he quickly realized what he must look like standing there staring up. Brogan locked the Bug with his key fob and canvassed the parking lot for witnesses to his weird behaviour. There were three vehicles parked there, but the third car he almost didn't even see. The black, four-door Sedan was hardly noticeable because it was parked at the far south end of the building, and the darkness of night engulfed the black car making it almost invisible. Even the two street lights in the center of the parking lot, which lit up virtually the entire area, would not identify the bulky beast. The other two cars were parked beside Brogan's, and he didn't see anyone else around.

With a small smirk hanging on his face, Brogan headed toward the store. "Better grab a cart," he thought as the automatic doors opened.

Fishing a loonie from his pocket he slipped it into the slot, freeing the cart from the metal chain gang. As he spun around the second set of automatic doors swept open, and a loud popping noise echoed from the back of the store. Brogan quickly squatted behind his shopping cart, recognizing the sound as gunfire and instantly his headache was gone.

Brogan's eyes darted around the store as he tried to see something, anything that would give him an idea of what was happening.

"I need to get in there… see what's goin on!"

Staying squatted, Brogan zipped through the second set of doors and spun around the corner, hiding behind a display of chocolate bars. Suddenly he heard a man shouting, followed by a woman's plea for her daughter's safety. Brogan peeked over the rack and immediately became enraged. The man yelling had a mother and her young daughter on the floor at gunpoint. Brogan's heart felt like it skipped a few dozen beats and a warm sensation flowed through his body.

"Here we go!" Brogan growled through clenched teeth.

As he leaned over to get a better look at the man with the gun, his nostrils flared and he realized he was grinding his teeth. Then Brogan spotted a pallet jack which had been left beside a pallet of produce, only a few feet away. A sadistic smirk crept out the corner of his lips as he whispered to himself, "Improvise!"

Brogan climbed onto the pallet jack and proceeded to ride it like a scooter towards the gunman; steering with both hands and pushing between the outriggers with his right leg. Each push bringing forth an inevitable end for the gunman.

As Brogan rode the jack closer to his target he could see the handgun being waved around; and the fiend was still yelling at his hostages. Ten feet from impact, the gunman looked up. Just as Brogan predicted, the fiend was so stunned he couldn't react. Brogan placed his foot on the center of the jack and jumped off pushing as hard as he could, almost doubling its speed. All the gunman could do was open his mouth in disbelief.

"There is no mercy when you mess with kids!" Brogan said as the pallet jack found its intended target.

There was no time to turtle or scream, let alone jump out of the way. The gunman's fate was sealed the moment Brogan decided to stop at the store. His injuries, most likely life altering, were partially due to Brogan's messed up morning, and the fact that he was still extremely revved up from the afternoon's events.

The jack handle struck the gunman's face at the same time the base hit his legs, shattering all on contact. The force of the pallet jack also snapped several of his ribs like twigs, and drove him into a wall that was stocked with fishing supplies.

Several more gunshots rang out from the back of the store, drowning the commotion, as Brogan introduced the gunman to "Uncle Jack". He immediately squatted beside the woman and her daughter. "Lady, you and your little girl gotta stay hidden," he said in a stern but reassuring whisper. "It's gonna be ok."

Even Brogan couldn't believe how much reassurance was in his voice. The woman and her daughter looked at Brogan with fear in their eyes, making him even more mad. As Brogan spun on his heels to leave, the little girl reached out and touched his arm. He turned and looked at her. "You and your mom will be ok," he said smiling at her.

She smiled back and whispered, "I know, you're here now."

Brogan slowly looked to her mother, "Do you have any idea how many there are?"

The woman was obviously shaken. "I s...s...saw th...three men c... come in," she stuttered. "The o...o...other t...t...t..."

The little girl touched her mother's cheek, then looked at Brogan. "The other two men have bigger guns," she whispered.

Brogan looked at the girl. "Thank you for the help little miss brave," he said in a low voice, and was gone.

As Brogan zipped passed the unconscious gunman, he noticed fishing hooks and lures were imbedded all over him.

When Brogan reached the end of the aisle he squatted down with his back against the shelves. He could hear another man yelling and barking orders at more hostages.

The aisle Brogan had just come down had nearly a hundred feet of canned goods on one side of it, and camping supplies on the other. As he peeked around the corner, he estimated almost double the distance to the next gunman. Brogan grabbed a pair of binoculars off the shelf across from him and peered at the second gunman.

"He's got a freakin' automatic!" Brogan almost blurted out loud, but caught himself.

He quickly flipped around the end display to the next aisle. "That cut down about fifteen feet," he thought taking another quick look at the gunman before spinning around to the next aisle over.

Brogan peered through the binoculars again and saw three women, one man, and two kids about the ages of nine or ten, huddled on the floor in front of the gunman. Their backs were up against the meat display, which ran across the entire length of the wall. To the right of the gunman was a back door that lead to the manager's office. Brogan flipped around to the next aisle, hiding again behind the display rack at the end of it. One of the women gasped as she noticed Brogan, making the gunman turn around. Brogan could see the gunman, but the gunman could not see him through the rack of batteries.

"Come on man, think! I gotta help those people…" Brogan thought as the gunman turned back towards the hostages.

With a smirk as quick as his mind, Brogan dropped the binoculars and reached out to the shelf in front of him, snagging a ten litre plastic jug of cooking oil, and returned to his squatting position behind the rack of batteries, his back still to the gunman. He squeezed the handle of the jug and peeked around the corner one last time. Without warning, Brogan flung his arm back and shot it forward like a catapult. It was a long, hard chuck for something so heavy. Brogan watched as the jug of oil soared through the air in a high arch, looking like a drunken turkey trying to fly.

Brogan leaped up and spun around the corner sprinting for the gunman. He wasn't a gun expert but had seen enough Chuck Norris movies to know the gunman had an AK-47, and hoped he wasn't experienced with that particular gun.

The jug smacked the floor behind the gunman sounding like a big belly flop. The oil spewed out of the broken jug and flowed everywhere leaving behind a huge, oil spill Slip 'n Slide.

"What the…" startled, the gunman spun around to see what the noise was.

Brogan had already dropped to his left side as if he were sliding into home plate. When the gunman noticed Brogan he took aim at him with his fully automatic weapon. Brogan slid through the cooking oil past the gunman, squatting into the meat display shelf. With an awesome force that caused the sneeze guards to pop out, he launched back through the oil at the hostage taker.

The gunman took aim, and fired. Brogan was sliding so fast that the bullets ricocheted off the floor right behind him. The gunman wasn't able to pull his barrel down fast enough, and each bullet released from his gun missed its mark. Floor tiles were exploding inches behind Brogan's feet, like miniature landmines being detonated as he slid.

A millisecond before Brogan reached his target, he did a one arm push-up bringing his right forearm in front of him. On impact he stretched up cutting the gunman just above the knees. The fully automatic weapon ceased fire and Brogan knew it was a good hit. Any football fan would have agreed that it was "the hit of the week". Brogan watched the gunman complete his second 360 degree spin in mid flight, before landing on his face with his arms stretched out in front of him. His body then folded over top of his head and arms, with a curdling, crunching sound, before flopping back to the floor motionless.

Brogan wondered if he had killed the guy, but the thought diminished as soon as he heard more gunfire. He scrambled to his feet, and crouched by the newly freed hostages. "Everyone ok?"

Not one person said anything, they just stared at him. Brogan thought it was because they were in shock, but he was only partially right. They were so stunned by his actions; it all happened so quickly, they weren't fully aware they were free from the hostage situation.

Brogan wasn't trying to impress anyone, if that were the case he would have chased the football dream. Instead he just wanted to help those who needed it. His awesome choreographed moves were pure and simple, it was his natural ability.

"How many more in the back? I heard gunshots coming from there."

Still there was no response. Brogan's eyebrows caved in towards his nose. "HEY! People!" he yelled as loud as he could in a whisper.

Startled, the lone male answered, "There's one more. He has the same type of gun."

Brogan noticed blood seeping through the man's pant leg. He reached out and grabbed one of the lady's scarves. "Keep this tight," he said tying it around the injured man's leg.

"You people need to go find a place to hide. I'm gonna throw this next guy's sorry ass out right here," Brogan said with a smirk.

Simultaneously all six people scampered to their feet trying to get away. Brogan watched as the freed hostages faded out of sight, then he turned and started for the manager's office in the back.

"If they'll point guns at kids and actually shoot one of the hostages, then anything goes," he thought.

Brogan could feel his heart pounding the moment he walked into this whole ordeal, now it seemed as if he was going to have a heart attack. Not only was his heart beating extremely fast, but he thought it might rip out through his chest.

Brogan shot to the back of the store and crouched against the right side of the door casing. "This last guy probably has less scruples than the other two. He's gonna get hurt!"

Still crouching, he crept around a bunch of stacked boxes and through the staff lunch room. His movements were stealthy and precise, adapting to all the objects around him. He could hear more yelling as he neared the manager's office.

From the staff lunch room door he had a clear view into the manager's office and the situation in there. He could see the third gunman standing over top of the manager's assistant, Erin.

Brogan had met Erin several different times in the store and knew she was a nice person. She was always happy and would bring a smile to the face of anyone that talked to her.

The fiend had his gun pointed into the back of her neck and was yelling and poking her with the barrel. "Open the freaking safe you stupid bitch or I'll blow your head off!"

"I...I...I...d...don't know the c...c...c..."

"Well you better f...f...figure it out!" the gunman mocked. "Hurry up you stupid stuttering bitch!"

"B...but I can't," she sobbed.

Brogan watched in pure horrid hatred as the gunman struck Erin in the back of the head. He knew it hurt, he heard it. But Erin was still conscious and alive. Brogan looked around for an idea, and found himself feeling bad for not knowing Erin's last name.

"C'mon...open that safe NOW!"

Brogan couldn't stand to see anyone being treated that way. Especially Erin, she was too nice of a person. He smirked as he purposely bumped a chair that scraped loudly on the floor. The gunman spun around quickly and looked out the manager's door toward the staff lunch room. "What was that?"

Brogan darted behind the bar fridge as the gunman started slowly toward the lunch room.

"You better have that safe open when I come back," he yelled over his shoulder at Erin.

Brogan could hear the gunman getting closer. From behind the fridge he could see the barrel of the gun as the gunman entered the room. He was moving slowly and carefully.

Faster than any snake strike, Brogan reached out and grabbed the gun barrel as if he were curling a dumbbell, smacking down on top of the gun with his other hand. The technique ripped the gun free from the stunned fiend's grip. It happened so quickly, he didn't have a chance to pull the trigger. Brogan stood holding the AK-47 by the barrel as the gunman stared, trying to figure out what just happened.

"You don't have the guts to use that…shit, you don't even know how to hold it," the idiot taunted.

Brogan did not respond, instead he just stared. The fiend started to get anxious as his eyes met Brogan's. "You know what? I'm gonna kick your ass, and then I'm gonna take her with me for a piece of dessert later," the fiend threatened, pointing toward Erin in the back room.

The fiend clenched his teeth as he thought about his plan of attack. Before he had a chance to move, Brogan lunged with a huge gliding sidestep and unleashed a right heel kick that connected with the fiend's rib cage. It sounded like Rice Krispies snap, crackle, and popping over a loud speaker. Brogan put a lot of force behind the kick, and he knew it did some damage. He watched the fiend fly several feet back into the manager's office. As he hit the wall, drywall dust exploded into the air filling the small office. The masked man was embedded in the drywall with only his feet, arms, and part of his head protruding from the wall. He looked like a wall trophy that was built and mounted by Red Green himself.

Brogan reached down and gently grabbed Erin's arm. He pulled her to her feet. "Let's get out of this office, it's full of dust and assholes...not good to breath in you know!"

Erin looked up at Brogan and saw he had a smile on his face. Even with everything that had just happened she still caught his little joke. She knew that Brogan was trying to help her deal with everything by making light of the situation. It worked. Even though she was understandably shaken up, surprisingly Erin was still quite alert. As Brogan was helping her out of the office, Erin caught movement out of the corner of her eye. She was just about to say something when Brogan pushed her to his other side. They both looked as the fiend was struggling to get free from the wall. Brogan gave Erin's shoulder a slight squeeze. "You best go to the front and wait for help."

Brogan was watching and waiting for the wall trophy to get free, when he felt a soft squeeze on his shoulder and heard an equally soft voice. "Help's already here, and if you don't mind I would very much like to finish this!"

Brogan turned and looked at Erin, puzzled. He could see in her eyes that she was more angry than scared, but still it bewildered him. Erin noticed the puzzled look on Brogan's face. "Brogan, he pushed that gun into my neck really hard, and I want him to know he can't get away with that!" she said with the same soft voice and more calmness.

Brogan noticed the change in her eyes and in her voice.

"Besides that," she continued, "he groped me."

Brogan looked at her, his eyebrows dove down. "WHAT!?"

He turned his head slowly back towards the now freed fiend. "You can stick around, but you might want to back up a bit," he said to Erin.

The masked man charged towards Brogan. "After a kick like that, and he still wants more? He's gotta be on something," Brogan thought.

Once he heard the explicit details from Erin, Brogan's blood seemed to boil. It could have been all the excitement and adrenaline that made everything seem like it was in slow motion for Brogan; but as the fight continued Erin watched in amazement. It seemed to her like everything, except Brogan, was moving slowly.

A knuckle dragger came from the fiend.

"ARE YOU SERIOUS?!" Brogan asked in a deep pissed off voice.

He ducked, smacking the back of the fiend's right elbow, making him miss his target and increasing his punching momentum.

Erin was standing far enough out of the way, and smiled as she watched the fiend's fist drive into a filing cabinet. He let out a horrific scream that turned into a growl as he shook his hand trying to get rid of the pain. "You dick...you're gonna die you son of a bitch!"

The fiend lunged at Brogan trying to kick him in the nether regions. But before his leg was halfway through its swing, Brogan unleashed his own kick. He made contact just above the fiend's kneecap and felt the crack before Erin heard it.

"AAAARRRRGGGGHH..." The scream was ear piercing as the fiend dropped, holding his leg, writhing in pain.

"Oh, does that hurt?" Erin asked sarcastically.

"Screw you bitch!"

Brogan took a step toward the grounded fiend and leaned over him wondering if he was done. "First you and your meatball friends come in here and take a bunch of people and kids hostage, and then you hurt and fondle this nice young woman?"

"Screw you f..."

Brogan reached out and back handed the idiot's face before he had a chance to finish his sentence.

The fiend rolled onto his chest without making a sound; then suddenly without warning, rolled back swinging a huge hunting knife. Brogan pulled his head back as the knife barley missed his throat.

Throughout Brogan's martial arts training he had taken thousands of knives and guns from people, but never from someone who meant him harm.

Before the fiend could swing the knife again, Brogan grabbed his hand and bent it back, while simultaneously twisting his wrist and pulling hard toward himself. There was a loud crack followed by a girly scream, and the fiend was on his stomach again. Without any hesitation Brogan took his belt off and hogtied all four of the fiend's limbs behind his back.

"You little shits are..."

Suddenly Erin flew past Brogan, and with a single kick to the fiend's jaw there were no longer any threats coming from the downed dirt bag.

Brogan was more bewildered about the kick than the entire ordeal at the store. He never would have guessed that such a nice, small girl had that much power. Staring at Erin, Brogan had a confused yet impressed look on his face as he played the kick over in his head.

"What?" she asked.

"Erin! That was awesome! I never saw that coming, especially from you! There's university athletes that can't kick like…like that!"

"Oh, that," she said blushing a little. "I have a tough older brother, and I played a lot of soccer."

Brogan's bottom lip covered his top lip; he raised his eyebrows and nodded his head once as if to say, "right on sister, serves him right!"

Erin smiled at Brogan and she reached out taking his hand in hers. "Thank you Brogan."

"No, thank you."

Erin looked puzzled. "You saved me and everyone else. What could you possibly be thanking me for?"

Brogan looked forward as they both walked towards the front of the store. "That guy talked too much. He was starting to get on my nerves."

Erin could tell Brogan was still trying to make her feel safe and help her deal with the stressful events that had just unfolded. She didn't say anything, instead she wrapped her arm in around Brogan's and leaned her head on his arm as they walked, signifying that she was alright and that she could not feel any safer than she did at that moment.

As they reached the front of the store, they could hear sirens getting closer. All the freed hostages were huddled behind a display at the front of the store. Brogan and Erin both looked at them.

"Why are you people still in here?" Brogan asked throwing his hands up in the air. "You should have evacuated the store."

"You guys, we're all safe thanks to Brogan. You can come out now," Erin chimed.

The man with the bullet in his leg looked at Brogan, "We tried calling for help, but…"

"The phones are dead," the two young girls interrupted at the same time.

"They must have cut the phone lines," the wounded man continued, "so Alice went outside to use her cell phone," he pointed to her as he spoke.

"She was shot at!" the two girls chirped again at the same time.

"What?" Brogan asked, his adrenaline surging again.

"As soon as she stepped out the front entrance, two shots were fired."

Brogan looked over at the front doors and then back at the group. "Everyone stay here and keep your heads down."

He made his way over to the front entrance, grabbed a cart, and shoved it hard out the automatic doors. As soon as the doors opened a shot rang out. It was like the gunman outside had never used a gun before and was nervously shooting every time he saw the doors open.

Brogan darted outside and saw a man, at the far end of the parking lot, standing beside his car fumbling with his gun. He now realized the black Sedan, that he hardly noticed earlier, was the get-away vehicle. Brogan instantly took off on a mad sprint, even before he could calculate how long it would take him to cross the parking lot. Everyone in the store was now standing and watching out the front store window.

The lone gunman could hear the sirens getting louder and looked up just in time to see a strange figure coming at him fast. He scrambled to get into his car, then aimed the big black Sedan right at Brogan. Brogan heard the car's tires squeal as the 4-barrels kicked in, but he never slowed down at all. Still on a mad sprint, Brogan now found himself playing chicken only without a car.

Inside the store, the group watched in amazement.

"He's crazy...he's not slowing down! That car's going to hit him!" said one of the onlookers.

Erin didn't really know what to expect out of Brogan next, but after what she witnessed earlier she knew everyone would be safe, especially Brogan. She nudged the wounded man with her elbow, still staring out the window. "Watch this!" she said loud enough for everyone to hear.

It's back right tire still smoking from the take off, the Sedan was now doing 70 km/h and barrelling down on it's intended target. The gap was closing between them fast. Without slowing down and with hardly any effort Brogan snagged one of the iron garbage cans, from the parking lot, with his right hand and swung it up to his left. With the Sedan right in front of him, Brogan jumped with amazing agility; especially considering the extra eighty pounds he was carrying. Just like a jack rabbit, his legs came up in front of him and his arms hung down between his legs with the iron can in tow.

Once again Brogan wowed Erin. Even the get-a-way driver was both freaked out and amazed as Brogan cleared the roof of his car by five feet. But before the black Sedan could escape from under Brogan, he dropped the garbage can like a bomber plane releasing it's weapon. The eighty pound iron can shot through the windshield breaking the steering wheel off at the base and landed in the get-a-way driver's lap, pinning his arms down. He started squealing when he realized the impact had made his legs go numb, impairing them so he couldn't use the brakes.

Spinning in mid flight, now facing the rear of the Sedan, Brogan landed smoothly in the parking lot. Bending his knees to absorb the landing, he looked like a ninja with his right hand out on the ground in front of him and his left arm out to his side for extra stability.

The sirens were numerous and deafening as twenty or more squad cars raced to the scene. As the first three police cruisers pulled into the parking lot they had to slam on their brakes, coming to a screeching halt. The get-a-way driver's foot was stuck on the gas pedal and the Sedan was still speeding across the parking lot.

There was a huge oak tree that had been growing in the front parking lot entrance since before the store was built. It had been hit by numerous vehicles over the years and graciously accepted every one. The Sedan slammed head on into the tree and once again the big tree was the victor. Police officers instantly swarmed the mangled car with paramedics following closely behind them.

"I hope he's not dead," Brogan thought as he stood up and started walking back towards the grocery store.

The police took their time getting everyone's statements and listened in amazement to what had taken place. They were all anxious to hear what Brogan himself had to say about the nights events; but by the time an officer finally got around to speaking with Brogan, he just wanted to go home. As they talked, other officers gathered around to hear Brogan's side of things.

"Listen, I'm exhausted, and there are a few details that still seem a little fuzzy," Brogan finally told the police officer taking his statement.

"Tell you what son, I'll drive you home so you can get some sleep. Then I'll come pick you up in the morning, and we'll head down to the station so you can finish giving your statement. Sound good?"

Brogan looked at the officer, "Thanks, but I've got my car, I don't need a lift home."

The officer shook his head, "If you insist on driving, then I'll follow you home to make sure you're ok."

"Yeah I'm ok to drive," Brogan said pulling his car keys out of his pocket. "You can follow me home if you want, but...can you keep up?" Brogan joked showing the officer he was ok.

The officer noticed Brogan's grin and nodded with a smirk.

As Brogan got into his Bug, the people that he helped save were still thanking him; they had been all night. He gave a subtle wave as he started the ignition, popped it into first and left the parking lot.

The whole drive home, all Brogan could think about was Rita. Not because she could have lost him a couple different times that day, but because of how he managed to make it through the day with all that had been tossed at him.

As Brogan parked and got out of the Bug, he noticed the police cruiser. "Forgot about him," he mumbled to himself as he shut his door and headed toward the cruiser.

"Thank you for escorting me home sir," he said shaking the officer's hand.

"You're welcome son. Now go get some sleep and I'll see you in the morning," he said handing Brogan his business card.

Brogan nodded and started to walk towards his building.

"I'm glad you're ok son. You were pretty lucky tonight," he said with a wink.

Little did he know about Brogan's natural instinct.

CHAPTER 5

FATE

B rogan had two extra drinks with Captain Morgan and was destined to wrestle with the couch. He finally passed out at 4:00am, six hours after Officer Don Fisherman escorted him home. Brogan didn't normally drink, but when the headaches would start, funny enough, a few wobblies helped ease the horrific dull pounding; although he never made a habit of it.

When he was young, Brogan complained three different times about severe, gut wrenching head pain. And three times Brogan's mother took him to see a doctor, a different one each time. All three times, each doctor said the same thing, "There seems to be absolutely nothing wrong with his head at all. Just a lot more brain activity than what we think normal. It's a good, healthy thing but could we run more tests?"

Geraldine never allowed them to run more tests, and always kept a close watch to make sure the doctors only examined Brogan's symptoms. She didn't want to have to answer a flurry of questions again and again about his internal setup. Unfortunately, this meant that Brogan never had a doctor to call his own.

Even though Brogan was young at the time, he could see the stress it caused his mother every time a doctor wanted to run further tests on him. So to save her the anguish of another doctor's visit, after the third time, Brogan did not complain about his headaches ever again.

Brogan quickly discovered that each time the immense head pain would come it would eventually dissipate, and learned to deal with the pain as it came. Besides that, he was an extremely fast healer.

Brogan also soon realized that the head pounding pain would start shortly after something exciting had happened to him…something to get his adrenaline flowing. A near fatal accident on his bike, a fight or confrontation, a rush from a roller coaster ride; any and all things that would jump start his heart and get it pounding faster.

It was 8:30am and his blood shot eye slowly crept open. He felt achy from just that simple movement. "Not a good sign," he muttered to himself.

He spotted a glass of day old water perched on the coffee table beside him. "Not gonna cut it," he thought.

Brogan reluctantly pulled himself to a sitting position. He figured he might as well get up and take a couple Advil. He remembered this type of pain, the mixture of a good work out and a little celebration. It only happened a few times, but he remembered it vividly. He sat staring at the flashing 12:00 on his old, but still working VCR. "Who knows how to set those anyway?" he mumbled to himself lost in thought.

Eventually he pulled himself off the couch and stumbled to the bathroom not really comprehending the great deeds he had done the day and night before. He decided to grab a quick shower before heading down to the station to meet Officer Fisherman.

It was apparent that violence had been escalating lately in Saddleback City. Every time Brogan turned on the news somebody had been harmed in one way or another. It was the main reason Brogan didn't like watching it. Saddleback City was very clean and respected until crime sprees suddenly started erupting throughout the entire city. Police patrol had been beefed up immensely, but it seemed to have little or no effect. The city even went as far as to hire other private security companies to help take some of the work load from the police; still with little effect.

Brogan could tell that Officer Fisherman was a very busy man, and he was glad their meeting didn't take very long. "Finally some time to relax," Brogan thought as he opened the door to his apartment.

"There you are!"

The voice came from the kitchen. It startled Brogan, but he instantly smiled the moment his eyes met those of the intruders. He could never forget what they looked like, but each time he saw those beautiful green eyes it was like looking into them for the first time.

"Rita, sweetie, what are you doing here?" he sounded surprised, yet excited.

"More volunteers showed up at the soup kitchen than what they needed, so I figured why not go spend some time with the one I love!?"

"That's awesome! It's the best news I've heard in a while."

They grabbed a cup of coffee and headed out onto the deck to chat. The soft sun threw warmth over the two love birds in the cool morning air.

"Do you want to go to the zoo?" Rita asked out of no where.

Brogan never liked the idea of animals being imprisoned for profit, but he knew how much Rita enjoyed going. "Sure," he smiled, "as long as I'm with you!"

Brogan always soaked up the love that oozed from Rita's smile. And time spent with her, he cherished.

"We might as well walk," Rita said. "It looks like it's going to be a nice day."

Brogan looked at Rita and smiled as they walked slowly in silence, holding hands, enjoying the presents of each other.

"What?" she asked.

"I'm just…oh I don't know. I feel like a garbage bag."

The smile fell off Rita's face and she stopped. "Sweetie, what's the matter?" she asked. "What do you mean you feel like a garbage bag?"

Brogan looked into her eyes again and smiled. "I'm Glad!"

It only took Rita a second to put the two together. "Oh I get it, you're a Glad garbage bag, hahaha, very funny!" she said smacking his arm playfully. "You're so cheesy!"

She turned and started walking again. Brogan was right behind her quickly grabbing her hand as they continued on together. They often went for walks, sometimes talking the whole time, and others not saying a word; either way they enjoyed their time together.

This time they were so involved with one another that they didn't notice the two noisy crows sparing over a piece of chocolate bar that had been discarded in the street. Nor did they pay any attention to the fender bender at the four way stop, that was incidentally caused by a dog chasing the tire of one of the cars.

"What would you like to see first?" Brogan asked even though he already knew the answer.

Rita looked at Brogan. "You know," she smiled.

Brogan smiled back at her with all his love. He knew that Rita had a soft spot for the baby monkeys, and now the zoo had a new baby gorilla.

They both bought a bottle of water and proceeded to stroll through the zoo making their way to the gorilla cages.

The Saddleback City Zoo was well known for its spacious generosity and exceptional living conditions for all the animals there. What the zoo had accomplished was far more sophisticated than any other animal compound in the world; none came remotely close to the Saddleback City Zoo. Specialist even went as far to say that the animals didn't know they were living in a controlled environment. When Brogan had heard that statement he said then, and still will, that animals can feel their freedom being taken away from them when being put in captivity. Although, he also knew the animals had the best treatment at the Saddleback City Zoo. The facility was quite amazing; they had state of the art technology for all the animals to live comfortably. It seemed to Brogan that the animals didn't mind their living conditions. They were treated with the utmost respect and had all kinds of room to roam. Each caged area was specifically designed to accommodate whatever type of animal was placed in it, and was enclosed with high endurance, high impact plexiglass; very much like that used in a hockey arena, only with an added extra strength fibre woven throughout the glass. It was designed by a young scientist/inventor by the name of Darnel Casts, who had also designed and fabricated most of the non-lethal weapons used by the Saddleback City Police Force.

The entire zoo was one huge fortress. The plexiglass barricades did the job that they were designed to do: keep the animals safe from people and people safe from them. And so far, there had not been one incident concerning anyone's safety since the zoo had been redesigned and rebuilt ten years ago.

Brogan and Rita held hands as though they hadn't seen each other in months.

"This is what it's all about," Brogan said to Rita as they strolled past the tigers.

Rita smiled. "I love you Brogan," she said without looking up at him. "Thank you for everything, especially coming to the zoo with me."

Brogan squeezed her hand a little. "There's no one else I'd rather go to the zoo with," he whispered.

Rita looked up at him with a quirky smirk. "You wouldn't be caught dead in here if it wasn't for me. I feel bad for making you come."

Brogan put his arm around Rita and held her tight. He wasn't too sure what to say to make her feel better, so he spoke from the heart. "I know it sounds cliché, but it doesn't matter where I am as long as I'm with you. Plus, most of these animals were saved in one form or another, so it's not as bad."

"Oh Brogan! We're here!" she said pointing toward the gorilla enclosure with excitement. "I can't wait to see the baby gorilla!"

Brogan looked toward the cage that he had seen so many times now thanks to Rita. The enclosure was amazing. There were all sorts of big trees, and vine like ropes hanging all over the place. Close to the plexiglass there were tires hanging from two huge, fake trees that had several big limbs extending out thirty feet or more. The fake trees were designed to hold numerous gorillas without being torn up like normal trees.

When Brogan looked he could only see two gorillas. "Where's the rest of them?"

Normally because the enclosure was so massive, they would let all the monkeys and gorillas roam around at the same time. But today there were only two gorillas out.

Brogan and Rita reached their destination further up the path, away from a crowd of people who had gathered to the side of the cage to listen to a presentation about gorillas.

Rita looked at Brogan. "Why do you think there are only two gorillas out today? And where is the baby?"

51

Saddleback City Zoo took pride in their collection of animal species, especially the gorillas; the male in particular. This zoo was the only one in the entire world that had, in captivity and living as if it were still in the wild, a full grown 680 lb silverback gorilla.

Rita looked puzzled. "Hmm, that's strange! Well, look how that ones acting. Maybe that has something to do with it," she observed looking toward the cage.

"Yeah, rolling around, beating the ground, acting foolish, living the life." Brogan snickered.

"Maybe that zoo attendant can tell us what's going on, and where the baby is." Rita said as she started back down the path towards the crowd.

Brogan could tell that Rita was a little disappointed; she was really looking forward to seeing the new baby gorilla.

Suddenly, a scream rang out delivering goose bumps with its sound. The shrillful screech echoed across the entire zoo. Brogan bolted toward the crowd of people where a woman was still screaming. "My baby! My baby girl! HELP!!!! Someone help her!"

There was a single door leading into the gorilla/monkey enclosure, and was the only remaining piece from the old zoo. It was made out of steel bars, and was the type of door that would be found in a penitentiary. The sign hanging from it read 'KEEP BACK SIX FEET'. A 'Z' pattern path through a small garden of assorted flowers lead to the barred door. The path was only for the zookeepers and attendants to use.

The woman had been trying to keep a close eye on her three year old little girl as her husband dug through her purse looking for some change. Their little girl, Sophie, had been running around smelling all the pretty flowers in the garden and tripped, landing right beside the barred door. Just as the woman turned to pick her daughter up, a huge, long, hairy arm shot through the bars on the door and snatched the little girl. Sophie was a small girl so she fit easily through the gaps between the bars.

As the female gorilla pulled her through, Sophie's little face hit the bars and she was instantly knocked unconscious. The guide, who was giving the gorilla presentation, was fumbling for the keys to the door abiding by the father's screaming demands. The gorilla had little Sophie, still unconscious, in her arms rocking her like a baby, as if Sophie was her own.

As soon as the guide opened the door, the father barrelled in after his daughter, but was instantly on the ground after receiving four brutal blows from the silverback.

As Brogan arrived, he could see Sophie's father trying to get up. He had a deep gouge just above his eye. The blood was gushing, blanketing his face, making it virtually impossible for him to see. He was still trying to get to his daughter, yelling her name as the blood gurgled in his throat. Brogan later learned that the injured father also had five busted ribs, and a collapsed lung.

The silverback then went and sat halfway between the injured father and the female gorilla that was still holding little Sophie. He started picking at the ground in front of him as if nothing had happened.

"Sophie...Andrew, somebody save them! HELP!!" the mother screamed hysterically.

"Someone hurry the hell up and get that tranquilizer gun here NOW!" one of the zoo attendants screamed over his radio.

By now the crowd was frantic. Suddenly everyone gasped as they looked towards the little girl. "She's free!" one teenage boy yelped.

Little Sophie had regained consciousness, miraculously freeing herself from the female gorilla, and was now stumbling towards her father. She tried to run fast but was still woozy from being knocked unconscious.

The crowd suddenly screamed in horror as the huge silverback swung at little Sophie as she tried to get to her father. From a distance the swing looked like it was going to hit her, but luckily Sophie was just out of his reach.

She was only fifteen feet from her injured father, when the silverback got up and started after her. Reaching out with his huge, hairy arm he swiped Sophie's legs out from under her. She screamed and flopped to the ground turtling as she landed. The silverback sat back down and let out a loud growl as he raised his big, hairy arm to take another swing at little Sophie.

When Brogan saw what was happening he quickly slammed both his fists into the plexiglass, letting out a loud aggressive yell. "HEY!!"

The plexiglass shook as if a hockey player had been checked into it. The yell startled the crowd, as well as the silverback. He spun around and immediately made direct eye contact with Brogan.

Brogan had felt helpless watching poor Sophie and her father, but now he was pissed.

Within a split second the huge silverback turned his attention and was on a mad sprint straight for Brogan. The entire crowd started moving back from the plexiglass as they watched the charging beast getting closer. Rita pulled at Brogan's t-shirt as she moved backwards with the crowd, but he didn't budge. The silverback looked rabid as it barrelled towards Brogan. Rita watched as her future stared down the charging beast.

For everyone there, including the zoo attendants, the sight of the 680 lb, ferocious beast barrelling towards them was the scariest thing they had ever seen. It was even scarier for Rita because she thought the silverback was going to blast through the plexiglass and attack Brogan. She stared in amazement as Brogan just stood there, unfazed. She knew how Brogan had helped several people at his work, but she didn't know in great detail exactly what he had done to help them.

The huge silverback covered a vast amount of ground in seconds. Brogan could not help himself, he had to do something to get the gorilla's attention off little Sophie. When the silverback had struck Sophie, Brogan felt a rush of heat. With the heated rush still coursing through his veins, Brogan continued to challenge his huge, charging adversary with only a sheet of plexiglass between them. The silverback grunted angrily as he sprinted straight at the challenger behind the glass without slowing. If anything, Brogan swore the silverback was gaining speed with each ground rumbling step. The crowd watched the silverback, in a state of shock, as every muscle rippled and every inch of his teeth gleamed in the sun. Brogan stood motionless.

Ten feet from the plexiglass the giant gorilla took flight and lunged at Brogan. Brogan never moved or blinked as the huge silverback landed on the plexiglass right in front of him. The sound and impact was felt through the ground by everyone there. Then as if nothing had even happened, the silverback calmly and nonchalantly walked back to his original spot and sat down, taking no interest in the injured man or little Sophie. Everyone was hoping that the nightmare was over, and the two would now be left alone until rescued.

Suddenly the female gorilla started towards Sophie and her injured father, kicking up a bunch of dust, dirt, and grass the whole way. It was scary enough seeing her barrel towards them, but the debris flying around added to the dramatic affect. She snatched little Sophie, who had made it to her father's side while the silverback was occupied with Brogan. The father tried to hold onto his daughter but he didn't have the strength. He could hardly breathe, but still tried to drag his bloodied, broken body towards his screaming daughter, as the female gorilla started dragging her away.

It seemed like an eternity, but finally a zoo attendant arrived with the tranquilizer gun. Two zoo workers scrambled to load the gun, and started firing on the female gorilla. With each shot fired the crowd became more and more frustrated as every tranq dart missed its target.

"THIS IS RIDICULOUS!" Brogan growled, as his adrenaline pumped through his veins. "We have to get that little girl and her father out of there NOW!!"

Brogan looked up as he started walking backwards, then bolted forward jumping towards the plexiglass. His foot made contact six feet up the glass. The runners he was wearing caught all the traction he needed. As he landed, Brogan reached out with his right hand grabbing a ten foot pole with a big hook on the end of it that was normally used by the zookeepers. As soon as the pole was in his hand, Brogan unleashed a powerful spring sending him airborne. The frog-like jump off the glass launched him several feet back, landing him on top of the information booth. He would have to jump fifteen feet to clear the plexiglass fence and the barbwire on top of it, in order to make it to one of the fake trees in the enclosure. Even though the top of the wire was two feet lower, the distance Brogan had to jump to clear it was virtually impossible.

Watching Brogan closely from the ground, Rita clued in to what he was thinking, but before she could scream his name, she witnessed him flying into a realm of disastrous repercussions. Brogan ran off the roof at full speed with the hooked pole still clutched in his right hand. The crowd stared in amazement, and Rita breathed a sign of relief as he cleared the barbwire. Brogan descended bringing the pole close to his body, then released it as though he was throwing a Frisbee. Before it had a chance to completely leave his grip, he clenched his fist catching the end of it. With a stretch that he would definitely feel in the morning, Brogan reached out and hooked the tree. Everyone on the ground was in disbelief, and gasped as Brogan swung up from under the branch and landed on top of it in a squatting position.

"Tarzan!" one of the kids screamed pointing to Brogan in the tree.

The female gorilla now had Sophie in her lap and was picking through her blonde hair. Brogan scurried on the fake tree limb, positioning himself over top of them; then started lowering himself down, wrapping his legs around the branch, as he stretched out with the pole. He stopped abruptly almost hitting the female gorilla on the head. The horrified onlookers gasped, and the female gorilla turned to look at the crowd.

Brogan took a deep breath and held it in while he reached down ever so carefully with the pole. He had to work fast, and was trying to time it just right. The female gorilla was now rocking Sophie back and forth, and Brogan knew he would only get one chance to get it right. As the female gorilla turned toward the crowd again, Brogan quickly hooked Sophie around the waist and pulled her up to him. It happened so fast the crowd barely saw it, and the female gorilla didn't realize what had happened until Brogan had little Sophie safe in his arms.

"Let's get you outta here and back to your mommy," Brogan said smiling at Sophie.

He started climbing back on top of the huge branch with Sophie, when the female gorilla realized her little replacement baby was gone. She stood up and let out a horrendous growl, alerting the silverback, then sat back down and started crying as she looked all around.

Brogan stopped and looked directly at Sophie, "My name is Brogan, and I'm gonna get you out of here and back to your mommy and daddy," he said in a very nurturing but stern voice, "but I need your help, ok?"

Sophie looked up at Brogan with her beautiful blue scared eyes and nodded yes.

"Good! All you gotta do sweetie is hang on to me as tight as you can."

Brogan didn't wait for her to answer. He scooped her up and ran to the end of the branch. He knew he couldn't make the jump back to the top of the information booth, even without Sophie. He also knew it would only be a matter of seconds before the silverback would try to return Sophie to the female gorilla.

Suddenly, Brogan spotted a greyish black blur at the base of the huge fake tree, and could hear the grunts starting. They were grunts that indicated the silverbacks climbing arrival. Within a few short seconds the silverback was on the same limb and was charging for them. Brogan held Sophie tight and started sprinting toward the silverback. The gap between them narrowed. Just inches from the silverbacks reach Brogan dove off the right side of the huge branch, jumping far enough to reach a rope that was several feet away. Falling fast, Brogan slowed their decent by squeezing the rope, wincing as it burned his hand. He was counting on the momentum from the jump to swing them far enough away from the silverback that he could find a way to safety. But the silverback was mad and in hot pursuit. Brogan and Sophie swung from rope to rope heading around the fake tree. The silverback went in the opposite direction, mimicking Brogan as he swung straight for them.

By the time Brogan realized the silverback was heading in their direction, it was too late and he could not avoid the collision. He quickly twisted his body to shield Sophie. "Hang on sweetie!" Brogan yelled as he squeezed Sophie and held the rope swinging like Tarzan.

Brogan tightened his entire body preparing for the impact.

The crowd below, which had been growing since the incident started, was frantic as the silverback slammed into Brogan and Sophie. Brogan quickly rolled off the gorilla like a running back would off a potential tackler, enabling him to escape the silverbacks clutches as the beast continued swinging around the tree. The maneuver sent Brogan and Sophie into a spin, which Brogan was able to stop by extending his free limbs. However, the rope they were on had wrapped around the tree once and was getting shorter as it worked on its second time around.

As the silverback met up with them again Brogan flipped Sophie to his left side, holding her straight out from his body, while swinging on the rope with his right hand; waiting for the last possible second before making his move. Just as the silverback swiped his big, hairy arm, Brogan released the rope and him and Sophie instantly started to fall. The silverback's missed swipe made him extremely irritated. Brogan quickly grabbed the rope again squeezing it with everything he had, making his hand bloody and raw as he managed to stop their descent ten feet from the ground; while still swinging at a tremendous speed.

By now the silverback had landed on the ground and was sprinting to the next rope. He jumped, grabbing it at the same height as Brogan and Sophie and was swinging straight for them once again, he now had a better line on them.

Brogan realized there were only two ways to avoid this massive silverback, and the drop would hurt. Still holding little Sophie out to his side, Brogan knew what had to be done. He stared directly into the silverbacks eyes and could see the anger and rage building from his frustration. Brogan was hoping the stare would aggravate the silverback enough to make him put everything into his next strike.

There were screams from the crowd as they realized they were about to witness another collision. At the last moment Brogan whipped Sophie across his body, using the momentum to dodge the silverback's swipe. More screams came from the ever growing crowd. Swinging at full speed, Brogan performed his next risky survival tactic.

"Trust me Sophie," Brogan said in a reassuring voice, as he tossed her straight up into the air, releasing the rope at the same time.

In a seemingly choreographed move, Brogan snagged another rope with his left hand as Sophie fell perfectly into place on his right side. The outcome surprised not only the onlookers, but more importantly the silverback. They now found themselves behind the silverback, just as Brogan had planned.

Little Sophie looked up at Brogan and smiled. Brogan wondered if Sophie, amidst all the scariness, could find humor in the fact that they were now chasing the silverback.

The silverback was twisting and writhing on the rope trying to figure out what to do to get at them. Suddenly Brogan saw nothing but bad things about to happen. The silverback had found footing, pushed off the tree, and was coming straight at them. Brogan quickly decided his next move and again it would be a tricky one, but his main concern was little Sophie.

"Hang on Sophie!" Brogan yelled so loud everyone on the ground heard him.

Sophie clung to Brogan even harder than she already was.

Brogan knew he couldn't avoid the silverback forever, and the people in the crowd were surprised he had lasted as long as he had. But Brogan had absolutely no intentions of giving up. He held Sophie tight to his chest and glared at his swinging, hairy adversary, as the sky became engulfed by a determined, massive beast.

A millisecond before impact Brogan squeezed the rope, pulling himself and Sophie upward as if doing a chin up. It turned out being more of a jerking motion than a chin up, but Brogan was almost able to pull them out of the silverback's reach once again.

Suddenly the silverback grabbed Brogan's left foot. Immediately Brogan scrunched up his entire body, desperately trying to hang onto the rope with the extra weight of the silverback. Brogan's eyes met the silverbacks, and seeing the look of "Gotcha!" Brogan reacted quickly. He swiftly brought his right knee down into the silverback's temple. It happened so fast and devastatingly hard that it caught everyone watching off guard. The massive silverback lost his grip on Brogan's foot and the rope, falling fifteen feet onto his back and hitting the ground with a huge thud. Bunches of grass and mud skewered about, and a mushroom shaped dust cloud hovered above the stunned beast like a miniature nuclear explosion.

Brogan knew there was no time to waste. He tucked Sophie in tight, sliding quickly to the bottom of the rope before letting go, and hit the ground running before the silverback had finished his disorientated landing. Within seconds he was passing Sophie back through the bars in the door to her shaking mother and waiting paramedics.

"LOOK OUT!" the crowd screamed simultaneously.

Brogan spun around realizing he was trapped inside with the biggest, strongest, and definitely the most pissed off opponent he had ever faced. The silverback had regained his composure and was barrelling down on Brogan. Screams could be heard outside the gorilla compound as the crowd grew frantic once again.

"Where's the freaking tranquillizer gun?"

"Reload that gun!"

"Help him!"

"Get him outta there!"

Brogan stood in front of the barred door and stared at the savage silverback charging towards him. Suddenly another surge of heated blood broke loose and flowed swiftly through his body. It felt as if his blood was on fire, and he couldn't help but wonder why his entire body was covered in goose bumps. Things instantly seemed like they were in slow motion for Brogan. It had happened to him before, but this time was different. Different in the sense where he felt more alert, and the surge of heated blood was making him vibrate as if he had just guzzled ten 5-hour Energy drinks.

"Wow," Brogan thought as he clenched his fists and felt the energy pulsating through his whole body. He was now 190 lbs of pure energy.

Without warning the massive silverback launched at his potential victim. Brogan faked as if he were going left. The silverback shifted his weight in mid flight, reaching to where he thought Brogan would be. Brogan quickly leapt to the right, faking out his would-be tackler. The silverback grabbed an armful of air and growled with wild frustration. Brogan had evaded the flying beast once again.

The massive silverback landed on the barred door with all fours, breaking one of the two oversized steel hinges. The door flopped down to one side, and the silverback took off after his intended target.

Brogan was sprinting for one of the big fake trees, when he felt the ground pounding and shaking behind him.

"BROGAN!" Rita screamed from the crowd.

It looked as though the silverback was going to catch him, but what no one knew was that Brogan purposely slowed down just enough for the silverback to catch up. Once again Brogan faked left, and could have sworn he felt the silverback's breath on his neck. This time however, the silverback was only fooled for a split second and was back on Brogan's heels reaching for him. Without delay, Brogan kicked in the after burners; the crowd was stunned by his speed. The silverback's sausage fingers skimmed Brogan's t-shirt, and a heart pounding roar burst from the beast. Brogan sprinted, picking up more speed with every stride, and grabbed a rope dangling from the big branch in front of him. His momentum carried him off the ground as the silverback jumped grasping for him.

Before the rope started swinging him back towards the big fury beast, Brogan climbed it another four feet so he was high enough off the ground that the silverback couldn't reach him. However, as Brogan swung past his opponent, he realized the silverback was reaching for the same rope he was on. Brogan scrambled to pull the rope up before the silverback could grab it, but was too late. The massive gorilla mitt wrapped around the thick tow rope like it was a clothes line. Brogan held on tightly as the silverback shook the rope violently, making it virtually impossible to hang onto. His fingers started slipping and just when Brogan thought he couldn't hold on any longer, the thrashing stopped. He could hear the growling beast beating his chest, and the ground. It took Brogan a second to focus, but he could see the silverback moving away.

Brogan's fingers were spent; he lost his grip on the rope, and dropped fifteen feet to the ground with a thump. He knew the fight was far from over. Quickly regaining his bearings, he looked around for the silverback and noticed him moving toward Sophie's wounded father, who had started crawling toward the barred door once he saw his little girl was safe.

Brogan could see the beast's rage building; he was pounding the ground harder, and his growls were becoming louder and more frequent. Brogan was amazed at the immense strength and speed of the silverback. To watch him from a distance was one thing, but to experience it first hand, one could not fathom.

Suddenly the massive beast started sprinting for the injured father. The poor man was barely able to crawl, so Brogan, as well as everyone in the crowd, knew he couldn't take another beating. Brogan figured it was his fault for the silverback turning his attention on the injured man, because he was the one who frustrated and aggravated the beast. The only thing that mattered now was saving Sophie's daddy.

Brogan took off running as fast as he could; from the angle he was approaching at, the silverback could not see him coming. He closed the gap between them at lightening speed, still unnoticed. The silverback's focus was on the injured man as he barrelled towards him with his huge, hairy arms raised, ready to kill.

Again Brogan felt like everything slowed down. He didn't know if he could save the man, but he did know he was going to give it everything he had and try for little Sophie. With both arms raised and unaware of what was coming, the massive beast made for an easy target. Brogan dropped his shoulder, raised his elbow and planted both in the silverbacks left rib cage, feeling the solidness of the beast on impact.

Screams could be heard from the crowd as Brogan delivered the hit.

"He's crazy!'
"What's he doing?"
Two young men both agreed, "That was a good hit."
It was a solid blow that surprised everyone, especially the silverback. As impossible as it seemed at the time, Brogan flew into the side of the silverback knowing full well it was going to hurt. Even though it was a blindside hit, Brogan thought it would have little affect on the 680 lb beast. Although Brogan only tipped the scale at 190 lbs, after the initial impact it seemed for a second to be an even fight. The fact that Brogan played football and knew how to lay down a hit helped. But the biggest contributor was that Brogan himself could put a hurting on anyone as if he weighed 400 lbs.

His high school football coach had loved having Brogan on his team for many reasons. Brogan was super fast, he could play both defence and offence the whole game, and he could play any position. But what the coach, the entire team, and the fans loved to watch the most was Brogan's hitting. He always amazed everyone with his hits and tackles because they were perfect and all legal too. Everything about them, from the timing to the crushing, and normally there was more than one person flying. To some it may have seemed barbaric or a little sadistic, but until you watched him in action you would not understand it.

With this particular hit, Brogan faced an opponent that did not see it coming, but in retrospect weighed twice the amount of anyone he had ever faced before.

This time the massive silverback didn't growl, instead a long, hurtful groan expelled from the now injured beast. The impact stopped his forward progress and sent him flying sideways. He didn't look so massive or scary as his seemingly lifeless body flopped, then grinded through the dirt to a rolling halt.

Brogan scrambled to his feet after the intense hit and started to regain his senses. He noticed some zoo attendants, and a few spectators from the crowd were dragging Sophie's injured father toward the barred door. And from the corner of his eye he noticed the silverback getting up.

Brogan winced in immense pain as he shot like a missile towards the now standing giant. The silverback had some new potential victims in sight. A hair raising growling yelp burst from his mouth as he prepared to charge the rescuers. Before he could take that first gigantic leap towards them, Brogan ran past at an extraordinary speed, tossing a left elbow on the way by. The silverback caught the elbow above his eye, slicing it open and immediately gushing blood.

Brogan had almost made it by, but the silverback's huge arm struck him in the hip. The impact resembled a football player being cut at the knees. Brogan went airborne with no control and flipped head over feet, twice. Still spinning Brogan landed hard on the ground, several feet away. Dazed, he scampered to his feet, but his left leg gave out. Down on one knee, Brogan looked up and saw nothing but pain, most likely death, coming in fast. The crowd's screams echoed throughout the compound. Brogan managed to stand up again, preparing for the inevitable. The silverback was relentless, and to the crowd of onlookers it seemed Brogan had no more flight or fight left in him.

"Slow motion again," he thought as he watched the silverback charging towards him.

As the thought flashed through his head, he also caught a glimpse of someone in the crowd. Out of all the spectators, and with all the confusion and action, Brogan ended up looking right into Rita's eyes; they were filled with immense pain and grief. It was too much for Brogan to take. His heart sped up and started pounding hard. He forced his beaten body to comply, and leaned back to a martial arts stance.

The silverback, with arms raised, came at him fast. And with super-human speed Brogan unleashed a straight front heel kick to beast's gut. The kick slowed and hurt the beast, and Brogan again felt the solidness of the silverback. But his long, hairy arms had found their target once again. Brogan quickly raised his arms up to block the strike, and instantly felt an ice pick stabbing sensation through both his forearms. The silverback only hesitated long enough for Brogan to realize what was coming next. Again Brogan raised his arms to defend himself, but the next strike from the beast fractured both of them and knocked him to the ground. The second fury of strikes was even more devastating. The silverback's arms rained down on Brogan repeatedly as though heavy logs were falling on him. With every strike Brogan tried to defend himself by kicking with his feet, and blocking with his already fractured arms. A couple strikes broke through Brogan's defence, landing on his head and slicing him open.

Suddenly the raining blows stopped. Brogan peeked through his arm defence, only to see the silverback crashing to the ground in a drunken, passed out state. Brogan, brutally dazed and injured, tried to make out what was happening. He could hear several different voices and feel people touching him. As he started breaking through his daze, he realized that he was now on a stretcher being carried by paramedics. He tried to look around but couldn't move his head because of the restraints they had him in. As the paramedics put him into the back of the ambulance, Brogan could here a woman's voice.

"You saved my little girl, thank you!" she said over and over.

Brogan raised his hand trying to say "You're welcome," when a familiar touch grabbed it. The touch brought a loving smile to Brogan's face, and held his hand all the way to the hospital.

"Brogan, I love you."

He looked up at Rita and smiled. He didn't say anything, but strangely enough he wanted to ask her to marry him.

"This is not the right time or place," he thought, as Rita ran her fingers through his hair.

Brogan replayed the thought of almost dying through his head. Then looked back up at Rita and smiled again, thinking "But it's never too late, not when there's a little thing called fate."

CHAPTER 6

REBORN

It was already day six of his hospital stay and Brogan was getting edgy. The only satisfaction he had was knowing that Sophie and her father were safe and healthy. That, and the fact that Rita would be back to see him again soon. She had been by his side almost the entire time since he was brought in. And although he wished she could have stayed with him the whole time, he understood she still had to go to work. Brogan knew he was being a little selfish, but who could blame him. She was the one woman that could dissipate his pain, heal his beaten body, and mend his tormented soul. He did feel bad that she took time off from her volunteer work, though he told her not to, but she wanted to be there for him.

His nurses were so friendly and were always cracking jokes, or teasing him about something. They were very accommodating for both Brogan and Rita, and had prepared the room so Rita was able to stay the night whenever she could.

"There you go sweetie, now you can stay the night comfortably," one of the nurses had said as she placed a pillow on the bed for Rita. "Now I'll leave you two love birds alone," she giggled as she pulled the door shut. "Buzz if you need anything."

The nurses had started teasing Brogan the moment they met Rita and saw how in love the two were. They warned them of the potential pain it could cause Brogan from Rita sleeping in the same bed as him. But, Brogan was willing to take the chance of Rita unintentionally hurting one of his injuries, and knew he was healing faster with her by his side.

Brogan had started feeling better the moment he saw Rita's face, smelled her sweet scent, and heard her loving voice. He smiled as he thought about his stay. The six days in the hospital had been nothing short of amazing for "the two love birds", as the nurses now called them. The two of them had so much time to sit and talk that they actually learned more about one another, making them even more in love; if that was even possible. Brogan's nurses thought it was so sweet how him and Rita were like high school sweethearts reminiscing about the past.

His third night in the hospital, Brogan suggested to Rita that they rent a movie after seeing their favorite movie on the list. Rita was sitting in the arm chair as *The Wedding Singer* started.

"There's room for one more!" Brogan had said patting the spot next to him in the bed.

Rita gladly joined him, and snuggled up sharing the covers. As they were watching the movie, two nurses entered the room. One had a huge bowl of popcorn, the other was carrying a couple of drinks. At first Brogan thought they were joining them to watch the movie. But to both Brogan's and Rita's delight, they handed the bowl of popcorn to Brogan, and placed the drinks down on the table tray.

"Enjoy!" they giggled as they left the room.

Each day in the hospital Brogan and Rita grew closer and closer, and Brogan grew healthier and stronger; unusually quicker than any doctors or nurses had seen before.

"Last night here!" Brogan said as he watched Rita slip on some pajama pants and one of his long sleeve shirts.

"Thank goodness!" Rita said climbing into bed with Brogan. Snuggling up to him, she leaned over to kiss him goodnight.

"Thank you for everything," Brogan whispered.

Rita smiled and touched his cheek; Brogan did the same to her. Rita leaned closer and pressed her lips to his. The kiss was long and desired but innocent; not like high school kissing, it was far more mature than that. It was a perfect moment for both of them, even if they were in a hospital; it was obviously irrelevant to both of them. Brogan's heart skipped a long beat and by the look on Rita's face, she felt it too. A tear bubbled from Brogan's eye and proceeded to roll slowly down his cheek.

"No Brogan, thank you," she whispered as she lovingly gathered the tear with her thumb.

Brogan had always known, but it was during that moment he truly saw everything so clearly; he would never love another the way he did Rita. And he would do everything in his power to make a safe and loving home for her, and someday their children.

They kissed again, said goodnight to one another, and laid in the hospital bed smiling to themselves, before finally drifting off to sleep.

By the fifth day of his hospital stay, Brogan had hardly any pain at all. However, it wasn't because of the painkillers or medication, it was something that had the entire medical staff bewildered. Some of the nurses said it was because love heals all, while others said it was because the treatment at Saddleback City Regional Hospital was top notch.

It was true that SCRH was a highly advanced facility. With money that had been donated, they were able to construct a new state of the art building with more advanced equipment.

But the doctors and nurses who had worked on Brogan knew that their equipment and care couldn't take all the credit. Brogan had several hairline fractures in both his arms that were healing at an unbelievable rate, and his concussion was no longer a concern. He also had eight deep contusions, held together by strips of tape, mostly on his head and arms that were almost fully healed. The doctors and nurses were baffled and stunned at his remarkable healing process. Brogan had endured a horrific physical encounter, sustained serious injuries, and was ready to be discharged from the hospital in less than a week; although they made him stay longer just to be safe.

Rita had overheard one of Brogan's nurses, who had been a registered nurse for twenty-five years, say it was, "Absolutely remarkable, but down right freakishly weird, how fast Brogan is healing".

The only conclusion the doctors could come up with, since Brogan refused to have further tests run, was that he had very good genetics. Some also believed that such quick healing could only be a miracle.

Brogan and Rita had been stealing kisses all morning, thinking they were being sly and sneaky about it. But all the nurses had noticed, and thought it was so wonderful.

"Out of all the frustration and ugliness in today's world what do we have? Huh? We have babies, and we have love. Then, every once in a blue moon we get to be witness to one of life's greatest gifts, true love. And if we are ever to be so lucky, maybe experience it first hand!" one of the nurses had said.

Rita leaned over kissing Brogan again, "I'll be back," she said doing a terrible Arnold Schwarzenegger impersonation.

They both stared at one another for a second and then started laughing. Rita explained to Brogan that she was going home to freshen up, and to pay her rent and a few bills. This was all true, but not entirely the whole plan. What she didn't tell him was that she wanted to buy him a little something special to celebrate his release from the hospital. She also wanted to take him out for dinner, and if he felt up to it, which she knew he would, maybe go see a movie.

Rita had just watched the man of her dreams, the man she wanted to marry and spend the rest of her life with, almost die trying to save a little girl and her father. She had watched as he put his own life in perilous conditions to help others, with no regard for his own safety whatsoever. And although she never ever wanted to be witness to such a scary scenario again, she couldn't help but have the utmost respect for Brogan and what he had done at the zoo. It also fascinated Rita that Brogan hadn't mentioned one word of what had taken place. She was even more intrigued that he had absolutely no qualms about helping perfect strangers.

Rita had always helped raise money for charitable events around her community, and she felt proud and good to do these things for people, especially children. But what she had witnessed six days earlier made her realize she could do more. Watching Brogan do everything in his power to save little Sophie and her father, flooded her heart with inspiration and incentive.

"I'll wait here." Brogan said jokingly.

Rita turned and started walking away still holding onto Brogan's hand. Their arms were stretched out, neither of them wanting to let go, their fingers running softly and slowly down to the tips. As their finger tips slid apart, Rita turned and winked at Brogan before leaving the room. She wanted to hurry so she could get her bills paid and have enough time to pick up a gift for Brogan, before returning to the hospital for his release. She quickly walked past the nurse's station, where she usually stopped to thank them and chit chat, but instead just smiled and waved walking fast out the front entrance of the hospital. All the nurses knew Brogan was getting released today and knew some of Rita's plans for a romantic night, so none of them thought anything about her not stopping to chat. The nurses had grown very fond of the "two love birds" in Room 44.

Rita ran down most of the three flights of concrete steps outside the front entrance and remembered there was a bank machine just down the street.

"It will save so much time if I use that machine!" She smiled unable to contain her excitement.

She made her way down the steps and turned right, walking past a bunch of bushes along the sidewalk before turning towards the bank machine. Without looking around, she wondered if anyone had noticed her teenage like urgency. Rita fumbled with her wallet trying to free her bank card, smiling as she thought about her evening plans. She slid her bank card into the slot and quickly punched in her pin number.

"Let's see…Brogan's gift, plus dinner, and possibly a movie." Rita spoke to herself as she added up how much money she needed before typing in $300.00 and pressing OK.

Rita's budgeting was second to none. She had saved enough money over the years to be financially stable in today's standards. She actually had enough saved in her two accounts combined to pay for the wedding and honeymoon, and still have some left to put a reasonable size chunk down on a house. Rita wanted to give Brogan the sense of security when it involved money. It wasn't that she was rich, she was just smart with her money.

A huge smile crept across Rita's pretty little freckled face as she waited for her money. "Hopefully he'll finally pop the question," she thought.

Brogan also had a huge smile on his face as he lay in his hospital bed waiting for Rita to return. He was excited to be getting out of the hospital, and thrilled to think Rita was taking him out on a date to celebrate. He was also feeling a little guilty about Rita having to use her vacation days from work to spend time in the hospital with him.

"This'll make up for it!" Brogan whispered.

Reflections of sunlight danced across his face as he slowly rotated the huge diamond ring he planned on giving Rita that night; on one knee of course. Brogan was happy to be giving Rita this particular ring; it was a very large ring that had been passed down in his family for several generations, and had been well taken care of by Geraldine over the years. "The sentimental value of this ring makes it priceless," he remembered her saying. "If you were buying it brand new, it would cost a small fortune."

"Isn't it too much?" Brogan asked his mother, being timid of accepting it.

"Look son, you take this ring and you give it to Rita." Geraldine had said. "You can tell her where it came from or just give it to her and smile every time she asks you how you picked it, that's up to you. But you take this ring, and make sure to see the look on her face when you slide it on her finger, it'll be worth more than the ring itself!"

Brogan became all warm inside, and it wasn't the ray of sunshine coming in through the curtain. It was Rita, and only Rita that could cause such a heated emotion. No one had ever touched his heart the way Rita had.

Brogan could remember his first kiss, awkward but still exciting. However it wasn't even close in comparison to the first time he kissed Rita's soft, loving lips. Strawberry lip balm took on a whole new meaning for Brogan.

Brogan was engulfed by love like a hand in a fur mitten on a cold day. The instant him and Rita locked eyes in JoJo's Java House five years earlier, he knew his heart would belong to no other. He only hoped that others could experience the love that him and Rita shared; and experience true and pure love that gives the warmth of security in a relationship.

Brogan wondered what else Rita had planned for that evening. It really didn't matter to him, as long as he was spending time with her.

Brogan felt good, and was anxious for the nurse to come in and tell him he was good to go. He knew he healed quicker than most people. He didn't really understand exactly how or why, but he knew his body could do extraordinary things. Especially when he was pushed to the breaking point.

Everyday through school, Brogan had to slack off or ease up on the playground, because he was extremely strong and fast. But how could he explain his miraculous healing capabilities to the doctors and nurses? The medical staff he had during this hospital stay were mystified by how quickly he healed. How could Brogan explain why he wasn't in a coma or even dead? Truth be told, he couldn't. He didn't know how his internal system worked. The only thing he did know was that he was feeling great, he couldn't wait to be discharged, and that he was looking forward to spending the rest of his life making Rita happy.

Brogan had actually wanted to leave the hospital on his second day there, but Rita and the medical staff were so concerned about his injuries that he agreed to stay for the short duration. The staff at the hospital had found out every little detail about the zoo incident from Sophie and her parents, who were on the next floor in the ICU. Brogan had gone to visit Sophie and her father a few times when Rita wasn't around, and had found out that Sophie's dad would eventually make a full recovery. He was very lucky he only received one third the beating Brogan had endured.

Brogan closed his fist around the diamond ring, put his arms up behind his head, and crossed his legs as he straightened them out. He wondered how long into their special night he should wait until he popped the question.

Rita snatched her money from the ATM before it was done being dispensed, and was startled by a voice behind her. She had so many things on her mind she didn't realize at first what the person actually said. Rita quickly spun around and had no time to react as two young males came at her. They pushed her back toward the bank machine making it difficult for passersby to see. She held the money tight to her chest trying to process what was happening. The taller of the two males grasped her hair, slammed her face into the ATM screen, and then grabbed for the cash. Rita still had a good grip on her money and kept moving around making it hard for her attacker to get it from her. Seeing that she was putting up a fight, the smaller male pulled out a knife. Rita scratched at his face trying to defend herself. Without hesitating he thrust the knife hard into her belly before she had a chance to scream, and just as quickly twisted it and yanked it free; bringing chunks of flesh with it. Her wound was horrendous because the knife used had four blades that swirled and crossed over coming together and joining at the tip.

Rita watched through blurry, tear filled eyes as the taller male ran off with her money and the other male chased after him trying to catch up. In shock, she held her stomach as she slid down the ATM until she softly hit the sidewalk. With blood trickling between her fingers, Rita slumped over.

A male nurse, who was quickly running out to the ATM so he could feed himself from the vending machine on his break, noticed Rita laying on the ground. As he got closer he could tell she had serious injuries due to the pool of blood around her. It had only been a few minutes from the time of the stabbing to when the male nurse found her, but she had already lost a lot of blood. Without thinking, he scooped Rita up and ran as fast as he could back towards the hospital.

As they topped the stairs, Rita started going in and out of consciousness. She could hear muffled cries for help as the male nurse screamed for assistance. She tried holding her head up to look for Brogan, but didn't have the strength.

One of the nurses gasped as she rushed over with a stretcher to help. "Oh my God!" she choked recognizing who the victim was, "the love birds…" she trailed off in disbelief. "It's Rita."

As they raced Rita down the hall they were all thinking how they had to pass Brogan's room to get to the ER. Simultaneously all four nurses sped up hoping to fly past Room 44 with no eye contact. Their main concern, of course, was Rita. But they didn't need anyone freaking out in the ER room either. And they knew, with the amount of blood loss, it wasn't looking so good for the little love bird.

Brogan could hear the commotion out in the hallway getting louder. He never liked to see people get hurt or be in pain, and wished he had a different room so he didn't have to witness people being brought into the ER. He knew they would pass by his open door, so he figured the polite thing to do was to not look. But for some reason, this time, an unearthly force compelled him to look and made his heart start to pound.

He watched as a bunch of nurses swiftly pushed a bed past his door. The squeak of the wheeling bed was loud and annoying to Brogan. He saw that two of the nurses were the ones that brought Rita and him the popcorn and drinks the night they watched the movie in Brogan's hospital room. And he noticed the pain on their faces as they sped by, which Brogan thought was a little unusual. He had watched this scenario several times since his stay in the hospital, and not once had he seen them looking so worried. Brogan also noticed how a couple other nurses looked in at him as they zipped by his door. It was a look that the other two nurses were smart enough not to let loose. And Brogan could not help but notice the worry in their eyes as well.

Suddenly Brogan felt sick. He was subconsciously already telling himself it wasn't true, but his gut wrenching pain and pounding heart told the truth. Somehow he just knew. It all happened so fast, and yet so slow, as they passed Brogan's door. The thing that made him jump from his bed was the bloody hand that hung over the side of the stretcher. His heart ached and was breaking as he refused to accept what was happening at that moment. Brogan ran after them shaking his head, praying it was all a terrible nightmare. He found himself outside the ER doors peering through the small windows. He knew that hand, he could never forget it; whether it was clean and smooth as silk, or covered in blood.

Brogan's legs went weak as he watched the doctors and nurses scramble around the bed. Even though he knew in his heart who was laying there, almost lifeless, he would not accept it. The ache in his chest was getting heavier as his heart started pounding faster and louder. Seconds dripped by like minutes.

Suddenly a nurse caught Brogan's pain stricken reflection in the window, and realized he knew it was Rita laying there. Within a minute two large security guards approached Brogan, merely to ask him politely to step away from the ER doors. The nurses didn't want any harm to come to Brogan, but they had to follow hospital procedure. They couldn't have him getting emotional and interrupting the doctors and nurses from completing their tasks. But before the security guards could say anything, Brogan caught a glimpse of Rita's face.

"NOOOOOOOOOO!" Brogan's voice was not his own. It was a blood boiling cry that formed painful goose bumps on everyone who heard it.

The security guards clenched their eyes tight as the hairs on the back of their necks stood straight up. The cry was heard by everyone in the ER, and was more heartbreaking than any cry of pain ever heard in the hospital before. The anguish everyone felt for Brogan was unbearable.

Brogan started to push through the ER doors and both guards put a hand on each of his shoulders. It wasn't for show or a display of any kind, it was simply instinct that made Brogan duck from their grasp and continue through the doors. He rushed to Rita's side, his legs wobbling like stilts, and looked at her as tears streamed down his cheeks.

"Brogan sweetie, you can't be in here right now," one of the nurses said as she frantically worked on Rita.

Brogan heard nothing but Rita's wavering breath through the oxygen mask, and had enough sense to stay out of the way of the medical team working on her.

"No...no...no..." he repeated in a soft, low voice as he stared in disbelief. "Hang on sweetie...you can't leave me..."

As they entered the ER to apprehend Brogan, the two security guards were stopped in their tracks by a single hand that the popcorn nurse held up.

"It's ok," she whispered, "let him stay."

The amount of blood that flowed freely without hindering or slowing was disturbing enough; but to see it happening to such a beautiful and innocent woman like Rita, magnified the heartache.

"Whoever did this, twisted the knife before pulling it out!" one of the doctors said hoarsely as he worked on Rita.

"The bastard knew the damage it would cause..." a male nurse said softly; glancing at Brogan he caught himself before he finished what he was going to say.

For the next ten minutes Brogan stood frozen as the medical team rushed around Rita frantically trying to save her life. This was a nightmare, a terrible nightmare, and Brogan desperately wanted to wake up and go on his date with Rita, just like they had planned. His heart was being torn from his chest as he wished, prayed, and demanded God to let him trade places with her.

Suddenly a sound snapped Brogan from his frozen trance. It was a continuous *beep*, one that pierced Brogan's heart and would change him forever.

"Clear!" shouted the doctor as he placed the paddles on Rita's chest.

Rita suddenly opened her eyes and slowly scanned the room of bloody workers until she found Brogan's pain stricken face. He rushed to her side again, folding her hand into his and smiled at her. He could see the seriousness of her injuries and didn't want her to see it in his eyes, but he could tell she knew. Rita strained to focus her vision on the man of her dreams and his smiling face. Gathering her last bit of diminishing strength she reached out and caressed Brogan's cheek.

"Brogan…" she blinked slowly, "thank you for everything Brogan…I love you…"

"I love you too Rita," he whispered, sliding the ring onto her finger.

Rita's weak smile grew as she gently squeezed his hand.

Brogan's immense, life altering pain got a million times worse as he heard the heart monitor flatline again. He tried to say her name, but "NO!…NO!" was all that would come out of his mouth.

Rita's lifeless body jolted from the shock of the paddles on her chest a second and third time. The continuous *beep* echoed inside Brogan's head paralyzing him.

"There's nothing else we can do," he heard one of the doctors say.

In a tormented state of disbelief, Brogan moved closer to Rita's side as the doctors and nurses made a path for him. He softly grabbed her hand and squeezed it. "I love you Rita," he whispered through his tears.

He stared into her eyes with pure love, all the while whispering a desperate last prayer for the Lord above to save her. With his free hand Brogan gently swept her fiery red hair from her face and softly kissed her cheek. His eyes filled with desperation and turmoil as he realized his prayers were denied.

Brogan leaned over his soulmate's shell and cried as he had never cried before. No one moved from their standing positions for a long time. They stared at Brogan hoping he would somehow be alright. Eventually one by one the doctors and nurses left the room. Brogan continued to cry, caressing Rita's sweet, innocent face with his trembling fingers.

The staff at the hospital had witnessed similar tragic scenarios before, but none as compelling or heart touching as the two love birds. It would be considered by all who witnessed it or heard of it, the most tragic and heart wrenching story ever to be told at the Saddleback City Regional Hospital.

The two popcorn nurses periodically went to the ER door window to check on Brogan, and hoped he would be able to survive this tremendous, sick act of loss and go on living his life.

"He hasn't moved for two hours, I hope he'll be ok," one whispered to the other with tear filled eyes. "It's going to take him a long time to mourn."

But what no one knew, was that Brogan had been reborn.

CHAPTER 7

CLOAK N DAGGER

Five weeks had passed and the messages kept building up on Brogan's voicemail, twenty-seven to be precise. The majority of them were from his mother, most of which he returned and tried not to breakdown sobbing uncontrollably every time. Geraldine knew Brogan would eventually be okay, so she tried not to call him too much; but she was his mother, she had to check on him regularly. The rest of the messages were either from Rita's parents, or from the boys at Mocor.

Rita's parents were really sweet people and had taken a liking to Brogan the moment they met him. But her mother's voice was identical to Rita's, making it virtually impossible for Brogan to handle hearing.

Brogan had not talked to anyone from his work since Rita's funeral. He had nothing to say, and he didn't want someone telling him when he had to return to work. The fact that there was a set amount of time off work when a loved one died, pissed Brogan off. He could hardly function day to day let alone perform his responsibilities at work. Besides that, he didn't really want to see or face anyone. He also didn't need to blow up at anyone right now; it wouldn't be a pretty sight.

Brogan had no plans for the future now. He only wanted answers and justice, but more than anything he wanted retribution.

Since that incomprehensible, nightmarish day, Brogan had phoned only three numbers. Of course his mother was the first, basically to assure her that he was okay. But he wasn't okay. A huge part of himself was taken away and destroyed that day. Brogan felt an emptiness at first, but that gap was quickly filled with questions, regret, fear, and anxiety. These things were soon shadowed by rage, hatred, and wanting revenge.

The second number that he called, and was continually calling on a daily basis, was to the Saddleback City Police Station. By now they knew Brogan's voice, and would automatically put him through to Detective Seymore Shane. Every single day for the last five weeks Brogan phoned and talked to Detective Shane; and he was always willing to talk to Brogan and discuss all, if any, progress on Rita's ongoing case. Detective Shane and Brogan had first talked at the hospital. It was there that Detective Shane made a mistake. After twenty-seven years on the force, he had made a common rookie mistake. He gave into the compelling nature of remorse for Brogan's loss and provided him with information pertaining to the case. He had told Brogan that there were two gang members involved in Rita's murder. It was the only information Brogan received.

Although Brogan talked to Detective Shane on a daily bases, it was the same conversation everyday... "There's no change, or any new leads yet Brogan. But the minute we learn of anything, you will be the first person I call."

What Detective Shane really meant was that he would tell Brogan as long as it didn't jeopardize the investigation anymore than his slip up at the hospital already had. He also promised Brogan that he would not let Rita's case go cold, and that he was going to catch Rita's killers and make sure they were brought to justice.

It made Brogan feel better knowing there was someone like Detective Shane working on Rita's case. In a weird way Brogan felt connected to him, but then again he was investigating the murder of his once future wife, why wouldn't he feel connected to him.

No one knew about the third number Brogan had called since the accident, except for the person he talked to. One week after the brutal attack, Brogan phoned the Saddleback City Traffic Control Center (SCTCC), and spoke to a traffic analyst by the name of Darnel Casts. Brogan tearfully and reluctantly explained what he was looking to get his hands on and why, and had offered Darnel money to get it. However, Darnel would not accept his offer. Just one video was all Brogan wanted, and went on to explain that the police would not let him see any of the surveillance footage of the attack. After hearing the full story, Darnel felt compelled to help the begging man, but still denied Brogan over the phone.

At the time, Brogan never put recognition to his name, but Darnel Casts was the one that designed the plexiglass fences at the Saddleback City Zoo. Brogan also never realized that the man he tried to bribe was the one who single handedly revolutionized the entire traffic control system in Saddleback City, benefiting both drivers and pedestrians. Any and everything to do with the roadways, intersections, traffic lights, and walkways were solely designed and engineered by Darnel.

Ten or so years back Darnel had approached the Saddleback City Council over his proposal to transform the traffic control system, making a safer commute whether driving, pedaling, or walking. At first they shot him down not only because his designs looked too futuristic, but mostly because the price tag to reconfigure everything was completely out of their budget and highly improbable. It took a lot of explaining and persuading, but eventually everything Darnel had presented started to make sense and look a little more feasible. Especially when he made the offer to personally oversee every aspect of the entire job from start to finish if they passed his proposal, promising nothing would be overlooked.

Saddleback City Council finally agreed that Darnel's proposed traffic control system would be a huge benefit for their city. Still, the problem was that the expense for the new system was double what they had in the budget. So Darnel made another bold move by donating half the cost of the extremely expensive system.

City Council was confident that Darnel was the right person to oversee the new changes, and was pleased when he accepted the permanent position of Traffic Control Supervisor. If anything he was overqualified for the position, but was happy to be supervising the system he designed.

The city's portion for the completion of the redesigned traffic control system didn't compare to the profits they had made so far. Now ten years later, Darnel's system had generated enough money for Saddleback City to climb out of debt entirely, and become financially secure as a large city. What started as a multi-million dollar idea, transformed into a very profitable venture. His system had put Darnel in the company of some very important and influential people, and had actually made him one of the important people himself.

The redesigned system had many benefits. Accidents and fatalities had dropped immensely, and emergency vehicles were on route without delay at all times. Not to mention the millions of dollars generated from photo radar, speeding tickets, red light runs, parking tickets, and many more traffic violations.

Darnel was wheelchair bound and had been since the age of twelve. His mother and father were taking him to the fairgrounds when their vehicle was struck by another vehicle. Darnel's parents, as well as both his legs, were taken from him on that horrific day twenty-five years ago. To this day, Darnel still had unanswered questions about the accident.

Darnel's uncle Reynolds was the one who stepped up to raise him, and always encouraged him to follow his dreams. He had been there every step of the way for Darnel, and Darnel's wall to wall university degrees were proof of that. Darnel was extremely skilful, he was a rebel scientist, a connoisseur of fabrications, an inventor, and always had something on the go. Everything was legal of course, but Darnel had a very vivid imagination, an abundance of energy, and access to all kinds of money. One of his favorite projects to date, was when he improved their existing, and invented new, non-lethal weaponry for the Saddleback City Police Force

His father, William Casts, was a very wealthy man. When he was alive, it was rumoured that the Casts family net worth was nearly five hundred million dollars. With his uncle's constant support, and all Darnel's accomplishments, Darnel was able to increase the Casts family net worth to over a billion dollars.

It took a while for Darnel to get the video footage Brogan was looking for; the one he said he wouldn't get. He had to take the necessary steps to ensure it could not be traced back to him, as it was illegal. But Darnel felt obligated to help his newly developed interest, if not for closure, then for his own studying purposes.

Brogan had only called Darnel one time, but that was all it took to peak his interest. Although after they're conversation, Brogan would never have guessed that Darnel was planning to help him. He honestly thought the phone call to Darnel was a dead end. But despite the fact that

Brogan still wasn't thinking clearly, he did feel some kind of connection with Darnel. And for some strange reason, Darnel had felt a connection with Brogan. The two men had only talked for five minutes, and Darnel empathized with Brogan's pain, but it was much more than that. Even though Darnel had a hidden agenda, which he never shared with Brogan, he knew he had to help him.

Darnel's redesigned and reconfigured traffic control system now had cameras everywhere, covering each and every angle possible in Saddleback City. What people didn't realize was how much could be seen and what was being recorded.

Darnel had to be very careful retrieving the information Brogan requested, as the consequences could be detrimental. If caught, he could lose his supervisor position, get charged or sued, and even do time. Darnel, however, believed the cause outweighed the consequences or repercussions. He not only granted Brogan's wish, he did it in such a way that there would be no evidence of tampering. If by chance anyone found something, the trail would lead nowhere, and he filtered every little video trail to ensure it.

The front entrance of the Saddleback City Regional Hospital faced a 'T' intersection with three sets of lights controlling it. Six cameras strategically covered all angles of the intersection. The police had already confiscated all video footage of the hospital for that day, but Darnel had his own little workshop that no one knew about, where he was still able to view the footage and see exactly what the police would see.

It had been five weeks after the animalistic attack and Brogan was growing more agitated. It seemed as though there would be no help or answers from the police, or anyone for that matter, and Rita's killer would never be caught.

Just when Brogan thought his tear ducts were dry, he found himself on his knees with his face in the floor, crying harder than the time before. Eating was now a chore for him, since he had no appetite, and he would only do it for the sole purpose of maintaining his strength. The money Brogan had saved for his future with Rita would now be used in any and every way, legal or not, to find whoever was responsible for her death. If ever there was a time for justice and truth to prevail, it was now.

Brogan cried so hard that his ears started ringing painfully, but nothing compared to his tormented heartache. He refused to accept the possibility of never finding Rita's killers; literally snarling at the thought. "If I don't find those animals in this lifetime," Brogan thought out loud, "I'll hunt them down in the next."

Brogan sat on the kitchen floor with his knees up to his chest for a long time, staring at one spot on the floor in front of him until he couldn't feel his legs anymore.

"I will find answers, I will find truth, I will find those animals," he said finally pulling himself up off the floor.

As he stood up an intense attack of pins and needles shot through his legs. Suddenly the silence in his apartment was killed as it filled with the blaring ring of the phone. Despite the numbness and uncertainty in his legs, Brogan was on top of the phone before the first ring was complete.

Unknown caller showed up on the phone display and he answered it before the second ring. He noticed his hands shaking almost uncontrollably as he put the phone to his ear and wondered if his voice was in the same state, making him hesitate to say hello. Brogan knew, in some weird subconscious way, that he had to answer this call.

"Mr. Cormie? Hello? Are you there Mr. Cormie?"

The voice sounded important and serious like a principal, but laid back at the same time. It eased Brogan's wrenched up aggression, a little.

"Yes, I'm here," he answered with no emotion.

"You still interested in borrowing that...movie?"

"Yes!" Brogan's heart pounded as fast as he answered. He knew exactly who was on the other end of the phone and what it entailed.

"Meet me in Sarsaparilla Park at six o'clock tonight."

Brogan shot a glance at the clock, 5:15pm. "Ok, where in the park?" He needed a precise location due to the size of the park.

"West gate."

"See you there Mr. Casts," Brogan said in a polite but anxious voice.

"Man, what are you doin' sayin' my name over the phone?"

"Oh...shit!" Brogan stammered, his voice was still anxious but became apologetic.

"Relax man, I'm just playin' with ya!"

"You got nothing better to do?"

There was a short pause.

"Now we're even eh?!" Brogan chimed.

"You and I are gonna get along just fine!"

"I'll see you at six," Brogan answered, "and please, call me Brogan."

"Done," Darnel replied.

Brogan hurried to get out the door. He had more than enough time to get to the park, but was anxious to get there. "Now where are my damn keys?" he said gritting his teeth.

Glancing in the mirror, he reached up and snatched the keys from between his teeth; not even remembering picking them up. "Wow!" he whispered, "I've gotta pull it together."

He walked into the kitchen and placed both his hands on the table. "Is this really happening? I've gotta calm down!"

Brogan was curious what would be on the disc, maybe faces or a license plate, and questioned if he was ready to see it. He hoped this would be the answer to his endless questions, but wondered if he would be able to watch his only true love be taken from him again.

"Whatever it takes!" Brogan said out loud as he left his apartment. "I will do whatever it takes to hunt down those animals, whatever it takes!"

He kept repeating it as if he was talking to someone, and in fact, he was.

He flew down the apartment stairs, tears of sorrow and joy streamed down his face. "We might have a break in the case sweetie," he whispered, his stomach rolling from nerves.

He blasted through the doors at the bottom of the stairs, leading outside. The sun wasn't visible through the tall buildings, but the brightness of the late day momentarily blinded Brogan. As his eyes started to adjust, he could feel the searing heat escaping from the asphalt pathway. Brogan turned to head down the path in the direction of the park, and jumped back a bit, startled, as a black man in a wheelchair sat staring at him. Brogan had a feeling this man was Darnel, mostly because of his stare. Likewise, Darnel knew the man standing before him was Brogan. The tears streaming down his cheeks sort of gave it away. Although Darnel had also done an extensive background check on Brogan the day he received his desperate phone call. He knew almost everything there was to know about him. He had even found video footage from both the fight back east between Brogan and Master Cros, as well as footage from the zoo incident.

Brogan stared at the man in the wheelchair saying nothing.

"What? You ain't neva seen a black man in a wheelchair before?" Darnel smirked as if the two men were old schoolmates.

It all came to Brogan as an overwhelming wave of emotions; thinking how Darnel had jeopardized his job, and much more, to help him. Brogan fought back more tears and the urge to hug Darnel.

"Sure I have, just not as muscular and handsome," he said razzing Darnel as he shook his hand.

Darnel reached into his inside jacket pocket and pulled out a disc far enough for Brogan to tell it was what he was looking for.

"I have your movie," Darnel whispered, sliding the disc back inside his jacket; the way a drug dealer would his goods, not giving them up until there was an exchange of money.

"So how much do you want for it?"

"I don't want any money," Darnel said as he looked around inconspicuously.

Brogan wondered what he wanted. "Can I have it?" he asked trying not to be overbearing.

Darnel shot a look at him so quick, it startled Brogan. He looked straight into Brogan's tear filled eyes saying nothing. It was a look without words that said it all, telling Brogan there was much more going on.

"Would you be interested in taking a ride with me Brogan?"

"Sure, where?" Brogan asked impatiently.

Darnel looked up at Brogan, "Look, we don't have time to discuss that right now. Just hop on and we'll get goin'."

There was an awkward silence as Brogan stared at Darnel.

"I'm just playin' man!" Darnel said breaking the silence. He popped his wheelchair up on two wheels and spun around. "I've got a ride for us."

Brogan noticed through Darnel's jacket, how big his arms were, and automatically knew Darnel worked out and took good care of himself.

Even though Darnel was in a wheelchair, from the waist up he was a power house on wheels. Some might even say he was on steroids, and although he looked it, it was all natural.

Out of nowhere a pimped out Escalade pulled up and stopped, the back door popped open, and a ramp unfolded in front of Darnel. Brogan stood staring in disbelief. "This guy is unreal," he thought.

"Hop in my friend, let's take a ride."

Brogan jumped in the passenger seat, still in shock, and looked over at the man that was driving.

"Brogan, this is Uncle Reynolds," Darnel said, "he's the one who raised me, and there ain't no one I trust more in this life! So you can guarantee you can also trust him."

In the past five weeks there was a couple times Brogan considered laughing, or even smiling, but thought he would be disrespecting Rita in some way; so he held them from escaping, even though he knew Rita would've wanted him to keep smiling. But for some reason, in this moment he found himself smiling again, and it felt good.

The seemingly tall, older, black man was wearing a black cowboy hat and was listening to Beastie Boys. Brogan also thought he saw a slight shape of a holstered hand gun under his suede coat, and got a sense that he was not a man to mess with.

Darnel reached up front giving Brogan a reassuring pat on the shoulder. "You have nothing to fear or worry about my friend, I'm on the level."

Brogan looked back over his shoulder. "So where are we going?" he asked.

"Back to my place. I have a big screen we can watch that movie on."

They had been driving a long time and Brogan could see the Rocky Mountains getting closer, they were quite a ways out of town. For the whole forty minute trip Darnel explained how there was more going on than what the police were saying. "Let's just say there are more previews on this movie than what was on the original."

"What does that mean?" Brogan thought, his interest peaked.

Brogan had never seen the original, he hadn't seen anything at all. He knew that Rita had been stabbed for the money she had withdrawn from the ATM. He also knew that the murderer had twisted the knife inside her so she wouldn't survive. But he had never seen any of the video footage, and if the police had anything as evidence, Brogan didn't know about it.

Brogan looked out the window as the pimped out Escalade slowed and turned right, then drove up a long horse shoe shaped gravel driveway. He wasn't really expecting what he saw, but as he stared out the window, it all made sense. On top of the big hill was a huge farm ranch. The three storey house had a classy, homey feel, and was very well maintained. The two front doors looked as if they were stolen from an ancient castle in England, only trimmed down to suit the style of the house; they were bigger than average doors, but not too gaudy. The porch was the entire length of the house and wrapped around both sides of the huge ranch style home. Brogan guessed it connected in the back with a big deck. It also looked as though the third floor was one big room with windows all around it, kind of like a huge lighthouse room. Brogan stared at the house in respectful amazement, taking in all the features.

"I grew up in this house." Darnel said startling Brogan. "My father built it with his bare hands for our family when I was two years old. And let me tell you, he left nothing out when he built it. He wanted my mom and I to have anything we needed. The front doors are from Ireland or something like that."

"England Darnel," Uncle Reynolds piped in as they got out of the Escalade. "You have ancestors who lived in a castle in England many, many years ago. When your father found the remains of the castle, the only things he was able to salvage were a bunch of stone he used for landscaping around here, and those beautiful solid oak doors. He had them shipped back, and with his own hands trimmed the doors down to fit, and viola." Uncle Reynolds pointed to the front doors proudly as if he had built them himself.

Darnel gave his wheels a push and darted out the back of the Escalade and in front of Brogan. "Yeah, what he said," Darnel said winking at Brogan.

"And that top room there, that is something you have to see for yourself. That'll be explanation enough," Darnel said pointing up to the third floor.

Brogan quickly noticed how everything seemed to be wheelchair accessible, which showed him that Darnel made sure he was able to go anywhere, to do whatever he wanted without someone having to help him.

"The house and surrounding ranch sits on one hundred acres," Darnel continued. "This is where our animals roam around," Darnel pointed. "Further back we have woodland."

"There is approximately fifteen hundred acres in total," Uncle Reynolds interrupted as he retrieved some packages from the Escalade.

"Follow me Brogan, we'll go inside and grab a cold refreshment," Darnel said rolling away.

"You've got a nice house here Darnel," Brogan said following him toward the front doors.

"If you like the outside, you're gonna love the inside my friend!"

Uncle Reynolds followed as the two men entered the ranch home.

Brogan whistled as he stepped into the front entrance. "Wow, how much does a traffic analyst make?"

Uncle Reynolds chuckled as he headed to the next room.

"Brogan, the position I hold with the city, well, let's just call it a hobby. I have been in business for myself for quite some time now. I forget exactly how many years it's been…"

"Nineteen years now Darnel," Uncle Reynolds replied walking back into the room carrying different packages. "You started when you were eighteen years old."

Darnel gave his wheels another push and motioned for Brogan to follow. Brogan was amazed at the huge front entrance and how it spanned out in different directions, leading to bigger rooms.

"I reinvent things in my spare time, and come up with new stuff from time to time."

Uncle Reynolds hit a button on the front entrance wall, and the big castle doors started to close.

Brogan watched as the doors creaked shut. "They sound exactly like they look," he thought.

Darnel led Brogan into a huge dinning room with a gigantic table. Suddenly a beautiful woman, with a physique that would make any man blush, entered the room. She was carrying two cold Alexander Keith's and handed one to Darnel and one to Brogan.

"This is my lead ranch hand Denise," Darnel said motioning toward her. "Denise, this is Brogan."

Brogan reached out and shook her hand. "That's quite a grip!" he said.

Brogan couldn't help but say something, it was a strong handshake.

Denise smiled. "Nice to meet you," she said as she walked away.

"You too, thanks for the brew!"

Darnel waited until Denise had left the room, then wheeled closer to Brogan. "I needed someone qualified to do certain tasks, Denise needed a job and a place to stay. She takes care of the horses, and all the other animals as well. She also makes meals along side of Uncle Reynolds. I sometimes dabble with cookin' myself; it seems to help relieve stress. And besides that Denise is usually in the kitchen when I am, she's a good teacher."

Darnel looking around to make sure Denise still wasn't in ear shot before continuing. "She's an ex-Marine that had a little scuffle with her commanding officer; she knocked him the hell out! Actually, she beat him to the point where…lets just say she got her point across! It's amazing how much she knows about everything, Jacqueline of all trades, queen of many. She is also head of my security."

"How many security guards do you have?" Brogan asked

"Let me see…four…nine…twelve….just one - Denise! When I hired her she proved she could handle anything I threw at her. She's a major asset to this ranch and my well-being.

Brogan and Darnel sat at the huge dining room table and continued to talk, and drink their beers. As they talked, Brogan was continually looking around in awe of Darnel's house. He noticed there were huge floor to ceiling paintings everywhere, and kept looking at one in particular. "Dogs playing poker eh?" he finally said.

"Yeah, it proves that what my dad used to say is all too true, 'the eyes miss most everything."

"Brogan, I am deeply sorry for your loss," Darnel said completely changing the subject. "I understand, in a sense, what you're goin' through. But I want you to prepare yourself for what you're goin' to see on this disc I have. What I have uncovered is bigger than you or I, anyone for that matter, but it involves everyone." He paused for a moment, "Uncle Reynolds?"

Uncle Reynolds suddenly emerged out of the next room.

"Can you do us a favor and…"

"The Vision Chamber is powered up and ready to roll," Uncle Reynolds interrupted in a cool but stern voice.

"Come with me," Darnel said pushing his wheelchair away from the table.

Brogan followed him, feeling his nerves starting to give.

Darnel stopped at the painting of the dogs playing poker, the one Brogan had been admiring earlier, and pushed a button on the frame that wasn't noticeable to the naked eye.

"My father used to say that a dog would make a good poker player," Darnel said as the painting started sliding to the left.

Brogan thought for a couple seconds before asking, "Why?"

"Because you never know what an animal is thinking," Darnel answered with a smirk. "They're unpredictable."

Behind the painting was a set of elevator doors that opened as the painting moved.

"All aboard," Darnel said wheeling into the elevator.

Brogan stepped onto the elevator not knowing what to expect. Out of the blue, Uncle Reynolds appeared and looked at Brogan. "Remember son, life is full of shit. You're gonna get some on ya, eventually. How much? That depends on you!" he said in a heartfelt voice.

The doors shut and Brogan could feel the elevator descending.

"Isn't Uncle Reynolds a wise and cheerful man!" Darnel snickered.

Brogan inspected the elevator on the ride down. "Who is this guy?" he thought.

A few seconds later the elevator doors opened. Darnel wheeled out and Brogan followed. As he stepped out, Brogan spun around in amazement at the amount of technology Darnel had in the room; it seemed almost futuristic, surpassing the Enterprise.

One wall served entirely as the TV, with a big screen measuring eight feet tall and sixteen feet wide, and had two dozen smaller flat screens surrounding it. The room also had a supporting surround sound system with speakers mounted everywhere. In front of the TV, not quite in the middle of the room, was a long computerized control desk. Across the room was nothing short of a recording studio, which housed state of the art equipment as well. In the center of this astounding room sat a massive glass table that was electronically capable of moving up and down, though right now it stood four feet off the concrete floor. The glass table top spread ten feet wide by ten feet long. As Brogan got closer to it, he realized why the size was needed. The entire table top was a map of Saddleback City, illuminated and computerized as well.

Darnel wheeled straight over to the control desk in front of the big screen, and proceeded to type on the keyboard.

"I can't understand why you call this the Vision Chamber," Brogan said trying not to sound too overwhelmed.

"You should see my theatre room," Darnel bragged.

Brogan stood beside Darnel and stared at the wall of flat screens. "You do pretty good for yourself with this ranch and all! You probably get all the channels for free, eh?"

"You have no idea my friend," Darnel replied in a dark comical voice.

As Darnel finished typing, all the screens started showing familiar images.

"Hey, that's the center of Saddleback City, and Sarsaparilla Park!" Brogan said astonished. "Holy smokes, that's the police station!" Brogan stood in disbelief pointing at the screens.

"Anything that the traffic control tower sees, I see...and then some!" Darnel explained. "Brogan, what we have here is a state of the art surveillance room, with technology so advanced that no one knows its full capabilities or potential...but me of course! Not only can I see everything the control center sees, I can also see everything that the police see. Plus I have a huge advantage; I can manually zoom in or out on any object or person with any camera throughout the city. I can also move each camera separately, to virtually anywhere I wanna look. All in all, if there's shit hittin' the fan, I have sight of it comin' and can duck, if you catch my drift."

Brogan looked at Darnel completely boggled as he continued to explain how he obtained the position he had with the city. "Don't get me wrong Brogan; I have been lookin' for answers myself for a long time. I worked my ass off to get to where I'm at today. Boy did I work! I took it upon myself to try and make a difference by getting involved with the city. I mean deeply involved, as you can see."

He paused before continuing. "My parents were taken from me years ago, that same day my legs were also taken from me, and I've been lookin' for answers ever since. I would trade all my limbs, my life, to have my parents back again. But Uncle Reynolds helped me realize, at a very young and naive age, that sometimes shit happens, and in order to do anything to stop or rectify it, you need balls, a good poker face, money, and as he says

"It helps to have a card up your sleeve". So here I am, not only showing you my hand, but also one of the many cards up my sleeve. We, and I mean all of us living in Saddleback City, are subject to fear, loss, and pain at some point in our lives. But don't you think it should be by the will of God, or even Mother Nature? Not by some freakin idiot gang member trying to make a name for himself in the gang rankings. This city has been in trouble for a long time, well before I lost my parents, or my legs; and it's obviously just getting worse."

Brogan listened to Darnel's story intensely, trying to process everything he was saying.

Darnel took a deep breath and continued. "I'm not going to lie and tell you I'm not still lookin' for some sort of retribution, because I am. My parents were murdered; they were taken out, on purpose. It was a professional hit, and I was basically supposed to be collateral damage. No one thought that this little kid would survive and come back lookin' for answers," Darnel said pointing to himself. "And if those responsible for my parents deaths know who I am and are keeping tabs on me, so be it. They will read in my psychologists file that as a boy I lost both my parents and my legs in the same automobile accident, that I was scarred for life, and turned into a computer nerd who was fixated on making driving safer for everyone. What I'll bet they don't know, and is another card up my sleeve, is that my nerdy position at work is a cover. And that I used my money, and the design of the new traffic control system as a tool, a Trojan horse if you will. I plan on finding answers for myself, and for you too Brogan."

Brogan felt everything Darnel was saying was true, but he wasn't born yesterday. He had been around and played enough sports to know a pep talk when he heard one. And that's exactly what Darnel's spiel was, a pep talk to win Brogan over. What Brogan didn't know, was that Darnel had seen the video footage of Brogan's fight with the silverback. Not only was Darnel in complete shock and awe, he became obsessively intrigued by Brogan, which was one of the reasons this meeting was taking place.

Brogan didn't have enough time to fully analyze the speech he just heard when Darnel touched his arm. "You might want to sit down," he said pointing to the chair next to him.

Brogan sat down without taking his eyes off the big screen. Darnel zoomed in by stroking a couple buttons on the keyboard. Suddenly, like a perfect angel, there was Rita, an absolute beautiful creature, hustling down the stairs outside the hospital. Brogan closed his mouth realizing it was completely dry. Tears began streaming down his cheeks, but he couldn't look away. All at once he could smell her sweet fragrance. It was almost too much for him to bear, but he forced himself to get through it as his heart started to pound faster. Brogan watched in splendid horror as Rita made her way to the bank machine, all the while with a smile on her face. Brogan choked on his tears and swallowed hard. Rita had just taken her money out of the machine when two males came into view heading straight for her. Brogan noticed how Rita's attackers never even saw how much money she had withdrawn. No sooner did she take her card out of the ATM and the animals attacked. There was so much blood and carnage for such a sweet little angel. It was too much for Brogan to handle. He was seething mad, and completely broken all at the same time. He could feel his blood boiling as it rushed through his body, but all he could do in that moment was double over sobbing uncontrollably.

Darnel waited until Brogan had composed himself, and together they went over the footage numerous times trying to see where the animals came from. Other surveillance angles showed they had come from different directions, and hooked up half a block away.

Darnel zeroed in on one of the attackers, and zoomed in, his face consumed the big screen. Brogan knew now that he would never forget the face of Rita's killer; his facial features were being etched into Brogan's mind. As he stared at the screen memorizing her attacker, he couldn't help but feel overwhelmed. He believed Rita had left him a clue by leaving a scar on her killer's face as she tried to defend herself. Either way, Brogan now had a face to put on Rita's killer. He now had someone to hunt down.

"That means the police have DNA!" Brogan yelled, jumping to his feet.

"Brogan, you can't talk to any cops, about anything you've seen here tonight," Darnel demanded.

Brogan watched as Darnel pulled out another disc and pushed it into a second slot.

"I know, I know! I can't say anything about this to them, cause they'll know I've seen the footage."

Darnel nodded without looking at him. "It's much more complicated than that."

Brogan looked up at the screen.

"This is fifteen minutes later, five blocks away, captured on a different camera."

Brogan watched completely bewildered, as the same animal who killed Rita, walked right up to a police cruiser parked on the side of the street; leaned into the drivers side window of the cruiser, then passed a wad of cash to the officer inside.

Darnel and Brogan watched the recording over and over, and from every angle possible.

"Ok, even though we can't make out the officer's face, we have the plate number off the cruiser, we could…"

Darnel looked at Brogan with empathy escaping from his eyes. "They change vehicles, different cops drive different cruisers all the time, and besides, we don't know who on the police force can be trusted. I know it sucks, but we need to dig further and get more incriminating evidence."

Overwhelmed, Brogan wiped his tears away and agreed not to discuss anything with anyone, at all.

"Can I come back tomorrow and view the footage again?"

"Dude, we're partners now, we'll work on this together until we get to the truth!" Darnel said with a big smile.

Brogan nodded, "Thank you Darnel."

Darnel returned the nod, "I'll get you a ride home my friend."

"Thanks, but I really feel like walking right now."

As Darnel watched Brogan walk away, he considered the potential dangers and ramifications of getting to the truth. He knew in this fight Brogan would not stagger, and felt there was a need for all the cloak n dagger.

CHAPTER 8

LOST n FOUND

Pain and agony made the long walk home not long enough. However there was no walk that could cure Brogan's pain. He felt as though all his energy had been drained, and yet he still wanted to keep walking. His thoughts were racing through his mind and he couldn't wrap his brain around them. "Nothing made sense...was Darnel insinuating that this conspiracy went as far back as to when he lost his parents? It seemed very unlikely, especially because Darnel lost his parents so many years ago. How could there be a connection between the two horrible crimes. The crime rate was getting worse in Saddleback City, and Rita didn't have any enemies." Although neither did Brogan, not yet anyway. "And what about that officer in his cruiser that horrible day, how was he involved, and why did Rita have to die so he could get his money?"

Unending questions and conspired theories pierced Brogan's mind like stings from a wasp. The truth was Brogan didn't have a clue why Rita's attacker would hand over the money to a cop right after committing a brutal murder a few blocks away. "A bribe or something, protection pay, what did it mean, and why?"

Brogan's head hurt. He kept running everything him and Darnel had watched over and over in his mind. "Everything between the two accidents seemed so irrelevant when compared, and yet somehow the sadistic criminal acts were related? But how? If the police were involved, then how much involved, and how many police?"

Brogan continued walking the long, straight, dark road, not even realizing he was almost speed walking. "Those animals had no way of knowing how much money Rita had even taken out," he thought out loud. "It definitely was a hit and run robbery, but why kill her?"

Brogan stopped dead in his tracks and tears streamed from his eyes. His whole body tensed, as he felt the overwhelming mental exhaustion. A minute slowly rolled by before he started to walk again. He wiped the tears away only to have them replaced by new ones, like a faucet that wouldn't stop dripping.

"It didn't matter how much money," he thought wiping his eyes with the backs of his hands. "It could have only been twenty dollars and those animals still... They wait until someone is using the ATM and then they strike? But they would have to make sure they had a way out, right?... No!" Brogan shouted answering his own question. "They strike whenever they feel like it, and they obviously don't care about being seen...Rita was killed in broad daylight."

Brogan's face scrunched up tight. "In the middle of the day, two gang members walk up, and take Rita's money and her life with no remorse? They gotta be crackheads! They show no hesitation either, so have they done this many times before?"

Brogan's mind was racing in a million directions. "This is insane! Why the hell was that cop taking money from that animal? That animal that JUST SLAUGHTERED MY RITA!?"

Brogan dropped hard to his knees on the asphalt and buried his face in his hands. This time there were no tears to wipe away, there was no sobbing or crying, there was no sound at all. For several minutes Brogan just knelt there shaking, his body tense again. Suddenly, he threw his head back and his arms up into the dark night sky, "AAAAAAAAAAHHHHHHHHHHHHHH," he yelled with all the strength he could gather, like it had been building for some time but was unable to escape his lips until now.

It seemed, at that moment, every noisy cricket went silent, all night crawling creatures went into stealth mode, even the wind appeared to have stopped blowing through the trees.

Eventually Brogan mustered up enough remaining energy to get to his feet and start walking again.

"Darnel's right," he thought feeling a sickening weight in his gut. "I can't talk to nobody, especially the cops!"

Brogan paused for a second and put his hand over his mouth, the way a grandfather would when you surprise him. "What about Detective Shane?" Brogan thought out loud. "Can I trust him? All I wanted was an answer! Not some great big conspiracy bunch of CRAP! What the hell is going on? The only person I can trust right now is Darnel! At least I think I can trust him. This is so messed up!"

Brogan carried on with his rant, questioning everything. "I've been calling Detective Shane every day since the attack. So what, I can't call him anymore? Or do I keep calling him so he doesn't get suspicious and think something's up? What if he's dirty, and has been giving me no information for a reason? I've gotta talk this over with Darnel." Brogan said, everything still racing through his head.

Brogan sped up as he continued his self induced conspiracy state. "I can trust Darnel, I have to! There's no one else. Besides, he brought me into his home showing me all his secret, high-tech equipment like he's Bruce Wayne. He told me he's on a quest to find answers and asked me to join him; and then opened my eyes to the fact that Saddleback City has slowly been consumed with corruption and crimes that could have been prevented."

Brogan recalled what Darnel had said earlier, "Even though right now everyone may not be affected by the overwhelming stench of crime building up in our beloved Saddleback City, be assured the wretchedness of evil will eventually touch everyone; and cause pain and wreak havoc on all our lives!"

Brogan's eyes widened and his mouth opened slightly releasing a sigh as Rita's face flashed through his head. His pace quickened even more as he humbly remembered all that Rita stood for. "Everything she did, she did trying to make a difference in peoples lives. She tried to help anyone and everyone she could, even those who didn't want help she found a way to help them. This was one of the many reasons I loved her so much."

Tears once again started steaming down his cheeks as he continued to reminisce. "Her passion for life; she was such a happy person, she just wanted to share the love and try to spread happiness however she could. All she had to do was smile and people were instantly changed for the better, at least for that day anyway. You tried to help so many people to make this shit hole a better place," he sobbed, "and this is what they do to you!

YOU DIDN'T DESERVE THIS...YOU DIDN'T DESERVE THIS..."
Brogan screamed into the empty night sky, then suddenly took off on a
mad sprint heading for home.

"I will trust this man who opened my eyes and made me realize there
is something wrong with this city. I will trust this man who helped me
put a face to the animal who took Rita from me, FROM EVERYBODY!
I will work with Darnel and try to do what Rita was trying to do...make
Saddleback City a better place to live. Rita, I love you so much, and I
promise I will find that bastard and make sure he never hurts anyone ever
again!"

Brogan's speed increased dramatically without him even noticing.

"A face with a scar," he said grinding his teeth, you freaks want to
act like animals? Then I will hunt you down like the animals you are!
God help anyone else who stands in my way of bringing Rita's dream to
reality! ...Time to hunt!"

Brogan made it home fast and went straight to bed. He was completely
exhausted from his journey home, not to mention the amount of horrible
and disturbing information he received that night; he was still trying to
comprehend it all. He was smart enough to realize he had to get some sleep
to help him think more clearly in the morning. Yet, as he laid in bed all he
could do was conjure up several different ideas, trying to devise a plan of
some sort, before sleep would blanket the pain for the night.

"I'll start hunting first thing in the morning. I love you Rita and I will
bring everybody involved with this down, I promise you my love," Brogan
whispered before finally drifting off into an uncomfortable sleep.

Since that dark day, Brogan had yet to dream of anything; he had
only nightmares haunt his subconscious state. Sleeping had become a
problem, because every time he closed his eyes the same nightmare would
resume. Except tonight was different, tonight Brogan deliberately kept that
scarred face in his head. He chose to enter the subconscious realm of the
unknown with that monster on his mind, if only to get an idea on how
to catch him. And it worked, his nightmare this time wasn't of a faceless
killer chasing Rita, surprisingly Rita was not part of his sleep at all. Instead,
this nightmare was of a new face, a scarred face that chased Brogan his
entire sleep, though he refused to wake up. Through the whole nightmare,

Brogan kept looking over his shoulder at the scarred monster hard on his heels and could not look away, he felt compelled to keep looking at him. Just as the scarred face was about to jump him, Brogan woke up, and as quick as it started the nightmare was over.

Sweaty and pissed off, he got out of bed and found himself in front of his closet. "First things first," he said out loud.

He proceeded to pick through all his dark clothes, pulling black shirts off the hanger until he found what worked best. "Easier to hide in the shadows, if need be."

Brogan suddenly started feeling an anxiety attack coming on and quickly sat on his bed. He held his hands out in front of him and watched them shake.

"C'mon man!" he said, giving himself a small pep talk, "you can handle this."

Brogan didn't know what to expect. But he knew that he had to do something before that fiend ruined more lives. "That monster needs to pay!"

He tossed the chosen dark clothes on his bed and headed for the bathroom. Brogan was preparing for a long excursion, not knowing what had to be done to find the answers he was looking for. First he had to find Rita's killer. Although he hadn't put much thought into what he would do once he found him. The only thing he could think about was hunting down this animal, and his pack.

"However long it takes, no matter where I have to venture, I will be relentless in my pursuit. You scar-faced bastard and all your demented fiendish friends are not going to like me at all. I'll tell you bastards RIGHT NOW! YOU ARE NOT GOING TO LIKE ME!" Brogan growled staring angrily into the mirror. "I'll hunt you down, and it's only a matter of time before I do."

Brogan looked at the clock as he changed into his new dark get-up. It was noon, and he was mad at himself for sleeping so long, but figured he must have needed the sleep. He looked out his window, and seeing nothing but cloudy skies, thought maybe there was a good chance of rain.

"Perfect! I think I need to go do a transaction," he said as he grabbed his wallet and headed out into the unknown, a sinister, cocky smirk forming in the corner of his mouth.

After visiting the bank machine outside the hospital, Brogan went to several other ATM's around the city, taking out money every time. Now with $380.00 in his pocket, Brogan sat down on the park bench outside his bank to regroup his thoughts and maybe rethink his strategy. He had questioned his so-called flawless plan right from the start.

"Maybe they only target women, or weak looking individuals?" Brogan thought wondering how he could possibly put a name to the scarred face that was now burned and etched into his brain.

He contemplated going to the police and telling them he just got mugged and saw his attacker's face. Maybe they might have his picture, and more importantly his name, on file. He wouldn't tell them anything, or even point out the guy if he found his mug shot, he just wanted his name. Unfortunately he would then be putting himself in the presence of cops that couldn't be trusted.

"Crap!" Brogan blurted out in frustration.

Reluctantly, and with no real choice, he decided not to associate with the police. Instead he figured he'd go to the mall, grab a protein drink, and clear his head.

"What are the chances of seeing him at the mall!?" Brogan shrugged. "I couldn't be so lucky!"

Before heading to the mall, Brogan deposited all but twenty dollars back into his account. He only had $400.00 in this particular account, and there were many more bank machines to visit. Plus, he didn't want to touch the money in his other account, it was his emergency fund. And he wanted it all accessible all the time, just in case something happened. Although he would never stop hunting whether he had the money or not. He couldn't, he owed it to Rita. It was all he could do for her now. Not having funds might slow him down, but it would never deter him.

On the way to the mall, Brogan wondered if his bank would contact him questioning the many ATM transactions, and to make sure his card wasn't stolen. He would have to come up with some sort of explanation so they wouldn't put a freeze on his accounts.

The mall was packed as usual, and the line at Juiced Boost was long, but worth the wait. Brogan finally got his protein drink and found a seat on a bench in the middle of the mall's hallway. Enjoying the air conditioning, he sat sipping his drink and indiscreetly watched every face that went by.

Suddenly a short, purple mohawk caught his attention. As the young, male punk sauntered toward him, Brogan couldn't figure out why he was so aggravatingly familiar to him.

The 200 lb, 5'10" mohawk punker had a stainless steel chain that ran from his left eyebrow back to his ear, then strung back over ending on his left nostril. The rest of his ensemble consisted of a skid row sleeveless t-shirt, jeans that were cut off at the knees, and a tall pair of big, black army boots. He was quite jacked and looked as though he could handle himself. He was with a guy and girl who were dressed similar to him, but had their heads shaved. Brogan tried not to stare, or be too obvious in doing so, though they were probably use to people staring.

All at once it hit him like a kick to the groin. "He's the other animal from the video....he was there when Rita was murdered!" Brogan was in such a state of shock that he didn't realized he was whispering his thoughts.

Luckily no one heard him. He had been focusing so much on the scar face fiend that he almost forgot what the other attacker looked like. But this mohawk punk was definitely him.

Brogan held his breath as the mohawk punk walked passed him, his body was rigid and tense with anger, frustration, and anticipation; but he refrained from grabbing the idiot there on the spot. He needed to find the right time and the right place to initiate physical contact and questioning.

Brogan waited until the three punks had passed him and were several feet away before he started to follow them. He followed behind them very slowly, imitating their walking speed, until they stopped to talk. Brogan quickly became interested in the bath towels on display in front of a shop. After two to three minutes of discussion, the mohawk punk kissed the girl and then did a funky handshake with the guy before they parted ways, and he left in the opposite direction as them.

"Patience...just hold back and wait," Brogan told himself. "He'll eventually give you the opportunity."

He was hoping to get this guy alone, where he could question him without anyone being nearby to hear. Brogan followed him all the way to the end of the mall, watching him spit on the floor every so often.

"Some piece of work!" Brogan thought.

Brogan took another sip of his drink, and almost choked on it as the punk suddenly spun around and headed straight for him. Brogan never looked up; he kept slurping his drink and walked right past him, watching the punk in the reflection of the store windows. When he got to the last store, Brogan turned around and continued following the punk again, holding back a little further this time knowing the punk had checked him out when they passed one another. Brogan knew, he felt it, in fact he thought for a split second that he was going to be jumped.

"I couldn't be that lucky!" he thought playing the scenario over in his mind. "Although it seems like he's looking for his next victim. Bastard won't get one this time."

Halfway back through the mall, the punk turned down a long corridor. Instantly Brogan spotted the washroom sign and proceeded to follow him, an appeased smile on his face. "This is it, you punk bitch, let's see how you do against someone your own gender and closer to your size!"

Brogan snickered feeling a small adrenaline surge starting to flow through his body. "Easy now, wait for it," Brogan reminded himself.

He watched as the punk entered the men's bathroom and disappeared out of sight, before sprinting down the hallway to catch up. He was at the men's room door in the blink of an eye.

When Brogan crept into the bathroom he noticed a man's legs in the first stall, and watched in astonishment as the punk swiftly reached under the stall and stole the man's wallet from the pants around his ankles. Brogan couldn't believe it. "You freakin animal!" he thought. "And you have the nerve to just stand there going through his wallet!?"

Brogan could feel his body heating up, as he walked aggressively towards the punk, to the point of almost exploding. Without blinking, Brogan reached out and grabbed the back of the punk's belt. He yanked so fast and fierce the fiend didn't have a chance to yell. The wallet spun in the air as the punk flew backwards and out the door, without touching the floor. With no hesitation Brogan jabbed out his left hand snagging the wallet before it started to fall, slid it under the stall to the man, and turned to chase after his prey.

Brogan moved so fast, he was out in the hall just as the punk crash landed. The fiend flew with such force out the bathroom door that he stuck in the drywall across the hall. Without recognizing his own strength,

Brogan picked the punk free from the walls clutches, and launched him again. This time grabbing him by the armpits and throwing him hard over his shoulder. The punk had just started to regain his senses from the first toss, and now found himself airborne once again. He smacked the hard mall floor with his chest and face, and slid dazed and confused, his arms dragged behind him accompanied by a terrible screeching noise as his skin scraped the floor.

"Perfect!" Brogan said noticing a maintenance room to his right.

He grabbed the punk's belt again, and in a back hand motion unleashed a horrendous yank and throw. The punk blasted through the maintenance room door and slammed into a large shelving unit on the far wall, scattering its contents all over the room. Brogan stepped into the four by eight foot room, shut the door, and locked it behind him. He took his time turning the lights on, figuring they would have more of a blinding effect if the punk sat in the dark for a bit first. The punk squinted when the lights came on as his eyes coordinated with his brain to focus.

Brogan noticed he was wearing a skull watch on his left hand, and thought he might be right handed. He couldn't see any signs of weapons on him, but figured if the idiot had one, he would have tried to use it by now.

"Tough bastard!" Brogan said noticing the punk was coming around quicker than he thought.

Although he didn't want him unconscious anyway, he still had questions he needed answered. Brogan watched as the punk clumsily climbed to his feet.

"What the hell! What's goin on…? Who the hell are you mother fu…?

Having no empathy whatsoever, Brogan open hand slapped the punk across the face. His head slammed hard to the side and bounced off the shelving unit before he fell to the floor shaking his head.

"What the hell man, you fu…"

Brogan cut him off. "You're trapped. You hear me? Trapped! There's nothing you can do," he said through his teeth like Dirty Harry, but in a much darker voice, making the hairs on the back of the punks neck stand up. "Now I have a couple of…"

Brogan was abruptly cut off by a right-cross thrown by the punk, and was surprised by the speed at which it came given the punk was still in a sitting position. But he was no comparison to Brogan, whose reaction time was second to none. Brogan effortlessly struck the top of the punk's flying fist, as if they were playing a harsh game of knuckles; and watched as the punk retreated his knuckle assault, wincing in pain, holding his hand close to his chest.

"What the shit man!?" he screamed.

Brogan noticed a change in the punk's demeanour as he realized there was nothing he could do. Brogan then leaned in close to him, knowing the punk would still be defiant, and spoke in the same intimidating voice. "How's it feel? I want to know how it feels when you are facing certain injury and there's nothing you can do about it! I'm curious to know if it's the same feeling you put all your victims through? …Now listen, and listen good, you…"

"Screw you…"

Before the punk could finish, Brogan stuffed two fingers up his nose, clenched down with his thumb, and started lifting. Instantly the punk was scrambling to get up as fast as he could so the pain wasn't so intense. Brogan assisted him, taking most of the 200 lbs. Although the pain was excruciating the punk was reluctant to heed to anyone. As Brogan helped him stand up, the idiot punk unexpectedly pulled an eight inch knife from his army boot with his left hand.

"Didn't see that coming," Brogan thought as his eyes darted around the small room, catching sight of a broom leaning against the wall.

The punk shot in with a bladed lunge and once again it was no comparison to Brogan's reaction time. He reached out and snagged the thick broom handle. The speed at which Brogan moved exceeded anything the purple-haired freak had ever encountered. The broom fell in a whipping motion, like a fly swatter swiping a fly from the air, striking the punk on the top of his weapon wielding hand with a thick, sickening crack. He screamed in pain knowing there were definitely broken bones in his hand. Brogan snatched the knife out of the air and stuck it in the wall just inches from the punk's head.

Knowing he was beat and trapped the punk was still arrogantly defiant. "AAAAhhhhhhhhh!" The sound was more of a girly scream than a manly yell. "You son of a bitch…you've got no idea…" he said as he slid down the wall into a sitting position.

He held both his arms close to his chest, and pulled his knees up under his chin as if trying to protect his injuries, and prevent further pain. With no hesitation or mercy, Brogan stomped the top of his foot. But before the punk could scream in more agony, Brogan stuffed a rag into his mouth. His eyes lit up with fury, and the punk could see it clearly as he stared into them.

"In case you didn't catch it the first time, you're trapped in here with me!" Brogan said in a growling voice, squatting in front of him.

He pulled the rag from the punk's mouth, and moved uncomfortably close to him. "Your friend stabbed an innocent woman at the ATM in front of the Saddleback City Regional Hospital over a month ago. I want his name and where I can find him."

Brogan stared into his eyes.

"I got no freakin idea what you're talking about...asshole!"

Neither of them blinked as they sat staring at each other.

"You're so far over your head dick wad, that you'll be dead before you make it home." The punk threatened realizing he got away with calling Brogan an asshole.

The instant the punk blinked, Brogan reached up and ripped the chain free from the body parts it was pierced to. As he started to scream, Brogan stuffed the rag back into his mouth. Although it was muffled, it still seemed loud.

Becoming very frustrated Brogan removed the rag from the punk's mouth and stared at him again, not blinking.

The punk was breathing much heavier, showing that he was getting extremely pissed off. "You got no clue dude...these guys don't mess around! They'll kill me...you...and everyone you know. Whatever it is you're trying to do...or find out...it's not gonna work! You fu..."

Before he could finish, Brogan open hand slapped him again, but much harder, causing him to squeal like a pig.

Brogan continued to stare into his eye's still not blinking or saying anything.

"I'm not telling you squat...you asshole!"

Brogan stuffed the rag back in the punk's mouth. "I'm done messing around!" he hollered. "Answer my questions, or I'm gonna get severely pissy!"

The punk's eyes told the whole story. He was scared, in pain, and wondering what was going to happen to him next. Brogan could see all this, but still kept staring into the monster's eyes with no remorse.

He fiercely pulled the rag from the fiend's mouth to ask another question, but didn't get a chance to speak.

"Screw you, you son of a bitch. I'll kill you, you're not safe anywhere. I'm gonna kill you. You won't even see it coming. Then I'm gonna kill your momma!"

The punk chose the wrong relative to threaten. Brogan's retaliation was extreme. He wanted to prove he was not playing around and wouldn't put up with anything from this punk, anymore.

As Brogan stuffed the rag deeper into the punk's mouth, he reached up with lightening speed and clamped onto the punk's left ear. Suddenly a tearing sound, like Velcro being quickly torn apart, echoed through the small maintenance room. The punk stared at Brogan with questioning eyes. The strike was faster than any snake, so quick he didn't realize what had happened. As he focused on the ear in Brogan's hand, his eye's got big and he started shaking his head in denial. He pressed his busted hand against the left side of his head as his eyes slowly made their way up to Brogan's, and locked.

"AHHHHHHHHH! AAAHHHHH…. AAAHHHHHHHHH!!!!" the agonizing screams were muffled by the rag, but were still very loud.

Blood bubbled from between his fingers as he whimpered in pain. Brogan reached up again and slowly removed the rag from the punk's mouth, and tossed the ear on the floor beside him like it was an everyday occurrence. This time there was no yelling, no cursing, and no death threats; only a stare of compliance.

"His name is…Mo Daft." The punk spoke softly staring at his ear on the floor. "He doesn't have a specific place he calls home…that I know of. He runs all over the city…and stays wherever. He hangs out…at the pool hall dance club…on 47th. Man, he gets crazy…getting jacked up on all types of shit, everyday. He's got knives and guns. He's nuts man! He'll kill ya…without even thinking twice. That's it, that's all I know…I swear!"

Brogan unleashed a right jab, from his squatting position, which landed on the punk's chin knocking him out instantly and making his head bounce off the shelving unit. The jab wasn't seen or heard, but would definitely be felt by the punk when he woke up.

Brogan listened at the door for anybody on the other side, then slowly opened it and stepped out into the hall. He strolled toward the mall exit feeling better, somehow knowing that things would work out. It wasn't a feeling of relief, or any type of happiness. It was something worth more. Brogan felt accomplishment, a purpose, for the first time since Rita's death. He had a name to put to the scarred face, and a little information to help him with the hunt. It made him feel better knowing there was a next step, and he was that much closer to finding Rita's killer.

Brogan wouldn't forget Mr. Mohawk either; he would let him roam free for now. "Besides," Brogan thought, "it would do no good at all taking him to the police, most of his friend's probably work at the station!"

Losing Rita would prove to be the most traumatic and devastating thing for Brogan. But now he had found a purpose to keep him going; another reason to do much more than just try to live without his Rita.

"These animals need to be dealt with quick and hard. I need to bring the fight to them with heavier repercussions. They need to be hit so hard and fast that it affects everybody involved."

Brogan now realized there were some very important people involved in this shit storm. And knew they would be more difficult to expose and bring down. "Some big and powerful figures were involved with taking everything I had, let's see them deal with me when everything's taken from them!" he said grinding his teeth with pure hatred and determination.

Brogan wasn't too sure what he was going to do next, but he did know he was going to fight till there was nothing left. He was a changed man now.

His mother had known of the potential beast lurking inside him since he was a boy. She had always hoped that if for some reason this part of him was unleashed, it would be harnessed somehow, and directed towards good things and helping people. Like lifting a vehicle off someone who was trapped, or saving people from a burning building.

Sadly, those who interfered with Brogan's new perspective on life would witness true savagery first hand. He was not one to be messed with. But now his pain and hate, combined with his amazing strength and abilities, would create something no one could ever fathom. His loss, that one act of horrific and devastating violence, had created a force in him that was comparable only to nightmares. The force was still not fully known, even to himself, but it was growing stronger and angrier by the day, with more reason to fear it. It was a force that was even more powerful and terrifying than love itself, and there would be no stopping or controlling him now. It was a force created from his love being murdered and taken from him. Before, Brogan was a man with a beast lurking inside him, waiting to be released. Now he was a beast within a beast, trying to break free.

Brogan exited the mall and shut the door without a sound. As he walked away he started humming part of Rita's favorite song, "I once was lost, but now am found."

CHAPTER 9

MATCH MADE IN HELL

B rogan had never been so violent or vicious, and still he had held back the rage with the mohawk punk. Even when he was younger, in sports and especially martial arts, he found himself holding back his aggressiveness. Holding back the potentially lethal arsenal of strikes he had learned and practiced religiously. Holding back the lurking beast that flowed through his veins, through his entire body.

When he was growing up it was about fun and competition, there was never a reason for Brogan to be mean. But it wasn't about fun or competition anymore, it was life, and it was real.

Brogan understood the hardships of life, some aspects anyway. He also realized there was always someone who had it worse. He knew that life could crap on anyone, at any point. And he knew it was how you cope and deal with the crap that determined who and what you were as a person. However, when you have someone to love, and they love you back, then the crap doesn't seem as bad. Whatever falls in your lap, you deal with, and it's easier to get through the obstacles that litter your path in life because you have that loving support.

Brogan's life was great, everything was going his way, but it threw him a curve ball, one that he never expected. A curve ball that took everything from him. It had changed him forever. He now had to adapt, and do anything he had to, to get the answers he needed. It used to be love that kept him motivated, kept him grounded. But the ramifications had already been released, and would end up on the heads of those involved with Rita's death.

Sometimes losing a loved one is not only life altering, it's also an opportunity for desperation to latch on, feeding and multiplying until it clouds your judgement; leading you down a dark path in life, a path no one should ever venture. But Brogan was different, he had very little limitations compared to the average man. After losing Rita he intentionally chose to walk the dark path. He knew it was a vicious cycle of pain, and chances were he would be trapped forever in the abyss of eternal suffering. Still he chose it in the hopes it would change things and eventually do good for people.

Brogan felt good when he woke up the next morning. For the first time since Rita was taken from him, he went back to his regular morning routine. He was glad to have the name and face of Rita's killer, and knew he was one step closer to hunting that monster down.

"I can't wait to tell Darnel what happened yesterday," Brogan thought.

He completed his usual set of push-ups, but kept going feeling more energized than he had in a long time.

Brogan knew if he could take this one animal off the streets, he would be saving numerous people from certain agony, or death. As long as this fiend roamed the streets, anyone in his path would find anguish and despair.

Brogan didn't know how, but he planned on ridding Saddleback City of this animal and anyone involved with him, no matter who it was. Subconsciously, Brogan was preparing to annihilate any and all that wreaked havoc and chaos in the city; anyone who brought grief and destruction to those who were innocent and trying to live a normal life, would be eradicated. He didn't care about the consequences or repercussions, he only wanted retribution.

"Mo Daft had his chance," Brogan thought grinding his teeth. "Even if he had problems as a kid, he still chose to bring misery to others. You chose to walk the dark path, well guess what?! I'm right behind ya!"

Brogan had no empathy or mercy for this animal, or anyone associated with him. Mo Daft not only made wrong choices, he went and pissed off the wrong guy.

On the outside, Saddleback City seemed like the perfect place to live. The people, for the most part, were friendly. There was beautiful mountain scenery shadowing the background, half the city was older style buildings, and everything blended together perfectly western. The problem, however, was internal, eating away from the inside and destroying the city at an astounding rate. Brogan learned that in the last five years, the crime rate had risen 60%, and was still climbing with the help of crooked cops.

Brogan knew he had to phone the only person he could trust, the only person with the funds to help him pursue and find his answers. He didn't quite know what to expect from Darnel. But he knew Darnel would be happy to help him, and had a feeling they were going to make a great team. Together they would not only find answers for Brogan, they would also find the answers Darnel had been searching for. However, little did Brogan know he would involuntarily and unknowingly be assisting Darnel down his own dark path.

Brogan phoned Darnel, and explained almost all that had happened the day before. After hearing everything, Darnel insisted Brogan come straight to his ranch with no stops. "Listen, this guy will have heard everything about you from the mohawk punk, and will be more prepared for you," Darnel warned. "If you go lookin for him right now he's gonna have friends, and they'll have more friends with guns! You get the idea? Brogan, you need a strategic plan of action. You need me!" Darnel ended his spiel with a smirk and a wink, even though they were on the phone.

Brogan looked down at the floor focusing on the conversation. "We gotta do something about this whole mess, or at least find someone who can help. We gotta make things better for everybody. This is stupid man, we got a whole lot of crap happening here and I don't know what the hell…" Brogan trailed off momentarily, lost in thought. "Darnel, if there is anything you can do…I mean, I can keep picking off all the little meaningless idiots in the hopes of getting to the bigger ones, the ones in charge of this whole mess, but that could take awhile."

There was a few seconds of silence and for a moment Brogan felt there would be no reinforcement from Darnel.

"I'm sending my uncle to come get you, to join our party, stay right there."

"Party?" Brogan said. "I don't want to intrude…"

"I'll explain everything when you get here. All I can tell you right now is…we might have to alter your attire. I think I have something in your size," Darnel said before hanging up.

"It must be some kind of code," Brogan thought. "Maybe he was trying to tell me someone was listening in on our conversation. Or, shit I don't know! But I'm not in the mood for some classy cocktail party right now."

Darnel's uncle Reynolds showed up within minutes of Brogan hanging up the phone.

"Weird!" Brogan thought, remembering how long a drive it was to Darnel's. "He must have been in the area."

Brogan tried talking to Uncle Reynolds on the drive back to the ranch, but it was mostly Brogan asking questions and Uncle Reynolds answering with grunts. Brogan needed to know how serious they were in helping him find the answers he was looking for.

"Brogan, there are a few more tools in Darnel's workshop that you might find…handy," Uncle Reynolds said without batting an eye; then burst into laughter with a viking type belly laugh that caught Brogan by surprise, making him jump.

"What do you mean?" Brogan asked.

Uncle Reynolds kept laughing, only a bit quieter, as Brogan stared at him.

"Well, whatever Darnel can do to help me find the animal responsible for Rita's death, I'll pay him back ten fold. I promise."

"You already have!" Uncle Reynolds said looking at Brogan with rigid, sincere eyes. It was the only time Uncle Reynolds took his attention off the road the whole trip.

Brogan had no way of knowing how extensive Darnel's scientific research was. As a child, after losing his parents and his legs, he buried himself with experiments and bent the scientific boundaries without anyone being the wiser. Darnel had kept a lot of things that he invented or modified to himself.

It was a fast trip to Darnel's ranch this time. So fast, that Brogan found himself clutching the safety handle and pressing his feet into the floor for most of the ride. Uncle Reynolds however hadn't broken a sweat; he drove that Escalade like he was a professional stunt driver.

Darnel was waiting outside, with a huge smile on his smug face, when they pulled up to the house.

"Where's the party?" Brogan asked stepping out of the Escalade.

"C'mon dude, we've got some work to do!"

Brogan noticed that Darnel seemed really excited, and truth be told Darnel was ecstatic.

Brogan followed Darnel inside and they headed straight to the painting of the dogs playing poker.

"Hey Uncle, could you put the Escalade in the garage?" Darnel yelled as they waited for the elevator. "I'm gonna tune the engine and add a couple things."

"Oh, so you want it submerged then?" Uncle Reynolds asked.

"Yeah, that would work better for what I have in mind."

"How many underground rooms do you have?" Brogan asked as they stepped onto the elevator.

"Put it this way," Darnel said, "Denise and Uncle Reynolds call it "a-maze-ing science"."

"Or I could just call you Bruce Wayne!" Brogan said with a smirk.

"Everything about this guy is cool and mysterious," Brogan thought to himself.

His thoughts were interrupted by the elevator doors opening.

"Ok, we need to find a way to get to where we want to go," Darnel said, immediately starting to form a plan of attack. "But when we get to wherever that is, we'll need several different ways out, just in case."

"Who's on first?!" Brogan joked, but was really impressed with the professional mannerisms that Darnel was portraying.

"Don't get the wrong idea Brogan, I'm no Sherlock Holmes or a detective by any sort, but I've got a lot of toys that will be of good use… and, I watch a lot of *CSI* and *Criminal Minds*."

Brogan smiled, "You offering to help is enough."

Darnel immediately got the control desk powered up. "Now where did you say this asshole Mo Daft lived?"

"I was told that he doesn't have a fixed address or anything like that. That's the catch, he's all over the city."

"You mentioned on the phone, a pool hall or something?" Darnel asked working his fingers madly on the keyboard.

"47th Ave., I guess it's some sort of dance club pool hall?"

"How'd you come across this information?"

Brogan thought for a moment. "Oh, I might have left a couple small details out."

Darnel looked over at him.

"Darnel, if I tell you, you can't tell anybody."

Brogan watched as Darnel smiled and raised his arms above his head. "Brogan, my brother from another mother! Look where you are dude! It don't get much more secretive or personal than this! Look, I'm in this for the long haul, whatever comes up I'm there. But I need to be kept in the loop," Darnel said grasping Brogan's shoulder. "I felt a connection with you when we first talked on the phone. I thought since you and I both shared the pain of losing our loved ones, we could try and do something about this shit storm in Saddleback City together. You scratch my back, and I'll pay to get someone else to scratch yours."

Both men smiled.

"Brogan, I know we just met, but I consider you my friend. And whatever we discuss, it stays between us."

Brogan nodded and proceeded to explain everything that he had left out from their conversation on the phone. He told Darnel every little detail about what had happened since he left the ranch that previous night, occasionally stopping to answer Darnel's questions like, "How big was this guy?" and "What kind of knife?" Brogan told Darnel everything in great detail and watched the smile on his face get bigger as the story went on.

Darnel threw in a bunch more questions once he had finished, and Brogan answered them all faithfully. It was definitely a bonding time between the two wannabe crime fighters.

"We're gonna have to mount a camera on you somewhere! I can't miss anymore of the action!" Darnel said, amazed that there wasn't a scratch on Brogan, but the other guy was missing an ear.

Darnel rubbed his hands together as he looked at Brogan with a sinister smile. "My uncle used to do that when he had an idea. What's up?" Brogan asked.

"I might be Bruce Wayne, but you're Batman!" Darnel said in a low voice, punching in a code on the key pad.

Instantly the table dropped to his level then tilted to an angle for perfect viewing. He punched the keys a few more times and the aerial view of Saddleback City popped up on the big screen.

"That's cool Darnel."

"Oh yeah, watch this!"

No sooner did Darnel say that, and the exact location and building appeared up on the screen, enabling Darnel to swivel and move the view of the pool hall 360 degrees in any direction.

"Very cool!" Brogan exclaimed, not able to hide any signs of being impressed.

The two men talked, and came up with a simple plan. Brogan would walk in the front door, take a look around, then turn around and leave. But if anything were to happen, he had two emergency exits to choose from: one on the right and one on the left towards the back of the room. Darnel also explained to Brogan that once he was outside, there were narrow alleyways on either side of the building. Each giving three additional exit options: going up, staying on the street, or going underground.

"Now Brogan, if you head east in either sewer tunnel, you will eventually come out in Sarsaparilla Park. If you head west, however, you'll probably get lost."

Brogan looked at Darnel.

"Brogan, this is dangerous! If at anytime you feel…"

"It's ok Darnel," Brogan said cutting him off, "I'm doing this!"

Darnel smiled, "*We*, are doing this!"

Darnel pulled a map of the Saddleback City sewer system up on the screen, "I'll print off a copy of this for you, just in case," he said discussing certain aspects of the tunnels.

Next Darnel pulled an aerial view of the buildings up on the screen. With another couple of key strikes and the view inverted.

"Here, right here, and over to there," Darnel said pointing at the screen. "There are fire escapes on the outside of the building on either side."

Darnel hit another key and the view started moving slowly north over the building tops.

"Now Brogan, if you do decide to go up, I suggest you head north." Darnel said, leaning almost right out of his wheelchair to point. "You'll have to jump from building top to building top. You said you used to free run, so that'll come in handy if you go this route! I'm gonna give you an ear piece so we can stay in constant communication."

Brogan's eyes got bigger, "That's a good idea!"

Darnel touched Brogan on the shoulder again. "No matter what happens, and wherever you end up, I'll have a ride there for you."

"What's on your mind Brogan?" Darnel asked noticing the weird look on Brogan's face.

"Everything is so well planned and organized, we don't even know if he's gonna be there," Brogan said.

"Well, then you ask a few questions to see if we can find him, and try not to ruffle any feathers."

Brogan smiled, "You know this is gonna cause a ruckus!"

"Don't worry, I've got a few tools you can take along that should help." A secretive smile crept across Darnel's face.

Brogan felt a surge of energy flicker through his entire body like chain lightening shooting across the sky. The feeling was an overwhelming rush of power. It was more than an adrenaline rush, it had always been like that; only now his rage seemed to enhance everything.

Brogan realized at a young age something was changing in him, and was getting more finely tuned as time went on. He also realized that when something in life triggered this feeling, everything came into focus for him. And if the event was threatening, life altering, or crazy enough, it sent him into overdrive. He would gain so much more strength and speed that it shocked whoever witnessed it, including himself. But what Brogan couldn't figure out was that the gain in his strength and speed stayed with him. He called it, "the next level". He always wondered how many levels there were for him, and whether or not his body could handle the next. But as the levels erupted, his body adapted to it.

"Thank you for helping me with all this Darnel, it really means a lot to me."

"We're helping each other Brogan. I like you. You and I have been through some serious crap in our lives. We met for a reason, I believe. I know life is full of tragic events, but when some animal takes everything from you…it's not right! Sometimes you gotta fight back! You are a good man Brogan. I'd be proud and honoured to follow you into the depths of hell to right all the wrongs for everyone in Saddleback City. Besides, I always wanted to fight crime…maybe get a small cape…although it might get caught up in my wheels if it was too long," Darnel said with a smirk.

"Darnel, we barely know each other, but I want you to know that I'm not only doing this for Rita, I'm also doing it for you too. You've had so much taken from you as well, and it's been too long. I will help you find the answers you've been searching for. I'm also doing this for the people who don't deserve to go through the pain that you and I have experienced. I'm doing this because it's the right thing to do…and I seem to be pretty good at it so far."

Darnel smiled again, "Brogan, I do believe this will be a very long and extremely fun partnership!"

Brogan placed his hand on Darnel's shoulder, "Let's go hunting!"

Darnel spun his wheelchair around. "Well, enough said eh! Follow me!" he said rolling onto the elevator.

Brogan stepped in beside him and the doors shut. Darnel pushed a button and they started moving.

"Darnel? It feels as though we're going down?" Brogan questioned, quite puzzled.

"That is correct, we are descending."

"Yeah, but weren't we just in the basement?"

Even though Darnel was looking straight ahead, Brogan leaned forward a little to look at him harder, and noticed he was grinning.

"Seriously! Who the hell are you? You're like a secret spy or something! Darnel, you continue to amaze me! You *are* Bruce Wayne!"

"Partner, you are in for a treat! Ala peanut butter sandwiches!" he joked as the elevator doors opened.

Lights started popping on, like silent firecrackers, in a neat, orderly line on the ceiling.

As they got off the elevator, Darnel explained how he paid for workers from out of the country to come in and do most of the work down on this level. And that each worker received $100,000 not only for the work they did, but also for their silence. He explained how they all signed a legal document swearing them to secrecy, that if anyone talked about any of the construction that had been done, Darnel would take the money back and everything else they owned as well.

The room was directly below The Vision Chamber, and possibly the entire ranch. Brogan couldn't believe the size of it. It was easily three times the width of the vision room, and four times as long. There was a long table in the middle, running a third the length of the room. Glass casings covered the walls around the first half of the room; housing a huge variety of weapons, chromed tools, and other stainless steel objects neatly stored in their specific places. There were also half a dozen suits in their own protective glass cases.

Brogan spotted something down at the far end of the room and tried to focus on it. "You have a shooting range in your basement that's under your basement!?

"Yes I do. I use it to test the cool weapons that I have designed and modified."

"You're like a scientist inventor meets secret agent!"

"I'll take that as a compliment. Now, we'll play with the weapons later, but first I want you to try something I've been working on for a long time. I'm thinking it's the solution to our little infestation of gangs in this city."

"Are you gonna load me up with gadgets like James Bond?"

"Well, sort of, only with a little more intimidation! Naaaaaw, James Bond ain't got nothing on this!"

As Darnel wheeled along the wall of glass cases he explained to Brogan about his passion for inventing, creating, and modifying. And how a lot of what he did couldn't have been done if his uncle Reynolds and Denise weren't around to assist him.

Darnel parked his chair beside one of the glass cases that was mounted into the wall. Brogan studied its contents in awe. "That's the coolest thing I've ever seen, it's really...intimidating! What is it?"

"This is your new best friend!" Darnel smiled. "I figure since you're gonna be starting shit, you might as well have the best toys money can buy to help keep you clean."

"Sweet!"

"Now listen Brogan, I took the liberty of straightening a few things out for you."

Brogan looked at Darnel. "What do you mean?"

"I know you haven't felt ready to return to work since the accident."

Suddenly Brogan was consumed with guilt as he realized he hadn't even had the decency to get ahold of anyone at his work. They were good people and were probably wondering how he was doing, and if he was ever coming back. He did enjoy his job. But since Rita was taken from him, he hadn't even given it a second thought.

"I contacted them, and if you ever decide to go back to your boring old job, you can, anytime you choose."

"Well it wasn't that boring," Brogan retorted.

Darnel smirked. "Oh I heard all about it! But compared to what you and I are gonna experience, endure, and encounter on this new adventure, you might never wanna change professions again!"

Then Darnel got serious, "And I figured…I know bereavement leave is ridiculously short, so I put $100,000 into an account for you. Nobody knows about it, and you will be the only one who will have access to the funds.

Brogan's jaw hit the floor. He was completely boggled. He stared at Darnel not knowing what to say.

"Darnel, you didn't have to…I mean…I appreciate it, but honestly…"

"It's nothing," Darnel said interrupting him. "I just hope you know how much I appreciate all you're doing."

Brogan turned back towards the glass case. "Wow, that's cool!" he whispered. "What would possess you to build something like this?"

Darnel gleamed with pride as he explained. "I finished it roughly five years ago. I built this thinking it would help the police force better handle overwhelming situations. With the crime rate increasing the way it has been over the years, Saddleback City needed something that would give the average policeman a huge advantage over not just one or two criminals, but the capability to go up against half a dozen, maybe more.

Nobody knows about this little project of mine. When I finished this beautiful sculpted piece of equipment, I proposed the idea to the police force. I didn't tell them I already had a prototype. I told them nothing about the design or any specifics. I was very careful about how I introduced the concept without giving away any vital description or information. They didn't go for the idea at all. It seemed no matter what I said, they had already made up their minds."

"How much?"

Darnel's one eyebrow went up. "It was gonna cost $250,000 for each police officer to be equipped. I explained that it could be done, and that not every single police officer had to have one. I told them they would only have to equip ten officers, and crime would dissipate in Saddleback City. I even suggested choosing one officer to equip to start with, just to prove it could still make a huge impact on the crime in the city. Still they said no. So I told them I would scrap this idea and proceed with making them a new non-lethal weapon, because that's what they wanted."

"You're telling me that they had the opportunity to clean up the mess in this city, and they passed on it because they might not see their annual bonus?"

Darnel nodded, "Yup! I guess they figured the cost outweighed their means. So in my spare time I modified it a bit more, added a few extra gadgets, and improved everything on it again and again to keep up with advancing technology. It was an ongoing piece of work. Now here we are five years later, and I'm pretty sure I'll continuously be working on it, there's always room for improvement. The amount of time, energy, and thought I've put into this project, I know it will keep you alive as you hunt the beasts that roam Saddleback City. It's gonna help us wipe out all the corruption."

Brogan stared at the glass case, deep in thought.

"You Brogan! You're gonna make a difference. I huge freakin difference my friend! Anyone who comes up against you, will soon realize they are in over their heads and are gonna need a lot of help. I'm not gonna lie to you Brogan, I've been looking for someone to assist me with trying this new piece of equipment for a long time. Look, you don't have to do this, but I feel it in my heart, in my bones that you are the chosen one."

Both men looked at each other and smiled.

"Sorry, that sounded a little corny! If a highly trained police officer used this, it would take at least four big, able men to stop him. But with your capabilities Brogan, it would take a small army to even slow you down! You'd be virtually unstoppable, a freakin force that has few, if any, limitations."

Brogan couldn't help but feel as though this were another pep talk.

"I'm in!" he said with no hesitation, "but that's a lot of money. What if I break it or something happens to it?"

Darnel leaned back in his wheelchair and smirked, "Ya know, I never once considered the money aspect of it. Once I started, and realized what I had created, I couldn't stop. I was a mad man for a long time with this idea; thinking that I could make a difference in this city. Nothing could deter me from working on it. I'd be down here for days! I can't describe it; it was like an unseen force driving me to complete it. I can't do much physically about the crime in this city, but I can offer my skills and knowledge. I now know in my heart the reason I had to finish it was because of you." Darnel pointed sternly at Brogan. "We were meant to meet and become partners, I see that so clearly now. This is fate!"

Brogan looked perplexed, "That's a bold statement, but I can totally understand why you believe that."

"Do I believe we're gonna change the world, probably not," Darnel said, his voice getting a little scratchy. "But believe this Brogan, we're gonna kick a whole lot of ass and clean up this city for everyone who deserves to live here. And we're gonna have a lot of fun doin it too."

Both men smiled.

"Can I try it out?" Brogan asked eagerly.

"YES!" Darnel shouted enthusiastically. "It's about time too! I thought you'd never ask. Brogan I want to make it perfectly clear to you, we are partners in this together. We make choices and decisions as a team. I realize there are gonna be times when it won't always work that way, and we'll have to fly by the seat of our pants. But this is yours as much as it is mine, we are partners."

"Darnel, the only thing I'm really bringing to the table is my problems. But I'm willing to do whatever I can to help."

Darnel gave Brogan a funny look and slumped into his chair putting his hands together. "I'm a stickler when it comes to perfection. I need my equipment and tools to be in perfect order. I have to have all my inventions working the way I want them to. I'll do whatever it takes to get everything functioning properly. This is an amazing piece of equipment if I do say so myself. I have designed it to over achieve in almost every scenario it encounters. And I wouldn't let you venture into a shit storm unless I was completely sure of its capabilities. I have done everything in my power to ensure it will perform with gratifying excellence. I've just been waiting for the perfect candidate to try it out. With you wearing it, the limits are… well, unknown at this point. But I'm pretty sure with this new toy you will exceed everything I have already calculated. There will be no animal you won't be able to track and hunt down!"

"I don't know man," Brogan said still staring at the glass case, "what if I try it out and it doesn't do what you…or I want it to do? What if I don't live up to your "calculations"? What if I can't make this work? Don't get me wrong, I'm all for it, I'm in. I just don't want to let you down."

"I believe you could take down six men without breaking a sweat. Now, your rage kinda throws a lot of my calculations out the proverbial window. Rage has power that the strongest man doesn't. If you can harness that, and I believe you can, then the amount of power you will possess will be astonishing. I have never seen anyone like you before. You move like no human I've ever seen playing sports or even fightin in the UFC. You move more like…well, an animal. Your instincts and reflexes have somehow fused, or maybe mutated, making you more aware of your body and surroundings. I don't know what it is about you Brogan, but there's no way in hell that you and this beautiful piece of craftsmanship I invented, don't match up. It is designed to exceed and excel in any and all performances, and apparently so are you."

Darnel placed his thumb on the bottom corner of the glass case, and the front popped opened.

"It looks like thick rubber, but feels really light," Brogan said examining it closer. "That's cool! How'd you get it to be like this?"

"I have taken what used to be known as Kevlar, and modified it to a rubbery, flexible, but somewhat solid state," Darnel said. "There's actually three different layers, each of which I have redesigned and modified. We could throw this at a bear, let him unleash a savage attack, and he would tire out before damaging it."

"Wow Darnel, this is amazing! …You're amazing!" Brogan exclaimed in awe of Darnel's work. "So, you must have a name for it!"

"This, my friend, this entire suit is what I call the BITTS. Body Impenetrable Transform Technology System. It is my idea of righting some wrongs and helping others from experiencing unnecessary grief. It's my invention, my baby, my masterpiece if you will."

It definitely was a masterpiece, a masterpiece of crime fighting weaponry, and Brogan knew it. He figured there would be very little stopping him once he was armed with Darnel's great invention. It looked as if it could withstand a small war.

Brogan pulled the suit out of the glass case. It was extremely dark grey, so dark it could be easily mistaken as black. There was an opening in the back from the waist up to the neck; everything else was one piece, including the boots and the gloves. Once Brogan stepped into it the rubber-like material formed to him enhancing his muscles.

"Wow dude, you look cool in that suit! It's a perfect match!"

"It's a lot lighter than I thought it would be."

"I know, ain't it cool, it's part of my design. It gives the illusion, on the outside, that you're heavier and more solid than you actually are, but inside the suit you won't feel that weight. It doesn't make you any heavier, if anything it should make you more stable and help with your striking and throwing power. That's where the "Transform Technology" comes into play. How do I explain it? The suit feeds off your specific body heat, sort of. It kinda forms to your body and allows all movements to be enhanced. It works with you, taking the energy that you're using at that moment and increases your strength immensely. It happens so quick the strength increase is right there as you fight, run, climb, etc. And now that you've put it on, no one else can wear it unless I bypass the electrical circuit.

"This suit has electricity running through it?!"

"No…well, sort of…not all the time anyway. Just short bursts, but I'll explain that later. You gotta try that on too." Darnel said pointing toward the glass case.

Brogan turned to see the matching dark grey headgear sitting on the bottom shelf. It resembled a tighter fitting, full face, motor bike helmet, with a small flat black eye shield; and had extra material, similar to a balaclava, connected to the bottom. He slipped the headgear over his head and immediately the neck material fussed to the suit.

"That's kinda freaky!" Brogan exclaimed as he felt the two materials fuse together.

"Yeah, I should have warned ya about my new and improved Velcro!" Darnel snickered. "Once the suit and helmet are put on, the material instantly connects."

"Wow, everything is so much clearer through this shield!"

"The light enhancer is an improvement on my previous version. It also has UV protection, night vision, and heat detecting sensors." Darnel continued, "Ok, now grab the two small wire loops that are in your arm pits."

Brogan looked down and grabbed both cords, one in each hand.

"Now pull those cords down."

As Brogan pulled the cords a fabric flapped out forming wings on either side.

"What the? Wings?"

"There's one more cord under your crotch area, pull that."

Brogan pulled the remaining cord and a web formed between his legs.

"Is this a glide suit?"

"Yes, it is a glide suit, only I have modified it and made the entire webbing out of the same material as the suit itself. If your body is as strong as I think it is, then you'll be able to manoeuvre it in mid flight, giving you the ability to dive and climb as you're gliding. That is until you reach your full altitude or your body's breaking point. But you'll be able to stay airborne for a long time if your body can handle the enormous strain that will be inflicted on you."

"This is something else...it's amazing!"

"Brogan my friend, you're gonna experience what it's like to be a flying squirrel! You're gonna have a blast in this suit! But you'll need to get some practice and flight time in before you start using the flight features right away," Darnel said. "We don't need you injured this early in the game."

Brogan nodded. "Understood!" he said pulling the cords and watching the webbings retract back to their original spots.

"Oh, I should also mention that this suit is bullet proof. Although I'm sure it would still sting to get shot!"

"I think I can handle that...for the cause, you know."

Brogan was referring to taking on any pain to carry on with Rita's cause, and Darnel knew it.

"How's your movement?"

"It's kinda like having a diving suit on, just lighter and a lot more comfortable."

"I'm hoping it doesn't restrict your movement too much, especially your running."

Brogan smirked, "Let's find out!"

Before Darnel could agree, Brogan shot to his right and headed for the far corner of the room.

"Wow, that was a fast take off!" Darnel thought. "He's so quick, clearly he's not restricted!"

Brogan felt stronger and extremely agile. He couldn't believe the freedom of movement he had, with this half inch thick suit on, and covered a lot of ground in just seconds. He ran up beside the wall and leapt, his right foot hit and five more steps followed along the wall. He was almost perfectly horizontal as he rounded the first corner of the room. Five more running steps covered the width of the far back wall, and Brogan was still horizontal. As he rounded the second corner, gravity started to take effect. He got three more running steps on the third wall and with a powerful launch, jumped and flipped sideways in the air, landing on the floor in a full out sprint.

He pushed himself to run faster, heading straight for Darnel, and decided to kick it up a notch. As his arms pumped harder, and his legs sped up, his speed was astonishing. Several feet from Darnel, Brogan dove as if he were diving for a Hail Mary. Darnel's mouth was wide open and his head went straight back, as Brogan soared over top of him. Darnel whipped his wheelchair around just in time to see the amazing landing. Brogan had soared past Darnel, and then made like he was diving into water. Right before he landed, he tucked and completed a single summersault effortlessly. Immediately after the roll, he started walking back to Darnel looking and checking the suit over.

"This suit is really something else!" he said taking off the headgear.

Darnel stared at Brogan with his mouth still open. "I'll tell you what Brogan, you're something else!" Darnel said shaking his head in disbelief. "I've never seen anyone move like that...that fast and agile, it's freakin amazing! To tell you the truth, I'm a little freaked out right now! How the hell did you run up...how'd you stay on the wall like that? I mean, I understand that you have momentum and your legs are strong, and you're fast, but wow!"

"Oh that's nothing, it just takes a lot of practice. I've been doing stuff like that since I could run," Brogan answered modestly. "So, how do I look?"

"Like a really mean, animalistic ninja! That was absolutely spectacular!" Darnel said, unable to let it go. "I pity whoever tries to tangle with you! How's the headgear feel? Does it fit ok?"

"Yeah, it fits great. Everything is enhanced, I can see so much clearer. It doesn't even feel like I'm wearing it."

Darnel pointed out two buttons, one on either side of his helmet. He explained that the right was for night vision, and the left was for seeing long distances. He could press the left button three times and each time he'd see further, like a high powered scope; pressing it a fourth time would bring it back to normal vision.

"Now, you also have two buttons on the left side of your hip," Darnel explained. "They're imbedded into the suit so not to press them by accident. The first button enables a palm trigger in you right hand. Squeeze your fist, can you feel that bump? That's the trigger, it will shoot out a grappling hook from the top of your forearm. It's connected to a very thin, but strong, fifty foot wire I invented. Squeeze your fist again, and it will retract."

Brogan listened intently to Darnel, "This will definitely help kick some ass, eh!"

Darnel smiled and continued, "Now, that second button will send out a 60,000 volt electrical surge on the outside of the suit. It works kind of like a taser; it interrupts the communication between the muscles and the mind, making anyone who comes into contact with it collapse. Originally it was designed for the police; if they got out numbered they could press this button in an emergency. The only downside is that it takes a while for it to recharge again. And don't worry, as long as you're in the suit you won't get zapped, even if you're in water."

Brogan was completely amazed with the suit, and with Darnel. He continuously checked the suit over and over.

"I know that you've been hurting for a while," Darnel said taking the focus away from the suit. "And I know you have one main target right now. Just remember there are a lot of animals in Saddleback City that will probably need to be dealt with along the way. I guess what I'm trying to say is that I hope you're in this for the long haul, cause I am. I want to bring the city back to where it use to be. When people didn't have to worry about losing someone they love to some meaningless crime."

Brogan reached out and shook Darnel's hand. "I will take down the monster who stole my love, my life, and anybody else who stands in my way. I will help you with whatever you need. If we can make a difference in Saddleback City where people are safer, and no one has to suffer because of some animals doing, then I'm in for good. I will make this my life! Darnel, because of you I have more to live for, to fight for, and now I even have an advantage with the BITTS! Thank you for your friendship and support."

Darnel smiled, "Will we be able to make a difference in Saddleback City? Only time will tell. But without a doubt, Brogan and the BITTS are a match made in hell."

CHAPTER 10

INCONCLUSIVE CHAOS

R eluctantly, and against Brogan's wishes, Darnel convinced him to hold off on hunting until he had gotten use to the suit. From using the grappling hook, to mastering the extremely modified glide suit. Darnel watched in bewilderment as Brogan quickly became accustomed to his new attire. In two short jaw dropping days, Brogan had become one with the suit, and Darnel watched in awe as Brogan continued to amaze him.

On the forth night of training in the suit, Darnel and Brogan sat down for supper.

"It's like I tailor made that suit perfectly to fit you," Darnel said as they went over their plan one last time.

Tonight was the night. Both men had studied and memorized the entire map, including the escape routes; and had gone over their simple plan many times in the last four days, each giving their own scenarios and what ifs, but agreed Brogan would have to play it by instinct.

"This is it," Darnel said when they were done supper. "Time to go to work!"

Uncle Reynolds had prepared the surveillance van for the occasion. Truth be told the full size van had quite a few tweaks and adjustments, all done by Darnel, his uncle, and Denise. The van had been modified into a four wheel drive that also had hydraulics to raise it for rough terrain, or lower it for better stability, as well as easier access for Darnel. It secretly held 460 horsepower under the small hood, along with a nitrous kit, making it crazy fast. Darnel had modified the suspension as well, and slapped some new tires on to make it virtually a pig in the mud. He also had a remote key that would lower the van and open up the back doors for his wheelchair. Once inside he could roll right to the drivers spot and with his modified wheelchair, strap the chair into the clamps and drive away. All of the van's features were operational from the steering wheel and dash board, with everything being computerized of course.

"Sweet ride!" Brogan said seeing the surveillance van for the first time.

"Any spy group on the planet would have surveillance van envy!" Darnel chimed as he wheeled up the ramp and into the van. "I've even got a small fridge for drinks."

Uncle Reynolds peeked around the front of the van, "I'm tagging along for the ride, just in case."

"No Uncle, I need you here watching the cameras and listening to the police scanners with Denise. You're our backup and someone needs to make sure everything is being recorded. We'll be in communication with the two of you the whole time."

It was starting to get dark and Brogan was getting anxious. He loaded the black suitcase containing the BITTS into the van. "Well I'm ready, let's hunt!"

Darnel strapped his chair into the clamps on the driver's side. "Tonight my friend, the animals who meet you will have stories to tell their cellmates for years to come!"

"Let's hope so," Brogan said with a smirk.

The van was silent as they pulled out of the driveway, both of them thinking how the beginning of the end of so many people needlessly suffering, was about to commence. They remained quiet for the entire drive into Saddleback City. Brogan was reviewing the escape routes, and Darnel was trying to think if there was anything they missed. Neither one of them had second thoughts about their plans for the evening; they weren't going to back down from any encounter, and would do anything to ensure the safety of one another. Both had their reasons for doing this; Brogan's were apparent, Darnel however kept most of his skeletons in the closet.

Darnel parked down the street from the Lucky Draw Pool Hall, the place the one eared punk mentioned, on 47th. Although another small detail Darnel hadn't told Brogan, was the fact that he had been watching this place for quite some time.

"That might be the reason for all the people out front," Darnel said randomly as he checked out the dozen or so people standing outside the entrance.

Brogan looked at him questionably.

"Well, if the police come to raid the place, they have to get through a bunch of drunkards, who are deliberately in the way."

"I guess that's kinda smart thinking for some stupid, drug dealing animals."

"Brogan, this is a rough bar, you're not goin in there without the suit. I know you can fight like a savage Bruce Lee, but if these bastards have guns, there's only so much I can do," Darnel said looking down at his legs.

"I think I'll go in and take a look around, have a beer, and ask a question or two. Then I'll come back to get the suit, and venture right back in there to ask a few more questions!"

Darnel looked at Brogan, "What kinda questions you gonna ask?"

Brogan smirked, "You know, I'm hoping that he's in there. But if not, I'll ask the usual… Where's that meatball Mo? Has anyone seen that asshole Mo? Questions like that."

Darnel smirked back, "Then I suggest you put that suit on now!"

Both men had their last chuckle before getting serious.

"Besides," Brogan said, his smirk melting from his face, "if they pull guns, I'm really gonna get pissed and kick some ass!"

It would have sounded silly coming from an unarmed man, but Darnel believed him.

Excitedly, Darnel started flipping switches and power bars, on the control panel. The monitors flashed on, and the rest of the equipment powered up.

"I placed a small camera in the front of your headgear so I can see everything, and record it. Actually, I put one on your back as well, so I can watch your back. There's also a transmitter in the BITTS' headgear remember, and there's a tracking device just in case we lose touch."

Brogan said nothing and simply nodded. He was feeling that rush and trying to control it, for the time being.

"But, since you're not wearing the suit in right away, I've put two cameras in this baseball cap," he said handing it to Brogan.

Brogan noticed a sewn-on picture of a handgun on the front of the cap.

"And put this in your ear. I'm your eyes and ears Brogan, but don't worry, I've got a little experience. I'll also be listening to the police scanner just in case they decide to crash the dance competition."

"Then, you'll keep an eye on me is what your saying?" Brogan asked without cracking a smile.

"I've got your back Brogan."

"I know you do Darnel, I know."

"Here put this on," Darnel threw an old leather jacket to Brogan.

"Now what does this jacket do?" Brogan asked as he slid it on.

"Nothing but help you look cool and blend in."

The two men pounded fists before Brogan got out of the van. He started walking towards the bar, scanning and sizing up all the people in front. He couldn't hear them from the distance he was at, and for Brogan it was an eerie quiet. As he walked with his thumbs in the front pockets of his jeans he had reached another level, and had all he could do to contain his inner beast.

"Can you hear me now?" Darnel suddenly chimed.

"Yes, I can hear you."

"Good, good, the two cameras are working fine too. Any sign of that Mo guy and you get the hell…"

"In and out, got it," Brogan said cutting him off.

As Brogan reached the front entrance, no one seemed to pay any attention to him. He quickly realized that these people were actually drunk and or high. "Just because they're whacked, doesn't make them any less dangerous," he whispered to himself.

Brogan wasn't scared or nervous of what he was about to do. The image of his beloved Rita being brutally murdered made him impervious to fear. He swaggered through the group of bombed dead beats, and into the bar.

"Good luck you crazy easterner," Darnel whispered into the earpiece as Brogan disappeared through the bar doors.

"Wow, there's a lot of people in there!"

Brogan said nothing as he made his way to the bar at the far end of the long room.

"What you want muscles?" the barkeep asked when he reached the bar.

"Draft."

The barkeep grabbed a half-ass clean mug and poured him one.

"Holy crap, that bartender is proof that Phyllis Diller and Jack Nicholson had a baby!"

As funny as Brogan thought that was, he kept his poker face and said nothing. The barkeep gave Brogan his beer, grabbed the money, and moved on to his next customer.

"That is one fugly woman!"

"That's a guy," Brogan said with the glass in front of his mouth.

He decided to stay at the bar and drink his beer, figuring he'd have a better view of the place. The first thing he noticed was hanging on the wall up behind the bar, and Darnel got a good look at it too.

"There's something you don't see everyday, eh!?"

Brogan nodded.

It wasn't the usual shortened baseball bat or small billy club with a sign underneath reading "The Equalizer". Instead, hanging on the wall was a huge deep-sea spear gun. In place of the pointed arrow head was an oversized, red boxing glove. Brogan looked down toward the bottom of the spear gun and read the carved quotation, "UNDISPUTED CHAMP". Then had to really focus to read the smaller writing below, "It Works n It Hurts!".

"Dude, that would definitely leave a mark!" Darnel said.

Brogan nodded and spun around to scan the dance floor.

"Looks like mostly women on the dance floor," Darnel said as he watched through digital eyes. "Hey, that's pretty good music!"

Some kind of techno music was playing loud, Brogan thought it had a good beat, but that was it. He then scanned the pool table area and noticed it was mostly guys.

"Brogan it seems like, from what I can see, a lot of the people there are gang members. The women hanging around the pool tables might be hookers, but the majority of them look like they're in the same gang."

Brogan took a good look around, and what Darnel was saying was bang on. They were wearing some type of black leather jacket or vest with the same colors. He couldn't make out what was on the backs of each one, but he figured it was their gang symbol.

"Dude!" Darnel startled Brogan. "Uncle Reynolds and Denise zoomed in on the back of their jackets. Apparently that's a gang insignia. It's a picture of a blood red grenade, with 'ATL' imprinted on it in black letters."

Brogan had noticed a massive biker in the far right corner over by the pool tables. He was on Brogan's left when Brogan entered the bar.

"You see him?" Brogan talked low.

"Yup I do," Darnel answered quickly, "and I'm running his picture through the police database as we speak... Huh?"

"What?"

"Well, his information comes up, but there's no other details; no criminal history, no gang connections, nothing."

"Weird. Why's his information even in there then?" Brogan questioned.

"I'm not sure... But you better stay clear of him! Holy crap he's a big boy! It says here, he's 6'6" and 340 lbs. I think it's true, although the camera does add a few pounds. He looks like he's solid muscle, eh?"

"Mmhmm," Brogan grunted out loud.

"What?" mumbled the drunk guy sitting next to him.

Brogan didn't pay any attention to him; his thoughts were on the massive man in the far corner. "He's sitting there for a reason," Brogan thought. "He's watching everybody who comes and goes. Guaranteed he noticed me come in."

"You know he's sittin there for a reason, right?" Darnel chimed, almost as if he were reading Brogan's mind. "And you know he was checking you out as soon as you walked in there."

Brogan didn't think the massive man was bouncing, not with those two girls hanging around him like that. But he was definitely of significance, possibly even one of the head guys of the gang.

"He's probably just a pusher, he gets other little idiots to pedal the drugs," Darnel suggested.

After watching for a while, both Darnel and Brogan got a good sense of the place and how it worked. Druggies and drug runners would come in and play pool or dance until they were gestured over by one of the two girls hanging with the massive man in the corner. Brogan watched several times as one of the high class hookers went over and stood beside the phone booth at the north exit. Then, whoever was looking to score would go pretend to make a phone call, and they would do the exchange as discretely as possible. But to Brogan and Darnel it was obvious what they were doing.

"So, have you recognized anyone in there yet?"

Brogan almost answered no, but caught himself. He took another swig of his beer. "Darnel, we might have a situation here!" Brogan said looking toward the entrance.

"What do you mean?…" Darnel's voice trailed off as he caught sight of what Brogan was talking about.

A beaten and bloodied familiar face came into camera view. He limped through the doorway, with both hands in casts, and three quarters of his head wrapped in a white hospital bandage that covered the left side of his face; and a bloody stain where his left ear should be.

"Holy crap, that's him!" Darnel sounded panicked. "You gotta get out of there…this is not good…not good at all!"

Brogan slowly turned to face the bar, and had another long swig of his brew.

"Are you hearin' me dude? Brogan…you gotta get the hell out of there…NOW!"

Brogan released a sinister smirk. "But I'm not done my beer," he replied in a low, calm voice.

Almost in a panic, Darnel started pleading. "Seriously Brogan, abort the mission! I repeat, abort the mission!"

Darnel could see Brogan through the big mirror behind the bar and watched to see if he was gonna take his advice and get out of there.

"Dude! I can see you, what are you doing? I know you're trying to watch your one eared friend, but forget about it and get back to the van man!"

"Yeah, that's right," Darnel said throwing his arms up in the air, "have another drink of your beer and wait till the guy that's now hard of hearing, compliments of yours truly, turns around and recognizes you. Then I can sit here and watch him tell that monster of a man; he'll bark an order, and I'll watch my partner get attacked by twenty or more gang members!" He said getting louder as he spoke. "May I remind you that you're not wearing the BITTS yet! Listen, just get up and walk out. You and I will re-strategize, and do this another night."

"The thing about it Darnel, is that if the one eared wonder is here, maybe Mo might show."

"I see what you're saying Brogan, but where you are right now, well, it's a death trap. Even with the suit on, I don't know if..." Darnel trailed off realizing Brogan already had his mind made up, and he wasn't going to change it. "Ok my friend, I'm here, so whatever your next move is, I'll support you. Besides, you're my partner, eh!"

If anyone were to look into Brogan's eyes, they would've immediately known some trouble was brewing. The rush had started when they pulled up, once inside it turned into a constant surge waiting to erupt.

"Darnel is right," Brogan thought, "I've gotta calm down and regroup."

Rita's smiling face quickly flashed in Brogan's mind. It happened fast, but the image was perfectly clear and traumatically surreal; causing Brogan to have another adrenaline surge, that forced its way through his veins. Tears started to build up and he fought them off with every ounce of his mental being. Suddenly another flash of Rita, only this time she was in the ER bed, bleeding and dying; yet still smiling at Brogan. His heart was pounding so hard that he could see his shirt moving in the mirror. His entire body was tense and ready to uncoil like a spring. The tears streamed through the defence, and flowed freely, there was nothing he could do but wipe.

Brogan kept his head down and prayed that his voice wouldn't reveal his case of emotional diarrhea. "Bartender, beer me!"

"What?! Come on now, I can't condone this type of behaviour!" Darnel said with both concern and sarcasm. "You're in serious shit if you have another beer! I will personally kick your ass...somehow."

At this point Brogan had no qualms of starting an all out bar brawl right then and there. He was very willing, and very capable, but severely out numbered. Unfortunately the only person who was thinking about him being out numbered was Darnel. Despite ordering another beer, Brogan knew why he was there, and he wasn't going to compromise that. He believed that anybody and everybody associated with Mr. Mo Daft was responsible for Rita's death.

"And I'm personally gonna hunt down every one of you sons of bitches!" Brogan said grinding his teeth, making it hard for Darnel to make out what he was saying.

"What? What did you say Brogan?"

The rolling tears were again beaten off by the rage, and the continuous surging adrenaline pumping harder through his veins.

A full beer mug came zipping across the bar, and Brogan snagged it before it flew past him. He pulled his money out and slapped it hard onto the bar. The barkeep walked over and scabbed the money off the bar looking at Brogan as if to say, "What was that about?"

The techno music was still thumping, but no where near as fast as Brogan's heartbeat. As he raised his beer, he noticed his hands were shaking, but brushed it off. Darnel noticed as well, but didn't say anything. Brogan took a long breathless swig of his beer.

"Can you please explain to me what you are doing?! Seriously, if you wanna drink, come out and we'll find a better bar."

Brogan placed the empty beer mug down on the bar without a sound. All he could think about was the cause, Rita's cause; to make this crappy place better. And for nobody to be hurt by these animals ever again.

Brogan turned slowly and started walking for the door.

"Right on my man, I'm glad you see things my way," Darnel said thinking Brogan was walking slower than usual. "Come back out to the van, we'll grab a pizza and go back to my place to plan for another night."

Darnel was watching the monitors as he spoke. Suddenly, they showed no movement. Darnel got an uneasy feeling. "So, what you want on your pizza?" Darnel stammered wondering what was going on, and why Brogan had stopped.

There was no answer and still no movement. Darnel felt timid to say anything else, so he just watched, and waited. He stared at the monitors, seeing exactly what Brogan saw. Darnel started to get freaked out when he realized the digital eye was focused on the bandage punk, who was now talking with the big guy in the corner.

Brogan's thoughts were getting faster and faster. "How could anyone hurt someone like Rita, so innocent…and just go on without any regrets… with no remorse. Who's next you animals…who's your next victim gonna be…?

"No!" Brogan snapped only loud enough for Darnel to hear.

Darnel couldn't take his eyes off the monitors as it started moving again, quickly. "Now what? What's goin on Brogan?"

"Well at least he's movin' towards the door, please don't do anything!" Darnel thought as he watched the monitors intensely.

"That's it! Keep on walking right out the door my friend." Darnel coached.

There were twelve pool tables in the bar, and Brogan had to walk down the middle of them to reach the front door. There wasn't any more people there than when he had come in, they were just getting louder. Brogan kept walking not saying a word, but Darnel noticed him glancing down at the pool tables.

"What's goin on Brogan? What are you thinking? Just come out to the van!"

His desperate pleas went unanswered. The digital eye went back up to the corner where the bandaged fiend was standing and talking.

"We're gonna test the suit tonight!" Brogan said eagerly.

Without looking down and with no hesitation, Brogan swiped a loose pool ball off the table he was walking past. Nobody saw the wind up or the release. It happened so fast that Darnel barely saw any movement, but was the only one who caught a glimpse of anything. The blistering white bullet sliced through the smoke filled room, creating a horizontal whirlwind in the smoke as it found its intended target; striking the one eared wonder right in the forehead. The sound was similar to an aluminium bat striking a softball, only more hollow. And was followed quickly by another unique sound, a dry, gurgling yelp. The force of the impact sent the unsuspecting punk's head back causing instant whiplash. The momentum launched him into some tables, knocking over two of his gang member buddies, the tables, and everything on them; sending debris everywhere. His lifeless body slammed into the corner wall and seemed to defy gravity for a couple of seconds before sliding slowly down the wall to the floor. A swarm of gang members rushed to his aide, causing such a commotion that Brogan was able to walk right out the front door undetected. Once outside, he headed straight for the van.

Darnel had seen the punk go flying, and a bunch of gang members running around in a panic, but he hadn't seen how it all started. He was reviewing the video as Brogan got into the van.

Brogan went straight for the black case that contained the BITTS.

"What happened? What'd you do in there?" Darnel questioned, still watching the replay. "You threw a...holy crap, you killed him! That was a really hard throw! DUDE...he's dead!"

"Naw, he had that thick bandage around his head! He's not dead, but he's gonna wish he was!"

Brogan squatted down to open the case. "I don't really know what possessed me to do that, I just had to. I didn't plan on it Darnel, it just kinda happened, like an urge; the scratch you gotta itch. The guy's a meatball anyway, he deserves that and much more."

"So you're goin back in there are ya?! Well that's just great, now that you've got everyone worked up and on the look out. And our friends have ventured outside now! No doubt looking for the culprit responsible for their buddy's possible amnesia, maybe even severe brain damage."

"Do me a favor, tell them I'll be out in a minute," Brogan said sarcastically.

"I don't know if that would be a good thing to do, these guys look pissed! You hit him in the head with...a cue ball!?"

"Well the eight ball was too far of a reach," Brogan said as he put on the BITTS.

Darnel stared at him, amazed that he was still cracking jokes when the situation had just gotten a lot more serious because of his little production.

"These animals have been fearless long enough! They walk around this city like they own it, and hurt whoever they want, whenever they want. Well, I'm about to put a whole lot of hurt on them! I'm gonna show them what it's like to be hunted!"

"Hang on...ok, now it's recording...repeat what you just said so you're last words can be an example of what not to do as a crime fighter," Darnel mocked.

"Darnel, these animals have to be dealt with, taken down, hell no, taken out! And I'm the one to do it!"

As Brogan continued to put on the BITTS, Darnel decided to lighten the mood. He spoke as if he were narrating a movie. "There's a new breed in Saddleback City tonight, a one of a kind. There's no other like him, he is unique. He does his hunting whenever he chooses, making him unpredictable. He is never the prey. As this subspecies of ninja, slash animal, prepares to venture out into the dark night, all creatures stir restlessly. His presence is felt by all with a sixth sense, and even those with no sense. He is unstoppable in tracking down those who prey on the innocent and the defenceless. He is relentless in his fight for righteousness and justice. He is empathy and relief for those who need protection against the dark and unknown. He is for the good; he is for the people of Saddleback City. He is the angel of amnesty, a force never to cross. He is a nightmare for those who oppose him. He is pure energy ready to explode. He is the answer to Saddleback City's prayers. He is the HUNTER!"

"I like that! It's got a nice intimidating ring to it. Now please tell me you're done!"

Darnel smirked, "Thanks dude, I've been trying to figure out what to call you, then it hit me. Since the day I met you, you've always talked about "HUNTING" these animals! Hence the new 'H' on your chest."

Brogan shot a quick glance down at his new symbol. "I like it."

"Brogan, you know these animals are all revved up now," Darnel said changing the subject. "Chances are, they're gonna be expecting something...looking for something."

"They're expecting some asshole that threw a cue ball. They're not expecting the Hunter!"

"Dude, that's such a cool name! Oh, by the way, I added a little something to your headgear, try it on."

Brogan slipped on the headgear. The bottom of the helmet sucked in snug to the neck of his suit.

"What did you..." As Brogan started to talk his voice was altered, "Cool!"

"I can change the tone of the voice to whatever you want. I just wanted to make sure no one would hear your actual voice."

"No, it's perfect! This will definitely add to the intimidation."

"Well, you look like a psycho ninja, and you sound like Darth Vader on steroids. You're gonna scare the shit out of a lot of those gang members tonight!"

"Correction, I'm gonna kick the shit out of a lot of those gang members tonight!"

"Holy crap you sound mean! Ok, what's your plan of action?"

Brogan shrugged his shoulders and said nothing.

"So what you're tellin' me is you're gonna walk right in the front door and start smackin' people around?"

"See, I knew you'd come up with a good plan!" Brogan said as he turned to exit the van.

"It's not a plan, it's a question! …Ok then, I guess we're gonna play it by ear, eh!?"

Brogan stepped out of the van without a care, staring at the front entrance to the bar. He wasn't worried about what was going to happen tonight, especially now that he was wearing the BITTS. He was actually excited to break it in.

"Good luck my friend, I'll be keeping an eye on everything and will be ready to help if you need me."

"They're the ones who are gonna need help!" Brogan said without taking his eyes off the bar entrance.

The way Brogan looked and sounded as the Hunter sent goose bumps up Darnel's arms. He watched as Brogan started across the street and almost disappeared as the BITTS camouflaged him with the shadows of the night.

You can get a lot of information about a person by the way they walk, and how they carry themselves, if you know what to look for. The Hunter's walk showed no signs of any weakness at all, his walk had purpose, it told whoever was watching that he meant business.

As the Hunter got closer to the building, some people in the group at the front door had already noticed this strange creature approaching. The Hunter stopped in the dim of the street lights, on the road. Most of the crowd was now looking at him.

"Hey little ninja boy, you're supposed to get the dope first, then go home and dress up!" yelled the big, black guy.

The entire group started laughing and pointing.

The Hunter just stood there.

An even bigger guy stepped forward. The white, redneck giant stood about 6'6", 345 lbs, and was wearing a ten gallon cowboy hat. "I reckon it ain't Halloween, so I'm thinkin' you're lookin for the star trek convention? It's down the street, freak."

Everyone started laughing again, and the big, black guy gave him a high five. That's when Darnel noticed they were wearing matching shirts. "They're bouncers here," Darnel informed Brogan, "Probably gang members as well."

"Seriously little ninja boy, if you're lookin to score, you gotta take that mask off."

The Hunter never moved, and stared down the massive bouncers.

"Ok little ninja boy, now I'm aggravated. You go home to mommy right now, or I'm gonna break your head off!"

Everyone in the group backed up as the two bouncers stood their ground.

"Ok Brogan, watch your back! These are really big men; you gotta make sure they don't get ahold of you. Holy crap, it's hard to sit here and watch!"

"Ya gotta call me the Hunter when I'm wearing the suit!" Brogan whispered so only Darnel could hear him.

"Ok, Hunter...or how about I call you "little ninja boy"!"

"You animals are done in this city," The Hunter said ignoring Darnel, and stepping toward the two giant men.

The mechanically altered voice sent shivers through the entire crowd. The big, black bouncer shot towards the Hunter, his speed hidden by his size. The Hunter stood and watched as the bull hurdled straight toward him at full speed. With big, sprinting lunges, the bouncer closed the gap between them fast. At the last second the Hunter crouched and shot forward with one huge leap. With surprising speed, he brought his right knee into the bouncer's thigh. The collision caught Darnel, and everyone else, off guard.

The bouncer did a complete flip in mid air, and landed on his face sliding to a painful stop in the middle of the road. He wasn't unconscious, just severely dazed with dead leg and brutal road rash.

The cowboy bouncer yelled and ran to aide his partner, but was too slow. The Hunter shot his right arm out, and the grappling hook followed. Before the giant cowboy even knew what had happened, it was too late. The grapple hooked the thick leather belt that the cowboy was wearing, and the Hunter gave a tremendous tug. All 345 lbs of the cowboy was launched forward. As he flew out of control towards him, the Hunter flicked his wrist and the grapple retracted.

Darnel giggled to himself as he watched the big cowboy flailing his arms trying to regain his balance.

The Hunter leapt in to meet his next victim, planting his right foot on the cowboy's knee and pulling the ten gallon hat down over his head, as he brought his left knee up under the cowboy's chin. The brutality of the hit devastated the crowd, making a couple of them puke. There were several loud cracks from the blow, and fragments of chewing tobacco stained teeth flew everywhere like shrapnel from a detonated explosive. Both Darnel and the Hunter knew he had to be in shock. A chunk of his tongue fell to the ground after getting caught between his teeth, causing him to bite it off. Pieces of his jaw bone were jutting out after they punctured through his cheeks. With his entire jaw destroyed he was barely conscious, but still standing. The mammoth of a cowboy suddenly dropped to his knees, then slumped to his side in a fetal position, passing out while holding his face. Both bouncers were down, and out of commission.

"Brogan…I mean Hunter, I added zip tie dispensers on the inside of both your wrists, there's a hundred in each roll. You know, the ones the police use when they don't have handcuffs… By the way, that's a pretty good start for the first day on the job!"

The Hunter snagged a zip tie, and fastened one thumb from each bouncer together.

"So what's our next course of action?" Darnel asked, seeing Brogan heading for the entrance.

"I'm going inside to have another beer."

"Yeah, that's gonna go over real well with the gang members in there! They're gonna be all over you the second you open that door."

"I'm just going in to stir up the nest a bit more, and then have another beer. No mercy, right?"

There was absolutely no hesitation from Darnel, "Right! No mercy!"

Once inside, the Hunter slowed his walk, checking out the situation he was putting himself into. The techno music was still thumping, and the dance floor was mostly full. Everyone not dancing turned and stared at the masked man, as he leisurely walked down the aisle between the pool tables. He was halfway down the long row when he stopped, and slowly looked around.

Immediately, two gang members grabbed pool cues and headed for the Hunter, when a huge voice rang out above the music stopping them dead in their tracks. "WAIT!"

The music stopped just as quick as the two guys with the pool cues did. The Hunter turned and looked at the massive man sitting in the corner.

"What the hell are you supposed to be, a ninja or something?!"

"Man, you gotta set these meatballs straight!" Darnel sounded agitated. "Tell them you're the Hunter, or you'll be known as little ninja boy!"

"THE HUNTER."

When Brogan spoke his altered voice seemed to throw the massive man off. It was metal, electric, and mean sounding, and it pleased Darnel when he heard it.

"What? Why 'the Hunter'," the massive man mocked, "I don't see any bow and arrows, or a gun!" A smirk spread like an evil disease across the massive man's face.

"I hunt animals, like you!" His metal voice rang out low, but stern and serious.

The smirk melted off the massive man's face. "I see you got past my watch dogs out front! I don't know how, but…Mr. Hunter is it? You've gotta be able to see the predicament you're in right now; out numbered and definitely out sized!"

"Seems fair to me!" The Hunter said slowly scanning the room.

No one laughed or snickered, no one hardly even moved.

"What makes you think you're going to take us all down, huh? I'm kinda leaning in favor of my guys kicking your ass! All I have to do is let them!"

"You hurt innocent people!"

"We're just trying to survive. If a few innocent people get hurt along the way, oh well, that's life in Saddleback City, eh boys! And if you're going around hurting those that hurt the supposedly innocent, then that makes you an animal too!"

The Hunter slowly scanned the entire room again, everybody was staring at him. "That's correct."

The massive man started belly laughing, and almost everyone joined in until he began to speak again. "Alright, you've got me very curious. If we're all animals here in my fine establishment, it's twenty to one odds and you're in over your head! HOW does the HUNTER expect to live TEN SECONDS after my signal?"

"I'm the alpha male!"

The massive man's eyebrows raised as everyone heard and felt the shivers that came with the altered voice. "GET HIM!" The massive man demanded in his own huge, deep voice.

Instantly the two guys with pool cues came rushing in. Immediately the Hunter grabbed one of the guy's hands and zip tied his thumb to the cue while instantaneously grabbing his other arm to block the cue from the second guy's swing. A loud crack rang out as the music started to play again, muffling the first gang members cries of pain from his now broken arm.

The Hunter planted his foot hard into the chest of his second attacker, shattering his ribs and sending him flying into a crowd several feet away; leaving him with a severe case of whiplash as well. Still holding the cue attached to the thumb of his first attacker, the Hunter yanked and tugged the pool cue, manipulating the guy's elbows to swing violently, striking the heads and knocking out three of his fiendish friends. Just as quickly, a bottle bearing fiend rushed in. With one quick violent spin, the Hunter released the pool cue with the gang member in tow. The momentum sent him flying hard into the bottle bearing fiend. Their heads collided with a hollow crunching noise, and neither one of them moved from where they landed.

"That's eight!" Darnel whispered in the Hunter's electronic ear.

More eyebrows were raised now, but no one was backing down.

"SERIOUSLY!" The Hunter sounded intimidating speaking with his altered voice.

Without taking his eyes off the monitors, Darnel kept checking the equipment to make sure it was recording.

A smaller guy then stepped out from the crowd and the Hunter looked over at him.

"LOOK OUT!"

The Hunter spun his head fast, his body and leg followed finding the sneak attacker in the gut.

Another guy came from behind with a broken beer bottle, only to find the Hunter's extremely heavy right heel in his sternum. No one heard several of his ribs crack, but the Hunter felt them under his foot. It was such a hard kick that the thug flew back breaking the legs of the gang member he fell into, eliminating both from the fight.

The Hunter spun around to find the small guy flying through the air. He caught him in mid flight with both hands and went with his momentum. The Hunter spun so fast and vigorous that the power behind the throw sent the little guy flying into another gang member that was running toward them. They slammed face to face with horrendous results, swapping both teeth and flesh during the collision.

Still, the massive man in the corner didn't move. "You getting tired yet?" he bellowed across the bar.

The Hunter stood and stared at him, "Come find out, pork chop!"

"BROGAN BEHIND…" Before Darnel could finish his warning, the Hunter spun around to see a knife wielding fiend climbing over a pool table.

The Hunter, too quick to defend against, punched the fiend in the face. It was a fast left jab that stunned him for a split second. If anybody blinked, they missed it. Just as quick, the Hunter ripped the knife from the fiend, and sank it deep through his hand and foot. It was fast enough that no one realized what happened until they saw their gang buddy stuck to the top of the pool table bloody and screaming. The ten inch blade went all the way in, up to the handle, and would be almost impossible to get out.

Amongst the excitement, Darnel noticed that people started to leave the pool hall, as screams of agony could now be heard over the dance music. He figured gang members would be the only ones left once everyone else cleared out; which could help them determine just how big this gang was.

One of the gang members had grabbed the "Undisputed Champ" off the wall, and was aiming it straight at the Hunter. There wasn't any noise from the shot, but it came faster than expected. At the last second, the Hunter threw a right hand block. His speed amazed all who were involved in the bar brawl. The big, red boxing glove deflected off the back of the Hunter's hand. Losing no momentum, it struck a fiend in the throat as he was sprinting towards the Hunter. The impact immediately upended the fiend and incapacitated him as his head slammed to the floor. The boxing glove lost some speed, but still bounced off the fiend and swung out heading again for the Hunter. There was nothing he could've done, it couldn't have been predicted by anyone, and it wasn't. The glove grazed the Hunter, but the rope that was attached to it somehow wrapped around the Hunter's waist. Immediately the fiend holding the gun, started to pull it making the rope tight. Two others came rushing in, one on either side of the Hunter, thinking they had him. When they got close enough, the Hunter reached out and grabbed two handfuls of their hair. Now in control of their heads, the Hunter lunged forward slacking the rope. With ambidextrous as one of his many talents, the Hunter simultaneously entangled both guys' necks in the slack rope. And with a strong tug, both men not only had bad rope burn, but also received multiple neck injuries, as they completed a 360 degree spin before landing. In a split second, the Hunter had the rope untangled from his waist and yanked it so hard, the guy holding the boxing gun flew in towards him barely touching the floor. He had mild separations in both shoulders from the initial tug. The smack on the floor told the rest on the story.

At the same time the Hunter heard a yell and caught a glimpse of someone flying through the air at him. He stepped in under the flying fiend, plucked him out of the air like a line drive, and drove him into the floor. It was a solid belly flop that dislocated his shoulders and shattered his pelvis.

"Hunter… there's another guy coming from behind…he's just walking though!"

The Hunter turned around to see what Darnel was talking about. The obvious gang member was walking, with no expression on this face, towards the Hunter.

The Hunter cocked his head, "What? You want a shot at the title?"

The gangbanger, standing 6', 220 lbs, slowly kept coming.

The Hunter quickly checked behind himself, and then started backing up. He made his way to the dance floor where several people, who obviously decided to stay, were cheering for him and waving him over. This didn't go over well with the massive man sitting in the corner, but still he didn't move.

On the dance floor people were patting the Hunter on the back, and touching him as if he was a rock star. But before long were backing up to make room. As the psycho, slow walking gang member made his way onto the dance floor, a familiar song started playing. Although it was the remix, it definitely couldn't be mistaken. *Saturday Night's Alright for Fighting*, by Nickleback and Kid Rock. The music got louder as the two men squared off in the middle of the dance floor.

"Are you kiddin me dude?" Darnel said as he watched in disbelief. "You know he knows that you know what you know!"

"I know!" the Hunter said under his breath as he slowly circled with the challenger, waiting patiently.

Darnel was in total awe of the events that had unfolded so far. "That dude knows you have skills! He's been sittin back watching you annihilate every punk in the joint, and yet he still wants to fight you?!"

"He's dumber than a cup of dirt!"

"That could be. He could very well be one sandwich short of a picnic… or he can really kick some ass!"

"Well, let's find out!"

"Ok, but cripes, watch yourself!" Darnel instructed.

The gangbanger moved first with lightening speed. He sprang forward, three feet off the ground with his right knee aiming for the Hunter's chest. The Hunter also lunged forward, with everything his legs could power, giving him a height advantage and positioning his right knee in line with the fiend's face. To the Hunter's surprise, the gangbanger managed to manoeuvre and duck in mid flight. The Hunter flew over top of him, and turned to find a side kick to his ribs as he landed. The crowd on the dance floor booed and hissed. The Hunter slid back three feet, still standing.

"See, I told you a bear could attack you in that suit!"

The Hunter recognized the Taekwondo kick, and circled with the gang member as they faced off once again.

"Extend your leg, then snap the kick," the Hunter sarcastically coached his attacker.

Suddenly the gang member came at him again, growling and flailing his fists wildly, peppering him with a barrage of punches and kicks. The Hunter retaliated with a superb block for every strike that was unleashed. He made a point to execute every block with perfection and exert little effort in defending the fiend's fists of fury. The crowd went wild as they watched the live martial arts movie. The short sparing match stopped, and both men circled each other again.

"I think you pissed him off!" Darnel's voice sounded hoarse, as if he had been yelling for awhile. He still couldn't believe Brogan's speed and agility.

Darnel knew he found the perfect partner, the perfect tool, the perfect weapon. He was so excited to see Brogan wearing the suit, and to have someone do what he so desperately wanted to do himself. Not only was Brogan a good match for the BITTS, Darnel knew the Hunter would do his bidding for him. Darnel felt like there would be nothing stopping him now. As long as the Hunter stayed on Darnel's side, there was very little that would derail their partnership. And that's exactly what Darnel was hoping.

"Catch your breath, let me know when you're ready!" the Hunters voice rang with intimidation.

With another huge lunge the gangbanger threw a knuckle dragger from the deep. The Hunter watched as the fiend's right arm swung forward. His fist came in hard and fast. The Hunter swatted the swing away, then threw a devastating right-cross making contact under the fiend's left eye. There was so much force behind his swing, it was intended to end the battle. The fiend's head whipped violently to the right, and his body had no choice but to follow. He dove face first into the floor, and surprisingly, bounced back to his feet before his slide on the floor came to a halt.

"This guy is tough, he's gotta be on something, eh!?" Darnel stated.

"I don't know, but I punched him really hard!"

"I'm tellin' you dude, he's messed up on something!"

As the fiend walked slowly back towards the fight, the Hunter couldn't believe what he saw. "You seeing what I see?!"

"Wow! Dude, you obviously hit him hard! That's what caused all... that!"

The fiend's whole left cheek, from beneath his eye, was torn and hanging down off the side of his face. The muscle and bloodied bone was what captured everyone's attention. But he was relentless, and his injuries didn't faze him in the least.

The Hunter readied as the fiend got closer.

With an open hand, the Hunter smacked the right side of the fiend's face, simultaneously kicking his feet out from under him in the opposite direction. The Hunter kept his hand on the fiend's face and assisted the spin. The fiend completed a full cartwheel before slamming into the floor. He had many broken bones, but there was one loud crack that echoed over the music. The Hunter noticed what caused the loud crack before anyone else did. The gangbanger's right arm was in a twisted position when he landed. As he lay there, his arm was still twisted, but jutted out in three different spots. Not letting his injuries stop him, the gangbanger got up, moving a little slower this time, but still headed for the Hunter.

"Hunter, take him out!" Darnel cheered enthusiastically.

"Oh, ok," the Hunter quickly replied, a hint of sarcasm in his voice.

"Sorry...sorry! I just wish I could help kick some ass!"

As the tough fiend neared the Hunter, he unleashed a hay maker from the left. His fist was inches from the Hunter's face when the Hunter made his lightening counter move. He squatted and spun with his right leg extended, sweeping the fiend's feet from under him. The fiend's legs buckled and gave way, bringing him horizontal, five feet off the ground. Before gravity could take effect, the Hunter gave a loud growl and jumped straight up driving his knee into the fiend's ribs; and watched as the fiend folded over his knee like a wet towel. The impact broke every rib on his right side, and sent him airborne once again. The Hunter's expert Muay Thai knee sent the tough fiend straight up, almost hitting the ceiling before dropping fast and hard to the floor. There were several different sounding cracks as he landed, the most significant damage concentrating on his remaining healthy ribs, and both his wrists. All his fingers were either broken and or dislocated, which added to the other numerous sickening sounds.

"There's no way in hell he's getting up from that! WHOOEE! That was an ass whoopin' and a half, eh!? I hope you've got some left for the big bastard in the corner?! What am I saying...of course you've got some nasty shit to unleash on that big, burley bastard...right? You better!" Darnel warned with enthusiasm.

The music stopped as well as everybody in the club. The fiend was back to his feet, swaying back and forth.

"There's no way he can take that and keep going!?" the Hunter thought. "SERIOUSLY!" he growled impatiently. "I'm done messing around!"

Just then the relentless fiend lunged at the Hunter with a strong, fairly quick, side kick, considering his condition. The Hunter slammed a hammer fist down on top of his calf muscle. The fiend made a low faint yelp.

"That's the only sound he's made this whole torturous one sided fight!" the Hunter thought as he continued with his combo of carnage.

The fiend's leg shot to the floor throwing his top torso forward. Faster than a blink, the Hunter's right fist came across striking his temple, immediately followed by a backhand jab, with the same hand. The two punches were so fast and fluent, that the second strike landed before the fiend's head could flop hard to the side from the first strike. There wasn't a millisecond that went by before the Hunter fired a left side kick of his own. Three strikes that would most definitely take this relentless fiend down. The side kick launched him back several feet onto the pool table. As quick as he landed on his back, he climbed to his feet and dove off the edge of the pool table, high into the air as if to throw one final, cage fighting Hail Mary. This time, his attack had a desperate shrieking scream attached to it. As he flew through the air screaming, there seemed no stopping this drug induced juggernaut. The Hunter dropped to one knee, aimed, and released his final statement. The grapple hook shot from the Hunter's forearm like a missile, zipping past the fiend's head as he was in mid flight. With a hard yank the hook snagged the fiend, and his body went immediately out of control. He hit the floor with immense force; his lifeless body flopped and turned over like a corpse falling out of the back of a hearse.

"WHOOEE! You know he's done! There ain't no drug that's gonna help him get up to keep fightin!" Darnel roared. "If he gets up, I'm drivin' the hell outta here."

The fiend laid on the floor with absolutely no movement. The fact that he was still alive and breathing was a miracle in itself.

"If he gets up now, that means he's a zombie or something, and you can't kill him! Then we'd all be food for freaky Frankenstein here!"

As Darnel continued his rant in the Hunter's ear, the Hunter turned his attention to the massive man sitting in the corner; and couldn't understand why the two women were still standing beside him after all the near murderous mayhem. The Hunter started to walk towards them, and still the massive man didn't move. As he got closer, one of the high class hookers ran into the nearby men's washroom. The Hunter had the massive man in plain view while he rounded the next pool table, then stopped and continued to stare at him.

Darnel took a deep breath, "Holy, he's even meaner lookin with that goatee. LOOK AT THE MARKINGS, AND THE SIZE OF HIM, HE'S HUGE!"

The Hunter rolled his eyes after Darnel's lame Crocodile Hunter impersonation. Unexpectedly the massive man spoke up in a very deep voice. "You gonna try'n take me out?!"

Brogan had never really fought a man that big before, he never had to. "What the hell!" he thought. "Can't be any tougher than the silverback!"

There was a loud creaking noise as he stood up out of his chair, and suddenly Darnel and the Hunter both realized how big and potentially deadly the encounter might be. The massive man stretched his arms straight up and growled.

"He's stretchin', getting ready to kick your ass because you messed up his fine establishment!" Darnel continued his rant.

Out of nowhere, the high class hooker that had taken off into the men's washroom came back holding a double barrel shotgun. The Hunter couldn't believe what he was seeing. Without any warning she pulled both triggers. A double shot to the chest sent the Hunter flying back, before landing on the floor, and skidding to a motionless stop.

Both girls immediately started walking over to the immobile, masked body. As they got closer, the girl reloaded the shotgun. Just as she locked the barrel back into place, the Hunter flipped up off his back, kicking both feet out striking their stomachs, then landed.

The shotgun flew out of the girl's hands and instantly she was on the floor convulsing and twitching as immense pain surged through her body. The second gang chick instantaneously started vomiting violently and eventually fell to the ground twitching uncontrollably in a pool of her own puke.

"That's just nasty, what the hell did she eat? SICK!" Darnel exclaimed.

Suddenly the massive man attacked with surprising speed. The Hunter jumped to meet him, striking him in the temple with his knee, and simultaneously bringing his elbow down on top of his head. The combination of blows had very little effect on the massive man. He grabbed the Hunter by the waist with both hands, and with a huge growl, tossed him up into the air hard.

The ceiling was twelve feet, and the Hunter would have most definitely surpassed that mark. In mid flight he spun his body around like a cat, and landed on the ceiling in a squatting position. Then sprang off like a sinister toad bringing both his knees down on the massive man's shoulders, and driving both his elbows into his head. The four strikes were hard, and severely pissed him off. He dropped to his knee in pain, and the Hunter lunged back, spinning in the air again and landed on top of another pool table in a crouching position with his hand out in front of him for stability.

The massive man shook his head and grabbed the bottom of the pool table next to him as he stood up. With another huge, deep growl, he flipped the pool table at such a speed that it was surprising to say the least. The Hunter dove up and over the table as it came crashing down where he had just been perched. The Hunter would have cleared the massive man, but he reached up snagging the Hunter's ankles as he flew over top of him. His flight was abruptly interrupted, as he felt his momentum change direction, and could instantly feel the overwhelming strength of this human giant.

The Hunter slammed into the floor and bounced, but before he had time to completely land, the massive man grabbed him again and tossed him hard, like a bail of hay. The Hunter tried to flip around, but was still a bit stunned from the slam to the floor. His shoulders and back hit first, as he crushed the rack of pool cues hanging on the wall. He was scrambling to get up as the massive man grabbed him by the leg and started dragging him backwards. With all his strength, the Hunter raised his free leg up high, and brought it down fast. His heel came down with great force, and landed on top of the massive man's bicep. His grip loosened and the Hunter was able to spin his leg free, leaping to his feet.

With a huge growl of his own, the Hunter unleashed a right leg kick that found a soft spot on the massive man's outer left leg. The Hunter knew about pressure points, and it showed, as the massive man's leg buckled under the intense weight, and he dropped to one knee. He was in pain and instinctively reached out with his hand to hold himself up as he fell. But the Hunter grabbed it, twisting it outward exposing his whole right side, and then gave him a quick, hard knee to his armpit. As the massive man toppled over, he latched onto the Hunter, pulling him down with him. The Hunter landed on top when they hit the floor, and gave him a fast, hard right and left elbow. He responded by wrapping his ape like arms around the Hunter. It was literally a bear hug. The massive man was trying to kill, and the Hunter was trying to survive.

"All available units respond to Lucky Draw Pool Hall. Shots fired! Repeat, shots fired! Proceed with caution!"

The radio call startled Darnel as he fumbled frantically with his electronic equipment. "You gotta get outta there Hunter!"

"I'm trying…" the Hunter grunted from the bear hug he was trapped in. "Crap, he's strong!"

"No! I'm tryin' to tell you the cops are comin'! So if you don't want to answer any questions, I suggest you kiss and make up, or knock him the freak out and stop playin' around!"

The Hunter managed to wiggle his hand down to his wrist, as the horizontal bear hug got tighter and tighter. The Hunter could feel the great pressure on his ribs.

"Make sure tongues are in the proper place, and not between the teeth!"

The massive man looked right into the Hunter's tinted face shield, "What?" he grunted as he squeezed tighter. "You got something to say before you die, little ninja bitch!?"

The Hunter wanted to make it perfectly clear that he was not to be messed with, so his intimidating voice got very loud. "HOLD ON TIGHT!"

The Hunter pressed the second button on his wrist, and instantly felt relief as the massive man's grip loosened. He wasn't able to completely let go of the Hunter as his muscles were contracting from the 60,000 volts shooting through his giant body.

Darnel had designed the shock to last three to five seconds, and both the Hunter and Darnel enjoyed watching every second of it. As soon as the shockwave died out, the Hunter got up and spun around quick. With two strong leaps he cleared the debris scattered all over the floor, and landed right beside the one eared bandaged bandit. He grabbed him with both hands and hoisted the unconscious fiend over his shoulder.

The Hunter looked back one last time and could see the massive man's body still twitching. But there was something else that caught his attention. Darnel saw it on the monitor too. "Did you see that?"

The Hunter quickly left the trashed, pool hall and headed towards the van. "Yup, I saw it."

"Well, you gotta go back and grab it!"

Suddenly the van's back doors flung open and the Hunter tossed the unconscious one eared wonder on the floor.

"What's this, a souvenir?"

"No, but I want to find out where he goes, and how!"

"Good thinking! Are you goin back to get that key?"

"Yeah, I noticed it when I looked back at the bear hugging behemoth. It must've fallen out of his pocket during the funky chicken dance he did! It looked like a room key or something."

"Well, here take this," Darnel said tossing the Hunter a key imprint pad.

"You never cease to amaze me! You're prepared for everything!" the Hunter said as he disappeared out the van door.

"Get the imprint, and get the hell outta there before…crap…too late!"

Suddenly the night air was broken up by sirens and screeching tires.

"The police are here, you better hurry up!"

The Hunter could hear the police outside as he was imprinting the key. Just as he finished, a swarm of police officers came busting into the pool hall. The Hunter jumped from pool table to pool table until he reached the exit door into the alley, then sprang ten feet off the ground to the fire escape ladder, and scampered like a rabid squirrel to the rooftop. He thought he had evaded them, until he heard some of them shouting. "There! Up there! He went over the roof ledge!"

"How the hell did he reach that ladder?"

"Never mind that! How the hell did he climb forty stories that fast?!"

By the time the police finally reached the rooftop, the Hunter was eight rooftops over, and twenty stories higher than they were.

His speed had increased immensely; he could feel it as he pushed himself to run harder. Even after everything the Hunter had done so far, Darnel still couldn't fathom how he moved so quickly.

The Hunter reached the edge of the seventy story building at full speed and dove off with absolutely no hesitation. Before he started to descend, he pulled all three cords for the glide suit. Instantly the strong western wind filled his wings.

"Hunter? Hunter! Where are you? I quickly took off before the cops saw me, and left the GPS monitor in the back of the van. Did you go underground, or did you go up?

The flight was exhilarating and surprisingly peaceful for the Hunter, despite the oncoming headache. He had never felt anything like it before. "It's a freedom you couldn't get from cruising on a Harley down the highway," he thought to himself as he soared silently through the night sky.

He felt good about everything that had transpired. He had wanted to stir the nest, let the animals get a taste of their own dish of crap, and that's exactly what him and Darnel accomplished.

Some of the peacefulness and serenity he was feeling at that moment came from the glide suit, but most came with Brogan knowing that he was one step closer to getting justice for Rita.

His speed and momentum helped him glide farther than in any of his practice runs on the mountains out back at Darnel's. He soared a long way, hardly losing any altitude, making the flight even more enjoyable.

"HUNTER!? I'm coming up on the first check point on Main Street. Where are you dude?!"

Out of nowhere two soft thuds landed on the roof of the van, and Darnel slammed on the brakes. The Hunter suddenly slid off the side of the roof, through the passenger window, and landed on the seat.

"Show off!" Darnel exclaimed. "Good thing I had that window down or your entry wouldn't have been that slick!"

Brogan smirked as he slid off his headgear.

"I see we're gonna have to work on the communication device in your headgear too. Seems to be on the blitz eh?!"

"Yeah!" Brogan said with a snicker, knowing full well Darnel knew he heard him, but just didn't answer.

The police searched everything at the bar, and only found a small quantity of drugs and a handful of weapons. They couldn't find a single thing that might suggest who this masked man was, all he left behind was unconscious bodies. And the fact that the police saw him there, gave them nothing to go on.

Detective Shane was the one in charge of investigating the mess, and he wanted answers. "I want to know what gang did this, and who their boss is!"

"Sir, it wasn't a gang."

"What?" What the hell are you talking about? Look at this place!"

"It was just one man sir. We think…in a mask!"

"One man? One man with a mask took out fifteen guys!? Without firing a single shot?!"

"Twenty sir!"

"What?"

"The masked man, he took out twenty ATL gang members sir, not fifteen."

The police reports said nothing about another gang, or any type of boss, but they all had one thing in common, a line reading "Inconclusive Chaos".

CHAPTER 11

TRACKING TRAFFICKING

T he drive back to the ranch was full of conversation. Brogan explained how the glide suit felt from the altitude he was soaring at. And answered any and every question Darnel had. He also changed out of the BITTS, and placed it perfectly back into the case, almost dotingly. Darnel explained how he planted a tracking device in the butt cheek of the one eared bandit, and dropped him off in an alleyway a few kilometres from the bar.

"I hope nobody got me dumping that poor bastard out on video! If anyone would've seen me, they would've thought I was dumping a body!"

"You were dumping a body! So, is it working?"

Darnel handed the tracking monitor to Brogan, "He's still sleepin! Hasn't moved since I tossed him out!"

"What's the range on this thing anyway?"

"Let's just say it doesn't matter where out little lab rat goes, we'll be able to find him! There's nowhere he can hide! If he goes into a bathroom at a truck stop, I'll be able to tell you exactly what stall he's in!"

"Cool, so we won't lose track then, right?"

"Brogan, I guarantee he will not be lost with the tracking device I injected into him. I've designed the transmitter to send out monitoring pulse radiation waves that are linked to my computer system only."

"What? English dude!"

"What I'm trying to tell you is, not only can we find our little lab rat anywhere, this monitoring device will also give us a complete layout of the entire building he's hiding in!"

"Wow! You are the man Darnel!"

"Yes I am! You have no idea!"

"Well I got a couple of ideas, but you already told me you weren't a secret agent...or a spy!"

"Nope neither of those, just a guy with a little money to play with, and a whole lotta time on his hands!"

Once arriving at the ranch, the crime fighters continued their discussion of the evening's events over some pizza and beer. Then headed for the information room to watch the video recordings of everything. Brogan sat, saying almost nothing the entire time they watched the video footage. Except when he had the revelation that the surveillance van should be called the "Eye Van".

Darnel had arranged the monitors so they could view each incident from both his, and the Hunter's point of view. They watched everything that was recorded, but focused mostly on the specifics of the fighting. Darnel found it amusing that Brogan couldn't believe it was him in the suit. "I really never knew I looked like that, I mean... moved like that!"

"Well, you were wearing a fancy new suit!" Darnel joked trying to take some credit.

"Too bad it couldn't disintegrate bullets!" Brogan quipped, starting to feel the effects from the shotgun blast.

"Ha! That would be something! Let's see the damage."

Darnel checked the marks and bruises Brogan received from the shotgun blast, and determined rest would be the best prescription, so both men decided to call it a night.

Brogan had been given his own room at the mansion so he could crash at the ranch after a night of crime fighting, and not have to worry about going home.

"Thank you me buddy, for being a great and wealthy friend!" Brogan said patting Darnel's shoulder.

"No, thank you my friend, for being a severe ass kicker!"

Darnel spun his wheelchair around, and popped a wheelie down the hall.

"We're going hunting again tomorrow!" Brogan said before Darnel got too far away.

"I expected as much!" Darnel answered without stopping his wheelie or looking back. "Let the hunt continue!"

Brogan slept hard all night and barely moved a muscle. Darnel, however, had other plans. He stayed up working on the BITTS, and a side project, until the morning, dosing off only a couple times in his wheelchair. Darnel wanted to tweak the Hunter's suit and check for any damage.

Morning came quick, and Darnel was surprised to see Brogan up so early. "What happened, piss the bed?" Darnel joked.

Brogan grunted as he stretched his arms above his head, "I told you, we got some hunting to do!" He grabbed a cup and poured himself some coffee, black as usual. "You didn't sleep?"

"Couldn't! I had some minor adjustments to do to the BITTS, and I added something too!"

"Oh yeah?! What?" Brogan was quite interested to know what else he had to play with.

"Well, for starters, you now have two grappling hooks, one on either wrist."

"That's awesome! That opens up a lot more possibilities, eh!?"

"They are endless my friend! I also added another inside layer of chest cavity, just in case you decide to stand there and take another shotgun blast!"

"Oh come on dude, she totally threw me off when she ran away like that! I thought she was scared, I had no idea she went to get a big ass gun!"

"Well, I've taken care of that as well! I added a monitoring pulse wave device to your suit. Now wherever you are, your surroundings will be scanned for more hostile gangbangers, so no more surprises...hopefully!"

"I'm sure that won't be the last of the surprises. So...that extra layer on the chest cavity, that won't slow me down will it?"

"Brogan, I really don't think we have to worry about that! You watched the video footage... It doesn't seem like you're too sore from last nights brawl either. Is there something you're not telling me? You're not an alien or a machine are you? C'mon man, you gotta tell me if you are...we're partners!"

"I will tell you everything I know, if we can eat while we talk."

It was a hearty breakfast, from eggs and sausage, to toast and fruit. Darnel hardly said a word as Brogan explained to him about his internal setup and how it made him function differently from everyone else.

"Well, that's all that I know," Brogan said taking the last gulp of his coffee. "A few doctors figured my internal system is totally different than anyone else they've ever seen or heard of. But like I said, the tests were never done to confirm their suspicions."

"So you've never had a complete check up?

"I never really had to. When I was younger, my mom was very protective over me, especially when it came to doctors asking questions and wanting to run tests. And since then I've been fortunate enough not to get that sick where doctors had to poke and prod."

"Wait a minute Brogan! No doctor has ever taken an x-ray of you before?"

"Just recently at the Saddleback City Regional Hospital. But they only x-rayed my arms for minor fractures."

Darnel took another bite of his food and sat back in his wheelchair with his hand over his mouth. "Let me see if I've got this right," he said still chewing his food, "what you figure, with no confirmed tests from any doctors, is that your body produces an extremely high dosage of adrenaline…" Brogan could tell Darnel's mind was racing. "Of course, that's it!"

"What?" Brogan asked.

"Your body produces all this adrenaline, which helps you heal faster. But what I don't understand, is why your body doesn't shut down after it has absorbed all the adrenaline it can handle." Darnel was trying to process what Brogan had explained to him. "I mean, how can your body control all that adrenaline? What happens to the extra that doesn't get used up? And what's with the severe headaches afterwards?"

"I don't know, I guess my innards are designed and setup for it. I can't explain it any better than that. Maybe the headaches are caused by the extra adrenaline."

"And every few years, or so, you get a little quicker?"

"No. It doesn't just happen every few years apart. It normally occurs when something happens to me or around me. It has to be a significant, exciting event to cause me to feel the rush."

"So, it's not every time you fight?"

"No, I still have the speed and power, but for this…whatever it is, to excel, it has to be a very hairy situation. I call it "the next step"!"

Darnel leaned on his elbows and raised his eyebrows. "Do you think you got to the next step after last night?"

"No, I'd be able to tell, so would you!"

"So each step that your adrenaline pumping body goes through, brings you closer to what?"

"That's a loaded question that I don't have the answer to. I used to wonder how many steps there were gonna be for me, you know, before I croaked or something. But after the fourth time it happened, I just kinda didn't think about it anymore."

"Last nights events had no effect on you then? You didn't go to the next stage in that scenario?"

"Nope. I was pretty much just pissed off and looking for a fight. Basically it has to be a drastic or very surprising event for it to kick in."

"Amazing, absolutely amazing!" Darnel said wiping his mouth with his napkin. "I'm so glad that you're on my side!"

"Not just on your side, we're partners!"

Out the huge picture window, both men noticed Uncle Reynolds had pulled the Eye Van around front.

"Looks like it's time to hunt!" They both announced simultaneously.

Darnel rolled up to the driver's position and secured his chair in place. Brogan climbed in and instantly started scanning the van for the black case.

"Don't you fret Brogan," Darnel said noticing, "That suit will go wherever you go!"

Darnel picked up the tracking monitor, passed it to Brogan, and started down the driveway. "I guess our little lab rat finally woke up, and is on the move!"

Their plan was simple enough, they would locate the lab rat, and follow him around in the hopes he would lead them somewhere important. They needed to get a better understanding of what was going on, how many gang members there were, and who was actually involved.

"I don't know if you've ever done surveillance before Brogan, but it might get boring."

"That doesn't matter, whatever has to be done. I'll watch grass grow if that's what it takes!"

As they drove back towards the city to find their bugged bandit, they discussed the events of the night before, again. They also agreed to keep a low profile, and only unleash the Hunter if need be.

"There's a lot of bad and mean people lookin' for the Hunter right now," Darnel explained. "Even the police! We need to lay low and observe everything so we can try and figure out what's goin' on between these ATL gang members and the police. I'm sure not all the cops are corrupt, but it would be great if we could get some evidence recorded."

As they entered the city limits, the signal on the tracking monitor started to get a stronger reading. They continued to follow the signal, when suddenly Brogan almost jumped out of the Eye Van. "There! Right there! Pull over, I just saw him!"

"This is exciting!" Darnel said enthusiastically as he quickly pulled over. "I've always wanted to be involved with crime fightin'!"

"You are involved! You're the reason we can fight and do something to make a difference in this city!"

Darnel gave a half assed smile. "I know I'm here in heart and spirit, and I know I'm supplying all the funds and toys, but I would really like to kick somebody's ass! I mean, as long as they deserved it of course."

Both men were getting frustrated and anxious as they moved their surveillance van nine times before the lab rat finally stopped for more than a couple minutes.

"Have you noticed that every stop he makes he seems to get a little heftier, and only stays for two minutes at a time?!" Brogan observed.

Darnel was in the back of the Eye Van scrambling his fingers over the keyboard. "I've noticed, and I'm checking every address he's stopped at, and…holy crap!"

"What is it?"

"I ran all the addresses through the Saddleback City police database, and just about every single place our lab rat has stopped is a known drug spot!" Darnel said wheeling back to the front of the Eye Van.

"So that means our little lab rat is their drug runner! That's why he looks a little bigger through the mid section after every stop. It's either money or drugs that he's packing," Brogan theorized.

"It very well could be something like that, it could be anything. All we have to do is be patient, and wait. Soon our little lab rat will slip up and give us something we can work with. I can feel it! He'll cough up another piece of the puzzle, you can bet your…"

"He's stopping again!" Brogan yelled.

Darnel immediately stopped mid sentence, curious to what Brogan was so amazed at. Both men stared as the lab rat climbed a flight of stairs to enter another building.

"What on earth is he doing at The West Hotel?" Brogan asked curiously.

Darnel reached into his pocket and pulled out the key he had Uncle Reynolds cut from the imprint pad, and handed it to Brogan. Brogan never took his eyes off the hotel as Darnel dropped the key into his hand. He quickly glanced at the key, and then fixated his eyes back on the hotel again. "This is not a coincidence, there's no way!"

"I'm guesstimating there's a one in a quadrillion chance that this is a coincidence, but my money is on no! The key has number 222 imprinted on it right? This is what I was tellin' you, this is the next clue, the next piece of the puzzle!"

"You're absolutely right Darnel. Let's see if this puzzle piece fits!" Brogan said holding up the key.

"Where's our little lab rat gonna take us? I'm guessing room 222!"

"It shows he's stationary, in what looks like a huge suite with a really odd layout."

Darnel peeked over at the monitor, "And he's alone too."

"I'm not sure what to make of this though?" Brogan said handing the monitor to Darnel.

Darnel studied the monitor quickly. "I'll tell you what Brogan! Somebody's got a lot of something in that room! That's why it looks like such a weird layout, compared to the rest of the suites on that floor! Look," he said pointing to the monitor, "there's two walls in that room that actually aren't walls at all!"

"What do you mean?"

Darnel passed the monitor back to Brogan and pointed out the difference in the walls. "You see? You can tell these are the actual walls of the hotel room, they're solid. But with closer examination, you can clearly see these ones aren't real walls. They look like outlines of boxes or suitcases. I'm not exactly sure what they are, but I can guarantee you they're not structured walls of the hotel room."

Brogan slouched down in the passenger seat, trying to be less visible to anyone outside. "When he comes out, I'm going in for a look!"

Darnel smiled, "I expected nothing less."

The West Hotel was an older building that had been renovated into the average three star hotel. It always seemed to be fairly busy, with families and businessmen coming and going. But now it made Brogan question how many of their customers were corrupt, and staying there just to "do business".

Only a few minutes had transpired and the lab rat was back outside again.

"He wasn't in there long!" Brogan said.

"Wait till he gets a little further away before you go check it out."

"Looks like our lab rat lost a bit of weight while he was in there too!"

Darnel peered through the binoculars and quickly studied the lab rat. "Oh yeah, he's not carrying anything anymore, that's for sure."

Before the lab rat came down the stairs of the hotel, he looked all around to make sure the coast was clear, and then egotistically sauntered down them.

Darnel dropped the binoculars. "He's not drunk, but I think he had a little something when he was in that hotel room."

"I'm going in to check it out."

"Here put this on, and stick this in your ear," Darnel said handing Brogan a baseball cap and an earpiece.

Brogan put the ball cap on, and stuffed the earpiece into his ear. With the key in hand, he headed for the hotel. In two strong leaps he was up two flights of stairs, and at the front door. He opened the door and went out of sight. Darnel unclamped his wheelchair again, spun around fast, and was in the back of the Eye Van flipping switches and pushing buttons. The main monitor came into focus and Darnel could see 222 from the baseball cap camera. Brogan pushed the key into the slot. "Hope this key works!"

"It will, have a little faith my friend!"

Brogan could hear the uneasiness in Darnel's voice, but said nothing.

The door popped open with a small squeak trailing behind it. Brogan slid inside fast and slick. As he ventured in, there was a bathroom on his left, an open walk-in closet on his right, and a short hallway that entered into a huge open room which included a kitchen.

"HOLY CRAP!" both men said simultaneously as they looked towards the kitchen area.

There were several hundred packages of drugs stacked from the floor to the ceiling, with small pathways to walk in and through them.

"There has to be millions of dollars worth of drugs there!" Darnel observed.

Brogan headed toward the left side of the room after something caught his eye.

"HOLY SHIT!" Darnel whispered, watching the monitor, as Brogan scanned the other side of the room where bigger, thicker packages were piled. "Look at all that money!"

Most of the money was covered with black plastic wrap, the same as the drugs, but there was no mistaking the two. The whole left side of the room was entirely money.

"Mostly hundreds," Brogan said flipping through a stack.

"There's gotta be millions, and millions Brogan!"

"So, maybe a billion!" Brogan said sarcastically.

"Maybe, smart ass, maybe!"

Brogan went over to the other side of the room to get a closer look at the drugs. It was indeed a white powdery substance.

"Ok Brogan, come back to the Eye Van so we can discuss our next move. And...you better make it quick!"

"Hang on one second, I want to check the bathroom, you never know, there might be drugs or money in there too!"

"That's great, but you gotta get outta there NOW! The cops are here!"

"What?! Stop playing Darnel!"

Brogan scampered to the window and looked out the curtain. Two big cops were walking up the stairs, each carrying a black bag.

"Did you hear me?! Get outta there Hunter!"

"You gotta call me Brogan when I'm not in the BITTS!"

"Listen up smart ass, you're about to get busted!"

"Let's see what they're doing here. If they're coming to do something in this room, we're going to record them!"

"Well you better hurry up and find a place to hide then, they might be heading straight for that room!"

Before Darnel even finished his sentence, Brogan went into the bathroom and jumped straight up; stretching his limbs outward, they landed on opposite walls without a sound. He felt the drywall buckle under his hands and feet as he applied the proper amount of pressure to keep himself perched above the door.

"Oh buddy, you got lucky! What if the bathroom was a little wider, eh?"

"It's skill, not luck! Are you recording, cause it sounds like someone's at the door."

Darnel could barley make out what Brogan was saying, but he answered in the same soft voice. "Yes I am. You're not even straining, are you?"

"As long as the drywall doesn't give, and no one decides to chuck a leak, I'll be fine."

"Brogan my rookie crime fightin friend, even bad guys gotta go!"

The door popped open fast with a big squeak and voices trailing behind it. Both cops were in uniform, one was taller and bigger, but both were definitely on steroids.

"This'll make the room a little smaller."

"Oh yeah, the Big Man will like that!" the smaller cop answered, with a heftier voice than expected.

"So, you still got some of that brick left?"

"Yeah, I dip in after every shift. You gotta relax from a shit day somehow!"

The bigger cop seemed naïve and hesitant as they both unloaded their black gym bags.

"You think maybe I could get a little bit from ya?"

"Man, just grab one from here, I don't think the Big Man is gonna miss two bricks."

"I've considered that. You gonna grab one too?!"

"No man, I told you, I still got some left at home. But where do you think I got that one from?!"

"But if the Big Man ever found out...he'd...!"

"I know man, that's why we make sure some asshole, under us in the ranks, takes the fall for it!"

"Oh, good thinking!"

Brogan removed his baseball cap and slowly lowered it down and out the bathroom door.

"Spin it a little to the left, you crazy eastern bastard!" Darnel whispered. "Perfect!"

The bigger cop took a brick and stuffed it into his uniform jacket. The footage that Darnel was recording was limited due to the small hallway. But there was no misunderstanding, the two dirty cops were clearly unloading drugs, right in cameras view.

"We've got to make sure we are scheduled for that task force raid this weekend, Big Man's orders! There should be a shit load of drugs!"

"Well, there sure was a lot at the last bust! And it's definitely easier to snag bricks from a raid, than the cop shop storage!"

"But the Big Man ordered another hit on the cop shop storage anyway! That's kinda funny, eh!"

The bigger cop nodded and finished unloading his bag. "I've gotta piss."

There was a quiet, girly gasp, and Brogan knew it wasn't him.

"C'mon man, piss at the coffee shop, we've gotta get outta here and I've gotta eat!

"Ok, stop yer bitchin!"

As they headed towards the door, their voices became as clear as crystal, "Dude, the Big Man is gonna be out of the city for a couple of days. He says he wants everything tightened up and watched closely! He's got extra guys on the clock because of the hit on Lucky Draw's last night. It got everybody pulling their shorts up! At least until we catch, and kill that guy. C'mon, let's go eat!"

The door shut and there was no need for whispering.

"Now get the hell outta there Brogan!"

"For sure me buddy, but I gotta chuck a leak first," Brogan joked.

He jumped down from his hiding place and was about to open the door to leave when Darnel startled him.

"WAIT!"

Brogan froze. "What? More cops?"

"No, two shady lookin characters just passed the cops on the stairs, and are heading inside!"

Brogan scooted back to the bathroom and placed himself perfectly where he was before. In no time the squeaky door shot open and Brogan felt the wall shake from the doorknob embedding into it. He waited until they were in the main room and then lowered his hat cam to the same spot as before. Both scruffy men were unloading hundreds of thousands of dollars, adding to the huge stacks in the room.

"This is primo shit man, everybody's buying! This is our biggest money drop off yet!"

"Yeah, I know. We should be allowed to take more than two bricks at a time; it sells so fast, we can't carry enough of it! And if we happened to get busted, the Big Man would get us out pretty fast."

"But this way we have to bring the money in more frequently. And stop complaining, the more times we have to pick up, the more times we get to sample our supply!"

"Could you imagine if the Big Boss Man found out we were doing that?! He'd have us shot!"

"Or put away for a long time!"

"Ok, let's get the hell out of here."

"After I piss."

"Hurry up man."

"Are you kiddin?" Darnel whispered throwing his hands up, even though no one could see him.

Brogan quickly reached down and unscrewed the light bulb on the vanity light. There was less of a chance that he would be seen if the light never came on. As he got back to his mounted position above the door, one of the men entered the bathroom. Brogan held his breath and tried to stay as still and quiet as possible. He wasn't scared, he was worried that if anything were to happen in the room, all the dope and money would be moved to another unknown location real quick, and they would have to start their search all over again.

The scruffy man flicked the light switch, but was unfazed when the light didn't come on. He finished his business and without any further chatting between the two men, they left the room.

Before Darnel could say the coast was clear, Brogan was coming out the front door, and within seconds was back in the Eye Van.

"I don't know about you, but I just started breathing!" Darnel said holding his chest.

"That was pretty intense! So, we've got everything recorded?" Brogan asked smiling.

"My friend, we struck gold! We've got faces and voices, with a lot of money and drugs in the background."

"Alright! Now what do we do? We can't go to any police, we don't know who's dirty or clean!"

"What we do now, my friend, is get more and more evidence, as much as we can. We'll dig until every last one of these bastards are dug up and revealed for what they truly are! We have to keep goin' till we hit the bottom, and find the source of all this bullshit corruption!"

"I've gotta be honest with you Darnel, it might be a good thing that you're not out there fighting these guys with me. You'd rough them up too much with that nasty temper of yours."

"You're one to talk now aren't ya!? Oh yeah...you gotta go back in and plant this somewhere."

Darnel handed Brogan a small surveillance and audio transmitter about the size of a thumbtack. "This is the sticky side, just press it against the wall or whatever."

"Are you telling me with all your wisdom, smarts, and technology, you're going to call it "the sticky side"?" Brogan snickered.

"Don't give me a hard time about this now, go and do your job."

Within two minutes Brogan had planted the device in the room and was back in the Eye Van. "There was a 'Do Not Disturb' sign on the door that I don't remember seeing the first time. Do you think the hotel owner or manager is in on this?"

"He very well could be, or the dirty police are tellin' him to keep everyone clear of that room. Maybe they have the room booked or rented as a police surveillance room. Grab the hand held monitor, let's see if we can find our little lab rat again. He might lead us to another piece of the corruption puzzle!"

"Holy crap, we should have been cops! Or detectives!"

"No Brogan my friend, we're too honest."

"True. I guess we'll have to stick to beating the snot out of these animals, eh!"

The crime fighting partners drove four blocks and quickly realized it was going to be a scorcher of a day.

"Are you ever gonna let me drive this beast?" Brogan asked as Darnel leaned over to crank the air conditioning on.

"You think you can handle her!?" Darnel asked razzing Brogan.

Before Brogan had a chance to answer, Darnel caught a glimpse of movement on the monitor and pulled over to the side of the road to take a look. Brogan immediately looked down at the monitor in his hand. The tracking device was proving to be an ingenious idea.

"Good eye! Our one eared little lab rat has come back to the surface again."

"I still can't believe you hit him in the head with a pool ball!"

"I took his ear off too!"

Darnel shook his head in disbelief. "Who are you kiddin, if our lab rat ran into you face to face again, he'd piss himself and then faint. …Hit him right in the head…" Darnel snickered as they positioned themselves for surveillance duty. "I gotta show Uncle and Denise that in slow motion!"

"According to the monitor, the lab rat got thirsty and went in this little pub here." Brogan said pointing.

"Yeah, looks like he's in a bathroom stall," Darnel added.

Even though he designed it, Darnel was almost as amazed as Brogan was with their new high-tech gadget.

Not too much was said for the next forty-five minutes, as they watched the monitor.

"He's gotta be breaking those bricks up for selling. Nobody craps for that long without getting dead leg!"

"Brogan my friend, I believe you would've made a fine detective."

Finally there was relief with movement, and the lab rat showed himself, stretching his arms above his head. He was squinting as the sun tried to blind his bar attuned eyes. He looked around trying to act inconspicuous, and then headed north. The first stop he made was in the middle of the city, at Sarsaparilla Park, to a fairly secluded bench which seemed his usual meeting place for dealing drugs.

Some of his customers looked the part of a druggie, no care about nothing but the next fix. Others would pull up in nice rides, with a sexy broad in the passenger seat. The rich closet snuffers would park a half block away, get out like they were going to buy the place, and then slowly make their way to the man with their needed nose candy. Sadly, a percentage of the customers were kids, barely teenagers.

When the first kid showed up, Brogan was enraged to the extent where he was willing to get out and jeopardize the whole operation. "ARE YOU SERIOUS!!!!? There is no excuse for treating your body that way, disrespecting yourself and putting toxic crap in your veins and up your nose. BUT, when you start selling to kids!…"

"Easy my friend, it's hard to watch but sometimes we gotta let certain things unfold, no matter how drastic, just to get the next piece of the puzzle."

In the two and a half hours of sitting and selling, the lab rat received forty-two visitors in total. The last two were cops who talked to the lab rat for about thirty seconds, without looking at him, before moving on. A minute after that the lab rat was on the move again. Darnel and Brogan followed in the Eye Van from a safe distance, and observed the lab rat starting to make a lot of random stops. Darnel made sure to take note of every address so later they could find out more information about who lived at each place.

At first, his stops were at nice houses and apartment buildings, relatively upper class. But they were completely thrown off by the next several deliveries the lab rat made. They watched as he entered businesses and warehouses, including lumber yards and different types of industrial plants. His stops were quick and under three minutes each.

"I had no idea it was this bad, it's like an epidemic, and I've been living in this city for five years!"

"Brogan, I've been livin' here my whole life and there's not a day that goes by that I don't see the city getting worse! It's falling apart at the seams more and more everyday. I've been lookin a long time for the ones responsible for taking my family, and my legs. Right where you and I are right now my friend, this is where all my years of investigating my parent's deaths has brought me. Right here, with you by my side."

"Darnel, I promise I will do everything I can to help you."

The Eye Van rolled slowly to a stop close to the next drop off location the lab rat made. Instantly, the Eye Van was filled with more rage, and both Darnel and Brogan contemplated getting out and beating the lab rat to a pulp. 'Junior High School' stood out in big white letters above the school doors. A young boy met the filthy lab rat in the parking lot, and was handed a sandwich bag packed full of little white bags; then quickly vanished back into the school.

Without hesitating, Darnel punched in the name of the school, got the phone number, and was already talking to the principal before Brogan could remove his staring eyes from what just happened.

"Good afternoon this is principal Benads."

"Yes, I'm calling with a concern in regards to one of your students!"

Darnel gave an immaculate description of the young boy who was walking around with thousands of dollars in drugs. He explained to the principal that he witnessed a black man give a bag of drugs to the young boy. But the description of the guy was off by every detail.

"Who may I ask is calling?"

"Oh, just a concerned citizen," Darnel said hanging up the phone to continue following the lab rat.

Minutes later Darnel and Brogan heard on the scanner that a police unit was dispatched to the school. The two crime fighting partners said nothing as they continued tracking the lab rat, both with huge smiles. They knew the kid was busted and that none of the drugs he had would get to any other kids, at least not today. They also knew that it was done in a way that wasn't too conspicuous. Although, both men were pissed to see yet another stop at another school. This time it was a high school, and it wasn't a kid in the parking lot.

"These animals have to be stopped, the whole organization!" Brogan said as both men took turns looking through the high powered camera; and determined it was in fact a teacher involved in this drug deal.

They were relieved, to a certain extent, that the older man received only two small bags, for personal use they figured.

The next stop for the lab rat was the biggest shock of the day. He strolled right up along side the passenger window of a parked police cruiser, handed the cop a huge roll of money, and walked away.

"Are you kidding me!? Are there any cops on the force that aren't corrupt!? How many can there be?"

"No worries my friend, we are recording everything! They'll be goin down with the rest of the scum in this city," Darnel said starting the Eye Van.

Brogan seemed perplexed, "What're ya doing?"

"I have a plan. Somehow we have to find out who can be trusted and who to stay away from, right?"

"I agree!"

"We might be takin' a chance here, but it's gotta be done."

To Brogan's surprise, Darnel drove back to the hotel. "You've gotta go in and get a brick, I'll explain when you come back."

Brogan didn't ask any questions, and was back with a single brick in under a minute. Darnel explained the plan he conjured up to Brogan, as they drove to the Saddleback City Police Station.

By the time they arrived at the cop shop, it was dark. Brogan put the BITTS on and sat with the headgear in his lap. "You think this plan of yours is gonna work?"

"It's a long shot, but we need to find an inside man that's not dirty or corrupt."

Darnel parked on the street, outside the police parking lot, in a shadowed area. Brogan put his headgear on, "Cowboy up!"

"Brogan, you're not gonna be fightin no one!"

"You gotta call me Hunter when I'm in the BITTS. And I'm just trying out a few different lines, you know, catch phrases."

Darnel passed another toy to the Hunter. "How bout, 'Round 'em up'!"

"Somebody will slap me if I say that," Brogan teased. "Are you sure these rubber suction darts won't do any damage? I've seen this guy, he's all business, and he carries two six shooters."

"I'm pretty sure the darts won't damage anything," Darnel reassured.

"Pretty sure? That ain't good enough dude, did I mention he carries TWO six shooters! And he drives a '77 Charger!"

"Who drives a sweet ride like that to a job like his anyway? Ya think he might be on the take?"

"Darnel, he was one of the first people who tried to help me; he talked to me when no one else would. I seriously doubt he's dirty, he just seems too grounded. He's very down to earth, and I think he's got a family too!"

"Well, if he's that nice of a guy, he won't mind you shootin' a couple rubber darts at his ride."

The two crime fighters pounded fists and the Hunter was gone. Darnel slipped on his black toque, and grabbed the one pound brick. He had already picked the Charger's lock by the time the Hunter had scaled the adjacent building to the police station. The Hunter would now glide to the cop shop roof, and wait. The police station was twenty stories, so the glide would be short but exhilarating none the less.

Darnel chuckled to himself as he pictured the Hunter standing on top of the police station, figuring he'd be the only one to ever do it. It was designed to be virtually impossible to climb from the outside, and just as impossible to break into or out of.

Darnel planted the brick on the driver's seat of the black Charger, and wheeled back into the Eye Van just as the detective was finishing his shift. The Hunter stood on the police station rooftop, and watched the detective as he walked to his car. The moment of truth was about to be revealed to them, whether or not they had an inside man they could trust.

Detective Shane opened his car door and stopped, he stared for a few seconds, and then looked around the parking lot. "Shit!"

The detective swiftly snagged the brick and locked his Charger door as he turned around to head back inside.

Darnel and Brogan had discussed earlier that if the detective was dirty, he would simply drive off with the dope on his seat and a smile on his face. But if he was a good cop, he would go back inside, after a long shift, to do more paperwork on the brick that landed in his lap.

SHOOMP!

The detective immediately spun around with his hand on his weapon, and saw the suction dart on his door. He plucked it off his beautiful car door, and ran his fingers over the spot of contact, then noticed there was a note attached. The detective unrolled the note from the dart, but bent over to check his door again before reading it. He stood back up and read the note out loud, "LOOK UP!"

The detective immediately turned in the direction that the dart came from, and looked up. He wasn't sure what to expect, but he wanted to know who was stupid enough to shoot shit at his car. His eyes elevated to the cop shop rooftop, where he saw a lone, dark figure.

"I guess he wants to talk," Detective Shane said out loud. "Well I want to talk about the respect of nice cars!"

SHOOMP!

The detective spun around and plucked the second dart off his car door. Still staring at the dark figure on the roof, he unrolled the second note.

"COME ALONE!" he read it with a quick glance and was staring again at the dark figure as he walked towards the police station.

"Tell you what prick, best stop shootin' shit at my car! And use a phone dammit!" he yelled as he entered the police station.

Detective Shane stepped onto the elevator and pressed the twentieth floor button. On the way up, he checked both his weapons to make sure they were loaded, but didn't button the strap on his hip holsters, thinking he might need them quick. Detective Shane stepped off the elevator on the top floor, and turned right. He walked to the end of the corridor, then opened the last door on the right, and climbed another short flight of stairs before opening the door to the roof. As the detective stepped out, he had an unwavering feeling, and was ready. The Hunter felt the same thing as the detective walked slowly towards him.

Detective Shane didn't pull his gun out right away, which told the Hunter he was confident he could pull it fast enough to save his own life at anytime.

The two men stood ten feet from each other in the center of the roof, and the detective placed his right hand on the side of his gun. "Hit my car again, and we're gonna have more than words! Who are you and what do you want?"

"You won't be needing the gun."

"How can I be certain? You shot my car!"

"I could've shot you!"

"Good point. What do you want from me? Did you put that brick of dope in my car?"

"Yes I did. It was a test to see if you were a dirty cop."

"I could still be a dirty cop, how can you be certain?"

"With your attendance record, and the number of arrests and convictions over the years, I was betting on you being a good guy."

"Alright, you don't mean me any harm, and I'm not gonna shoot you. So…who are you, and what do you want?"

"I want the same thing you and every other good citizen in this city wants."

"Ok, so you want less crime and a million dollars, what does that have to do with me?"

"I was thinking we could help each other clean up the city."

"Who pays your salary? Cause the last time I checked, that was my job. And you still haven't answered my question. Who are you? I mean, I get the fact that you're dressed up all scary, and would probably like to jump from building to building beating up bad guys. But who are you, and why not let the police, like me, fight the crime in this city?"

"Cause there are dirty cops littering the streets with drugs; the same drugs that your fellow coworkers have already seized, they are reselling. I need an inside man, and you need a vigilante to fight the way the police can't.

"Where did you get all this information?"

"I know there's a huge internal investigation in progress right now because of drugs mysteriously disappearing from the evidence room. And I also know the police heading the investigation are dirty cops. Detective Shane, I know you fight the battle everyday, but it's a losing battle. Day after day you relentlessly chase these animals down, and you feel that you're making a difference? The statistics show that crime has risen drastically each year for the last five years! You could use my help!"

"You're right, but how am I gonna help you? Anyway you could help me, would be against the law."

"I know where there's a huge pile of drugs and money, stolen from the police impound and drug raids."

"I was hoping you were a nice guy trying to fight crime, but if you tell me it was you that stole…"

"No!" the Hunter said, cutting him off. "I had nothing to do with any of that, except for the brick in your car, but I'm trying to find out who is responsible for all the corruption in the city."

Detective Shane couldn't get over the Hunter's altered voice. He was a grown man who had been in numerous gun battles throughout his career, and had never wavered or backed down from doing his duty. But the altered voice sent shivers up and down his spine. It gave him the same feeling he had the first time he discharged his weapon on duty, killing a young man. A dark penetrating vibe that leaves a memorable imprint of fear, for life, when something triggers it. Detective Shane didn't think this dark masked stranger was a psycho, maybe a little fantasy orientated, or animatedly ambitious.

"So you think by wearing that outfit, and teaming up with me, that we're gonna clean up this stinking city?"

"Yes!"

"You're drunk, or stoned," Detective Shane said shaking his head. "Something isn't right upstairs. Everyday I see crap going on everywhere, and everyday I see the evil take a bigger grip on this city. Of course I'd deny it to anyone! I figure if I do my job the best I can, maybe I can make a difference, even if only a small one. Then the people of the city would see me doing my job, and feel safe. But everyday I can feel my grip on the situation getting looser, weaker. At this point, I would like to believe a dark stranger could rid the city of the scum and give it back to the people, but I'm a pessimist! Perks of the job! And life just isn't that way. This is not Gotham City and you definitively aren't Batman!"

"But I do have information, and proof that no one else has. I thought you would be more interested in the stolen drugs and money."

"I am interested, but how much are we talking about? I don't have time to waste on little fish. If there's gonna be any changes made in this city, I reckon we need to find the bigger fish."

"I'm guessing everything that was stolen from the police impound is there, and more. You better bring a big truck!"

The Hunter explained everything that Darnel told him to say, to the detective; everything from the hotel room full of drugs and money, to the cops who were involved.

Detective Shane listened intently, taking all sorts of notes. "If all this information is true, then I reckon I'll have to pick and choose my team members carefully!"

"Select only the ones that you are absolutely certain of, and be careful."

176

After their conversation, Detective Shane had more belief in the dark stranger than he had when he first saw him.

"I'm sure you're aware of the brutality of these animals, but you'll have to watch your back more than ever detective. If one of the dirty cops catches wind that you know anything, given the right opportunity, you're dead."

"It's gonna take some time to assemble a team of my liking. Wait a minute!" Detective Shane said changing the subject like he just had an epiphany. "That was your non lethal carnage at Lucky Draw's, wasn't it?! It all makes sense now!" he said knowing for sure that the dark voiced stranger was in fact the real deal.

"I only went in for a beer."

"A sense of humor, down to earth, and obviously severely pissed off about something," the detective thought, taking in everything the dark stranger said, even noticing his slight hand gestures as they talked. "So you went in for a beer and they didn't like your costume!"

"They didn't like anything about me!"

"How do I contact you if I need more information? What if you can't find me?"

"I think I'll be able to hunt you down," the Hunter said starting to walk towards the north edge of the roof.

"You didn't answer me, who are you? What do I call you?"

That familiar feeling of seeing your first horror movie, came flushing over the detective as the dark stranger stood on the roof's edge, then turned and answered.

"I am the Hunter."

With a massive and powerful lunge, the Hunter dove, and dropped out of sight. He pulled the cords and set his glide suit as he started his descent. Detective Shane ran to the roof's edge just in time to see the Hunter scrunch into a ball in mid air, then spread open with wings before the dark night engulfed him.

"And stop shootin' shit at my car, dammit!" Detective Shane yelled down into the darkness of the night.

As he made his way back inside the police station, the detective was baffled, and impressed. He made it to his office on shaky legs, shutting his door behind him. Sitting at his desk, he pulled a half empty bottle of Captain Morgan and an oversized shot glass from the bottom drawer, and filled it to the top. He watched his hand shake as he raised the nerve calming beverage to his lips.

The detective wasn't scared; it was an adrenaline rush from the unknown that teaming up with the Hunter brought. The excitement he felt for what was to come was overwhelming, and even with the second glass, his hands were still shaking.

"This is nuts! He's nuts!" Detective Shane said in a hoarse whisper. "He should call himself nuts, or suicidal nut job, or something! This is never gonna work! Or will it? I mean, this guy takes out a small gang, a small army, with little effort apparently. He's jumping off buildings and flying into the night. Is this too good to be true? This guy comes to me and offers to help clean up the city, by any means necessary. This is huge, if he is what he claims he is, if he's for real."

The detective sat quietly in his chair sipping at his drink, replaying the events of the night, contemplating his own sanity for believing this could be real.

"Detective Shane, old buddy, the Hunter is real!" he finally said out loud thinking he was also a little nutty for talking to himself all night.

The detective's hands weren't shaking as much after his third glass. For the next couple hours he tried to wrap his brain around everything that was explained to him on the roof. He went through piles and piles of names for recruiting members for his secret squad, and discovered there weren't many police officers who he could truly trust. There were hardly a handful, but he figured maybe he could receive some help from the RCMP, if need be. He wondered what had pushed the Hunter to play this darken comic reality role. What made him snap, bringing him to the point where he put on a costume to fight bad guys that would most definitely try and kill him? His only conclusion and only hope was that the Hunter was the real deal.

On the drive home in the taxi, the detective wondered how all this would play out. It seemed insane and baffling, a masked man tracking trafficking!

CHAPTER 12

FRIGHTENING FURY

After a short, hard sleep, Brogan and Darnel discussed the meeting with Detective Shane over a morning snack. The two rookie crime fighters filtered every little detail they could think of.

"I ran his postures through a character mood analysis recognizer."

"A what?" Brogan asked confused.

"It's a program I designed that allows us to read someone's body language."

"Can it tell what someone is thinking too?" Brogan bantered.

"That would be something, but no smart ass. What I'm saying, is from the way Detective Shane stood, and how he moved about as he talked to the Hunter last night, my program will give a close reading of his mood at that time. I also ran his voice through a similar program I designed as well."

"Ok, you've got me really interested now. But I can already tell you what Detective Shane was feeling! He was feeling like pulling those big ass Dirty Harry guns out of his holsters and shooting twelve into me after I shot his car!"

"Brogan, I told you that nothing will penetrate the BITTS. Although a nasty gun like that... well it's gonna hurt like nothing you've ever felt before, especially that close! But according to these readings, he was excited to see you, like an old schoolmate. He didn't want to kill you, although his adrenaline was pumping! The thought of shootin' you might have crossed his mind, you did shoot shit at his nice ride!"

"You gave me the gun and ammo, and told me to do it!"

"But," Darnel continued, ignoring Brogan's comment, "the readings tell a lot about his character and more. It shows us we can trust him."

"Well, I believe if you underestimate him, you're done! I think he's the real Dirty Harry, and Clint Eastwood created the movie character from Detective Shane's experience and personality traits!" Brogan said.

"Yeah, the voice analysis program told me that he was in no way nervous or ready to run, let alone back down from the Hunter. Nope, our Detective Shane is a true-blue cowboy that you don't want to piss off! He's the right guy to have on our team," Darnel said with reassurance.

"Even with the BITTS on, I felt intimidated by him. The way he sauntered up to me like he was a bouncer confronting an underage, troublemaker at the bar."

Darnel wasn't too sure whether to believe that the Hunter was intimidated, by anything. Especially dressed in the BITTS!

"So how long before Detective Shane is ready to go?"

"I'm thinking a week, maybe two. But every little decision that's made in our fine police precinct is being recorded as we speak."

"Wow Darnel, you've got a set of brass berries on you! Don't get me wrong, I know you're a genius and I think it's a really good idea to use audio devices and record them, but wow!"

Both men knew they were rookies at this game, but they had to have every advantage over these animals, who were ruthless and unforgiving; any weakness or mistake and they'd be dead.

"So, what do we do until Detective Shane is ready?" Brogan asked.

"My friend, we keep rattling the cage! Which means the Hunter needs to scope out his next prey!"

"I was hoping we were gonna do some hunting! What's our plan of attack this time? I'm sure you have some kinda ingenious plan already formulated in that computerized brain of yours?!"

"Well, we need to get more evidence. The more we have, the more animals we can take down. So I was thinking we need to get more dirty cops on video, and any other faces that may also be involved. Regardless, we need to flush out the dirty cops, and the idea I have is bound to work wonders. The Hunter needs to get out more, you know, spend more time with nature and the animals. We unleash the beast from the east like never before, and throw him to the animals of Saddleback City. Fear will spread through the criminal grapevine like crack through their veins. The Hunter will be on every animal's trail. They'll be so overwhelmed and distracted with the Hunter's unravelling vengeful rampage, they won't even realize what we're actually doin! We hit every drug dealer, every drug house, and especially every shipment of drugs or money that goes on in this city."

"Dude, that's a lot. There's no way we can cover the whole city and every single…"

"Let me finish, my friend!" Darnel interrupted. "We only focus on what the ATL gang members are involved in. We keep clear of the hotel drug room, but we immobilize and shut down the handful of their bigger business deals and operations!"

"I do believe you are a genius me buddy!"

"They're gonna have to dip into the stash at the hotel if the Hunter stops all other drug operations. If we leave the hotel room open and accessible, it'll be the only resource of drugs and money, in turn helping us get more evidence on video. As long as no one realizes we're setting them up to be recorded at the hotel, this plan might actually work. They'll be lookin over their shoulder, but it'll be the wrong shoulder! If the Hunter shuts down everything, but the hotel drug room is still open for business, these animals will start using up their storage fast. They'll be forced to replenish it by stealing more from the cop shop evidence room, which will also be caught on video. And hopefully this plan will expose most of their bigger players!" Darnel explained with purpose.

"Simple but effective! Regardless of whether they go to the evidence room or come to the hotel, we're sure to get more of the ATL members, and dirty cops on video."

Darnel believed, and had Brogan convinced that they were going to take down nearly the whole ATL organization. With the Hunter attacking their bigger criminal activities all over the city, and eventually a hit on the hotel room, Darnel was certain it would all lead to the demise and fall of the ATL gang. He believed all his calculations and detective work gave him a strong scientific estimate of what they were dealing with.

"These animals must feel that fear, no matter if it's fear of being busted, beat up, not getting that next fix, or even the fear of not making the next delivery," Darnel said counting his fingers as he listed everything. "Whatever the reason, they need to feel fear. Once these animals lose grip of one thing, they'll start messin' up with other things as well."

"I agree, they need to hear the footsteps!"

"Ahh," Darnel said getting what Brogan was trying to say, "if they hear footsteps, they lose concentration, and drop the ball!"

"And that Darnel, usually leads to an incomplete pass!"

"In turn, bringing business profits way down, which could possibly flush out the head ATL boss. Whoever he is, he'll eventually have to surface to try and straighten out his business problems. Or should I say... problem! If the Hunter keeps kickin' ass, then we'll be victorious! Besides, every one of these bastards deserves to be hung by their balls," Darnel said.

"I tell you what, I'm not getting involved with any ball hanging! But the Hunter will kick a couple of these assholes in the nuts for ya!" Brogan said stretching his arms above his head and leaning side to side in his chair.

"You hurting? You look stiff! I can't have my star player going out playin' in this condition! You need a massage!"

"Dude, if you start trying to rub my shoulders I'll..."

"Don't flatter yourself! I'm talkin' about getting a professional in here for ya!"

"No, no, I'm fine."

"Are you sure?" Darnel questioned, watching Brogan try and stretch it out.

"Darnel...the Hunter is pissed!" There was a small quiver in Brogan's voice. "These animals are in for a treat. They fly around on their drugs, worshipping the evil that pays them with a high. They take orders from others, and follow through with them no matter how sick or demented the orders are! They rejoice in the relentless struggle the innocent must endure...these freakin animals DON'T DESERVE TO LIVE IN TODAY'S SOCIETY!"

Brogan slowly and smoothly inhaled deep, to the point that his chest would not expand anymore; then exhaled every molecule just as slow and smooth. "Darnel, you've been such a good friend, there's no one like you. But there's no one like me either. If these animals knew what was coming, they'd be out of town already. I'm telling you, my crime fighting partner, you better hold on to your digital balls, and keep that video surveillance steady! The Hunter is gonna do more than stir the nest, I'm gonna annihilate every single animal until their kind is extinct! I know there's always gonna be more bad guys, I'll deal with them later. Our main goal is to take back Saddleback City. These animals are never going to be safe anywhere! This is why Darnel, I think the Hunter should hunt all the time!"

Darnel looked at Brogan with big eyes. "In broad daylight? There's a thousand percent more of a chance of you getting caught, being hurt, or ending up dead! Even the good cops will shoot the Hunter, look at him, he's freakin scary!"

"Exactly my point! Let's add to the intimidation. If the Hunter is willing to risk everything at anytime, day or night, they'll soon realize they're not safe, ever."

"Everyone will also think the Hunter is completely NUTS!"

"They might not be too far off!" Brogan said almost serious. "These animals want to dish out pain and suffering to the innocent, I'm gonna show 'em pain! They can't fathom the amount of force I'm gonna bring down on them! Darnel, I'm revved up, let's go hunting!"

"I love it when you say that. Almost as much as I like watchin' the Hunter kick ass!"

They packed the Eye Van with the equipment they needed. On the way into Saddleback City, the crime fighters agreed to set up the surveillance camera outside the hotel first. When they got there Brogan put on a disguise, making it look like he was an electrician working for the city, and made sure he had everything he needed to set up the camera. He quickly climbed a light pole that was mostly hidden by some older trees, set up the small digital camera, and was back in the Eye Van within minutes.

"Is the camera still working in the hotel room?"

"Oh yeah," Darnel said pointing to one of the many monitors, "hasn't stopped recording."

Brogan knelt on the floor staring at the black case in front of him, lost in his own thought.

"You're really serious about this aren't you Brogan?!" Darnel said after giving him a minute.

Brogan slowly opened the case and stared at the BITTS. Without looking away from the suit, he answered with an unsettling voice, one filled with pain and pure rage. "I've never been so serious in my life. These animals…they will fear the Hunter!"

Darnel was caught off guard a little, not by what Brogan said, but how he said it. It was eerie, calm, and to the point.

Darnel spun his chair to face Brogan straight on. "Words gonna travel fast! Once you hit that first spot, the next will be harder, and each place we hit will continue to get tougher. They'll beef up security, and take the necessary precautions to protect their investments. And you better believe they'll be ready for a good fight. They battle cops with automatic weapons, imagine what they'll use against the Hunter!"

"Is this your best pep talk, cause it needs a little work!" Brogan joked.

"I'm just tryin' to prepare you," Darnel shrugged. "I want my friend to keep me entertained for a long time!"

"Every time the Hunter hits, it'll be harder! The more prepared and better armed they become, the more nasty and vicious the Hunter will be!" Brogan said with harmful intent.

Darnel had only heard Brogan grind his teeth on three different occasions, this time it sounded like he might have to visit a dentist.

"We're fighting a losing battle, the same as Detective Shane," he said through his teeth, "I don't like to lose!"

Darnel looked up and tried to keep his true feelings hidden. He spoke cautiously, so not to let any cracks in his voice show through. Although he was relentless in his fight, he had a big heart for the people he cared about. And all joking aside, he knew how dangerous the crusade, him and Brogan were about to begin, actually was. "Brogan, I got your back! No matter what!"

"I know you do, that's what makes us good partners! Now, don't be going and getting all sappy on me. We're going to fight each battle with all our pain and rage. We will find the answers you've been searching for Darnel. And I will find the animal that took my Rita…my everything from me!"

Both friends knew, and experienced first hand, what it was like to lose someone they loved. Unfortunately, the knife piercing their hearts was twisted and driven deeper by the fact that the animals who did it never got caught.

Darnel cleared this throat. "I've mapped out various stops our lab rat has made, and there's three 'TAZ's' we can hit really fast."

"Perfect!... But what the hell's a 'TAZ'?" Brogan asked trying to decode what Darnel had just said.

"Target Attack Zone," Darnel said with a chuckle. "They're only a few blocks from one another, no one will be able to alert anyone else or get backup in time."

As Darnel rolled to a stop near the first TAZ, Brogan put on his headgear then looked over at Darnel, "Time to hunt!"

The Hunter shot across the street and went to the right side of the house. Without hesitating he jumped off the fence, grabbed the second story window sill, and dangled there while he reached up and slid the old house window open. It squeaked as it reached halfway. Hanging on the window sill with both hands, the Hunter put his feet up against the house and sprung straight out, his body now horizontal. He pulled hard with his arms, and Darnel watched in amazement as the Hunter shot in through the window. He landed on three limbs without making a sound. His stance enabled him to defend himself from any angle, as he scoped the interior premises.

The Hunter's prowl was that of an animalistic ninja, constantly alert and ready to attack.

Suddenly a lone figure emerged from a bathroom. He pulled his zipper closed, and looked up. There was no time for him to scream, he was frozen from the shock of the masked intruder. With a monstrous leap, the Hunter was on the gang member like a rabid tiger; his feet landed on the ATL gang member's knees. Grabbing the back of the guy's head with his left hand, he brought a right elbow down hard on his neck. The gang member's knees buckled as he lost consciousness. The Hunter held the guy's head and rode his body to the floor, then pulled the unconscious body into the bathroom and out of sight. With lightening speed the Hunter grabbed the guy's arms, crossed them behind his back, and zip tied his thumbs tight to his legs; ensuring not only discomfort and pain, but also no escape.

The Hunter then crept down the hallway further. A squeak in the floor gave another gang member away, but unlike the first guy who was caught off guard; this one was ready for a fight. He flew out of a small closet in the hallway with both arms raised above his head, wielding a ten inch knife that he planned on sinking into the Hunter's back. Before he had taken a full step the Hunter throat chopped him. If the strike was any harder, it would have crushed his larynx. Instantly he dropped the knife and grabbed his throat with both hands trying to breath. The Hunter snagged the knife before it hit the floor, then punched the fiend and spun him. With the same speed and technique he used on the first fiend, the Hunter zip tied his limbs. He then smacked the gang member's neck and stuffed him back into the closet, unconscious. Propping him up against the closet wall, the Hunter drove the ten inch knife through the guy's jacket collar and into the wall.

The Hunter heard Darnel snickering as he shut the closet door.

"What? He decided to come out of the closet, and I decided to put him back in there!" the Hunter said feeling the need to give Darnel an explanation.

"That's funny," Darnel said as he quietly chuckled to himself. "When the police open that door…they're gonna shake their heads! What the hell was he doin in there anyway!?"

The Hunter checked each room on the second floor only to find they were all empty, until he walked up to the last door of the hallway. It was shut, unlike all the others, so he opened it with caution.

"Again with the bricks of dope!" Darnel exclaimed as he saw everything that the Hunter was seeing, "I told ya! These are all the same bricks; they're all from the police evidence room. The only difference is there's not nearly the same amount as in the hotel room, and there doesn't appear to be any money in there either. It's still enough to put everyone in this house away for a long time though. I'll send Detective Shane an anonymous text letting him know that the stockpile of drugs from the evidence room has been moved to this shady apartment!"

The room had less drugs compared to the hotel room. But there were dozens of automatic rifles, shotguns, and a whole slew of hand pistols in a huge trunk that was opened on the floor.

"Darnel, are you getting all this? There's enough weapons and ammo in this room to start a small war in this city!"

"I'm afraid it's only gonna get worse."

The Hunter turned to make his way towards the stairs. Heading down them he could hear some slight sniffling and a loud boisterous laugh.

The fifth step down let out a loud creek, and the laughing quickly stopped.

"Hey shit heads!" came a loud booming voice, "yer gonna get punched the hell out if ya keep messin' around, dicks. I'm tellin' ya for the last time!"

The Hunter's eyebrows went up, and a sly look came over his face. He went back up a step, and then stepped down again. The stair let out another loud squeak that cracked an echo throughout the whole downstairs.

"That's it!" came the booming voice again, "I've had enough! I ain't takin' this shit no more! We got a shit load of dope here, an you two assholes want to play around, makin' noises n shit!? I'm kickin' both yer asses when I come up dair!"

There were thirty stairs, and a long slow left turning railing. From the top of the staircase you couldn't see the bottom, until you rounded the corner. The gang member who was yelling and threatening the two unconscious gang members upstairs, was now on his way to satisfy his paranoid state.

As soon as the Hunter heard one of the steps creak, he sprinted off the top of the stairs with feet flying first. He ran his left hand on the railing to guide him as he flew to the bottom, clearing all the steps on the way down. Before the fiend made it to the fourth step, the Hunter struck him with both feet in the chest. The impact drove the fiend off the step and clear across the twenty foot entrance of the house, losing consciousness, but not altitude as he flew back towards the wall. His arms and legs were trailing behind the rest of his lifeless body, like a flag in the wind. His ass hit first and sank deep into the drywall, freaking out the two stoners in the room on the other side of the wall. Suddenly all they saw was an ass staring at them through the wall, like a mounted moose head. Scrambling to get to their feet, and grabbing for their guns, the two stoned ATL members looked as though they were auditioning for *The Three Stooges*. By the time they had their guns and made it to the doorway to see what was going on, the Hunter was preparing for his next strike.

Both stoned fiends bumped into one another as they tried to fit through the doorway at the same time. They finally made it out of the room only to be greeted by a dark creature standing in front of them. Although both men had guns, they stood frozen, staring.

Drunk, stoned, or sober as a judge, the first time seeing the Hunter usually had the same affect.

With a sharp, fast, outward smack, the Hunter disarmed the thug on the left. Still the fiend just stood and stared. The Hunter then unleashed a flat palm to the solar plexus of the fiend on the right. The force behind his palm sent the fiend flying backwards through the room, over the coffee table, and softly slamming him into the couch flipping it over.

The still standing fiend swiftly pulled another small pistol from his back, and tried to control his shaking hands as he pointed it in the Hunter's face. The Hunter's reflexes were too quick, especially for the stoner. He instantly slapped the top of the gun, then backhanded the fiend in the nose. The gun dropped to the floor as the fiend stood dazed with his arms at his sides. The Hunter quickly reached out with both hands and grabbed the fiend just above the elbows. With an immense tug, the Hunter managed to not only dislocate both the fiend's shoulders, but also separate his forearms from his elbow joints. It wasn't instant, not at all, but the amount of pain was all too apparent once the fiend started shrieking.

The punk couch tackler managed to get to his feet and started climbing over the flipped couch, but was having a hard time as if he were trying to climb a six foot fence, drunk.

The other fiend was still screaming in pain.

"Hunter, dude, put these idiots out of our misery!"

No sooner did Darnel get those words out, and the Hunter stepped past the fiend, then reached back getting a good grip. It happened so fast that Darnel had to play it back in slow motion. It was a hip toss executed perfectly, and harder than any other throw the Hunter had ever done before. The screaming fiend rolled off the Hunter's hip and flew across the room as if he had been shot from a canon. In mid air, and halfway to his dismal destination, both ATL gang members locked eyes, and knew it was inevitable. The punk on the couch reached his arms out as though he was going to catch his flying fiendish friend. But the screaming fiend slammed face first into him, crushing his arms like empty pop cans as they caught the inside ribs of his flying buddy. The collision sent both men flying, and shrieking in pain. The screams stopped abruptly as the two entangled punks slapped against the wall with all their weight and momentum. Darnel's stomach churned as their bones popped like a sadistic bag of popcorn. It was an eerie sound, the popping was almost simultaneous, yet you could still hear all the individual breaks.

"That was insane Brogan!"

"HUNTER!"

"Ok, sorry...Hunter! Jeez! Man, that's gotta be play of the week for sure! HOLY CRAP! Batman who? I'm tellin' you right now, you should be in the UFC!"

"You really enjoy watching someone getting beat up don't you!"

"No...well yeah, I watch the UFC...but with you it's different! I've never seen anyone move like you, not even an animal, and the power you possess is never-ending excitement! And you've got this wild side that emerges when you get pissed! Like that throw! I'm outright amazed! Watching you doin this stuff gets me all fired up! I want so bad to be smackin' heads too!"

"I tell you what Darnel, the next meatball that jumps me, I'll bring over and you can pound on him."

"Cool, but that's not the same dude..."

"Ok, I won't bother."

"I mean, if you get the chance to throw one my way, I should have a little something for that special occasion!"

"I'd be curious to see what gadgets you'd come out with! I'm gonna check the rest of the rooms on the main floor," the Hunter said getting back to business.

He went room to room hoping to have another gangbanger jump out at him. It was an exhilarating feeling. The rush was something Brogan always secretly enjoyed, and used wisely. It always gave him that extra umph, although he had never tried to hurt anyone intentionally. It's not that he never thought about straightening out a few people here and there throughout his life, but he realized the consequences and repercussions that would follow if he ever did let his anger loose. But now, he had a new reason in life.

There comes a time in a man's life when he decides enough is enough. How he chooses to handle the situation that brought him to that point, changes him forever in both his mind and his heart. It can mutate the soul into an unrecognizable creature. Some pick evil to fill their empty and unknown needs and wants. Others pick the good life and try to live with peace and serenity, maybe even trying to spread the love. A handful of people will be caught in the middle, doing a little of both, just trying to survive life.

The Hunter was finally the one person willing to stand up and become the force that would help everyone. The one person who would make a difference, by any means necessary. The one that would help all that needed it, with instinct, anger, and, whatever else he wanted to blend in with his broken soul. The decision had been forced, and final. Any and every animal who preyed on the innocent in Saddleback City was now going to be hunted. It was inevitable, and it was going to get vicious.

The Hunter walked out of the room he had just checked, and Darnel suddenly gasped as an ugly face popped up on his flat screen monitor. A skinny ATL gangbanger had snuck up behind the Hunter. He was so slick and quick that is startled Darnel. The Hunter heard Darnel's gasp, but it was too late! The hideous looking man yanked out a .45 handgun with extreme quickness, and pulled the trigger the second the barrel touched the back of the Hunter's head. The bullet disintegrated on impact with his headgear, and drove the Hunter's head forward. The ugly guy started yelling, laughing, and cursing as he looked down at this forearm and saw fragments of meat and blood covering it. It was the hardest strike to his head the Hunter had received yet. The shot rang in his ears a bit, and pissed him off a lot.

"ARE YOU SERIOUS?!"

The Hunter spun around grinding his teeth hard. His left elbow came roaring back, slicing the air with a whistle, then collided with the ugly guy's cheek and jaw. Before the guy's head had a chance to fly to the side, the Hunter spun the opposite way and followed through with a right elbow, harder than the first. But surprisingly the ugly fiend was still standing. The Hunter then grabbed the guy's unrecognizable hand and wrapped it around his neck choking him; and tenderized his mid section with ten super fast punches. The fiend fell to one knee and looked up barely conscious.

"Cowboy up, meatball!" the Hunter growled.

Darnel couldn't believe what he was seeing; his masked partner was heading back to the Eye Van dragging his semi conscious victim behind him. Darnel opened the back doors and the Hunter flung the ugly guy in. Darnel glanced at the Hunter with a questionable look on his face.

"Partner," the Hunter said not giving up Darnel's name, "I want you to meet one of the meatballs that tried to kill the Hunter. Meatball, I want you to meet the man responsible for the Hunter still walking upright and breathing!"

Once again Darnel surprised and impressed Brogan. With a huge right-cross, from a big black man in a wheelchair, the Eye Van rocked as the fiend flew out the back doors and onto the ground unconscious.

"WOW! That felt good!" Darnel said shaking the pain out of his hand.

"Wow is right, that's quite a punch you're packing there!"

Darnel didn't say too much, not with words anyways, his smile said it all! Both men strapped in and started driving.

"You are the man Darnel, I've said it from day one! This headgear you designed is really amazing! My ears are ringing a little and it made me a tad pissy, I'm not gonna lie, that hurt. But I'm alive to fight another day! It's another life saver designed and fabricated by the D man, eh?!"

Darnel kept driving and looked straight ahead as he answered. "To tell you the truth my friend, I didn't test the helmet to that extent, but…I'm glad it works!"

"What!?"

"Did you realize that you were in and out of that place in no time?" Darnel said changing the subject. "It was freakin quick considering what the Hunter had to contend with in there!"

"I'll beat it," the Hunter said with a cocky nod. "Where and when is the next animal den?! And don't change the subject! What do you mean you didn't test the helmet to that extent?"

"Look, I ran every test that I could conjure up in my weak and fragile state of mind. Just not that one!"

"Well Darnel, I feel much better knowing that you're glad the helmet passed the needed requirements through experiments you never thought of! ...weak and fragile, my ass!"

"That guy came out of nowhere!" Darnel said pulling into the shadows at their next stop.

"I know, he slithered up on me like a snake!"

"I was watching the monitor, then like a big freakin ugly zit, pop, the ugly weasel was starin' right at me! It totally freaked me out!"

"What do we know about this place?" the Hunter asked getting back to business.

"The information I scabbed off the police database has informed me that this joint is always jumpin! It's an apartment building complex type of deal. There's one particular room on the third floor where the drug dealers hand out, I guess there's three of them. The rest of the building is like a party dorm, all the people that live there buy their drugs off these three animals. The police have raided this apartment fourteen times, and nothing ever sticks! Everyone who lives in the building has a cover up to help the dealers every time the police show up. I'm sure some of the police force does business here themselves!"

"That's awesome! It means that every single person in this building is gonna be pissed that I'm messing with their dealers and supply. And they're all suspected animals that feed off the fear of the innocent in this city. Time to hunt!"

"There's a good chance these idiots are armed. But as long as you keep the headgear on you'll be fine!" Darnel joked.

"Alright smartass!" the Hunter said as he disappeared.

"Dude, no goodbye, no hug?" Darnel razzed.

The Hunter made his way to the right side of the building, and spotted an emergency fire escape ladder.

"Just be extra careful in there," Darnel warned.

"How about I be extra mean!" the Hunter said as he leapt up the ladder three rungs at a time like a frog on steroids, reaching the roof in seconds.

"I can see you Hunter, you're right above the balcony! So what's the plan? What silent and sneaky technique of break and enter are you gonna show me tonight?"

"Check this out!" the Hunter said sprinting off the edge of the roof, diving into the unknown. He turned as he flew through the air with his belly up to the sky, with no care of what was waiting on the inside. No care, only anger.

The Hunter reached out with his right arm and fired his grapple. It ripped, and grabbed ahold of the metal and stone building. He feathered the grappling hook trigger to shorten the line as he swung closer towards the open balcony door. It was all perfectly timed, as the Hunter shot in through the open door and picked his first prey.

There was heavy metal music blaring, and the few people in the room were head banging to it. The Hunter was in and out fast, like a light switch turned off and back on. Everyone in the apartment thought they saw something, but the fact there was a party crasher wasn't registering. Nobody had any idea what had just happened, and no one noticed one of there dope buddies was no longer with them.

Again the Hunter shot in, snagged the closest guy, and just as quickly shot back out the balcony door. He feathered the grappling hook and it swung them out past the balcony. Once outside, the Hunter let go dropping the dope fiend three stories. Although the impact was fast and hard, to the Hunters and Darnels surprise, he bounced on the lawn. He had several broken bones and a few dislocations; he wasn't going anywhere, and neither was the first punk picked from the room, laying beside him.

Another gangbanger started to emerge from the balcony doors, which the Hunter was hoping for. The fiend had barely stepped outside when both of the Hunter's feet planted on his chest. The impact was like being struck by a pick up truck. The strike was deliberate and focused on the fiend's chest, but his flight path was unknown.

The crushing impact sent him flying back through the balcony doors and clear across the room. He lost no altitude at all, like a straight twenty foot drive. The two guys standing at the far wall drinking their beer and smoking their crack didn't have any idea of the gross devastation about to befall them. The three gangbangers were bound together by sheer force and energy. The multitude of breaks, dislocations, and their short groans were muffled by the loud music. The psychological effect and the many injuries all three sustained, would keep them off the streets for a long time.

Immediately after the chest kick, the Hunter retracted his grappling hook and it pulled him back out the balcony doors, and up to the roof. Just then, another gang member came out with a fully automatic rifle.

"Darnel, make sure you get me on video, fishing!"

"Boy, what the..."

The Hunter shot his grappling hook out and downward, past the railing on the balcony. He gave a small tug, then released. The grapple came back through the rungs snagging the guys leather belt. The Hunter gave a huge tug, and the fiend with the automatic rifle flew towards the railing with no self control. With a quick flip of the wrist, the Hunter released the grapples grip and brought it back to his arm. As the gangbanger flopped over the side of the railing, the gun went flying and his scream lasted to the thud on the ground.

"Well, you don't have to worry bout that guy anymore!" Darnel said pointing out the obvious.

The Hunter watched as another guy came out onto the balcony. As the gangbanger bent down to pick up the gun his fiendish friend had dropped, the Hunter shot his grappling hook down and snagged him from behind. With a strong, quick pull the gangbanger flew off his feet, shooting straight up until he was eye to eye with the Hunter. The gangbanger blinked in the second of weightlessness, and with a deep, short growl the Hunter pulled the grapple wire. As the grapple hook retracted to the Hunter's arm, the flying fiend struck the gravel and tar roof face first. He then rolled twice on the roof before bouncing up again, shooting over the side. Darnel and the Hunter watched with puzzled smirks as the flying fiend dropped out of sight. He plummeted three stories to the hard ground.

The two crime fighters didn't hear a thud, only a short girly blat. A couple of seconds drooped by before they started snickering.

"Dude, what are you doin? Y'know he's dead!"

"I didn't mean for him to shoot off the edge of the roof like that! I thought he was heavier, that's why I pulled so hard."

"Right, you can use that for your defence. Ok, so how many more are left?"

"I'm heading down to check right now," the Hunter said as he jumped out from the edge and dropped down to the balcony. He stepped to the side of the doorway, and quickly peeked inside. "I see two guys inside. Maybe

I'll climb on the outside of the building around to the other side and go in through a window, being stealthy until I can sneak up and ambush them from behind!?"

"That's a brilliant idea, in fact I was just thinking the exact same th…"

Before Darnel could finish his sentence, the Hunter strolled into the room. With a short glare both gangbangers knew they were destined to meet the masked intruder's wrath.

Guns suddenly started firing, with two unsure, trembling fiends behind them. The Hunter jumped side to side with a forward momentum, trying to dodge the rounds from the two handguns, but was unsuccessful. He was struck several times, and made his last lunge towards the two fiends from several feet away. Landing in front of them he quickly grabbed one of the fiends by his gun wielding hand and yanked hard. There was a loud crunching, popping noise, and then yelps, like a dog that had been kicked. The next strike would end the pitiful yelps. The Hunter jabbed the fiend in the face, jerking his head back and bringing his feet off the ground as if he were just clothes lined. As his head bounced off the wall, the semi concussed fiend caught a glimpse of why he wouldn't have a memory for a few weeks. The Hunter's sharp, fast right elbow struck his chin and it was lights out with definite reconstructive surgery in the near future. The other gangbanger didn't even run, he stood trembling trying to reload his handgun.

The Hunter turned to the last simpleton standing, and watched him finish loading his gun. He then pointed it at the Hunter's head. With a quick sidestep, the Hunter dropped down to a crouching position, and slid forward to stand beside the fiend. With the speed of the Hunter, the gangbanger still had his arm straight out to shoot. The Hunter grabbed the fiend's gun hand, and squeezed his right shoulder at the same time. Then swiftly brought his right knee up and connected with the guy's elbow; the screams were deafening. The guy's arm folded over the Hunter's knee, in the opposite direction.

"That doesn't look right," the Hunter said still holding the wrist of the guy's broken arm. "Let me fix it for you!"

The Hunter smacked his elbow with a palm jab. The fiend's eyes started rolling to the back of his head as the Hunter tossed him. The fiend flipped end for end and slapped the wall with a devastating crunching sound.

Both Darnel and the Hunter were surprised that no one else had come into the room to see what the commotion was.

The Hunter zip tied the two fiends, then searched the dope pedaling pad and found roughly $100,000 in a black bag hidden in a closet. "I think we should do some good with this money," the Hunter said throwing the black bag into the Eye Van. "Whattaya think?"

"Sounds good!" Darnel replied. And the two headed to the next TAZ on the list.

The Hunter took some more hits as their crusade went on into the night.

"So how many shots did you take that time?" Darnel asked as the Hunter climbed back into the Eye Van after clearing another house of unwanted pests.

"I'm ok Darnel," the Hunter said taking off his headgear. "What's our next target?"

"Brogan, it's been a long, hard fought day! We should call it a night! Can't you hear all those sirens! C'mon dude, we've gotten a lot accomplished, call it a night. I'm tired anyway."

"I know we have, but I don't want to quit! I want to do more!"

"Look at it this way, we got more done today than the entire police force has all year! It was a good huntin' trip my friend, very good indeed. But for you to be able to keep doin great things, and keep making a difference, you need to rest."

The drive back to Darnel's wasn't a short one because of the long day the two crime fighters had put in. As soon as they got back to the ranch, Brogan went straight to bed and was sleeping before his head hit the pillow. Darnel on the other hand went down to the surveillance room to watch everything on the big screen. Uncle Reynolds and Denise were curious about the outcome of the day's events, so they joined Darnel. Darnel explained things as the three watched the video footage of the Hunter. They all agreed his moves were so fast and agile it made him blurry, definitely a display of frightening fury.

CHAPTER 13

WILD WEST

It had been five days of the Hunter's relentless reprisal to the animals he hunted down, when Denise insisted the sixth day he had to rest. She was better equipped mentally, and had five years experience as a military nurse before she joined the Marines. Brogan felt guilty for taking time to rest, but knew it was necessary if he wanted to keep fighting full throttle. He spent the day napping and eating; then got a good full night sleep.

Brogan threw both his arms over his head as he sat up in bed and stretched. His eyes were adjusting when they ventured over to the nightstand where a plate of fresh cut fruit and a tall glass of orange juice had been placed. He swallowed four big gulps of juice and stuffed a handful of assorted fruits into his mouth, just as the door flung open.

"Good morning my friend, feelin' better eh?! I'm glad. Now get dressed, we've gotta go! I've got some new information…"

Brogan squinted looking up at Darnel as he finished chewing his mouthful of fruit.

"Giddy up!" he said jumping out of bed, and started to get ready.

"Dude, you sure you're feelin' alright?"

"Yup! Looking forward to hunting! Why do you ask?"

Darnel looked Brogan up and down as he walked across the room in his boxer briefs to grab his pants. With a couple of snickers he rolled his chair over to Brogan and started poking him quick and hard with his forefinger all over.

Brogan flinched every time, "Hey! What the hell?!"

197

"Go take a look at yourself in the mirror," Darnel snickered, which erupted into a huge belly laugh as he wheeled out of the room.

Brogan walked over to the mirror, with his pants in hand, and smiled as he looked in wonder. A snicker slipped from his tight lips.

"I heard that dude!" Darnel chuckled from down the hall.

There were several small, and a few large, dark bruises spread sporadically over his entire body. Brogan shrugged, knowing it was part of the job, then finished dressing and stuffed another fistful of fruit into his mouth before leaving his room.

As Brogan ventured outside, Uncle Reynolds and Denise were just finishing packing the Eye Van. Darnel was already strapped in.

"Ok, let's go huntin'! …You see!" Darnel said shaking his head, "It doesn't sound right when I say it!"

"Cause my voice is altered?"

"No, even when you say it without the headgear it sounds cooler!"

Brogan looked at Darnel as he got into the van, and smiled. "Maybe you should find your own saying then! And by the way, you better watch your back!"

Darnel figured Brogan would get him back sometime, his bruises looked very tender.

"So about this new information?" Brogan asked curiously.

"I heard about a huge hit through the red and blue grape filled donut vine. I tapped into the fine detective's office line, and found out everything we need to know. Apparently Detective Shane overheard a couple of his corrupt coworkers talking about some meeting at The West Hotel. So he rallied his team to keep some eyes on the corrupt coworkers, and stake out the hotel. Needless to say it was a good lead, but there's a standoff between the Saddleback City Police Force and a fraction of the ATL gang as we speak!" Darnel said.

"Well what are we waiting for!" Brogan said eager to get to the hotel.

Suddenly Uncle Reynolds and Denise climbed into the Eye Van.

"Can I help you two?" Darnel asked staring at them questionably.

"Look Darnel, Denise and I are a comin', and there ain't nothin' you can say or do! Now go strap yerself in front of the computers and make yerself useful, I'm drivin'!" Uncle Reynolds said sternly.

Denise helped Darnel get strapped in at the back as Uncle Reynolds clamped the driver's seat back into place, and sat down. Darnel knew better than to argue with his uncle when he was so insistent. Plus it would be easier for him to fill Brogan in on all the details with the computer in front of him.

"Did you know every place we've hit all belong to one massive gang!" Darnel said not wasting any time.

"Naw, that can't be. Some of those gangbangers weren't wearing any colors or symbols."

"Yeah well, I don't know how to say this without sounding like a complete idiot, but my calculations were off."

"Off? Which ones?"

"About everything, the size of their organization and the amount of fire power they have. Somehow they even got ahold of some of my weapons, no doubt police issued!"

"How?" Brogan almost demanded.

"The amount of influence, power, and money their leader has, must be extreme! Not only do they have a lot of money, but this one person controls everything Brogan! Think about that my friend…everything! Every bike gang, street gang, punk gang, and almost the entire police force! Well, maybe not the entire force…yet, but a big enough part where anything in the storage unit and impound at the cop shop is accessible! My research has found all new evidence; not only lawyers and defence attorneys but also judges, and who knows how many on the city council, are all somehow involved in this shit storm. For all we know, it could be the whole lot of them sittin on Saddleback City Council! This new information is astonishing, and it seems to keep growing with each bit of evidence I find. The entire outfit goes by the name, ATL Gang, which is what we saw on some of those gangbangers jackets at Lucky Draw's."

Brogan let a small smirk slip from his lips. "Let me guess… All The Losers!?"

"Ha! No my friend, Above The Law."

Hatred seemed to seep from Brogan's pores causing his face to scrunch up. "We'll see about that!"

Then a concerned look spread over his face. "What about Uncle Reynolds and Denise? No offence Denise! But if they're in the Eye Van and we're seen, or a stray bullet...you know?"

Instantly Uncle Reynolds piped in, "As long as Denise, Darnel, and myself stay in the van, we'll be safe. I reckon you'll be the one in a serious pile of bull droppin's out there!"

"And Brogan, don't forget who you're talkin to. The Eye Van is virtually a tank on wheels," Darnel added to ease Brogan's mind about the idea of Denise and Uncle Reynolds coming on such a dangerous hunt. "The windows are fabricated out of the same material as the plexiglass at the Saddleback City Zoo, and the entire Eye Van is sprayed with the same substance as what the BITTS is made of. I even designed a layer, like the Hunter's suit, into the tires. The results were actually quite impressive... Anyway, it would take a fleet of tanks to take out the Eye Van! Besides, it's really freakin fast, they'd never catch us!"

Unexpectedly the police scanner cut Darnel off. "Shots fired! Shots fired! Officers down! All units respond to The West Hotel!"

Uncle Reynolds pushed the pedal halfway to the floor and tried to keep the Eye Van on the road. The ass end of the van squatted, the front raised, and a massive racing growl seeped from under the hood.

Darnel grabbed the sides of his strapped in wheelchair, "You ok up there Uncle?"

Talking through his clenched teeth, Uncle Reynolds kept both eyes on the road, and both hands on the wheel. "What? It's not even to the mat yet! This things got a little more get up and go! What the hell is up with this steerin' though?" Uncle Reynolds asked scanning the control panel. "I feel like we're all over the road."

"Because we are! Push the yellow button on the steering consol Uncle!"

Denise reached over and pushed the button. The Eye Van dropped, bringing it closer to the ground and distributing its weight more evenly. It was now less top heavy, and more like a race truck. Uncle Reynolds felt the difference as soon as the van was lowered, and pushed the pedal closer to the mat. The ride was quick and relatively smooth.

They came to an abrupt stop closer to the hotel than expected. The entire hotel parking lot, and most of the surrounding area, had police cruisers scattered everywhere. Red and blue flashes lit up the entire block, like spot lights on a stage. The only sirens that could be heard were the ones off in the distance, on route to the hotel. The scene was pure chaos. The SWAT team and officers were scrambling around in bullet proof vests, as civilians ran for safety.

Brogan quickly dressed into the BITTS as stray bullets pelted the van. "Well, I see the Eye Van is bullet proof. Tell me Darnel, has this test already been preformed, or is this a preliminary run with all of us being the crash test dummies?" Brogan razzed.

"Just keep that headgear on Brogan, and…"

"I know, I know, I'll be safe. And call me Hunter when I'm in the suit!"

In a blink the Hunter was out of the Eye Van and charging the hotel. Bullets were flying from every direction, and it made the Hunter angrier to think an innocent person, especially a kid, might be hit by a stray bullet.

"Hunter, you be careful, and kick some ass! You gotta put on a good show, Uncle Reynolds and Denise are watching! Oh, and the police scanner has informed us that there could be anywhere from twenty to thirty ATL gang members throughout this hotel."

"That's it? Didn't you just say the gang was huge?"

The three in the Eye Van could tell by his voice that the Hunter was running hard.

"And I'm sure you've guessed, they're all armed to the teeth! Apparently the ATL gang is tryin' to protect their investment!" Darnel said.

Suddenly a voice caught the Hunter off guard.

"Let the hunt begin!"

"Was that Uncle Reynolds?"

"Yes it was me. I got a little excited in the moment! Are you sure you don't need some help out there? I served my country, I can fight!"

The Hunter picked up his speed. "Let's see if I can bring the numbers down a bit first. I'll let you know if I need backup."

He instantly spied his first prey, and surprised himself by running even faster. He pushed his legs to the limit, he had to, there was a female officer wounded and taking cover by a squad car. Standing over her screaming and pointing an AK-47 in her face, the ATL fiend had already shot her in the upper leg, and was about to kill her. At full speed, the Hunter blindsided the gang member as if he were laying a hit in a football game. Only this full force hit had a lot more aggression behind it. The ATL member lost consciousness instantly upon impact. Giving a huge push at the end of the hit, the Hunter launched the gangbanger's lifeless body further, sending him twice the distance in his flight. His body slammed into the passenger door of a police cruiser, caving the door halfway into its interior, and attracting some unwanted attention.

The female officer stared up at her dark, masked savior in awe. Blood from her leg wound was starting to pool under her. "Who are you?" she managed to whisper.

Suddenly Darnel started to yell, "Behind y..."

The Hunter spun his head fast and saw an M-16 pointed right at them. Just as the Hunter crouched down to shield the lady of the law, the ATL fiend emptied his new clip into the Hunter and the police cruiser. The cop car was rattled with several rounds, two of which sunk into the cruiser beside the officers head, the remaining found the Hunter. With each bullet that hit him, the Hunter felt more rage, and cared less about the pain.

Suddenly there was a steady sound of an empty gun clip trying to find a bullet. The fiend had his finger locked on the trigger. Instantly the female officer drew her ankle backup 9mm pistol, and another sound emerged. It was a deep dark growl, and before the officer's weapon was fully drawn, the Hunter was on a hard sprint. The officer fired three shots at the ATL fiend as he fumbled, trying to reload another clip into his gun. All three shots struck the gang member in the chest. The newly advanced, police issued, stolen Kevlar vest he was wearing might have saved the fiend from certain death, but it would not save him from the disturbing pain he was about to experience.

The vest displaced some of the kick, but it made little, if no difference. The Hunter's right heel found the fiend's rib cage. As his leg extended in an upward motion, several ribs cracked and shattered as the pain stricken fiend was sent airborne from the donkey kick. The fiend was still conscious and in pain, as he flew backwards into a parked police cruiser. His lower legs struck the back side of the police car, and there was a loud clatter of cracking as the fiend's top torso slammed onto the cruisers trunk. His head whipped down smacking the trunk top, as the bottom part of his body flipped up and over. It was a disturbing image as the ATL member flipped several times in the air, and came slapping down, face first, onto the pavement.

The Hunter scanned the chaotic scene to determine his next plan of attack. It was easy for him to distinguish the cops from the ATL gang members, but not so easy to pick out the dirty cops from the good ones.

Squealing tires caught the Hunter's attention. A gang member was using a small, blue four-door car as a weapon against a group of five police officers; one of which was Detective Shane, who was leading the five man cop crusade, firing both his six shooters whenever he could. The cops had barricaded themselves behind a police cruiser for protection from flying bullets during the gunfight. With so many police cruisers in the street, if the blue car hit the cruiser they were behind all officers would unknowingly be sandwiched between two cars. The Hunter's heart skipped a few beats, and he felt that surge he knew so well hit his body like an adrenaline tidal wave. He could feel every muscle strain in his legs as he took off and pushed himself to run faster. The car was traveling fast and the Hunter knew there was no way he could reach all the police officers in time.

Suddenly the gang member driving the blue car bailed out, and the car raced forward heading for the barricaded officers. The Hunter could feel the extra strength in his legs, and his speed increased. This time he felt different, as if advancing again to another level.

The Hunter knew he couldn't use his grappling hooks to save the officers because there was too many of them. But he knew he could reach the car before it collided into them. Moments from the five cops being sandwiched, the Hunter dropped his right shoulder and laid down a destructive hit like never before. He ploughed straight into the backend of the driver's side, over the rear tire. The heroic impact was felt through the ground by all five cops.

The cars deadly westward direction had been diverted to a southerly, suicidal end as it slammed into another parked police cruiser, injuring no one.

The only one hurt was the gang member who launched himself from the blue missile. He had dislocated his shoulder and popped both his knees out when he jumped from the speeding car; and was trying to crawl back to the hotel, when the Hunter spotted him. The crawling creep saw the Hunter storming towards him and froze.

An ATL member inside the hotel noticed the Hunter walking towards his wounded ally, and instantly changed his target from the many police officers to the Hunter. Bullets bounced off the dark figure as he remained in pursuit of the now frozen creep.

The Hunter grabbed a partially open car door as he neared the gangbanger, and with a quick, hard tug, the door slammed into the frozen creep's face. The damage was fierce; he lay motionless on the pavement, no longer a threat.

The Hunter went back and scooped up the wounded female officer and ran her over to the Eye Van. "Stay behind this van and you'll be safe," he said placing her down on the far side of the van.

The female officer was intrigued and startled by the dark saviour's voice. But before she could thank him, or ask any questions, he was gone.

Without any care of the flying bullets, the Hunter scanned the mini war zone for his next prey. He darted in front of the hotel receiving several rounds over his body, sprung on top of a police cruiser, and dove through the air. In mid flight the Hunter shot his grapple hook through one of the second floor windows. It flew over the shoulder of a gang member that was firing an M-16, and still in flight the Hunter gave a huge tug. The small, sharp, steel hooks ripped into the soft flesh of the fiend's shoulder, right through his Kevlar vest, straight to the bone. The fiend was plucked from the window still firing his M-16 uncontrollably until he hit the pavement.

In the chaos of the gunfight, rounds were flying from every direction, and the Hunter knew some of the cops were shooting at him. Some were shooting at him because they had no idea this dark avenger was on the "good guys" side, others were trying to take him down because they realized he was a good guy.

The Hunter finished his dive through the air with a front roll summersault, and noticed a gang member squatting beside a parked car. He slammed into the unsuspecting fiend as he finished his summersault. It was a devastating hockey check that definitely would've made Don Cherry's *Rock'em Sock'em* series. The gang member was already tense from the gunfight with the cops, which made the collision even worse for him. The Hunter checked him into the car so hard, it shattered both the front and back passenger windows blowing them out like a concussion grenade had gone off inside the car. A huge imprint of the gang member's body was now visible in the door. Surprisingly he stood up, dazed and confused he reached out to steady himself. The next three strikes were almost simultaneous. The Hunter punched the gang member in the elbow, then kicked him just above the knee throwing him off balance, and punched him in the face with a fast left jab as he fell forward.

The three strike combo was so fast that Uncle Reynolds stared at the monitor in disbelief. "I reckon we're gonna watch this again later, maybe slow it down a bit though!"

Darnel smirked, "Uncle, that's why I have all these cameras, so we can go home and see what the Hunter actually did. I'm tellin' you two, he's so fast you can't blink or you'll miss something!"

Darnel turned back to the monitors trying to help the Hunter as he scanned the scene. "There's four officers pinned down to your right, you gotta help them!"

The Hunter spotted the four officers behind one of their cruisers that was being shredded by five ATL members with assault rifles, unloading clip after clip. The Hunter ducked and sprinted low behind the parked vehicles, sneaking up on the trigger happy fiends. He jumped over the last car, drop-kicking the first gang member, sending him crashing into the fiend beside him. It was a rib crackling kick.

"I call that the cattle cruncher!" the Hunter grunted.

"Dude, that was terrible!" Darnel said shaking his head. "How about the stampede stunner?"

"Or the buckin' bronco!" Uncle Reynolds piped in.

Suddenly the three remaining ATL members turned there attention, concentrating all their rounds on the Hunter. Several sharp bullets struck him before the Hunter quickly squatted, ripping a large manhole cover from the street to shield himself.

"Darnel, some of these bullets seem to be stinging more!"

"Those odd rounds are probably cop killers, you know, armor piercing bullets!" Darnel explained.

"Great!" the Hunter replied sarcastically.

"You'll be fine, just duck n dodge, stop getting shot so much!" Darnel razed.

Bullets were embedding and bouncing off the Hunter's street shield with a deafening echo. In an instant the sound of rounds rippling off the thick steel was replaced with the distant sounds of gunshots, and three fiends fumbling to reload. From a squatting position the Hunter stretched his left leg back for support, and slid his hands from the sides of the manhole cover to the top of it. He raised the cover, swinging the steel shield over his head far behind him, and fired the ferocious Frisbee. The 120 lb saucer flopped end over end through the air like an obese turkey trying to fly. The airborne rotating disc struck two of the three fiends at waist level, instantly shattering all their bones from the waist down. The third ATL member held up his M-16 assault rifle and aimed it at the Hunter. Before he could squeeze off a cop killing round, a single shot rang out louder than any other since the shootout began. The Hunter watched as the fiend received a round to his side, just under his arm pit. The shot launched him sideways several feet before he landed on the concrete. Instantaneously the Hunter looked to his left and saw Detective Shane standing there with a trickle of smoke oozing from the barrel of his intimidating .44 hand enforcer.

"You see Uncle, Dirty Harry! I told you too Denise, this Detective Shane is one tough, scary cowboy!" Darnel said repeatedly pointing at the monitor.

The Hunter nodded to the detective. "Didn't take him long to return the favor" he thought.

Continuous rounds were pelting the police in the street. Because of the barrage of bullets, all officers were pinned down and couldn't fire off any shots. Several officers had already been wounded, a few with serious, life threatening injuries. It seemed those few officers mysteriously received their wounds from behind.

The Hunter quickly spotted his window of opportunity on the second floor. He sprinted for the hotel, and from several feet away the Hunter dove upward as if going for a Hail Mary pass.

The three crime fighting passengers in the Eye Van watched with anticipation, not knowing what he was going to do next.

Once reaching the full height of his dive, he spread out horizontal, soaring like Superman. Before descending, the Hunter shot out his right arm and the grappling hook obeyed, fetching the roof's edge. Instantly the Hunter retracted the hook and it propelled him straight up through the window. He flew in like a maniac, causing the five ATL members in the room to attack. Instead of firing their weapons, all five rushed the dark intruder without thinking.

With the grapple hook still attached to the roof, and plenty of wire to play with, the Hunter decided to wrap it up quick. He darted in to meet all five charging idiots, with the unseen wire trailing behind him. The gangbangers immediately unleashed a heavy lashing on the dark intruder, each one throwing numerous punches and kicks, and even striking the Hunter with their weapons. The Hunter ducked and dodged the determined degenerates. He blocked some of the strikes to make it seem like he was actually fighting, but none of them caused him any pain or worry. A bunch of seconds flew by and the Hunter shot out of the six man rowdy riot rampage like a squeezed zit. The five fiends hadn't realized that during the scuffle scrimmage, the Hunter's thin grappling line had been meticulously woven around them. In a blink, the Hunter viciously yanked the grappling hook and the wire synched tightly around the five fiends like a giant anaconda. Grunts and groans of pain and clanking bones filled the room, and the Eye Van, as the gangbangers were slammed together.

"There's no mercy," Uncle Reynolds said with a concerned look on his face. "He's relentless...mean!"

"Don't think for one second that if these animals cornered any of us, that we wouldn't be screaming for the Hunter to save us!" Darnel barked defensively.

"I'm just sayin, I reckon these fools would've already realized what a huge problem they have on their hands... the Hunter!"

All five fiends were seriously injured, and tangled tightly together.

"That's quite the mess," Darnel said shaking his head. "Disconnect the wire and the grapple hook from your arm, and leave 'em tied up."

The Hunter was quick to object. "I don't think so! I might need this later! It'll only take a few seconds to undo these hog tied idiots...besides, it might be funny."

"What?" All three in the Eye Van asked simultaneously.

The Hunter moved quick to free his grappling wire from the fiends, periodically punching the mound of meatballs as they spun and flopped on the floor being unravelled. He purposely punched every accessible pressure point as he pulled his grapple hook from the entangled pile of punks. Every strike was fast and hard, adding to their pain and injuries. It took less time to untangle the grapple, than it did to tangle it, and the pain stricken punks weren't going to be a problem anymore.

The Hunter had started retracting his grapple hook back into place when a simultaneous trio sounded from the Eye Van, "Look out!"

A huge man had snuck into the room, and was barrelling toward the Hunter. At the last second the 6'3", 250 lb giant kicked the Hunter in the center of the back, causing him to fly forward. The kick was felt, since it landed on his spine, and the force sent him shooting through the window. Luckily the Hunter's grapple hook was free from the fiends, and still attached to the roof. The giant man headed for the window to witness his wreckage, and had no idea that round two was about to begin.

The Hunter swung out far; with a wide arc he gained a tremendous amount of speed, and returned to finish the fight. Both the Hunter's feet introduced themselves to the giant man's chest as he appeared in the window. The Hunter could tell the guy was solid, but the kick sent him flying across the room, sliding on the floor. The giant man scrambled to his feet before coming to a stop. It surprised the Hunter to see a man that size, with that much agility.

The Hunter promptly flicked the grapple wire, the hook detached from the roof's edge and retracted to his arm. The giant man was not impressed, and charged like a savage bull with his shoulders down ready to tackle and tear apart. The Hunter shot in cutting the distance in half. He ducked under the giant's arm and delivered a left elbow to his ribs. It stung the giant, but hardly slowed him down. Before he could turn around again, the Hunter darted past him with another two elbow jabs. One to his lower back, making him arch in pain, and a right to his chest, which threw him off balance as he tried to find his breath. His recovery was fairly quick, but short lived as the Hunter met him with two flying knees, sending him soaring backwards. Although the giant's quickness allowed him to grab the Hunter by the waist.

"Get outta there Hunter!" Darnel yelled.

Instantly the Hunter unloaded a barrage of bombs, with astonishing speed and immense force behind each punch. The giant kept ahold of the Hunter's waist as he received twice the thrashing that any professional fighter could take.

"You need Denise to come in there and knock that big, burly bastard out for ya?" Darnel joked.

The Hunter continued dropping hard, devastating Muay Thai elbows on the giant's face. As the giant's back hit the wall the Hunter felt his grip loosen. Ten more hard, fast fists took turns as they found their mark again and again. Blood was bursting though every deep cut from the magnitude of every strike. Another short, hard right jab to the dazed giant's face caused his head to jerk back viciously and sink into the drywall, preventing him from falling to the floor.

The Hunter lunged backwards landing on the other side of the room. As his feet made contact with the floor, the Hunter was sprinting full out at the giant, with no compunction. Halfway to his target, the Hunter pounced landing on the giant's chest with all fours. With the amount of force behind the Hunter's rage, the outcome was inevitable and similar to a pedestrian, car collision. Both men crashed through the wall and into the next room, with 2X4's, and drywall debris flying every which way. The Hunter rode the giant's body like a surfboard through the wall, his massive melon bouncing off the floor as they skidded to a stop.

The Hunter, still perched on top of the now unconscious giant's body, scanned the room slowly. As the drywall dust settled, the Hunter spotted four silhouettes, which quickly doubled to eight. The initial crash through the wall startled the eight menacing men. Every gangbanger in the room watched in horrid anticipation as the dust settled. The sight of the dark figure in the middle of the room, perched on one of their own, made the hairs on the back of their necks stand up. Nobody moved as they stared at the dark, masked intruder that resembled a slumbering creature of the underworld. Every man in the room now knew the Hunter was a force to reckon with, and most of them were regretting their decision of joining the gang life, if only for a conscious second or two.

Seconds trickled by and there was still no movement. The dust started accumulating on every motionless object. Suddenly a small cough to the Hunter's immediate right broke the silence, and the rumble was on. The Hunter sprang to the left, kneeing an ATL member in the chin, and fired his grapple hook into another member's forehead. The Hunter's knee was a bit more devastating than the hook, but both were successful in knocking out the two ATL members. His knee had broken every jaw bone and luckily for the fiend, he was out cold quick. The grapple hook, on the other hand, wasn't so quick to disperse unconsciousness. Immense burning formed in the guy's forehead, like a severe ice cream headache. He reached up with hardly any control over his arms, and cupped his face with his hands. The burning sensation intensified and the gangbanger fell straight back, bashing his head on the floor.

A hard right-cross knocked a third ATL member down on all fours. As he pushed himself up to continue fighting, the Hunter kicked both his arms forcing them to bend in the opposite direction. Each kick was unseen, but loud and nauseating, leaving bone breaking results. The ATL member rolled on the floor screaming in agony, before the Hunter's foot stomped the screaming out.

Everything was happening so fast it was hard for the three in the Eye Van to comprehend the Hunter's relentless rage.

"LOOK OUT!" Darnel yelled again, and the Hunter reacted on cue.

Without warning a fourth gangbanger pulled out a sawed off double barrel shotgun. With searing speed, the Hunter grabbed the gun, and pointed the barrel at another ATL member's chest. The gangbanger pulled both triggers before he realized what the Hunter had done. The recoil cracked the wooden stock of the gun against the fiend's face. His head riffled back and his eyes rolled up into his head as he slumped to the floor. The shotgun blast struck the fifth ATL member in his bullet proof vest, and sent him flying backwards across the room with intense chest pains.

A sixth gangbanger dove at the Hunter with lightening speed. The Hunter sidestepped and reached out with a fast and strong grip; his gloved fingers dug in behind the ATL member's collarbone, and with a riveting yank, the Hunter pulled the guy in for one last head to head.

In the Eye Van, all three were sickened by the brutal head butt, but still found humor at the fiend's face mashing into the headgear camera. The Hunter let go as he finished his face to face negotiation, and the momentum sent the sixth gangbanger across the room. Suddenly the Hunter side kicked to the right and struck the seventh ATL member in the ribs. The devastating blow caused the badly broken brute to fly up against the wall. The impact exploded half a dozen bricks from the exterior wall into the parking lot. The lifeless body slid down the wall and flopped to the floor.

The eighth gangbanger stood staring at the Hunter, his mind racing, trying to decide what he should do. He then raised both his arms in the air, and got down on his knees, giving the illusion that he was surrendering. But instead drooped his hands down the back of his neck, inside his Kevlar vest, and squeezed the handles of two large knives. Several razor sharp blades swirled and connected into one blade, making both knives very deadly. The Hunter stepped closer and the thug brought both knives out with a fast barnyard swing, one at each leg. The tips of each knife found their intended targets, as the eighth evil doer struck both the Hunter's upper legs. The result of the savage, slicing attack was life altering, and bloody, as the sharp blades slashed through arteries and tendons. But the BITTS proved impenetrable. The knives unexpected, abrupt stop, caused the fiends hands to slide down over the twelve inch swirling blades. They shredded the idiot's hands, leaving stringy pieces of flesh dangling from his wrists. The gangbangers mouth stretched wide open spewing shrieks as he dropped to his knees, realizing what had just happened.

The swirling blades triggered an image of Rita laying in the ER. It flashed fast through the Hunter's head, and his rage built with a grimacing growl. Still screaming in pain, the gangbanger looked up at the dark intruder with bulging eyes. At the peak of his cry, there was a fast clap, as the Hunter slapped the ATL member's ears with open hands. Instant pops indicated that his ear drums had burst. The gangbanger threw his shredded hands up to cover his ruptured ears. His stringy, bloody hands knotted together and draped over his head like dreadlocks. The Hunter grabbed the fiend's wrists, yanked him to his feet, and booted his chest with a heavy left foot. His screams of agony ceased, as his unconscious twitching body skipped across the floor, like a drop of water in a hot pan. There were no words from the Hunter as he continued his collision course with certain intent.

Uncle Reynolds and Denise would both look at Brogan differently from now on. They realized this seemingly glorified gore was not the Hunter's desire. But they now could see the horrific pain Brogan was enduring from losing Rita. Watching the Hunter pound punks with such rage and wrath told all three in the Eye Van that there was still a tremendous amount of pain. Enough to drive weaker men insane.

The Hunter could hear several fully automatic weapons firing from the next room. He wanted to stay clear of being shot again by the armor piercing bullets. There was no need to take unnecessary damage this early in the battle, so he would have to improvise.

Suddenly another image of Rita, smiling this time, invaded the Hunter's thoughts. A low agonizing growl started to build in the Hunter's gut, and it slowly built up pressure. His body surged with adrenaline like never before. He paced back and forth until the growl became disturbingly wild. Just when the Hunter thought he was going to explode, he reached down and picked up an overturned fridge. There was a lot more power skulking inside him. He could feel it, but wasn't able to harness it anymore.

The amount of power and rage behind the flying fridge was enough to deliver carnage in the next room. The 400 lb flying food keeper slammed through the wall and ploughed clumsily into the next room. It freaked out the five men inside as the wall exploded and a white whale flew in. Bones cracked and ligaments tore as the fridge found three fiends, eliminating two of them from the equation. The third fiend survived the fridge attack, receiving only a broken left arm and some fractured ribs. But standing back up wasn't the smart thing to do. The Hunter followed the fridge through the wall, like a running back follows his fullback through the line.

The fridge door ripped off on impact and was soaring across the open room. With no hesitation the Hunter snagged the door out of the air and slapped the third injured fiend's whole body with it. More bones crunched as he flew across the room, no longer a threat.

Spinning around to finish the last two, the Hunter received a butt of an M-16 on the left side of his neck. The forth gangbanger hit his target, and the fifth was winding up to do the same. Quick as a blink, the Hunter grabbed the guys head and blocked the rifle swing. The fiend found the floor fast and started drooling from the blow to his head. Another furiously panicked swing found nothing but air. The rifle made a heavy whistling sound passing under the Hunter's feet as he jumped to avoid the swing. Before the gangbanger finished his backswing, the Hunter landed a Muay Thai elbow on top of his head. He folded to the floor with severe damage to his spine as his body weight collapsed on his own misguided limbs.

The Hunter moved on, and the three in the Eye Van watched with anticipation as he checked four more rooms without incident. As he came up to the next room, the Hunter could definitely tell it was occupied by quite a few ATL's. The sound of gunshots persistently polluted the air. The Hunter opened the door and shot in. There were ten ATL members, all concentrating their murderous attempts towards the police outside. The Hunter snuck up between two gangbangers, and with bullet speed shot both his fists sideways into their necks. Unconsciousness settled into the unsuspecting animals as two others turned around and charged. The Hunter quickly recognized the two charging idiots as the dirty cops from the hotel. More adrenaline started rushing through the Hunter's veins. He lunged forward and slid six feet into his next two targets releasing a gut punch for each of the poisoned police. Both bodies flew backwards out the window with tremendous force. The dirty cops screamed as they fell two stories, before the eerie sound of their broken bodies caving in a police cruiser's roof.

Six gangbangers remained in the room, two continued to shoot at the cops outside, while the other four ran at the Hunter. They flew forward with fists of fury and the Hunter retaliated with his own ominous onslaught. The four threw punches and kicks with evil fibre behind them. Each time the Hunter received a shot, he gave four back. The amount of anguish and anger behind the Hunter's strikes was causing the four fiends to feel the pain, and slowed them down.

"Take this, ya scurfy pigs!" shouted the skinny fiend at the window as he threw a grenade at the cops outside.

The grenade put a big dent in the window casing, then bounced to the middle of the room, where it came to a rolling stop. All fighting ceased, and every man stared at the bomb. Two seconds seeped by in slow motion, and then panic set in for almost everyone. ATL members ran in all directions trying to find some sort of sanctuary. Reacting on his instinct to protect, the Hunter ploughed through the standing jumble of gangbangers and dove on the grenade as if it were a fumble. The BITTS absorbed most of the explosion, but it still had the same ear ringing damage; and the Hunter felt like he had received a foot stomp to the gut from Andre the Giant.

The fiends were still focused on holding their ringing ears when the Hunter attacked. The three in the Eye Van had no idea how many strikes the Hunter let loose as the cameras caught the six fiends collapsing to the floor.

"That's another one we'll have to watch in slow motion when we get back home!" Denise chimed.

"Hunter!" Darnel interrupted as the Hunter was about to leave the room. "I just noticed the tracking monitor is lit up, our little lab rat is in the next room over, and he's got seven friends with him."

The Hunter grabbed two unconscious bodies off the floor, one in each hand, then spun viciously around twice before releasing them. Both bodies blew through the wall scattering debris everywhere, then came to a scrunching halt in the middle of the room; surprising the ATL gangbangers. All eyes were fixated on the dark intruder who had just blasted through the wall. Nobody moved, or attacked, they just stood and stared.

Suddenly two huge pit bull's shot out of the ATL group, flying through the room side by side as they lunged at the Hunter. It was an attack that was not only animal instinct, but had definitely been rehearsed several times before. The Hunter spun sideways as the dogs flew past, snapping at him, trying to grab a bite. Too quick for anyone to see the Hunter reached out snatching each dog by the back of their necks. With a snapping, snarling pit bull hanging from each hand, the Hunter stood in a Taekwondo stance to indicate he was ready to rumble.

None of the fiends fired a shot from their weapons, but used them like baseball bats instead, swinging at the Hunter like they were trying to hit a home run. The Hunter turned towards the fiends, attacking with his K9 nunchucks, and unleashed a barrage of bites. Every time one of the fiends delivered a shot, they received several bites from one of the defending pooches. Pieces of bloodied flesh spurted into the air, and shredded pieces of clothing fluttered throughout the room as the brawl ensued. In the end, every fiend was on the floor in critical pain, either sobbing or screaming as they held onto their bloodied limbs; which had received numerous bites and dozens of puncture wounds from the savagely sharp teeth.

The lab rat had come out of the attack with less wounds than his comrades, and Darnel wondered whether the Hunter had planned it that way on purpose.

Both pit bulls were shaken up and seemed to have very little fight left in them, but tired or not, they were born and bred to bite.

Suddenly the lab rat scampered to his feet and tried to make a run for it. The Hunter quickly underhand tossed both dogs toward the escaper.

One of the dogs chomped on the lab rat's right ass cheek, as the second dog found his left one. Once attached, both dog's found the remaining fight inside them and viciously started shaking their heads. With the dogs not touching the floor, and hanging from his ass, the lab rat ran around the room squealing. The three in the Eye Van, and the Hunter, could not help but find the scene refreshingly amusing. Then to everyone's surprise, the lab rat jumped out the window with the dogs in tow, falling two stories and performing a sinister belly flop on the asphalt. Both dogs released their grip on impact and scampered away. The lab rat lay unconscious with several broken bones from the fall, and two big chunks of pants and meat torn from his ass.

The Hunter looked outside to see how the cops were doing in the gunfight.

"LOOK OUT!" Three different voices rang in his ears, as a huge set of arms wrapped around the Hunter picking him two feet clear off the floor.

With both power and speed, the Hunter's elbows found their mark as he continuously threw them backwards. The downpour of elbows was distracting enough that the attacker loosened his tight grip; allowing the Hunter to spin his body around face to face with his willing prey.

Darnel gasped as he recognized the Hunter's attacker.

The Hunter was shocked when he realized it was the same massive giant from the fight at Lucky Draw's, but surprisingly he had no marks on his face from their previous encounter, and now had a goatee.

Another blitz of fists and elbows rained down on the giant mans neck, head, and face. Deep cuts formed and his flesh split open exposing meaty tissue. Once again his grip loosened and the Hunter unleashed more devastating punches to the giant's melon, allowing him to drop from the python grip. Now on his feet, the power behind each strike would have a long lasting effect on the giant. The Hunter unleashed an ear clap followed by chops to the neck, and several quick boxing punches. The massive, suspected gang leader was teetering, and the Hunter exploded a bunch more elbows and flying knees. With each blow, blood was flying off the giant like a dog shaking water off his back. With one last attempt to squash the dark intruder, the massive monster blasted the Hunters chest with an exceptionally powerful, punch. The Hunter flew backwards smashing through the window.

"That felt like the silverback's crushing blow," he thought as he shot his grapple hook through a different window in the same room.

The massive man had somewhat regained his bearings and started walking towards the window to see the destruction he delivered to the Hunter. Before he got halfway across the room, the Hunter swung in through the other window landing on the giant. The impact caused his feet to shoot out from under him and sent him crashing into the small kitchen. The Hunter followed fast with every intention of finishing the big burly bastard off, but he wanted him to feel the effects for a long time. Cupboards busted open as the giant ploughed into the kitchen, with pots and pans littering the floor. The Hunter reached down and scooped up two, twelve inch cast iron frying pans from the floor. The Hunter unleashed several super fast heavy shots in a row, all to the giant's head.

"TIMBER!" Darnel yelled as the giant fell slowly face first into the floor, shaking the entire building.

The Hunter sprinted for the window and dove out through it as if there was water to land in. A bunch of police, and a few others, witnessed the strange, dark figure stunting through the window, and had no idea he was a good guy.

The Hunter shot the grappling hook out, latching it onto another open window. Swinging like a modern day Tarzan from his high-tech vine, the Hunter spotted several ATL gangbangers firing on police.

Five police officers had taken cover behind a bullet riddled squad car. The animals were trying to steal back the large amount of drugs and money the police had already retrieved from the hotel and packed into a SWAT van.

The Hunter decided to take a big risk and try another indoor attack. The radius of the Hunter's long swing enabled him to bring his momentum to a body breaking speed. His intentions were realized too late by the group of ATL members inside the room. They didn't have enough time to yell, let alone point their weapons at the fast approaching dark figure. The Hunter aimed for the middle of the pack and tightened up for the collision. The force that the Hunter unloaded, from his human cannonball state, was overwhelming and merciless. He bowled through the tightly formed group, his speed hardly diminished. The swing enabled the Hunter to fly out the other window, and up on the roof.

The Hunter was retracting his grappling hook long before any of the ATL members were back to their feet. None of them knew what hit them, and three of them were out cold. The five that stayed conscious through the human wrecking ball ordeal, were still quite dazed and did not see what was heading for them next. The Hunter stretched out his arm, as he stood on the roof, casting his grappling hook down in through the window, fishing for fiends. His first cast snagged a big fighter, with a massive pull and a quick flick, the large gangbanger flew off the ground. He struck the wall with bone crushing force, not making it out the window. Before the first fiendish fish had landed, the Hunter's grapple got another nibble. This time, the hook sank deep into the shoulder of his catch. One of the three prongs on the grapple hook snagged the edge of the guy's bullet proof vest, allowing the other two prongs to pierce straight through his shoulder. The snagged ATL fish screamed in agony as he reached out and grabbed one of his buddies. The Hunter let loose a deep growl and yanked viciously. With his reflexes being so quick, there was no time for the two gangbangers to stop the inevitable. Both flew off their feet and were heading for the roof, towards the Hunter. Police on the ground could see the dark stranger fighting the ATL gang, and continued to watch in awe.

Suddenly the Hunter sprinted off the roof and dove straight for the two on their way up. They nearly reached the roof when the Hunter met them in mid flight, with no mercy. The airborne collision sent both gangbangers flying; their lifeless bodies flopped and flapped uncontrollably through the air, until they struck the pavement hard.

After his mid flight strike, the Hunter completed a front roll, allowing his feet to make contact with the ground first. He landed in an all out sprint heading for the two remaining ATL members; who opened fire, striking him all over with armor piercing bullets. One ATL member reacted quickly, and was able to elude the Hunter, but only for a moment. As he ran away, the Hunter swiped at him, catching one of his legs and sending him skidding along the pavement. The slower of the two received full punishment to his guts, and went down raunchy and unconscious. The stench was overwhelming and the Hunter knew the gangbanger's bowls had blown out. The Hunter spun around to see the luckier of the two running away with a limp.

As he stood surveying the premises, he noticed the gunshots were few and far between, meaning the police were finally getting the situation under control. Then suddenly loud shots rang out from behind a Sedan; the driver's door had been ripped clean off. The Hunter spotted another ATL member, leaning against the passenger door, shooting at the police. The Hunter took off on a sadistic sprint that would lead to the unsuspecting gangbanger incapable of eating solid food for awhile. His feet shot in through the open driver's side, before colliding with the closed passenger side door. The door broke free from its hinges and slapped the squatted shooter like a beaver's tail smacking the water; with devastating results. The Sedan's door sandwiched the gangbanger into a parked police cruiser. The way his body slid off the cruiser and slumped to the ground indicated he had broken too many bones to fix all at once.

The Hunter then spotted the limping ATL member heading for an alley. "Where you going meatball!?" the Hunter whispered.

With three giant sprinting leaps the Hunter dove upwards and shot out his grapple hook. The hook snagged the roof's edge and the Hunter was swinging once again. The limping fiend reached the entrance to the alley, thinking he was going to get away. Suddenly a kick to his side slammed him into a dumpster. The Hunter started walking towards the fallen fiend and stopped dead, staring at him as he stumbled to his feet.

Darnel gasped, "Holy shit! That's him! That's the bastard!"

Both Uncle Reynolds and Denise stared at him blankly, not knowing who "the bastard" was.

The Hunter's arms went limp and drooped beside him. His knees buckled, noticeably, and he fought to stay on his feet as he stood face to face with Rita's killer. Horror-stricken and numb, the Hunter watched as the coward turned and tried to bolt. Limping as fast as he possibly could down the dark alley; not knowing he had inadvertently led Brogan to become the Hunter. The limping ATL member knew this dark stranger was the one taking out his gang buddies, and that he had to escape to save his own ass.

Images of Rita flashed through the Hunter's head, as he watched the escapee hobble down the alley. He couldn't help but think of the old scary movies he used to watch, when the person running away would constantly look back over their shoulder. As a kid, Brogan remembered thinking, "Stop looking over your shoulder, you'll be able to run faster!" Although it wouldn't matter if this fiend was riding a rocket, the Hunter would catch him.

Surprising to the three in the Eye Van, Rita's killer limped out of sight while the Hunter stood staring, completely lost in his memories of Rita. Suddenly a loud gunshot nearby acted like a starter's pistol, snapping the Hunter out of his loving and desolate thoughts. His legs exploded as the adrenaline rush surged through his body as if his blood was on fire. The continuous rush pushed the limits of the Hunter's own physical boundaries, making the BITTS throw back crazy readings and information about the Hunter's heart rate and more.

"That doesn't look like the Hunters usual sprint," Darnel said as he watched him take off after the fiend. "He looks more like a rabid animal."

Although the growl that erupted from the depths of his pain and suffering did not sound like any animal ever heard before. It was filled with torment and absolute rage. With each sprinting stride the growl intensified.

Rita's killer could hear the growl, and panicked more the closer it got. Sweat dripped from his face as he ran up to a building, and checked every door looking for an escape.

"FINALLY!" The fiend yelled bolting through the open door he just found. Slamming it shut behind him, he quickly grabbed a chair to prop up under the doorknob. He knew he would have to keep running to elude his pursuer, and was happy to see an elevator in front of him as he spun around. The older building was being renovated, and he hoped the elevator was working. He jumped onto it quickly pushing the top floor button, hoping there was a way to escape from the roof. Before the elevator doors closed, he watched in horror as the door he barricaded, disintegrated into small unrecognizable fragments. A dark figure stood motionless in the doorway, fixated on the fiend. A high pitch squeal seeped out of the fiend's lips as the elevator doors closed. The Hunter had a feeling the fiend was headed for the roof, and decided to take the buildings outside fire escape, to meet him there. He jumped from the doorway, across the alley to the adjacent building; ricocheting off it and landing on the fire escape ladder. Once on the stairs, the Hunter continued his hunt, not touching any of the ten steps between each floor. With one or two short, strong leaps the Hunter would round the corner and spring for the next landing.

The rooftop door burst open, and the frantic fiend emerged panicking, looking for a way out of his predicament. As he stepped out onto the rooftop, he instantly received a foot to the chest. He flew back slamming into the rooftop door, that he'd just closed behind him, then stumbled forward towards the Hunter. The Hunter reached out and grabbed a handful of the fiend's police vest and pulled it hard. He flew forward, and the Hunter watched as the fiend landed and skidded along the gravel and tar rooftop.

"OK MAN…I GIVE UP!" The gangbanger pleaded for his life as he came to a grinding stop, and made it back to his feet.

"I DON'T!" the Hunter taunted as he delivered a devastating left kick to the fiend's ribs, and a right palm to his chest.

Even with the Kevlar absorbing most of the impact, the power behind the palm strike broke three of the fiend's ribs and launched him backwards again.

"What the…Shit!…Man!…What are you doing?" The fiend protested as the Hunter grabbed ahold of his Kevlar vest and spun around dropping to one knee.

The overhead throw from behind launched the fiend twenty-five feet, and this time he didn't skid across the roof. He slammed into a large air-conditioning unit that stopped him from going over the edge, and surprisingly, slowly returned to his feet despite his intense pain.

"Who…are you?" Rita's killer asked as he swayed back and forth. "What do you want from me?!"

"YAAT…" the Hunter growled.

The dark, disguised voice sent shivers down the fiend's spine increasing his pain.

"You stabbed and killed an innocent woman outside the Saddleback City Hospital. WHY?!"

The Hunter could see in his eyes that he was replaying the scene in his head, wondering how to get out of the situation he was currently in.

"Man…I was higher than a….it's a new drug man! It wasn't my fault!" he said, thinking that if he sounded truthful then maybe the dark strange creature would have mercy. "I don't remember much. It was a new drug. It was harsh. I really didn't know what…what was really going on. Man, it was sort of like a movie…or a video game. Y'know? I was high man!"

The Hunter's reaction was too fast, and with no hesitation it was virtually impossible to see coming. Both his fists exploded into the guy's chest and abdomen. Then everything seemed to turn into slow motion as the Hunter walked to the edge and watched Rita's killer fly off the roof and out twenty feet before gravity took affect.

"I was high," he pleaded one last time, an expression of pure fear on his face as he fell.

"I WAS IN LOVE!!!!" the Hunter yelled anguished, and suddenly thought that maybe fear wasn't enough for Rita's killer to endure. There was no pleasure, no retribution in watching him fall to his death. It was more like watching a bug get flushed down a toilet.

Then a soft flash stopped the Hunter in his tracks. It was so bizarre that it grabbed and squeezed, not only his attention, but his heart as well. Rita's voice drifted clearly through his head. "No," she whispered.

The Hunter immediately dove off the roof pulling the wing cords for the glide suit. With his arms tucked and his feet together, he started gaining on the flailing, falling felon. The Hunter came in fast and caught up to the fiend who had already fallen twenty stories. He wrapped his legs around the fiend's waist, and the fiend grabbed, with all his grip, whatever he could on the Hunter. The Hunter spread out his arms, opening his wings, but their descent slowed very little. Twenty-five feet from the ground, the Hunter shot out his grappling hook, aiming for anything in the dark alley. It snagged a window sill, flipping both men into the air and sending them flying in different directions. The fall was fine, but the landing was brutal. Rita's killer was still conscious, and the Hunter wasted no time grabbing and zip tying the fiend's limbs in behind his back.

Sirens could be heard in the night sky.

The Hunter then turned and started heading for the shadows of the alley.

Several police officers, including Detective Shane, had witnessed nearly the whole ordeal, except for the landing. Flashlights, guns, and badges filled the once dark alley.

The Hunter felt better knowing Detective Shane would recognize that scumbag as Rita's killer, and he would do what was best. Nothing would keep Brogan from the trial of this horrific crime, in the Wild West.

CHAPTER 14

TRIAL AND ERROR

"I shoulda let him drop to his death! He wouldn't have felt a thing; he might have had a heart attack and died on the way down."

Darnel threw a fatherly stern glance at Brogan, "Dude, there's no way you'd be able to live with that on your conscience. Especially after hearing Rita whispering as clear as though she were standing right next to you."

Brogan was antsy and aggravated.

"Oh I think I could go on living, and I'd have no qualms about looking in the mirror either! All I'm saying is that it's been six months already, he's gonna get off!" he roared angrily.

"Brogan, at two o'clock this afternoon, YOU, my friend, and I will be watching and smiling as they sentence this animal...to life!"

Brogan immediately picked up on Darnel's hesitation. "Rita's killer and the rest of the ATL idiots will get nothing. They'll have some freak lawyer come in and get them all acquitted, you watch!"

"Brogan I'm tellin' you, those ATL members and the handful of dirty cops will be doin time. You helped me gift wrap all the video surveillance and audio evidence, and deliver it to Detective Shane. You saw how much incriminating evidence we gathered together, there's not a jury out there that wouldn't convict every last one of those gangbangers once they see all that evidence. They can't get out of this one my friend, none of them can."

Brogan wanted to believe Darnel but he couldn't bring himself to feel as confident about the trial. Darnel poured more coffee in Brogan's already half full cup. The aroma of coffee triggered a deluge of emotion, taking him right back to the first time he saw Rita in the coffee shop. It seemed, recently, almost everything triggered flash backs; anything to bring him closer to Rita again, in any form.

Darnel smirked as he topped up Brogan's cup. "Y'know what your problem is?"

"Enlighten me Darnel, you wise ass…I mean wise old bastard!"

"For months and months you've done nothing but fight crime."

Brogan slurped his coffee and squinted at Darnel, "So?"

"When you first started fightin crime as a superhero, you had some pretty nasty guys to contend with. The amount of guys you were roundin' up and handing over to the police for lock up was never-ending…until the shootout at the hotel. Before you had competition, now there's nobody to give you a go around! Well, except for that skinny purse snatchin kid. Y'know, the one in the Grab n Go parking lot!?"

Brogan's eyes got big, "Yeah I remember that little putz, holy crap he was fast!"

Darnel smirked knowing it would irk Brogan. "Y'know Brogan, you're lucky you caught him!"

"What?! Are you kidding me, I was all over him! Sure he's probably the fastest kid that I've ever chased down, but I totally caught him!"

"Sorry my friend, I've seen the video footage, and it doesn't lie. The kid clearly slipped going around the corner, that's how you caught him so easily."

Brogan's eyebrows grew closer, "No way man! Whatever!… Are you serious! C'mon Darnel, don't tell me that now! You know it took me seven minutes to chase him down, it was an exhilarating hunt. But I wanted that trophy, because that kid was so freakishly fast!"

Darnel felt bad and gave up his poker face, "Dude I'm messin' with ya! You totally ran down that little punk!"

The troubles and tribulations that Brogan and Darnel had encountered over the last several months had definitely brought them closer. They were more like brothers than partners now.

Both men snickered and Darnel leaned over and punched Brogan in the shoulder.

"Holy, c'mon man, not so hard, eh!"

"Brogan, you need a challenge, or you start getting restless. Hence you worrying about the trial. In the last several months we've busted up the ATL gang immensely, and crime has dropped in Saddleback City. But most importantly, we caught and handed over the animal responsible for Rita's death!"

"I know Darnel, but with all that freaking evidence, they should all be behind bars already!"

"I agree with you my friend, but we have to wait out the justice system, and hope they deliver the maximum sentence for each asshole! Patience my friend, patience!"

Darnel gave the best fake optimistic smile that he could muster. "Besides, the amount of credit that Detective Shane will get for all your hunting, he'll make sure nothing goes awry."

Brogan couldn't hide his unbelieving expression, "For some strange reason Darnel, I think it's way out of our league, and way out of reach, even for Detective Shane's fierce long arm of the law!"

"Well, we have an hour before the trial starts, let's get ready and get a good back row seat at the courthouse! Y'think it would be too obvious if we took some popcorn!?"

Both men let out a half assed chuckle.

"Oh yeah Brogan, Denise did your laundry for you, and left it on your bed.

Everyone at the ranch was absolutely delighted to have Brogan stay and help out there. He was highly appreciated, even loved. He was family now. And they were intrigued when the beast from the east was unleashed and caught on video. They believed in everything the Hunter was doing for the people of Saddleback City, and they enjoyed watching how he did it.

"I'll have to thank her for doing my shorts," Brogan said with a concerned look on his face. "Don't you see anything wrong with that? I'm a grown man, I can do my own laundry!"

"Denise considers you family now. Sure she doesn't say much, but what she lacks in conversation she compensates everywhere else. In other words, she's just doing part of her job. And she's told me before that she really likes doin laundry, calms her or something like that. Anyway, don't try to take anything away from her, she'll knock you out dude!"

"Then I'll just thank her, and be on my way."

Brogan and Darnel shared another laugh, but both men knew Denise wasn't someone to tangle with.

The Escalade glistened in the hot, unbiased, afternoon sun as Uncle Reynolds chauffeured the two crime fighters, dressed in their civilian's, to the courthouse. Once there, Uncle Reynolds parked up the street to stay clear of the media frenzy at the front doors. Their plan was to find a spot at the back of the courtroom, lay low, keep quiet, staying unseen and unnoticed. They would show composure, be calm, and there would be no outbursts from either of the two justice seekers, no matter what the outcome.

The anticipation was excruciating, and Brogan was on edge. The reason for today's trial was why Brogan became the Hunter. It had consumed his entire existence and was something he had been seeking since that dreadful day Rita was taken from him.

There was only one defendant being tried in the courtroom today, but most of the courtroom was filled with ATL gang members, proudly wearing and flaunting their gang symbols and colors. The ATL members and dirty cops who were busted at the hotel raid had later court dates. The dirty cops were being investigated by the one and only Saddleback City Police Force, which probably meant other dirty cops would do the investigation and come up empty.

The two secret crime fighters never spoke as they made their way towards the courtroom, but they were getting good at reading each other. Both of them were blown away by the amount of people that showed up for the hearing. A lot were friends of Rita's who came to finally see justice served for their dear friend. Others were there because that same bastard on trial for murder had previously hurt them and gotten away with it. Mr. Mo Daft was not well liked by anyone, except his gang banging buddies.

Going into the courtroom was a frisk frenzy as everyone was checked for weapons. When Darnel and Brogan entered they noticed friends, family members, and some strangers all sitting on the right. Basically everyone whose lives, at one time or another, had been touched in a negative way by Mr. Mo Daft. And they were all seeking retribution for his wrong doings. Also on the right were three prosecutors with their legal team, and a handful of police officers in case things got out of control. All the justice seekers barely filled the right side of the courtroom.

Darnel and Brogan sat at the back on the righteous side. On the malevolent side, there wasn't even standing room. It was a packed house, starting with three lawyers, and what seemed to be all of the ATL gang members, except for those awaiting trial. There were security guards strategically positioned on both sides of all the courtroom doorways. But no matter how many security guards were there, all the ATL members packed into the courtroom, was all too intimidating.

"It's freakin eerie in here, eh!?" Darnel whispered, Brogan hardly hearing him.

He was talking about the silence that came from the left side of the courtroom. The right side had created a soft buzz as everyone whispered among themselves. But the left side was a pure hush.

Brogan nodded wondering if there would be some kind of half assed rescue attempt if this animal was found guilty. Anything was possible with this gang.

Darnel leaned over with the same torturing whisper and Brogan strained to hear. "If anything erupts in here, we're severely outnumbered!"

Brogan nodded and scanned the room quietly.

"I wasn't lookin' for that type of answer!" Darnel yelled as loud as he could in a whisper. "I was kinda hoping you would say something in the lines of, "Oh Darnel don't you worry about a thing. I got your back and there won't be nobody hurtin' you"!"

As both men waited patiently for the trial to begin, they noticed Detective Shane sitting in the second row behind the three prosecutors. And they both, for a few reasons, felt reassured knowing he was attending the trial. Knowing that tough, son of a bitch was nearby and on their side was more than a confidence builder. Just then Detective Shane turned and shot a quick glance at Brogan as if to say, "We got the scumbag, and he's going down!"

"Did you see that?" Brogan questioned. "How'd he pick out where I was sitting so quickly? He must have seen me come in. I'm just glad he's on our side!"

Brogan had still kept in constant contact with Detective Shane the whole time he was crime fighting as the Hunter. And Detective Shane was quick to contact him when Rita's killer had finally been arrested; leaving out the fact that a masked superhero was the one who actually caught the animal.

Without warning everyone's attention was drawn to the huge oak door at the front right of the room, as a long mournful creak was released from its seemingly old, weary hinges. Brogan gasped slightly as a large creature emerged from the backyard of the house of law.

"What the hell!?" Brogan almost broke a whisper in the silent room. "Darnel! Are you seeing this? That's him...right?" Brogan tried very hard to contain his panic in a whisper. "I mean, except for the uniform and the beard thing, that's him! That's the massive guy from Lucky Draw's and the hotel!!"

"He had a goatee at the hotel...but not at Lucky Draw's..." Darnel trailed off, trying to figure the whole thing out. "Holy freakin crap, what's goin on here?"

The massive man lumbered out and took his place beside the judge's bench. Brogan's eyes spanned quickly over to Detective Shane hunting for some kind of reaction, but immediately realized he didn't recognize, or even know this huge gang affiliated hooligan.

"I told you something was weird about his whole thing! I got no idea what," Brogan said trying hard not to break the whisper mode. "But something is definitely messed up!"

"Calm down," Darnel whispered. "Let's see where this is goin."

Both men were certain this man was the monster from both Lucky Draw's and the hotel, and possibly even the ATL gang leader.

Suddenly his voice boomed across the room, startling most people. "The jury may enter."

One by one, twelve jurors spewed slowly from a hidden door, until all the seats were filled. Each jury member had to walk past the oversized bailiff to take their judgemental place. The burly bailiff stared down at them with a look of disdain, as if he were somebody special.

"All rise, the honourable Judge B. Mannly is presiding!"

"His voice is different somehow…" Brogan thought as the burly voice grumbled loudly across the courtroom.

"The voice is different!" Darnel leaned over to whisper.

The first to stand, with hardly any ruckus or noise, was the entire left side of the room. They were quick and uniformed in doing so. Everyone else noticed, and scurried to stand accordingly. Suddenly the oversized oak door, leading to the judge's chambers, moaned once again.

Some used to say it was designed and built that large to accommodate the egos, and suspected drunken dodder.

The judge's black wardrobe was the first to be seen, followed by more black robe, then a huge hand emerged from the clothe. Brogan felt the bench against the back of his legs shake as the whole courtroom audience gawked in incomprehensible panic. Several people gasped as the honourable Kodiak ducked down to enter the courtroom. Brogan had never seen a man so massive. There was too much of him to size up. The judge even had to turn sideways a bit in order for his shoulders to fit through the door. His enormity filled the courtroom with an ominous feeling as he made his way to the bench. Standing just shy of seven feet, he was pure intimidation, adding his 500 lbs plus made him immeasurably menacing.

"What the hell has he been eating? Hay!" Brogan almost squealed as he tried desperately not to break the whisper barrier. "Look at the size of him!"

"This is Mr. Mannly," Darnel said recognizing the judge, "he entered the strong man competition years ago! Y'know, where they flip tractor tires and lift cars? He won every year he competed, in every event. Apparently nobody could even come close to matching his strength. Rumour has it Mr. Mannly once open hand slapped a very large man, and killed him!"

"And now he's a judge!?!" Brogan asked, completely flabbergasted.

"Mr. Mannly father's money somehow got him out of every bit of trouble he ever found himself in."

The Kodiak judge climbed his law-abiding throne and sat down in the oversized chair. "SIT," the judge's voice lurked above everyone with an overwhelming resound.

The entire courtroom sat quickly with little noise. The amount of anxiety generated by the sight of the judge was enough to convince any criminal to confess. Even though his true physique was not totally visible due to his mammoth black robe, Brogan could tell by the way he walked into the courtroom, that he was an able and muscular man.

"Powerfully built, eh!?" Darnel continued softly. "Rumour also has it that the judge's father used to feed him steroids. And apparently the father suffered a stroke when his son, Mr. B. Mannly, the judge here, turned the tender age of sixteen," Darnel's whisper became almost unheard. "Some have said that it wasn't a stroke that killed him, apparently there was an argument at his father's mansion, and his young son open hand slapped him…"

Brogan turned and looked at Darnel, putting two and two together. This tidbit of information was followed by one uncompromising and convincing nod. Brogan's eyes slowly veered back to the Kodiak judge, and he found himself sizing him up again.

The courtroom was silent and everyone stared as a police officer escorted Mr. Mo Daft to his seat. Darnel could hear Brogan grinding his teeth.

"BEGIN," the monstrous voice struck every spine in the room.

The older prosecutor stood up and proceeded to build up enough courage to speak in front of this prestigious bear.

"Your honour, ladies and gentlemen of the jury, we are all brought together here in this courtroom to determine whether or not this affiliated gang member is guilty of his despicable crimes, most importantly, murdering an innocent woman. Does he deserve to spend time in prison? My vote is yes! His guilt is obvious! This man is accused of racketeering, extreme vandalism, verbal and physical aggravation of innocent people, numerous counts of assault causing bodily harm, uttering hundreds of death threats, theft throughout the entire city, uncountable burglaries of private homes, dozens of convenience store robberies, thirteen grand arson's, this list is never-ending. How the hell is this man not already behind bars you ask? I'll tell you how! Bullshit luck, that's how! You have to understand something, I'm not here today to make sure you convict this man for all those crimes I just listed, although he should be! My main focus here today in this courtroom, under the forever powerful and watchful eyes of God, is to make certain that you the jury, find this man guilty of murder! Murder of an innocent woman, who was in the wrong place at the wrong time!"

Brogan tried to contain his emotions as the prosecutor continued.

"Saddleback City is not ours anymore, it belongs to the gangs, it has for a long time. We need to make an immediate example out of Mr. Mo Daft, to show the ATL gang that this is our city!" he said turning toward the left side of the courtroom, directing his statement at the ATL members. "We built it, and we want it back! The people of this fine city would like to have BBQ's without having to worry that a stray bullet from a drive by shooting will strike a loved one! Not only do these monsters have control of our city, they have control of our hearts as well. The amount of evidence against the accused, Mr. Mo Daft, is overwhelming and proves his guilt without a doubt. What you, the jury, have to do is convict him! Ladies and gentlemen let me assure you, once all the evidence is presented, this man will be found guilty today. There's no doubt in my mind. In short, we are here today to make our streets and city safer, and to prove to all gangs that they have not won, that they are not in control, and that we are not going to back down. We deserve to live happy lives, so let's put this gangbanger away for a long time!"

Not once during the prosecutors opening arguments did the Kodiak judge look up from his notes.

"Once they show the jury the evidence we handed over to Detective Shane, we can all go home and that animal will finally get what he deserves!" Brogan whispered madly without taking his eyes off Mr. Daft.

Darnel nodded in agreement, noticing Brogan was keeping a close watch on Mr. Daft.

The only sound in the courtroom was the judge flipping though his papers.

"DEFENCE."

Each time the burly voice rumbled over the courtroom, the intimidation thickened.

The defence attorney quickly stood up, his chair scratched the floor loudly as he scuffled out from behind the table. He then marched over to the twelve jurors; without looking directly at them he cast a cocky look and swaggered back to his table. Picking up some papers, he licked his thumb and flipped a page, then another, as though he were actually reading his notes.

"I'm not going to lie to you people," he finally said. "My client is not a totally innocent man! He has bent the rules and broken the law, then had the audacity to break the rules that were set for him the last time he was in court. But there's not one single person in this courtroom that is totally innocent, sorry your honour. Everyone is guilty of something… whether it be big or minuet. My client is a lot of things, but a killer? …I don't think so," he said sarcastically, shaking his head. "My client has only ever been accused of assault. Why choose to murder someone now? Let me see if I get why we're here today…my client assaults various people, all at different times throughout his life. Every person that has pressed charges against him have been considered "big men". My client claimed innocent in every case, and rightfully so, self defence is not a crime. And now the prosecution is accusing my client of murdering a 115 lb innocent woman, for money? I'm sorry, I don't see that happening. I mean, come on ladies and gentlemen, every single assault complaint against my client was from a larger man than him. My point is, my client likes the excitement, the rush and the challenge of being the under dog, and trying to prove his point. My client did not kill that woman! Show me proof that he did! With proper treatment, I believe my client can function in today's society. He is not a killer. And if he is found guilty, then we will see an innocent man convicted of something he did not do, and a punishment handed out to a man whose freedom will be stripped from him. Not only that, but his name and reputation will be tarnished for as long as he lives. That's a big thing to take from somebody who's innocent. Plus, the real killer will still be out there somewhere, ready to kill again at anytime. Mr. Prosecutors, you best have some hard evidence! What right does anybody have to overlook their own impurities, big or small, and try to manipulate the justice system to cart this man off to prison? To prove a point?! Show us proof! Thank you your honour."

Darnel looked down at Brogan's hands as his knuckles cracked and popped. He was clenching his fists so tight, his hands were completely white, there was absolutely no blood getting passed his wrists. Darnel placed his hand on Brogan's bouncing leg, snapping him out of his tensed up state. His leg instantly stopped bouncing, and the blood started flowing through his hands again. But he was still pissed to see the swagger and the smirk from the defence attorney as he returned to his seat, as if they had already won the trial.

The Kodiak judge signalled for the prosecutor to begin, "PROCEED."

Just as he stood up to start, a member of his prosecuting team approached him from behind in a controlled panic. A look of anguish spread across the prosecutor's face as the man whispered bitter nothings in his ear. The message continued for several seconds before the man was gone as quick as he appeared. The prosecutor looked as if he were going to have a nervous breakdown right then and there. His legs buckled beneath him, he reached for the table and slowly lowered himself back into his seat. It was noticeable and heart wrenching to see this from the man who was going to rid the city, and world, of Rita's killer.

"PROBLEM?" the burly judging voice echoed throughout the room again, and everyone jumped simultaneously.

The prosecutor sat there not saying a word, or even moving, as if he had just slipped into a comma.

BANG! The gigantic judge's paw smacked the top of his desk, and the entire audience jumped higher in their seats.

"PROBLEM?" the judge asked the prosecutor again.

"I'm sor...sorry your honour... Umm...I don't really...I don't really know how to say this!" he sputtered. "Uh...I've just been informed of a certain matter pertaining to our case...could your honour grant us a thirty minute recess?"

"WHY?"

"For my team to look over the new information and quickly discuss it."

"NO!" the judge said loudly, his voice echoing through the courtroom. "PROCEED!"

The prosecutor stood staring, like a deer in headlights, clearly panicked. "Well...ok..." he said nervously. "We...uh...we have no evidence, your honour!" he finally blurted out.

The right side of the courtroom quickly filled with gasps and murmurs of disbelief.

"WHAT!?" Brogan yelled, almost falling off the bench.

He turned to Darnel looking for answers, but realized by the look on his face that he was just as baffled.

BANG! Everyone went dead silent as another open hand slap found the top of the judge's desk.

"NO MORE OUTBURSTS!" the judge commanded before turning his attention to the prosecutor. "EXPLAIN."

The prosecutor looked completely sick. "Well your honour, my young associate just informed me that everything, all the evidence we had on Mr. Mo Daft...well, it mysteriously went missing! It's gone!"

"YOU LOST YOUR EVIDENCE?"

The question was controlled, but a hint of sarcasm could be heard and felt, as if the judge's time had been wasted. Although, observing the judges body language, Brogan thought there was more to it than that.

The massive judge leaned back in his huge throne, and clasped his massive mitts together, as though he were going to say a prayer.

"CASE DISMISSED!" he bellowed without any hesitation or thought.

The courtroom exploded with cries, mumbled sarcastic remarks, and muffled pleas for help, for the judge to reconsider.

Brogan instantly felt a rush through his body, and jumped to his feet grabbing the bench in front of him. Darnel leaned over and tapped Brogan's hand as he noticed the wooden bench splintering under his intense grip. "Not here," he whispered

"But your honour..." the prosecutor pleaded.

"BUT WHAT?" the judge sounded annoyed.

"With all due respect sir, the amount of evidence that was accumulated against Mr. Mo Daft was very substantial. In fact, your honour, there was a lot of evidence, in this case alone, that would help bring down a huge chunk of the ATL gang. All we're asking for is a little more time to figure this mess out."

"DO YOU HAVE ANY EVIDENCE PERTAINING TO THIS CASE?"

"No your honour, we have no evidence," the prosecutor answered reluctantly.

"I WILL PERSONALLY SEE THAT A PROPER INVESTIGATION BE EXECUTED IN ORDER TO FIND OUT WHAT WENT WRONG IN YOUR CASE MR. PROSECUTOR! THIS HAS BEEN A BIG WASTE OF TIME FOR EVERYONE! NO EVIDENCE, NO CASE!"

This time the judge used his mallet to smack his desktop, but it was no where near as loud. With a crack of his mallet, his ruling was final.

Detective Shane hung his head, and the two crime fighters sat, bewildered, as their entire year of hunting was dismissed with one hit of the mallet. Everyone in attendance on the right side of the room, was appalled and in shock by the judges decision. But nobody there was more devastated about the outcome of this courtroom injustice than Brogan. He sat with his head in his hands, thinking of Rita. He had let her down, and somehow he was going to make it right. This was not the end. His thoughts drifted to Rita's mother and how he had spoke to her the other night on the phone about the trial. He promised her, knowing the evidence against him, that Rita's killer would be brought to justice. How on earth was he going to explain this to her?

All Mr. Daft's supporters stood up and vacated the courtroom, unified, with little sound. There was no cheering or clapping, not even a pat on the back, they just up and left. Like they knew that it was going to end like this. The righteous side stayed to discuss their disgust.

"Darnel I told you something was screwy…I knew some kinda bullshit would end up clogging the wheel of justice! Freakin MEATBALLS!" Brogan's voice grew louder the more he spoke. "Aren't you mad, upset, anything?! C'mon! We busted our butts for that evidence! Especially you Darnel. You edited every little piece of it, so neither of us could be linked to anything! Countless hours, for what?!"

The two crime fighting friends made their way back to the Escalade with Brogan griping the whole way. Once inside their ride, Brogan continued to vent to Uncle Reynolds as he drove back to the ranch. "And that gigantic judge tossed it right out! 'NO EVIDENCE…NO CASE'." he mocked. "BUULLLSHITTTT! I'm telling you something right now, I almost lost it in there! I mean come on! All the evidence went missing…really? How the hell does that happen? Bunch of FREAKIN MEATBALLS! And Darnel's not even upset!!!" Brogan said chucking a hitchhiking thumb at Darnel.

"Is this true Darnel, you're not angry about any of this?" Uncle Reynolds questioned. "Everythin' we've all been doin, Brogan taken all those beatin's, and you ain't mad?"

"Well, I reckon I'm getting upset now!" Darnel said imitating Uncle Reynolds old western talk. "I reckon we be gettin' the gloves out when we get home, eh?!"

Darnel's eyebrows raised and produced a quirky smirk. Uncle Reynolds caught it right away. "I reckon you won't be smirkin' when I stop this truck, pull you outside, and put an ass whoopin' to ya!"

Darnel's smirk turned to a big smile. "Listen, just because I'm not freakin out doesn't mean that I'm not angry about the turnout. This time he got lucky, but next time we'll deliver the evidence seconds after they call for it in court!"

Brogan shunned the idea. "Dude, it took us a long time to gather all that evidence, we had three banker boxes full of evidence against the ATL gang! How long is it gonna take us to build that up again? Besides that, they're gonna be more careful from now on! There's no way we'll ever get the same quality evidence again! We had a lot of names and faces in that evidence. Darnel, I'm with ya, I really am, but I'm beyond pissy about this! It's not fair!"

Darnel lost his smile, "Brogan my friend, I have dozens of copies of all that evidence! I even have all the original audio and video evidence. Do you really think I'd only make one copy? If anything were to happen to any of us, the proper people and authorities would be informed of certain information."

"What?"

"You guys must think I'm slow or something. You dweebs! Honestly?! There is definitely something goin on here, bigger than what we originally thought. Think about it, all that evidence gone! It would take a lot of powerful people to make that happen. You actually thought I didn't have a back up plan? C'mon guys, I ain't no Einstein, but I got back up plans for my back up plans! Heck, I've even got back up plans for your back up plans!"

"If you say back up plan one more time, I reckon we won't wait for no gloves!" Uncle Reynolds threatened.

All three men discussed the case as they drove back to the ranch. Both Brogan and Uncle Reynolds felt a little silly for not considering the fact that Darnel is a genius, a natural leader, and would most definitely have their backs.

Darnel had been on his laptop the entire ride.

"What you got going on there?" Brogan finally asked.

Darnel passed the laptop to Brogan.

"Who do those two remind you of?"

Brogan's eyes got big as beach balls. "What? Where is this?"

"That my friend, is feedback from my camera mounted at the back of the courthouse!"

From the laptop screen they watched as two extremely large men, resembling the bailiff and the juggernaut judge, exited the courthouse and met a third huge man, who also looked like the bailiff.

"What you're watching," Darnel explained as the three huge men climbed into a black four-door Cadillac, "is the massive Judge B. Mannly, and his two huge older brothers, that just so happen to be twins! One's the bailiff, the other owns and operates several shifty businesses throughout Saddleback City! How messed up is this now?!"

Brogan leaned back in his chair trying to make sense of the whole messed up day.

When they arrived, the three men scurried into the ranch house and down into the information room. Darnel punched away on the keyboard as Brogan and Uncle Reynolds stared at the big screen. The more information Darnel pulled up on the screen, the more pieces of the puzzle started falling into place.

"Yup, that judge is a big man!" Darnel said pulling up more information.

"Judge B. Mannly!" Darnel and Brogan said suddenly in unison, remembering the ATL gangbangers and a handful of dirty cops talking about the "Big Man".

Darnel's fingers went supersonic on the keyboard, and started filling in the holes from their own private ongoing investigation that they hadn't figured out before. Like, how could so much drugs and money be stolen from a police impound, or how could so many ATL's be getting away with so much crime without getting caught.

Darnel stumbled on even more information about the judge. He had been purchasing hundreds of acres, large pieces of land, and pre-existing buildings along with the lots.

"Wow, this judge has a lot of money!" Darnel almost whispered as he scrolled through the information.

For the next several hours Darnel worked on the computer while Brogan slept, and subconsciously waited. Finally the verdict was in. Darnel rolled into Brogan's room with two coffees, and looked at Brogan with great despair.

"Don't just stare dude, tell me what you know!"

"Brogan, follow me to the info room."

Once there Darnel pointed and explained what he had unearthed from this heaping pile of crap. "With this new information, well, my calculations were off, a lot more than what I originally thought. Since I started linking other crimes, even the really violent ones, to information pertaining to the twin brothers and the judge….ooooh baby were my numbers off!"

Brogan stopped drinking his coffee. "What do you mean? What numbers?"

"Brogan, I'm calculating well over two thousand ATL gang members. All the other crimes I linked together…it's actually…it's quite impressive, from a criminal's perspective! They have organized, or basically taken over, every gang, big or small. As well as every two bit dealer and whoever else they want to recruit, and are now running all the criminal activities in Saddleback City! All criminals report to the ATL gang!!"

"Holy crap! That's a lot of bad guys Darnel! Y'know what that means don't ya?! It means I'll just have to start kicking more ass!" Brogan smiled and waited for a similar reaction from his partner in crime, but got nothing of the sort.

"Brogan," Darnel said seriously, "I've been trying to figure out a way that I could help you more when we are out hunting. But it's hard, I'm stuck in this chair, and there's only so much I can do with the computers and high-tech stuff. So I called a few contacts, pulled in a lot of big favors, and spent a crap load of money, and…well, I think I found a way to help you kick more ass!"

Brogan's eyes got a little bigger. "You added something to the BITTS… or a bunch more! What'd you put on it this time, a bazooka?" Brogan chimed sarcastically. "Throwing stars that explode?"

"Brogan, there's way too many gang members for the Hunter to handle alone," Darnel said with the most serious look on his face that Brogan had ever seen. "It would take forever to make a dent in their armored numbers! So...I recruited a partner for you!"

"ARE YOU FREAKING KIDDING ME!? No! No way! You're my partner Darnel. I don't want... I don't need another partner!" Brogan began to pace. "LOOK! I've got you, Uncle Reynolds, and Denise! We don't need anyone coming in and messing things up! Y'know, Denise could put on a similar suit and kick some serious ass! Y'know that, eh?! I don't want another partner! It's been you and me from the beginning, and that's the way it should stay!"

Darnel started wheeling his chair through the doorway into the next room, leaving Brogan confused and rambling. He looked back over his shoulder as he exited the room with a smile. "There's someone I would like you to meet, wait here for awhile!"

ABOUT THE AUTHOR

Johnny Morice is the author of The Hunter, which is his first book of many to come. He grew up reading comics and has always been a superhero fan. He is also a longtime writer of "Stoems", which are his creation of short story poems. His training and several years working security, along with his vivid imagination, and love of writing all help contribute to the non-stop action from his superheroes. He lives with his wife and two children in Coaldale, Alberta, Canada.

Edwards Brothers Malloy
Oxnard, CA USA
September 2, 2014